ALISON INGLEBY

Expendables

The Wall Series Book 1

Dedication

For Sam. I'm only brave enough to fly because I know you're there to catch me if I fall.

A Note on Language

This story is set in a future London and is written in British English. For my readers who are more accustomed to U.S. English spellings and terms, I hope you don't find this too distracting.

1

Aleesha

I awake with my face pressed into the cobbles, surrounded by the stench of vomit, piss and dead rat. Daylight filters down between the tall buildings. A dull, soft light, the sun hidden behind layers of dense cloud.

Where am I? Slashes of red graffiti designed to look like a bloodbath mark the metal door on the opposite wall. *Shankster territory*. My pulse quickens as memories return.

A Shankster party. Monotonous beat of the music. People dancing, drinking, making out. The wild-eyed contortionist with dreadlocks to his waist who could invert his body into a perfect circle. Fighting my way up the stairs to the upper rooms. Pushing past the guards. And *him*. Green-eyes. The new leader of the Shanksters. My target.

My mind goes blank. *What happened next?* There's a tang in my mouth, faint but recognisable. *Tronk*. Oh, yes. That.

I'm in Green-eyes' lap, laughing as he plants rough kisses down my neck. Whispering in his ear that we should find somewhere quieter. A small room. The guards retreat. Just the two of us. But when I open my mouth to speak – to finally get the information I've come for – he silences me with a finger and holds up a tiny packet of white powder.

A flash of pain radiates up my arm and I realize I'm grinding my knuckles into the ground. It does little to temper my frustration. *You idiot! You could have been raped. Killed.*

I close my eyes, wishing I could make the world disappear. But it's cold lying here and, to top it off, it starts raining. Soft droplets dribble down my exposed thighs. Feeling around for my dress, I find it scrunched up around my waist. *Urgh.* I yank it down and clamber to my feet, which I realize are bare. It appears my shoes were another casualty of last night's failure. At least I didn't wear my good boots.

The one advantage tronk has over liquor is that there's no hangover. My head now feels as sharp and clear as this time yesterday. Though perhaps that makes the inevitable walk of shame even worse. There's a titter and I realize I'm not alone in the alley. Great. Being perved on by a group of scrawny kids was *not* how I'd planned my night to end.

"'Ey, we thought you was dead," one of them comments in a part-curious, part-bored tone.

"Sorry to disappoint."

I attempt to stride past them purposefully but fail miserably when my bare foot skids on a patch of unidentifiable goo. There are a few giggles from the audience.

"Shut it." I glare at them. "Shouldn't you lot be in school?"

A small girl with matted blonde hair shrugs. "What for?"

It's a fair question. School is a bit of a half-hearted affair here in Area Four, both from pupils and the authorities. You don't complain that all they're teaching you is a load of crap, and they don't complain when you skip class.

As I round the corner of the street, a hand lands on my shoulder and there's a familiar voice in my ear. "You were supposed to report back two hours ago." His voice is mild.

Perhaps it's the Irish accent that makes him sound so laid back.

"Well, since you knew where to find me, why didn't you come and w—" I check myself hurriedly. I have no doubt he knows that I've spent the best part of the night and this morning asleep like a drunk in a back alley, but that's no reason for me to admit it. "Get me," I end lamely.

"Never wake an angry woman, that's my motto. I knew you'd come around eventually."

Great, now he's mocking me.

Murdoch leans back against the wall and folds his thick, stocky arms. "So, did you get the information?"

I make myself look into his clear blue eyes. If you look away, they know you're lying. If your eyes flicker, they know you're lying. But if you're confident, if you know the tricks they look for, it's easy.

"Sure, I got something, but you're not going to like it."

The words trip off my tongue before I can stop them. *Oops.* That was *not* what I had planned to say.

He arches an eyebrow. "Okay then, so what is it?"

"I got to the new leader. Had him right in my lap, so to speak." *Technically, I was in his lap, but the end result would have been the same. If I hadn't screwed up.* "They definitely have some involvement with *them*." Murdoch nods, knowing I'm referring to the Brotherhood. "But we were interrupted, and then he zoned out on," I take a deep breath, forcing myself to get the word out, "tronk." *All the best lies have a bit of truth in them.*

"Dammit, I knew I shouldn't have trusted you."

For a second, I think he's going to hit me and my hand's halfway to my knife before I remember that I don't have it on me. *Damn this stupid outfit.* His fist slams into the boarded-up window an inch from my head.

3

"The previous gang leader refused to help *them*. Green-eyes wanted to avoid taking part in a leadership challenge, so he cut 'em a deal. Though, I'm not sure he'll be in charge for long. All is not happy in Shankster HQ."

"And their contact in the Brotherhood?" he whispers, glancing around nervously.

"I-I didn't get that far."

Frown lines appear on his forehead. "I can't work out if you know the truth and you're just hiding it from me, or if you don't know jack."

"If you told me what you wanted the information for, then perhaps it would be easier for me to help you," I say sweetly.

Murdoch's gang is still a mystery to me. Since he approached me a month ago and blackmailed me into working for them, I've been trying to find out more about the Chain. But no one I've spoken to has heard anything about them. I don't know if that's better or worse than the rumours about the Brotherhood. People don't talk much about them, either, but that's out of fear.

Murdoch's face darkens. "That wasn't part of the deal. You do as we ask and I keep your secret, secret."

"And help me find out what happened to my mother," I remind him.

He nods. "Sure, but you're a long way from that. If you can't even complete a basic task, we have no use for you."

My fingernails dig into the thin skin on my thighs. The pain helps to control the rising anger in my belly. "I've made contact. He'll be more receptive next time. I'll get him drunk. He'll speak more freely then."

And where are you going to find the money for liquor?

"If you go again, you go with someone. I don't trust you on your own."

"I told you, I work alone." Folding my arms, I meet his gaze. He looks away first.

"Fine, but if you don't have anything to report tomorrow, the deal is off."

He stalks away and I slump against the wall, closing my eyes. *How the hell do I find out about the Shanksters' link with the Brotherhood by tomorrow?* What I'd told Murdoch was mostly rumour, I've got no way of knowing if it's true, but I had to get him off my back somehow.

For now, though, I have a more immediate problem. Getting home safe.

"Aleesha?"

My eyes snap open. The man in front of me is short, not much taller than me, with the left side of his head shaved and the remaining hair braided tight. A snake's head tattoo pokes out the neck of his t-shirt. I breathe a sigh of relief. "Jonas, right?"

He nods suspiciously. "What are you doing out here?"

"I could ask the same of you. I wasn't aware Jay or Dane had authorized any contact with the Shanksters." I glance significantly at the graffiti-covered building behind me, but the gesture is too subtle for him.

Jonas frowns and is about to reply when footsteps approach. I vaguely recognize the newcomer, a squat boy with greasy tendrils of hair, from the Snakes' HQ. He squints at me. "What are *you* doing here?"

"Jay's business." Smiling sweetly, I add, "But I could do with a hand getting home."

Their muttered voices follow me as I walk down the street. I step carefully to avoid the shards of broken glass, metal and other hazards embedded in the filth that covers the road.

Luckily, it's been dry for a couple of days. If the streets were flooded, it would be impossible to see anything.

My breath hisses through my teeth as I snatch my foot away from whatever has just stabbed it. Lifting it up, I examine the sole, trying not to fall over or hop around on the other leg.

There's a shriek from one of the hobies lining the street. I look up to see Jonas walking away from her. "Here y'go." A pair of battered shoes are thrown in front of me. "We'd better go before she decides to get 'em back."

I yank out a splinter of glass and flick it away. The shoes look barely cleaner than the street, but they'll have to do.

"Thief!" the woman yowls behind us. I glance back, but she's too scared to come and reclaim them. She waves twig-like arms, her skeletal frame tottering on swollen feet. I grimace as I slip my feet into the over-large shoes, wondering if foot rot will be another price I'll pay for my weakness last night.

"Come on, she's just a tronk addict." Jonas pulls at my arm.

He's right. The signs are there as the woman sinks back into the line of hobies: hollow cheekbones, a desperate gleam in her bulging eyes.

That could be you if you don't give it up.

No, it won't. I'm smarter than them.

Are you really?

Yes! I made it off the streets and I will stay off the streets.

But what about the tronk?

I'm giving it up, alright?

The voice in my head falls silent. "As if I don't have enough to deal with."

"What?"

"Oh, nothing," I say, realizing I'd spoken aloud.

I'm glad of the escort on the way back. Walking practically

naked through Area Four in broad daylight is guaranteed to get you into trouble, but the boys manage to handle most of the attention. I dismiss them at the end of the road and walk the last fifty metres to Jay's place by myself.

Jay lives in two small rooms above a closed-up kebab shop. I guess it's my home too – or as close as I come to having one – but it feels wrong somehow to call it that. Too permanent. It's not bad as far as places to live go and way better than many I've stayed in, especially now the kebab shop is closed. The smell of the filth they cooked was enough to drive you mad.

I key in the code to the faded green door. The room inside contains a large battered table and a couple of chairs. Jay is in the adjourning bedroom, humming some mindless tune. He sounds like he's in a good mood, at least. I push the button on the hotplate. The orange light doesn't come on.

"Electric's off."

I turn to see him slouched against the doorframe, a slight smirk on his face. The black tattoos that wind around his arms darken his copper skin and his t-shirt is a little too tight over his shoulders.

"Three days of sun and the panels can't even give us an hour of electricity?" I mutter, jabbing the button again. *Dammit, no water then.* Reaching down for a bottle of Chaz, my hand finds only empty air.

"Sorry, this is the last one." He brings his arm out from behind his back and waggles the blue bottle gently so the liquid sloshes inside. A knot of anger tightens in my stomach. I grab the bottle from his hand and gulp down the contents. It barely wets my dry throat.

"Any food?"

"Do you even bother to collect your rations?"

I don't answer. What do I tell him? That I can't collect the crappy government rations all citizens are entitled to, and that if I tried, I'd be arrested on the spot? That all this time he's been harbouring an illegal?

He runs a hand over his short dark hair and sighs. "Nothing here. There are still some bits left from the depot raid at HQ, though. We'll head there later."

"Fine." My stomach growls and I can feel myself getting twitchy. Hangry, Jay calls it. Angry because I'm hungry. Maybe he's right. Or maybe anger is just part of who I am.

"You look a bloody mess. Where have you been?"

"None of your damn business." I bang the bottle down on the table, the plastic making a satisfying crunching noise. "It's not as if you were around last night."

But thank god he's not in the mood for a fight.

"Hey, I was just worried about you. I haven't seen you all morning." He begins to massage my shoulders, and the twitchiness subsides.

"I was supposed to be meeting a friend at a party. They didn't turn up, so I was about to leave, but they had …" My voice trails off. I don't really need to explain any further, he can fill in the gaps.

"A friend?"

Ah, yes. He knows as well as I do that I don't have any friends.

"I don't think you've met her." I shrug nonchalantly. "She's just a dweeb."

He seems to accept the explanation. "You should watch who you hang around with. You don't need no dweebs when yer the boss's lady."

I smile and stand on my toes to kiss him on the lips. "Not quite the boss yet," I tease.

8

He grins and pulls me in for a hug, planting a kiss on my neck before pulling back and holding me at arm's length, his nose wrinkling.

"Eeewww, you stink!"

I grimace, realizing he's right. "Yeah, I'll have to ask the hobies to keep their alleyways cleaner."

"Well, it's your lucky day. We have water! And I got it heated up before the leccy went off. Come on, I was about to jump in." He flicks my long braid so it swings from side to side.

"We have water?" I push past him and race for the bedroom. He laughs and follows, scooping me up and throwing me onto the bed. The bowl of steaming water is balanced on the wide windowsill; another bucket to stand in is underneath. Washing water is too precious to be wasted.

"Me first!"

Jay rolls his eyes. "Okay, but only 'cos you smell so bad."

I quickly strip and step into the plastic bucket. There's even a sliver of soap. Heaven. I wash down fully before dunking my head into the water and scrubbing at my hair, which hasn't been cleaned properly in weeks. It feels so good to get rid of the itchiness. When I've finished, the water is grey and murky.

"Huh, so much for a clean wash." Jay hands me a threadbare towel as I step out of the bucket. He tips the water back into the bowl.

"It's warm still, at least." I dry myself quickly and dress. It's good to be clean again. And wearing proper clothes that cover my body.

While Jay's washing, I return to the main room and use the tip of my knife to ease up the half floorboard in the corner. The fake wood is chipped and scratched. This old building used to have real wooden floors, having been built back when there

9

was enough wood in the world to waste on construction. But the floors have long since been ripped up for firewood and replaced with this synthetic stuff. Nestled inside the void under the boards is a metal lockbox containing my secret stash of chits, spare food and – when I have it – tronk. Today, it also holds a small amulet threaded on a thin cord.

"So, what you want to do for the rest of the day?"

I whip around, but he's still in the other room. Heart racing, I retrieve the amulet and replace the lockbox and floorboard.

"Haven't you got stuff to do?" I ask, walking back into the bedroom.

He shakes his head, sending water droplets spinning over the bed. "Nope. Dane's gone off somewhere and everyone's kind of in limbo at the moment, so I have a free day." He hesitates for a moment, looking at me. I don't like that look. It means he has something planned. And that usually means trouble.

"I thought we could go take a look at the Wall."

That was not what I had expected. "Why do you want to go look at the Wall? It's just a waste of time."

Jay steps out of the bucket and begins to towel himself down. "Well, what would you rather be doing? Lying around here all afternoon or hanging out with your dweeb friends?" He makes a twisting motion with his hands. Loser. I can't help but smile. And he's right, there isn't much else to do.

"Okay then, we'll go see the Wall."

A ray of sunlight lands on the small piece of green glass in my hand, sending speckles of jade dancing across the ceiling. After fastening the cord around my ankle, I walk over to Jay and wrap my arms around his warm chest, resting my head against his back. He smells of soap. Clean. The soap reminds me of my mother. Wherever we were, however little we had, there was always soap. I was always clean.

He pats my hand. "Hey, let go, girl; otherwise, we'll never get out of here." But his tone is soft, teasing. This is the Jay I like. I just wonder how long he'll stick around.

* * *

Area Four runs right up to the Wall, and half an hour later we're sitting on a flat-roofed outbuilding, legs dangling into the street below. In front of us, almost close enough to touch, is the Wall: the barrier that divides London. In most parts of the city, there's an empty area in front of it, where they knocked down all the old buildings. They call it the dead zone, 'cos if the Metz find you squatting there, you're dead. But here, the buildings crowd in toward the Wall so it's only a few metres away.

It's not a wall at all, really. At least, it's not made of concrete or Plexiglas or metal. It's just a shimmer of colours in the air. Bright, moving patterns of light. But it's more lethal than any concrete or Plexiglas wall. It separates us: Outsiders from Insiders. Its beauty and colour is almost mocking, like they're saying 'this is what it's like *Inside*'. Just to remind us of our drab, grey surroundings.

"Have you ever been on the other side?"

I shake my head. What a dumb question. No one I know has ever been through the Wall.

"I wonder what it's like."

I've rarely seen Jay in this kind of mood. Angry and sullen, yes. Reflective and thoughtful, that's just not really Jay. I sigh.

"Pavements of gold and orchards of fruit, if you believe what Dane says."

He snorts. "Dane don't know nothing. He's never even tried to get past the guards."

11

"Well, he'd be stupid to try. No one can get past unless they want to let you in." The only way to get inside the Wall is through the gates. There are three of them: East, North and West. The south side of the city is bordered by the swamps and the river, a mile of water that floods what used to be the southern part of London.

We're in the east of the city, but the East Gate is way up in Area Six. No one from Four ventures that far north. From what I've heard, Insiders can come and go through the gates as they please (not that any of them would choose to come out here) but as an Outsider, you can only get through if you have legit business Inside. They check your chip to make sure. As I'm not a legal citizen, I don't have a chip, so there's no way of me getting Inside.

"They only have two guards on duty, right? It can't be *that* hard to get past."

I snort. "Two on each side. And they filter you through those arches that scan your chip."

"Is that what they do? I thought they were just there to make the gate look more …"

"Ornamental?" I supply.

Jay frowns.

"Impressive?"

His face clears. "Yeah, that."

It can be frustrating being with Jay. And he's pretty smart, for an Outsider. No wonder Insiders don't want to mix with us. It would be tedious as hell. It's a fact of life: Insiders are more intelligent than Outsiders. It's designed that way. As an Insider, you get a hand up in the world from the day you're born. I seem to be an exception to the rule. I'm smarter than most Outsiders I've met, even though I was born in Area Five. Which is well and truly Outsider territory. And as I'm an illegal, there's no way any of the tiny cells that grew to become me could have been genetically enhanced. For some reason, my mother chose not to register my birth or even the fact that she was pregnant. According to the system, I don't exist. I guess when it comes to intelligence, I'm just lucky.

I glance at Jay. His head is slightly turned to one side and he's gazing at the shimmering light. It's his "thinking" face. I wait patiently. Finally, he stretches out his arm, fingertips only a few inches from the Wall, and looks over at me.

"Really? I'm not going to be carting your dead body back home, you know."

He grins. "Loving girlfriend, aren't you."

He shucks forward so he's perched right on the edge of the roof. I glance down nervously. The drop into the alley isn't too far – six feet, maybe – but if he falls, he'll definitely hit the Wall.

"Don't be an idiot. Remember what happened to the guys at the raid when the barrier came up? They didn't even scream. Dead in seconds."

Jay pulls back. "Yeah, yer right. I'd forgotten about that." There's a tremor in his voice.

"You'd forgotten?" My attempt at sarcasm fails and my voice shakes even more than his.

"Not forgotten the raid, obviously ..."

Just forgotten those who'd died. Gang members die every month. But there were nine who didn't make it back from the raid and it was only a month ago. Still, apart from that, the raid had been a success. It was the first time anyone in this part of the city had attacked a government depot and actually come away with stuff. Food. Weapons. If it hadn't been for that one guard who managed to somehow get the barrier working again, we'd have got even more. And those kids would still be alive.

The raid had been Jay's plan. Or, at least, that's what he'd been made to believe. I suspect Murdoch and the Chain were behind it. The guy with the brains behind the plan, who Jay had "recruited", was one of theirs. But telling Jay that would mean explaining about Murdoch and admitting I was working for the Chain as well as the Snakes. And then he'd get mad.

"Let's just stay away from it, okay?" I scoot back from the edge, but Jay doesn't move.

"Have you ever heard about tunnels under the Wall?"

"Nope. Who's been spreading rumours now?"

He shrugs. "I overheard someone on the street talking about it the other week."

"Maybe there are tunnels," I start carefully, "but most of them would have been flooded in the Great Flood, and even if they're dry, they must be hundreds of years old. More than likely they've caved in, or are about to."

Jay smiles wryly, giving me a gentle shove. "Always got an answer for everything, haven't you?"

I smile back and shove him harder. "Someone's got to think through your crazy plans before you go off and get yourself killed."

"Well, how about *you* use that great brain of yours to figure out a plan to get us into that place." He pushes me again, but I'm still off balance. I teeter, my limbs flailing dangerously close to the shimmering Wall as I try to stop myself falling.

"Hey!" Jay's voice carries a trace of alarm and he reaches out to grab me, but he misjudges the movement and knocks me instead, and it's enough to tip me off my precarious stance. The slick fabric of my top slips through his fingers. There's a scream, and I realize it's coming from me, but it sounds so far away. Time slows and it feels as if I'm floating down, not falling. Bright colours dance across my eyes and I see nothing apart from the Wall.

"Oww!"

I roll once, twice, three times. Pain shoots through my left shoulder and there's the iron-tang of blood in my mouth. My breath comes in gasps. Colours still flash across my vision like bolts of lightning. I close my eyes.

What's happening? Am I dead? Surely, if you're dead you're not supposed to feel pain?

I open my eyes. Cobblestones. *Clean* cobblestones. Almost gleaming. I run a finger over them. Gritty and rough. But no shards of glass, no empty chocco wrappers or old rat bones. No puddles of mud or vomit.

Hardly daring to breathe, I push myself up, ignoring the flash of pain at my elbow and shoulder, and look around. Towering above me is the Wall, the nearest mast visible along the long, narrow street.

In front of me are old-fashioned, brick-built houses. I take a step forward. "I'm alive." My words ring out in the silence. Somehow, miraculously, I *am* alive. And what's more, for the first time in my life, I'm *Inside* the Wall.

2

Trey

"Goldsmith, are you paying attention?" Mr Peters frowns at me over the top of his wire-rimmed glasses. I jerk upright in my seat. "Y-yes, sir!"

My cheeks burn as I realize my entire history class is looking at me. They're probably thinking I fell asleep again. Tired out from rugby practice, unlike the rest of the boys who seem to have boundless energy. Sometimes, I wonder if my parents paid for any genetic enhancements at all for me.

The truth is, I'd been distracted by a strange tingling sensation in my right forearm. I examine it as Mr Peters goes back to droning on about the refugee crisis of the 2050s. It *looks* normal. The tingling disappears and is replaced by a throbbing as if my pulse has been magnified a hundred times.

My arm moves two inches to the right. A moment later, it twitches again and moves back to the left. *Am I going crazy?*

I stare in horror as my forearm begins to flop limply from side to side like a fish out of water. Every five seconds. Like an independent limb.

Flip. Flop.

It feels odd, like there's an invisible puppet string attached to my wrist, reaching up through the ceiling to an unknown

16

puppeteer. I lift my arm experimentally. It responds to my mental command, as if there's nothing really wrong with it. Then my wrist jerks back.

Others begin to notice. At first, there are just a couple of nervous titters and a few sidelong glances. No one wants to draw attention to themselves. Peters' detentions are the worst. I push my hand into my desk, tensing the muscles in my forearm, willing them to stay still. One. Two. Three. Four—

The spasm throws my arm into the air. It lands with a thud back on the wooden desk. A ripple runs through my elbow. The next time, my whole arm moves, like a shockwave rippling through my muscles. There's a slight tingling sensation in my arm, a bit like the sensation you get when you knock your funny bone. I wonder if I've somehow trapped a nerve.

"What are you playing at?" Theo leans over to hiss in my ear. "Surely, you don't want detention again?"

"I'm not *doing* anything," I mutter back under my breath. *Should I excuse myself, say I'm not feeling well?* Nerves grip my stomach. Heat rises in my cheek. *What's happening to me?*

The sniggers are louder now. Chairs scrape as my classmates turn to look. Smythe seems to have developed a coughing fit at the back. Mr Peters is still gazing into the holo. "The geopolitics of the time and lack of strong leadership from the major world economic players resulted in the failure of the Berlin Refugee Summit to find a solution to the migration problem," he says.

I lift my arm, but at that moment it jerks so violently that I end up slapping myself in the face.

It is too much for the class. I think Jones is the first to break, or perhaps it's Branson, but the rest of the class follows quickly, unable to contain their mirth. Mr Peters spins around, his eyes narrowed.

"What is going on, boys?"

I hate the way he calls us boys, as if we were still in prep school, not in our final year.

My arm chooses that moment to spasm again. A bubble of hysterical laughter rises in my throat. *Must not smile.* But just thinking that makes the corners of my lips start to twitch. I grab my right hand with my left and push it down between my legs, meeting Mr Peters' gaze.

"Is there something wrong, Goldsmith?" He punctuates each word with a trace of sarcasm. He has a well of it. I can read his thoughts. Detention. Maybe a trip to the Head. A letter home.

"N-no, sir." *Damn this stutter.* Deep breaths. A wave travels up my arm, each muscle fibre passing the movement on to the next. Up to my shoulder and back down again.

What is happening to me?

"Is there something wrong with your arm, Goldsmith?" He walks over so he is standing in front of my desk. His cold eyes, so pale they're almost white, stare down at me. "Put your hands on the desk where I can see them."

I hesitate for a moment, squirming in my chair. My face is burning.

"Now!"

I place my hands palm down on the desk. Both of them are trembling. *How long has it been since the last spasm?*

Mr Peters reaches out, and at that moment I feel my muscle fibres twitch. My forearm jerks upwards, knocking his arm aside. The laughter in the classroom dies and suddenly I'm enveloped in silence. I feel the blood draining from my face through my chest to my feet. I grab my arm before it spasms again. It writhes in my grip like it's trying to break free of my body. I stare at the desk, not daring to look up.

"Go and report to the medic, Goldsmith. Johnson, go with him."

Glancing up, I see Peters has already turned to walk back to the front of the class.

"And the rest of you will stay behind for an extra fifteen minutes."

There is a collective groan. The feeling of relief fades. *Great, now I'll be in everyone's bad books.* I keep my head down as I walk to the door, avoiding the scowls of my classmates. As I pull open the door I glance back toward Peters, who is standing back in front of the holo. He catches my eye briefly and shock ripples through me.

His face is white and drawn, as if he's seen a ghost, and he looks as though he's aged ten years in the space of a minute. In that split second, I realize that he *knows* what this is. And from the look on his face, it isn't good.

* * *

Theo's footsteps pound the corridor behind me as he hurries to catch up. I want to keep running, to tell him to go away and leave me alone to deal with this *thing*, but he's one of the few people I'd count as a friend. I slow to a walk.

"You'll apologize to the guys from me, Theo? I can't believe Peters gave everyone detention. And right at the end of the week, too." Unlike me, Theo is popular with our classmates. He does well in classes and is good on the rugby pitch – both things I come pretty much bottom in. I sometimes wonder why he hangs around with me at all.

"Sure, but I don't think they'll mind. That was the most hilarious thing I've seen all week!" He nudges my arm conspiratorially. "How did you do it? It looked like all the bones in your arm had disappeared!"

My arm chooses that moment to spasm again and whacks his left arm.

"Hey, man, cut it out! We're out of class now." He rubs his arm.

"I *can't*. It's not something I did. It just happened."

"What do you mean? Is there something wrong with your arm?"

"Clearly! I mean, it was fine when class started. And then suddenly *this* started happening." My now independent limb jerks again. "Any ideas?" Theo is going to train to be a doctor when he leaves next year, so he spends a lot of time with the medic.

He looks thoughtful. "I've never heard of anything like it before. But don't worry, I'm sure the medic will have some information on it."

The medic is in the next block, on the ground floor. St George's prides itself on being a "traditional" school, which means everything is firmly set in the 2000s. I think the school building itself is even older, perhaps dating back to the early twentieth century, which is probably why bits of it keep falling apart. The medic is about the one concession to modern-day life they've allowed, probably because there would have been an uproar from parents if their darling boys couldn't get fixed up at the touch of a button.

The corridor is empty. A background hum of noise comes from the classrooms off to the right. On the other side, a row of arched windows look out on the gravelled landing area set into the huge expanse of green grass. A tightly packed row of tall, dense trees marks the school boundary. The late afternoon gloom is already setting in. In a few hours it'll be dark.

"Hey, have you heard what's been happening back in London? Apparently, things are getting feisty outside the Wall. There's a new gang who are murdering all the other gang leaders."

Theo is a mine of information about the Outside. His father runs the main broadcasting agency in town, which is the only one that reports and broadcasts on both sides of the Wall.

"Isn't that what they do? Fight each other?" I don't take much notice of the news, or what happens Outside. Something my father enjoys reprimanding me about.

"Not *everywhere*. Though in some areas there's quite a lot of it. Haven't you ever been Outside?"

I shake my head. "No, why would I? Have you?" I stop and stare at him respectfully. No one goes Outside, at least, not out of choice. The Wall was built to keep Insiders safe. Visiting the areas Outside the Wall may be exciting, but it's not worth the risk of being hurt.

Theo snorts. "Sure, I have. Been out with the reporters a few times. It's pretty grim. You know those holos Peters showed us last year of life before the Great Flood? Kind of like that, but with more water and mud and less electricity. You know, you'd have to pity the Outsiders if they weren't so stupid. Some areas aren't too bad, though. Six and Fifteen are almost as nice as Inside and you probably won't get mugged." He grins wickedly. "You'll have to come out with us sometime."

"Maybe." *Or maybe not.* I get to spend little enough time in London as it is; I don't want to waste it risking my life getting lost in the slums.

We get to the ornately carved wooden staircase that leads down to the ground floor. Theo slid down it once for a dare, got caught by Purley, and ended up scrubbing toilets for a month. If it had been anyone else, they'd probably have got expelled.

"What on Earth are the Metz doing here?"

I pause with my foot on the second step and look past Theo through the window. Two black pods with distinctive slashes of yellow are hovering over the landing site. "I thought they didn't leave London?" I join Theo by the window to get a better look.

"They don't usually. At least, there are branches in other cities, but they're mostly kept busy there. I don't think there's any law enforcement out here in the countryside, is there? Apart from the Farms which have their own security teams. But I don't remember the Metz ever coming here before."

Old memories stir at the back of my mind. *Armed figures, all in black apart from two bright yellow slashes on either side of their helmets; gunshots firing, screaming, a cold fear that left my teeth chattering.*

"They came here once." My voice comes out slightly unsteady and Theo flashes me a look of puzzled surprise. I swallow hard, pushing the memory back. My hands are clammy. "When the rebels broke into the school and took a load of us hostage. I was pretty young; it must have been before you arrived here." I smile weakly. "To be honest, I don't remember much about it, just being terrified and my teacher grabbing me and running from the playground." *And then they shot her in front of all of us.*

The pods are now on the ground, spilling men from their bellies like ants. "Fifteen men and dogs?" Theo sounds excited. "It must be something pretty serious for Pickles to have called them in. The fence is still down, isn't it?" The fence is our main security net that surrounds the school in an impenetrable electric field. Rumour has it that it's had a few technical problems since a squirrel managed to short circuit the system.

"What are you doing out of class?" Purley, our house master, is running up the stairs. He looks flustered and his lips are drawn into a thin line rather than his usual half smile. "Goldsmith, the Head wants to see you – I was just coming to find you. Johnson, get back to class."

"Bu—" Theo starts to protest, but Purley lays a hand on his arm.

"Just go."

Reluctantly, Theo turns and walks back down the corridor. Purley practically drags me down the stairs.

"I-I was supposed to be going to the medic."

Purley shakes his head. "The medic won't help you. John comm'd me to tell me what happened. Thank god he came to me rather than going straight to Eric."

John? Eric? Since when did teachers use first names when talking to students?

At the bottom of the stairs, rather than taking the corridor that leads to the Head's office, he sets off in the opposite direction. I practically have to run to keep up with him. "What's going on?" He doesn't answer. My arm jerks again, throwing me off balance. *Has someone poisoned me? Why does Purley look so scared?*

"This way," he gasps, short of breath, and sets off down the corridor to the design and tech blocks at the end of the school. Halfway down, he pauses by a set of fire doors that lead out onto a small garden. Chest heaving, he turns and grabs my shoulders. My right arm judders away. Purley's shorter than me, though much stockier. A few extra decades of good food hangs around his midriff. I heard a rumour he was once the best prop in the rugby team, back in his day.

He pulls me in so our faces are only six inches apart. I stare at the mole on his cheek, wondering why he hasn't had it removed. It has tiny grey hairs poking out of it.

"Darwin, listen to me, we don't have much time. The Metz have come for you. They've activated your chip. That's why your arm feels outside of your control."

"W-w-why?"

"You don't know?"

I shake my head and a troubled look crosses his face. "There was no reason given. Perhaps something your father … I don't know. I was in Eric's office when they called in. They have a capture-or-kill order for you. I don't know what you've done, Darwin, but they're treating you as a serious criminal. Do you understand?"

He gives me a shake to emphasize the message. My brain feels like it's stopped functioning. Every thought swims through mud. *Capture, kill. Capture, kill.* A cold numbness starts in my stomach, like I've swallowed an ice cube whole, and begins to spread outwards. "They're going to kill me?"

"They might try. Mr Pickles has to comply with their demands of course – we all do. He'll delay them as long as possible, but you must get out of here. Now! The fence is offline, otherwise you wouldn't have a chance. The gates have already been locked down. But you're a good climber – I've seen you. If you can get on top of the tech building, you should be able to jump over the main wall into the forest."

"What do I do then?"

"Run. The effect of the activation will start to spread through your body. It's intended to stop criminals escaping. As soon as you can, you must dig the chip out. He grabs my jerking arm by the wrist, turns it so my palm faces upwards and rests his index finger on a point about a third of the way up my forearm. "It's in here. You may have to dig deep. Do *not* let them catch you." He emphasizes each word with a jab into my shaking arm.

"Now, go."

I'm not sure I can move. My feet are firmly rooted to the worn flagged floor. Purley pushes me toward the door. "Go!"

I stumble forward, my feet trying to catch up with the movement of my body. Purley is already hurrying back down the corridor. The door swings open. The fresh air helps clear my brain. The refrain continues in my head.

Capture, kill. Do not let them catch you.

Life returns to my legs and I begin to run.

3

Aleesha

"Jay?" My voice feels loud in the silence. The constant hum of the city (of the city *Outside*, I should say) has gone. There's a sound of a child laughing (laughing?), but it feels like it's a long way off. The quiet is oddly unnerving.

I do a quick inventory of my injuries. My left shoulder and elbow are bruised and the top of my sleeve is torn. Thank goodness for long sleeves, otherwise, I'd have lost even more skin. Everything else seems okay, barring a few bruises, which I always have a good collection of.

A wave of dizziness hits me and I close my eyes until it passes. Hunger. I haven't eaten since before the party last night.

The Wall looks just the same from this side. A shimmer of colours swirling like water flowing along shallow indentations. I can see the vague outline of buildings on the other side. Not the low roof we'd been sat on, but the tall townhouse behind it. There's another series of masts, thinner and shorter than those linking the sections of the Wall, that sit inside the Wall. It's almost as if there's an additional barrier on this side of it, except there's nothing visible between the masts. Unless it's invisible.

I take a step toward it with my hand outstretched, then snatch it back when I realize what I'm doing.

You went through it once, why not again?

I take a deep breath. For some reason, I went through the Wall without it harming me. Logically, that means I should be able to pass back through the Wall again. Unless it's different from this side ... But why would it be? The Wall exists to keep Outsiders out, not to keep Insiders in.

"Jay?"

No reply, but then, if I can't hear the noise from Area Four, he probably can't hear me. The Wall must block the sound. He'll be worried. I should go back.

But what if this is your only chance?

I glance over my shoulder at the narrow passageway leading through a gap between the houses. It tugs at me. I'm Inside. *Inside.* I can't miss this opportunity. Jay would understand.

My feet carry me down the alleyway, fingers brushing the smooth walls on either side. A gust of wind carries on it a fresh, slightly sweet smell. I follow it to the end of the alleyway. A low railing fences off the front garden of the house.

It looks like a picture. Even though it's winter, the colours are bright and vivid. Who knew there were so many shades of green? What few plants survive Outside are either grey from the dust brought in by the winter rains or burned yellow by the summer sun. Here there are green-leaved shrubs, red-tipped spiky looking plants and a tall tree with tiny dark green needles. They surround a patch of what must be grass. Grass! I wonder what it feels like to lie on. To smell.

The windows of the house are empty and dark. Is anyone home? Along the side of the garden a path leads to a door painted such a bright red it makes my eyes burn to look at it. Black letters mark it out to be number thirty-four.

A flicker of movement in the corner of my eye makes me duck back behind the shelter of the wall. I look around frantically, scanning for the source of the movement. There it is again. Something coming toward me. A dart? A knife? I jerk back, raising my arm protectively in front of my face. But nothing hits me.

There's a short, high-pitched noise. I lower my arm carefully. Behind it, a tiny bird comes into view. It's perched on the top of the wall and is so small, so delicate, that I stop breathing in case the slight breeze of my breath knocks it over. Its back and head are black, like a cloak hiding the blue and yellow flashes underneath, and its tiny eyes are so dark and bright they look like tiny jewels set into its face. It's the most beautiful thing I have ever seen.

The bird turns its head to the side, as if to assess me better, and chirrups again. Then it spreads its fragile wings and swoops down into the garden. I lurch around the corner, not wanting to lose sight of it. It lands on a thin glass cylinder that's hung from the tree with the needles. There's a small perch for it and it pecks at a tray at the bottom of the cylinder.

Squinting, I can just make out what looks to be seeds filling the container. Seeds. My stomach growls and I fight the urge to hop the fence and run to the feeder. *They have food to waste on birds?*

The sound of nearby voices makes me pull back again into the alleyway. A young child chattering away to a lady who must be her mother. Or perhaps a guardian. They walk past the end of the alley without looking down it. When I look back into the garden, the bird has gone.

Fighting the urge to raid the contents of the bird feeder, I set off down the street. Black lamp posts are placed at regular intervals and I bet these ones actually light up when it gets dark, unlike those in Four. No scrimping on electricity here.

Rows of houses line the road, each with their own perfectly manicured garden. Behind them are more houses, then taller apartment blocks painted a dazzling white. *How do they keep them so clean?* It's strange that they kept these old houses when there is so much demand for space. Perhaps it's because no one wants to live in an apartment that close to the Wall.

Further into the city, shining glass towers reach up into the clouds. I wonder if it makes the people inside them dizzy, looking down from the top. They must be able to look across the Wall from that high up.

My heart hammers in my chest as I force myself to walk calmly but purposefully along the pavement. The streets are so neat and clean and made from a strange material that feels almost springy underfoot. But they're deserted. *Where are all the people?*

Another road comes in from the left, and I can see people at the end of it and hear the familiar noise of a busy street. Hurrying, I head toward it. On my own out here, I feel vulnerable and alone, but where there are people I can become one of the crowd. Safety in numbers.

Except I am not one of *this* crowd.

As I weave my way between women clutching shopping bags and young children playing in the street, stares follow me and the busy chatter that I long to hide in fades as I pass. Panic begins to bubble in my stomach. *Is it so obvious that I'm an Outsider?*

I feel a slight tug at my leg and look down into the curious round face of a small boy. He is dressed in a bright blue shirt and set of black trousers with strange red elastic bands that stretch over his shoulders. He looks like pictures I have seen of children's toys, not a living, breathing child.

"Why are you wearing funny clothes?" he asks in a shrill voice. "You look like the big black spider."

He seems impressed with himself at this analysis and stands back, staring up at me until a woman pulls him away, casting a dirty glance in my direction. I look down at my black, mud-stained trousers and ripped top, then around at the vast array of colours being paraded past. The boy is right. In Area Four, black helps me blend in, helps me disappear into the shadows. Here, it makes me stand out.

A breath catches in my throat. I look around desperately for somewhere to hide. I spot a dark alleyway between two brightly decorated shops. I stumble through the river of people, slipping between them, trying not to knock into anyone, waiting for someone to grab me, to find me out. To arrest me.

Outsider.

Finally, I make it. The shadows have never felt so welcoming. My breath comes in gasps, adrenaline surging through me. I need a disguise. Something to help me blend in.

Ten minutes later, with a shocking pink skirt and a blue scarf that I found discarded in a rubbish bin, I venture out onto the street again. This time, no one gives me a second glance. The skirt is long, covering my legs and the top of my boots, and awkward to walk in. I shuffle forward, my senses overloaded by the bright colours and smells.

Area Four just smells of decay. There are a million variations of the smell of decay, but they're all kind of the same. But here, there are so many different smells. They waft out of shop doorways, float down from the green balconies above me and brush off the people I walk past. Sweet, warm, fresh, perfumed. I don't have names for them all. My nose can't take them all in.

My mouth waters. Then one smell stands out. Pausing, I close my eyes. I know this smell.

My mother had taken me north, to the very top of Area Five. We'd crept out in the early morning before anyone else was awake, weaving through the empty streets in the dark. When I'd asked where we were going, she'd replied that we were going to get bread. I was confused as we already had bread at home, but my mother had said this was different bread. *Real* bread.

Eventually, we ducked into a tiny courtyard and there was *this* smell. The smell of freshly baked bread. My mother had knocked on a door and a man had come out. I heard the clinking of chits. So many chits! And she came back with a lumpy package.

We'd found a bench to sit on and she'd unwrapped the loaf reverentially. "This is what you should be eating, Aleesha." Her voice had been sad, but I barely noticed, so eager was I to eat the bread that smelled so good. My mother ate slowly with her eyes closed, savouring every mouthful. It was as if she was trying to transport herself to another place in another time.

We never had the bread again. I'd asked for it, over and over, but she just hushed me and said it was for special treats only. A few months later, she disappeared for good.

I follow the smell to a baker's shop. Loaves of bread are stacked up in the window: light, golden, crisp loaves, and darker round ones with seeds scattered on top, and small rolls, piled high. The smell makes me dizzy. My stomach's demanding food. I finger the chits in my pocket. Do I have enough?

Inside, there's a queue of people waiting to be served. To one side is a display cabinet where tiny painted cakes seem to rotate in mid-air. Some have flowers on top, others are filled with something white and puffy.

31

"Can I help you?"

I start, and meet the eyes of the man behind the counter. He frowns slightly. *Can he tell?* I point at one of the loaves behind him. Any one will do.

"This one?"

I nod. He wraps it up and holds out a scanner. "Your arm, please?"

I freeze for a second before I realize what he wants. Of course, payment. He wants to scan my chip. Except I don't have one. I feel heat rise in my cheeks and the murmurings of people behind me. I pull out the chits from my pocket and hold them out. My hand shakes.

Please, take them. Please.

The shopkeeper eyes the scraps of metal in my palm. "We don't accept those in here." There's a flash of pity in his eyes, but his voice is hard and cold. He glances toward the door. Turning, I spot a security guard blocking the entrance. My pulse quickens. What have I got myself into?

"I-I'm sorry." I don't know if he catches my words as I turn away, pushing past people toward the door.

The security guard grabs me. "Just wait, now." She pulls the scarf back off my face, then frowns in confusion. I look around wildly. The shopkeeper is talking into a comm device on the wall. *What's wrong?* I tug at my arm, but her grip is firm as she pulls something from her belt. "Stand still, I just need to ID you, make sure you're legit. Then you can go."

Dizziness washes over me. I feel myself sway and hands push me down until I'm sitting on the floor. Something's pressed into my hand. "Eat this," a soft voice says. A shout of protest from the shopkeeper, followed by a tart reply from the woman next to me. "It's alright, I'll pay for it. Can't you see she's half

32

starved?"

A golden bread roll. Crisp on the outside, soft inside. So different from the chewy, tasteless grey rations the government calls bread. I rip it open, stuffing it into my mouth, barely chewing.

"She's not registering." The guard stands above me, flicking through her device.

"I've reported it. Metz will be on their way. Just get her out of the shop, will you?" The shopkeeper sounds frightened.

I go cold. *The Metz are coming.* I have to get out of here. If they get their hands on me, I'm dead. Or worse. I've heard that the criminals they don't execute, they take to the Farms where they set them to work eighteen hours a day picking fruit and vegetables – all the jobs the robots can't do. You work until you drop dead and then you get replaced with another unfortunate soul. There's always a ready supply of 'criminal' Outsiders.

And there are rumours of even worse places. The Labs. They need people for experiments, for testing the latest beauty and gene therapies. You don't have to work so hard there, but your body is used as a test bed for whatever they want to roll out next.

That's what happens to criminals. And make no mistake, I am a criminal. Even if my only crime is being alive.

I struggle to my feet. The guard has a vice-like grip on my arm. She's dragging me toward the front of the shop. I stumble after her, out into the fresh air. Away from the smell of the bread, my head clears. A murmur runs through the bright chatter of the people outside.

"Ah, here they are." The guard sounds relieved.

The black helmets of the Metz officers stand out above the heads of the people in the crowd – two slashes of yellow on either side the only colour in their uniform. The crowd parts to let them past. My legs turn to jelly. I want to run, but I can't lift my feet.

The Metz officers form a semi-circle in front of us. Four of them. Slightly different heights and builds but otherwise identical. The guard pushes me forward and retreats a step. She doesn't want to be near them any more than me. People gather around us, keeping their distance.

The Metz officer's hand is like a pincer on my shoulder, but even without it pinning me in place, I'd be unable to move. It's as if my heart has stopped beating, and without the warm blood fuelling my muscles, my body is weak and lifeless.

"Name!"

I start, my muscles twitching involuntary. The voice is gravelly and toneless, giving no clue as to whether it's male or female. Or even if it is human at all. There are rumours about the Metz, but I had scoffed and dismissed them as fairy tales. Now, staring up into one of their impassive masks, I'm not so sure.

Breathe. Think. "Miranda. I-I think there's been some mistake."

I need a distraction.

The grip on my shoulder lessens. I take half a step to the side and cast my eye around the street. People all around. Shops with apartments above. An ancient encased clock high up on the wall, polished to a shine.

The clock.

"Stay still!" The bark is like a shot. My muscles obey instantly.

The officer reaches to its belt and pulls out a black collar. I gulp, my mouth suddenly so dry that there's barely enough moisture to swallow. My hands begin to tremble. *No, no, no.*

Unable to move, I watch as the officer holds the collar up and opens it wide enough to fit over my head. The crowd falls silent, hypnotized. When it is on me I will lose any ability to fight back, to lie, perhaps even to think. That's how they control people. Make them into mindless slaves. *What will it feel like to feel nothing at all?*

My fingers claw at my legs. There's something I need to remember. *The clock.* My middle finger catches on the raised seam of my knife pocket.

The black figure takes a step toward me, then a second. Slowly, as if it is relishing the process. Everyone's eyes are on the collar. Inch by inch I work the knife up and out, into my hand. I look for any gap in the protective black uniform. Any chink in its armour. There is none. The collar comes down.

Now. I step back and throw the knife. It hits the antique glass cover of the clock. It shatters, the noise cracking the silence like a whip. Shards of glass rain down on the people below. They scream, cover their heads, fight each other to get out of the way.

The Metz officer reaches for me, but in that split second of chaos, I have gone. Three paces to the crowd and I'm pushing through, slipping like an eel between people. Few try and bar my way; they're all looking at the clock and at the screaming, bleeding people below, trying to work out what has just happened.

"Stop her!" A bellow from the officer. I glance back. Two of them are pushing their way through the crowd, but they're bigger than me, especially in their uniforms, and the throng of people is too thick. I break through the crowd and run. I'm fast. But not as fast as the Metz. My only hope is to make it to the Wall before they catch me up. I'm pretty sure they can't go through the Wall, and it'll take them forever to go up to the East

Gate.

Streets pass in a blur. The tall buildings hide the Wall from view so I just keep moving, hoping I'm going in the right direction. I'm starting to tire when finally I find myself in a neighbourhood of terraced houses. Behind them looms the Wall. I've never been so glad to see it.

I run at it full tilt, knowing that if I stop to think, I'll wimp out. *What if last time was just a fluke?* I wonder if this will be my last thought in the world. Colours swarm in front of my eyes, then a brick wall rises up in front of me too quickly for me to stop crashing into it. My left shoulder gets the brunt of the impact again and I bite my lip to stop myself from crying out.

The smell of rubbish, dirt and stale beer hits me like a hammer. My lungs constrict and I have to force myself to breathe. I never realized Area Four smelled this bad.

I stagger along the street, desperate to get away from the Wall. Then I realize I'm not in Area Four. I'm further north. Must have come through into Area Five.

Resting my hands on my legs, I try and catch my breath. Black dots swim in front of my eyes and my legs are weak. Slowly, my heart stops pounding and I can stand again. It's only then that I think about the screams of the people who were standing under the clock, defenceless against the daggers falling on them. Children's faces. Cries of pain. Guilt stabs at me. But what choice did I have?

None. There was no choice.

4

Trey

Pain shoots up my shoulder as I hit the forest floor. I roll to absorb the impact, then get to my feet. Except my legs are weirdly unresponsive, and my momentum carries me to the floor again. The woody smell of damp earth is so different from the odourless environment of the school. Dampness seeps through my thin shirt, chilling my skin.

Do not let them catch you. Purley's words ring in my head.

I test my legs again, then set off, weaving through the trees. It is deathly quiet; the only sound my own rasping breath. Thin, bare branches whip my cheeks and pull at my hair. I've never been in these woods before. We always used Breacher's Wood on the other side of the school grounds for our cross-country practice. It's crazy, really, how little I know of the world outside those high red brick walls. The world outside London, or, more specifically, the central part of London enclosed by the Wall. How little it mattered until now.

Sliding down a gentle slope into a gully, I leave a skid-mark in the carpet of rotting leaves. Damn. I might as well have a horn blaring out my presence. I picture the black figures streaming out through the school gates, or perhaps out the back gate – that would be closer to the woods. The image spurs me on to run faster. I am a good runner. Not great, but good enough. Even so, it feels as if a hand is already clamped around my chest; my legs are weak, as if the dogs are already pulling me down.

Another rise, then a drop down to a second gully. I leap over the stream at the bottom. The bank on the other side is steep, but there are plenty of tree roots and I haul myself up with my one useful arm, not caring that my feet slip and slide on the damp wood.

A howl slashes through the silence. My body freezes, my legs suddenly locking in place and causing me to crash head first into a tree trunk. *Dogs.*

I've never seen the dogs the Metz use, but I've heard they are specially imported, bred from the wolves of Northern Europe, that even once trained they are still wild and barely controllable.

How far away are they? It's impossible to tell. My mind is racing, thoughts flying off in so many directions I can't concentrate on anything other than keeping moving. *Focus.*

My arm whips into a tree and pain combines with the ache of my muscles from the constant jerking. My back and left shoulder begin to twitch. Is it spreading? What did Purley say? *Remove the chip. If you remove the chip they can't track you.* The thought of physically cutting something out of my arm makes me want to vomit. Not that I have a knife to even attempt such a measure. *Keep moving.*

A few minutes later, I emerge from fighting my way through a dense green shrub into a dell. In the centre is a pile of scattered blackened wood. Three larger logs form a triangle around the fire pit. On the other side of the dell, rubbish had been piled, then scattered by animals searching for food. I've heard stories about illegals living in the woods. Perhaps this is one of their camps.

I run across the dell, heading for a break in the vegetation on the other side. A crunching under my feet stops me. Crouching, I feel around in the leaf litter until my fingers close on a shard of glass about two inches long, tapered to a point. Clutching it, I set off again, up a long hill.

The day is fading, the deepening gloom accentuated by a misty drizzle that clings to my hair and eyelashes. The forest feels deserted and dead. *Where are the birds? And the animals?*

A line of evergreen trees marks the crest of the hill. Panting, I push through them and stop dead. In front of me is a low wall surrounding a large green lake. Marble horseheads curve over wallowing pigs around a three-tiered fountain that's topped by naked women reclining in a variety of postures. Waterlilies cover part of the still water of the lake, the surface broken only by the occasional leap of a golden fish and light droplets of rain.

I know this place. It's an ancient ornamental lake that's part of the grounds of a large house not far from St George's. We used the lake for swim training a couple of years ago, before the hidden weeds took over and made it too dangerous. One of the boys got his leg caught and nearly drowned. Somehow, I've gone back on myself. I must have been travelling in an arc.

A volley of barking rips through the silence. It sounds close. I shiver, my arm trembling as I dip the piece of glass in the water and wipe it on my shirt. It takes a conscious effort to lift my jerking right arm onto the lake wall in front of me. I kneel on my wrist to stop it moving. A wave of dizziness washes over me. *I can't do this.* But the refrain resounds in my head.

Capture, kill. Capture, kill.

The tiny white mark on my forearm looks up at me, daring me to do it.

The glass shard is cold and sharp on my skin. A thin red

line of blood drips off my arm. I don't like the sight of blood. Especially my own.

Deep breaths. *Be a man.* My father's voice in my head now, goading me on. Before I can think further, I plunge the point of the glass into my arm. Blood bubbles up, cascading into the lake, dying the water a murky brown.

The pain hits a second later, along with a tang of bile in my mouth and an uncontrollable urge to vomit.

Find it. Get it out.

How deep is the chip? I move the piece of glass around, tearing skin and muscle, but I can't see anything through the blood that wells up from the wound. The pain is unbearable. My legs go weak and I lean on the lake wall for support, tears wetting my cheeks.

I'm about to give up, to admit defeat, when I feel the glass tap against something hard. I slip the point of glass underneath it and begin prising it up to the surface.

My vision blurs. I close my eyes and force myself to breathe deeply. *One more go, then you're done.* Opening my eyes, I turn my arm upwards and see it: a glint of gold amid the blood that continues to pour from my arm. So much blood. Does a person have that much blood in one arm or is it draining my entire body? The glass shard is slick with it, my fingers slipping.

I grit my teeth and wiggle the point under the tiny fleck of gold. With a ping, it flies out of my arm and lands on the grass beside me. The glass slips from my fingers and falls with a faint splash in the lake.

I sag against the rough wall, wave after wave of nausea washing over me. A breeze cools the sweat on my forehead. The taste of blood is in the air, in my mouth. Although … I feel around with my tongue and realize I've bitten through my cheek. The barking of the dogs is closer now. They can't be far away.

The tie around my neck is wet and awkward to undo with one hand. It's even harder to bind my arm, but by holding one end in my teeth, I manage a rough knot. The blood immediately soaks through the blue and yellow stripes.

Only now do I realize that my right arm has stopped jerking. I flex my fingers experimentally, then lift my arm up. It works! It hurts like hell, but it is *my* arm again, responding to *my* commands.

My gaze falls to the small gold object glinting on the grass. It takes me three attempts to pick it up, and when I hold it between my thumb and forefinger, I can only just make out the detailed etchings that identify it as a microchip. How can something so small be this significant?

It is surprisingly heavy for such a tiny thing, but not heavy enough. I think for a minute, pull off one of my shoes and socks, then replace the shoe. I drop the chip into the bottom of my sock, find a large stone to add to it and tie a knot in the top. Pulling my arm back, I throw the sock out toward the middle of the lake. It's a weak left-handed throw, but it goes a fair way out. A renewed round of barking from the approaching dogs masks the splash.

I hope Purley is right that without the chip, they can't track me. Because I know I can't go much further tonight. My mind is numb. The chase is over. All I can do is find somewhere to hide and trust what Purley said was true. I turn and leave, slipping between the trees like a ghost in the dusk.

* * *

When I awake, I'm so cold and in so much pain, I wonder how I slept at all. It feels as if every muscle I possess has been stretched, torn, or bruised. As for my arm, well, at least the pain has muted to a dull throb, though I'm afraid to remove the tie and check the wound underneath.

Last night I managed to clamber into a huge oak tree and wedge myself into a nook, and glancing down now, the forest floor seems far below. A flash of movement catches my eye and when I look up, a small brown bird is perched on the branch opposite, looking at me quizzically. It chirrups, and from another tree comes an answering call.

A ray of early morning sunlight filters through the trees, faintly bathing my skin in warmth. The grey damp fog of the previous day has gone. Sun. Warmth. Hope. I wrap my arms around my legs and shiver, my clothes still damp from yesterday's rain.

Removing my shoes and remaining sock, I stretch out my bruised, blistered feet. The crinkled rough bark feels familiar under my toes. I could be back climbing trees in Wales. *If it wasn't for the pain. And cold.*

What next? I can't stay here forever. I have to find my father. Dad will know what this is all about. He'll know what to do. Which means I need to get to London. It's about fifty miles away. Only half an hour in a pod.

A bark shatters the peaceful silence. My muscles tense; my body alert before my brain has fully caught up. Another bark, followed by a yipping noise. I sag back against the tree trunk. A pet dog. *But where there's a dog, there'll be a house.* A village. Which *may* just mean a pod point. And if there's a pod point, I can get to London to find Dad.

My tight, uncomfortable shoes go back on. The sole of one is half hanging off. Climbing down, I drop the last few metres from the tree to the ground, bending my knees to absorb the impact.

I find the house at the bottom of the hill. One in a row of ancient brick-built terraces. Smoke rises from the chimney. As I watch, a small dog races out of the open back door and battles excitedly with a long stick. A woman carrying a basket of washing follows it. She hums tunelessly as she hangs the washing up on a long line strung across the garden. So, this is life in the country. Burning wood to stay warm and having to dry your clothes outside.

The woman calls the dog back into the house as she returns with the empty basket. I study the items hung on the line in disappointment. It seems to be bedding and towels, not the jumpers I was hoping for. But a replacement bandage would be useful. I creep down to the side of the house, behind a bit of an outhouse that extends from the main building. Peering around the corner, I try and see in through the windows, but the morning light reflects off the Plexiglas.

I creep out and snatch a pillowcase from the line before retreating back behind the outhouse, my heart hammering in my chest.

Then I spot it. A hooded jacket thrown casually over a bench on the other side of the garden. It looks warm. A shiver runs through my body, my thin, damp shirt clinging to my skin.

Remember, you are better than them. My father's voice in my head, along with an image of some Outsiders fighting over a bag of potatoes as they run from the market stall.

Never steal. Never fight.

But I'm so cold. You can die from the cold, can't you? Surely, he wouldn't want me to die over a jacket.

You could return and pay them back once this mess is sorted out.

Surely, they won't miss one coat?

I run across the garden before I can change my mind and grab the coat, pivoting to dash back to the fence. Then I'm off running down the lane, my flapping sole loud on the hard surface.

Further down the road, I come across the rest of the village and a pod point. Two pods stand charging, both with green lights, ready to go. Sobbing in relief, I slap my hand against the square black access pad of the nearest one, leaning my head against it, my breath misting the smooth surface as I wait for the door to slide open.

Nothing happens. I pull back puzzled and try again, more carefully this time. The doors remain shut. *Why isn't it working?* I run across to the other pod. This time I try my left hand, though I know you're supposed to use your right. Nothing happens. Right hand. Nothing happens.

The chip.

Of course. I don't have my chip. Why didn't I think about this earlier? Without the chip I have no money, no way of getting food or help from a medic facility. No way of accessing transport. Without it, I'm no longer considered a legal citizen.

What have I done?

Cutting out your chip is punishable by incarceration at the Farms. Or death.

Now that I've stopped running, the throbbing in my arm returns. I unwind the blood-soaked tie and force myself to look at the wound underneath. It makes me nauseous: a red, weeping, swollen lump of flesh. I focus on tearing the pillowcase into strips and rebandage it. The blood seeps through, but at least I don't have to look at it. The coat is thick and warm. Pulling the hood over my head, I curl up next to the pod, wondering what to do next.

The sound of footsteps instantly alerts me. I relax as I see a couple approaching the pods. They look old, the woman leaning on the man as if for support. As they get closer, I see she's fighting to hold back tears; the stains on her cheeks the evidence that she has not been totally successful. I wonder if they're altruits: grandparents or great-grandparents who give up their lives so their grandchildren can have children of their own.

The man gives me a puzzled glance as they approach the pod furthest from me.

"Wait!"

My stiff muscles protest as I stagger over to them. The woman is already seated inside, her head bent.

"Sorry, do you mind if I join you?" I pant.

Fear registers on the man's face and he steps inside and reaches to close the door. I suddenly realize how I must look to them. A filthy, hooded figure. A bandit. I pull the hood back from my face and reach out an arm to hold the door open.

"Please?"

The man frowns at me, suspicious. "You're not from this village. What are you doing here?"

"I-I'm at the local school," I say. "All our pods are busy and my father called me back to London urgently – a family emergency."

"St George's?"

I nod. His eyes flick down from the oversized jacket to my filthy trousers and battered shoes. "I can't imagine St George's would have let you out in this state." He moves toward me, his arm out as if to push me away.

A howl carries on the wind and we both freeze. A second follows it, unmistakable.

45

The man frowns again. "That sounds like Metz dogs. Wh—"

I lose what he says next as the pod begins to spin around me. My head feels light, and when I close my eyes, I lose my sense of which way is up.

"Harold, catch him!"

The voice seems to come from a long way away. All I can hear are the baying wolves chasing me down. My body jerks. *Have they got me already?* There's no pain, though. At least, no more than before.

"Come on, boy, wake up."

Harold's rough voice cuts through the images. I blink and I'm back at the pods.

"Get in."

Before I can move, he's hauled me into the pod and closed the door. I collapse onto one of the soft seats, still not able to trust my legs. The pod hums and begins to lift off the ground.

Leaning forward, I look out through the two-inch strip of clear Plexiglas and see the village is already far below. Then the pod speeds up and the ground below becomes a blur of movement.

5

Aleesha

The screens in the square are blaring out adverts for beauty treatments, gene therapy and the latest tech devices. I perch on the edge of a dry fountain and rip into the protein bar I managed to find in a back-alley food store. There aren't many that accept chits in this part of Area Five. After the bread, the bar tastes like what it is: artificial junk. I choke it down anyway. Food is food.

There are three tiers of food in this city. At the bottom are the government rations: a basic entitlement for every citizen. It's supposed to be enough to live off, but if you look at the people who *do* live off it, you wonder how the government reached that conclusion. I think they just packed a load of vitamins and chemicals into some substance they made in a lab and labelled it as food. It doesn't even look the same. You feel a bit happier for eating it, but a few hours later, you're starving again. I guess they didn't feel they needed to make an effort with it since it's only Outsiders who eat the rations.

Then there's the stuff you can buy in the shops. It's factory produced, too, but because they're selling it, they put a bit more effort into making it attractive. The lurid packaging is about the only splash of colour out here. I bet people Inside don't even notice it; there are so many other things to distract them.

It's junk food, mainly. Chocco bars, candy, fake-meat burgers, protein bars. The burgers are pretty good, actually, but expensive. And Chaz. Water is always in short supply Outside, so they sell a lot of Chaz. Again, it's all fake food.

At the top of the food chain is the real food. Bread. Fruit. Cheese. Even meat from actual animals, although I understand it's stupidly expensive, even for Insiders. But there aren't many places you can buy it Outside and it's out of most people's budget. There are some shops up in Area Six that cater for the better-off Outsiders – those who work Inside. I've heard there're even some Insiders who are forced to live in Six until an apartment comes up Inside. I guess, technically, that makes them Outsiders, but I bet they don't think so.

A fanfare of noise blasts out from the screens announcing the start of the news. That's all that's on them: adverts and news. And the news is all about what's happening Inside (*their* news, not ours). Which may be why most of the screens in Area Four have long since been destroyed or stolen. No one wants to see perfect people in their perfect world when your own world is crap. And why would they bother replacing them? It's not as if anyone in Four can afford to buy the products and treatments being advertised.

The mention of Area Four catches my attention. The newsreader is interviewing a tall white man in a government suit. He looks thin and harrowed. The text at the bottom of the screen reads: *Statement from Andrew Goldsmith, Minister of Education and Health.*

"… and as I said, my colleague, the Secretary of State, is due to give a statement on this later."

"But what are *your* views on the gang problem, Minister? One of your manifesto commitments was to tackle gang violence Outside the Wall through increasing access to education."

The Minister looks uncomfortable. "We are making progress with that. Steady progress—"

"Have you actually implemented any of the programmes yet?" the newsreader interrupts.

"Yes. We have a pilot running in Area Eighteen at the moment that is going well." He holds up his hand to stop another interruption and looks directly into the camera. "We know many of our citizens live in fear of their lives from these gangs. Rising gang violence, particularly in the east of the city, is a real issue, but one we are addressing firmly. Our aim is to create a safe environment for all Outsiders. We will be stepping up measures to flush out these gangs in the problem areas and there will be a greater Metz presence on the streets."

A greater Metz presence? That's bad news. And what does he mean by "measures to flush out these gangs"? More Cleanings, perhaps. The thought makes me shudder. The protein bar sits heavily in my stomach and I start to feel a bit sick.

Stupid politicians, trying to prevent violence with more violence. But because it's on *their* orders, it's okay. He clearly knows nothing about how gangs actually work. Admittedly, there's a lot of fighting between the gangs, but that's just one side of the story. They don't show us looking out for the people on our patch, do they? Keeping a watch for imminent Cleanings so we can warn people.

Half the food we got from the raid on the depot last month went to people on our patch who were starving, trying to live off the government rations. I'd like to see how long *he'd* survive on the Outside living off that crap.

The news has moved on. There's an interview with a

Population Control Officer who talks about the rising number of illegal births she's having to manage.

Manage. As if it's just about writing an extra birth certificate or producing more chips. Why not tell people the truth? There are more babies to get rid of. To *dispose* of, as I overheard the PCO in Area Four say once.

Getting up, I stuff the plastic wrapper into my pocket. The sky has darkened while I've been sitting here. Time to get home before it rains.

"And now, an announcement from the President."

My head snaps up. He comes onto the screen, all smiles. It must be about three years since I last saw the President on a screen, but he seems to have aged a decade. His thick, black hair is now mostly steel grey, contrasting with his deep brown skin. Worry lines score his previously smooth forehead, but his eyes are still hard and cold.

"… there has been a rise in gang violence Outside the Wall for some time. However, I would like to reassure you all that we have control of the situation. Whilst this has not been an easy process, we have been steadily infiltrating and removing the heads of the most dangerous gangs. We look forward to a more stable situation for our citizens who live Outside the Wall."

His voice grates like an iron rod on brick. Is it just my imagination, or did he emphasize the word "citizens"?

"I know there have been rumours of an uprising. Please be reassured that these rumours are totally false. The Wall is impenetrable. And our priority is to ensure peace and harmony for *all* our people. Thank you."

He disappears and the breath I'd been holding rushes from my body. The first heavy drops of water speckle the worn stone of the fountain. The rain has come.

* * *

"Hey," I say, sauntering into Jay's apartment.

The look on his face is priceless. Like I've come back from the dead. Which I suppose I have.

In two bounds, he's across the room and wrapping me up in a crushing embrace, stroking my hair, running his hands down my back. I wince as he presses against my bruised shoulder, but he doesn't seem to notice. It's like he needs to touch every part of me to reassure himself that I'm alive, a solid person and not just a figment of his imagination. A shiver runs through me. I've never felt this wanted, this *needed* before. I didn't think he cared about me that much.

Finally, he holds me at arm's length. His eyes hold a mixture of guilt and relief. *Of course, that's why he's glad to see me.* He thought he'd killed me.

"I don't understand," he says finally. "You hit the Wall. I *saw* you go through it. I thought you were dead."

"So did I," I admit. "But somehow not. I just fell straight through it."

"So, you went Inside?"

I nod.

"And how did you get back?"

"The same way."

"And it didn't hurt you? Why?"

I shrug. "I don't know."

What do I say? That I seem to be able to do what no one else can. I don't know what it means, but I'm sure it can't be anything good. *Is it because I don't have a chip? Can all illegals pass through the Wall? I can't tell him that ...*

"So, where have you been? Why didn't you come back through straight away?" There's an edge to his voice as anger creeps in.

Anger that I kept him waiting so long.

"I'm sorry. I was just too afraid to go back through straight away, in case it wouldn't work again and I couldn't get back."

I recount my explorations Inside and my encounter with the Metz. Jay brushes this off, more excited about what the Inside is like. He quizzes me about every detail. The sights, the smells and the people.

"All perfectly beautiful," I confirm. "Not a blemish among them. And they're so *big*. It must be those enhancements they all have. I felt like a midget next to them. I swear, they thought I was a kid at first."

"Well, you are a little on the short side," Jay teases.

I punch his stomach gently. Jay's pretty muscular for an Outsider, probably because he doesn't have to survive solely on the government rations.

"Short and sweet?"

He grimaces. "I'm not sure sweet is exactly the term I'd use …"

He loosens my braid, running his fingers through my hair until it hangs straight down my back to my waist.

"Short and *sexy*?" I purr, doing my best coy glance.

"That's more like it," he growls and picks me up. I wrap my legs around his waist and he carries me into the bedroom, planting kisses on my neck and shoulder. He pulls off my top, frowning at the graze that runs down the top of my left arm.

"From the fall?"

I nod.

"I'm sorry," he says quietly, looking away.

"Hey, I survived, didn't I?" I pull his face toward mine for a kiss. "Nothing's broken. Bruises'll be gone in a few days."

But he's more tender than usual as he undresses me. His

caresses are gentler, as if he's afraid of breaking me. And there's a look in his eyes that I've rarely seen before.

* * *

"I've bin thinking."

"Oh?" Jay thinking always gets me worried. It's not that he doesn't try. I can see the concentration on his face, trying to get his mind to work. But he comes up with an idea, then his brain shuts down before he can finish figuring out the details. It's not his fault. I find it frustrating, but most Outsiders are the same, especially in this part of the city.

"Maybe there's something wrong with the Wall. Like it's not working properly and that's why it didn't kill you. Maybe the power shut off, like when we took down the barrier around the depot?"

"But when we shut the power off to the depot barrier, the whole thing went down. There was nothing there. Just the masts."

"Maybe. But maybe whatever it is that kills you isn't working. Or just parts of it kill you. I mean, *you* got through. And there's no reason why you'd be able to get through and others wouldn't."

Oh, yes there is. But I can't tell Jay my suspicions because that would be admitting I'm illegal. And the punishment is the same for harbouring an illegal as it is for being one. The Farms. Or death. However lovingly he looked at me earlier, I'm not sure he's prepared to risk his life for me.

"I've no idea why, but we've seen people get killed by the Wall and there's no safe way of testing it. If you're wrong, you die. It's not worth it."

I prop myself up on my elbow and look down at him. "You always wanted to be able to get Inside, right? Well, now I can.

53

And maybe if I can figure out why I can go through, you'll be able to, too. But let's keep it to ourselves for now, okay?"

The last thing I need is Jay telling everyone that I can somehow get through the Wall. Some of the kids in the gang are dumb enough to think they may be able to do the same. But if it is the chips, then surely someone would have worked that out by now? I can't be the only illegal Outsider around.

"Or maybe you really are an Insider," Jay says, stretching as he gets up off the bed. The mattress rebounds, the imprint of his body disappearing in seconds. "I'm going for a piss."

The door to the apartment slams. We share a toilet with the other residents of the building. Once, these houses would have had indoor bathrooms, showers and flushing toilets. But there hasn't been enough water to pipe through for decades.

The government fitted incinerating toilets but they broke down so much, eventually someone installed a composting one. Barry Crapper collects the waste and sells it back to the government for the Farms. He's a bit of a legend in Area Four, is Barry Crapper. Local boy made good. Of course, he lives up in Area Five now and I hear his kids are going to an Area Six school.

Maybe you really are an Insider.

Jay's words echo in my head. I stretch my leg up to the ceiling, twisting my ankle so the amulet on the cord around it twinkles. My mother gave it to me on the day she disappeared twelve years ago. It's the only clue I have to my father's identity. A gift he gave to my mother before I even existed.

My mother gave birth to me on the plastic floor of our one-room ground floor apartment in the rougher part of Area Five. She cut the umbilical cord herself and wrapped me in a scrap of the spare bed sheet that she'd torn up for the purpose. I was never taken to a hospital and my birth was never registered.

Keeping my illegal status hidden was a challenge. No one can hide a baby when the apartment walls are paper-thin, but she contrived to be out every time the local Population Control Officer came around to check my papers. She told the neighbours that my father worked away a lot, travelling to other cities on business trips. I doubt anyone believed her.

We moved three times in my first year, each time getting further from the East Gate, until we ended up in a part of Area Four where the PCO was known to be less concerned about records, if you made it worth his while. My mother did.

She told me all this when I was four. Except the bit about what she did to keep the PCO off our backs. I only figured that out later. At the time, I didn't think it was odd that the man came around so often to "check our papers". Always at night. And for some reason, I couldn't stay in the apartment when he was checking them. He'd give me a candy and tell me to scarper for half an hour.

Of course, after she disappeared he wasn't quite so kind.

My mother never told me who my father was. I suspect that he doesn't even know I exist. But from the hints she dropped, I wondered if perhaps he was an Insider and if that's why she hadn't registered my birth, because she couldn't admit who he was.

The apartment door slams again. "Are you coming to HQ?"

I pull on my spare set of clothes and join Jay in the main room of the apartment. "Yeah. I just need to clean up my arm. You go ahead."

"Better hurry, a storm's coming."

A crack of thunder drowns out his next words as he hurries back out of the apartment. The patter of raindrops on the

Plexiglas windows intensifies.

I lift the loose floorboard and retrieve the lockbox underneath. I'm pretty sure I still have some pills in here left from the depot raid. There's a clatter as something falls back into the void. A knife! I'd forgotten I'd hidden a spare one here. I usually carry three or four at a time, but the one I'd used to distract the Metz was my best throwing knife. This one doesn't balance quite so well, but it's better than nothing.

I pop a pink vitamin pill and a blue anti-infection pill, then go up to the roof to fetch some rain water from the tank. It's a large tank, but thirty people live in this block, so it's rarely full even after a storm.

Back in the apartment, I set the water to boil and examine the damage to my arm. The graze has already scabbed over and I figure it's probably best left alone. I dab around it and use the rest of the water to rinse out my torn top.

There's a flash of light at the window, followed by another roll of thunder. Rain hammers down, forcing droplets of water through the edges of the window frame. Trickles of water run down the wall.

"I'm going to get bloody drenched," I announce to the empty room.

Ten seconds out in the rain and I'm as wet as I'm going to be. My legs stay pretty dry, but I haven't saved up enough yet for a waterproof top and my t-shirt instantly sticks to my skin.

The streets are already filling with water. They always flood this time of year. I saved every chit I could get my hands on for a year to buy a pair of government-issue boots. Without proper boots, likelihood is you'll lose a foot to rot.

"Password?"

The bored gang member on security duty barely gives me a

glance as I answer and step past him to the back door. Inside, the thick walls muffle the sound of thunder somewhat. Squeezing the water out of my hair, I walk through and into the main hall.

The headquarters of the Spitalfields Snakes is a huge, old brick warehouse. Half of it is completely derelict, but what remains houses most members of the gang. The focal point is a huge hall that rises the full height of the building. Most of the original windows that line the walls have been boarded up, but the skylights in the roof have somehow survived. Usually, the sound of rain on the glass is soothing, but tonight it's almost deafening. It looks as if the storm's going to stick around.

A roped-off ring with padded mats stands in the centre of the room. It's empty tonight, but there's usually a wrestling or boxing match going on. In the far corner, a short, skinny man is taking out his anger on a punchbag. Next to him, a kid bashes a knife into shape with a makeshift hammer. Against the far wall, a mural is in progress. From what they've painted so far, it looks like another blue snake.

Every gang has a colour they use to denote their territory. For the Snakes, it's blue. The shades vary as paint cans are hard to come by, but every street, every alleyway in our area is marked.

"Hey, Aleesha, I've not seen you here for a while." The friendly greeting barely veils the underlying threat.

I plaster a smile on my face and turn to the willowy, dark-haired girl. "Megan, nice to see you. And, Anelia." I nod to Megan's shadow. "How are you both?"

Megan answers for both of them. "Fine." Her eyes narrow. "Who's that stranger you've been hanging around with?"

"Stranger?" I widen my eyes, all innocence.

She snorts. "Don't give me that. The big guy with the funny accent. He's not from around here. Does Jay know about him?"

Murdoch. Either they've seen me with him or Jonas has been gossiping. "Why do you think I was talking to him?"

Megan looks confused. "I don't know why you were talking to h—"

I walk away, strolling over to Jay. As usual, he's surrounded by a crowd, mainly younger gang members, all trying to prove themselves to him.

"Where's Dane?" I ask, looking around the hall. Jay usually sticks as close to the gang leader as possible.

Jay shrugs. "Said he had a meeting tonight and he might be back late."

I roll my eyes. I'd bet my last chit Dane is shacked up with the latest in his string of women.

Someone asks Jay a question and I use the opportunity to slip away and circulate the room, listening in on people's conversations. The atmosphere in the room is unusually tense and people talk in hushed voices. The Brotherhood comes up again and again. They've taken over the Dragons. The new leader of the Shanksters is under their control, too. Bigland Boy's leader was found half dead by the river. There are questions. What do they want? Are we next? Where's Dane?

Rumours. There are no facts, just rumours. The Brotherhood are an unknown terror. No one seems to know who they are, where their base is, or what they're trying to do other than taking control of the gangs. I've never felt such fear in this place before. Not even during Metz raids when the streets outside were swarming with black-clad figures.

People eye me warily. They tolerate my presence, but don't invite me to join their conversations. Are they frightened of me? Do they see me as Jay's spy?

I hunker down on a step and lean my back against the cold

brick wall, staring at the rivers of water lashing the skylights.

Is it possible to be lonely when you're surrounded by people? To be in a place you belong and don't belong?

Sometimes, I feel like I'm the shell of a person, going through the motions of surviving while searching for that something, that place that feels like home. Until today, I had thought that place was Inside the Wall. Now I realize I'm just as out of place there as I am here.

My belly churns and a bubble of emotion rises to my throat. I swallow it back down. I don't cry. Ever.

Will I ever find somewhere I belong?

6

Trey

The old couple drop me off at the Angel pod point. Apparently, it's the closest station to Great Percy Street, but when I get down to street level, I wonder if they've made a mistake. The top of the Wall shimmers above the mid-rise apartment blocks; the occasional pod flying in over the top of it. Our apartment is surrounded by tall glass towers and I can't remember being able to see the Wall from the local area. My geography of London is hazy at the best of times, but I'm pretty sure I'm in the wrong part of town. I'll just have to find my way on foot.

41 Great Percy Street, London.

Mum made me memorize our home address when I was five years old in case I got lost. It's seemed pretty pointless until now as I've never been allowed out around London by myself. Which is ridiculous when you think about it – I'm practically an adult. But it's always fun hanging out with my sister, Ella, so I never minded that much.

I wander down a street lined with identical apartment blocks. White to reflect the summer heat, with a dark patterned design probably marketed as decorative, but really there to incorporate the solar panels necessary to power each building's cooling system. Tiny tables and chairs compete for space with potted lemon trees and hanging tomato vines – everyone trying to make the most of their small balconies.

My arm is throbbing again. It's so tender, even brushing it against my body sends flashes of pain shooting up my arm. I flex my fingers. Everything still seems to work, so I can't have done that much damage, can I? I just need to get to a medic before it gets infected. Perhaps it's already infected. How do you know?

Someone crashes into my shoulder.

"Watch where you're going!" A man in the blue suit of a government official scowls at me.

"Sorry," I mumble. I'm about to walk away when something stops me. I know his face; I've seen him before. My mind is so slow, so fogged, it seems to take forever to find the memory. Then it comes to me. He works with my father. One of Dad's junior ministers, I think. He came to the apartment once when there was some government emergency. A riot. Father left with him and didn't return to the house for three full days.

I run back and grab his arm. "Excuse me! Do you know where I can find my—" I blurt the words out before I can stop to think. "Andrew Goldsmith?"

The man doesn't reply. He searches my features as if he's trying to place me. "I haven't seen Andrew for a couple of days. He didn't turn up to the office yesterday." He frowns at me. "Haven't I seen you before? Are you his … nephew?" He sounds puzzled.

I stare back at him blankly, unable to form a response. If he works with Dad, surely he knows he has a son? A lump forms in my throat. *Am I such a disappointment to him that he doesn't even admit I exist?* I've never been the perfect son he wanted;

I've always struggled in class and been at the back on the sports field, but I'm his *son,* for goodness sake.

"Wait, haven't I seen you on the news recently?" The man reaches for my arm, but I pull back, suddenly wary.

Why would I be on the news?

"Darwin. Darwin Goldsmith, that's it." He lunges for me, but I manage to dodge and step back. He seems half angry, half fearful.

Why is he afraid? What are they saying about me? I don't wait to find out. After a couple of paces, he gives up the chase and waves his hand in defeat. I don't stop until I'm two streets away in a large square thronging with people.

Wandering through the crowd, I get some strange looks. *What must I look like to them?* Filthy clothes, falling apart shoes, and an oversized, hooded jacket. I look like a tramp. An Outsider.

A fanfare announces the hourly news bulletin that interrupts the barrage of advertisements on the screens that line every building of the square. A few people look up, but most just carry on about their business.

The President comes on, talking about the rise of gang violence Outside the Wall. There's something about the possible opening of trade relations with France. Boring politics. I look away, and when I glance back up at the screen I'm staring at myself.

Huh?

I blink, wondering if it's some kind of trick. But I'm still there. White-blond hair, a bit shorter than it is now, blue eyes, a nose that's just a bit too large for my face. I'm smiling. Last year's school photo. Underneath it, text scrolls across the screen. *Illegal boy on the run. Report any sighting immediately to the Metropolitan Establishment.*

62

I run down streets, picking turns at random. I have no clue where I'm heading, I just know I need to get away. Away from the photographs of me on every building down every street. Finally, I pause in a dark alleyway behind a row of shops. My head's spinning and I stumble like a drunk, trying to keep my balance. *Stop. Think.*

Plan. I need a plan. I've still got a few hours of daylight. *What would Dad do? He'd have a plan for this. Think.*

But I disappoint my father again. I can't come up with anything better than trying to work out which part of the city I'm in and where that is in relation to home. Perhaps then I can stick to the back roads and get there before dark.

I carry on walking, searching for something, anything, that I can use to help locate my surroundings. The streets are narrow and the buildings are old, which makes me think I'm in the east of the city. Ahead of me is an intersection with a small square. A stone pillar flanked by two soldiers and topped with a lion stands proud in front of an ancient, stone-columned building that was once the financial heart of the city.

The man's words come back to me. *I haven't seen Andrew ... he didn't turn up to the office yesterday.*

My father not turn up for work? Not possible. I don't think he's missed a day's work in his life. But if he isn't at work, then where is he? *Have the Metz gone after my family, too? And why are they saying I'm illegal? Because I cut my chip out?*

I slide down the rough stone wall, feeling overwhelmingly tired. *Perhaps I'll just close my eyes for a minute.*

"Hey, are you okay?"

A hand on my shoulder rouses me. A pair of bright blue Smokers are standing in front of me. They're this season's style and at the more expensive end of the range. Another pair of feet joins them, this time dressed in boring black Klacks. Though, I would gladly take a pair of comfy Klacks over these stupid leather school shoes.

Blue shoes, black shoes. Black shoes, blue shoes. For some reason this makes me giggle. The colours begin to blur together. *Blue shoes, black shoes.*

The blue shoes move as their owner bends down and peers at me.

"Goldsmith? Is that you?" The voice is vaguely familiar.

I look up. It takes my brain a few seconds to process the boy crouched in front of me. James. Percy James. In the year below me. Runs cross-country. Fast. I look from him to the man standing beside him; his father, presumably. I wonder why he's not at school, or even in his uniform. Then I remember. Yesterday was Friday, which means today is Saturday.

"Hi, Percy." My voice is cracked and I clear my throat and try again. "How're you doing?"

"Are you drunk, boy?" His father's face comes into view. He does not look happy.

I take a deep breath and push myself up off the ground, but I can only really use my left arm as my right is too tender. Still, I manage to make it to my feet. Just.

"No, sir. I'm sorry. I'm just feeling a little unwell, that's all." *Now that is the understatement of the year.*

"What happened to you? I heard you'd run away, that the Metz ..." Percy's voice trails off as if he's unsure what to say.

I'm not totally sure I can trust Percy. I'm not sure I can trust anyone at this point. But I'm out of options.

"Please, help me, Percy. I—" I reach out and grasp his arm. "The Metz set dogs on me. They were trying to hunt me down, to kill me." I can hear my voice getting higher pitched and force myself to take a deep breath. "I haven't done anything wrong. I mean, they must think I've done something, but whatever it is, I haven't done it. I swear!"

Percy's expression sways between sympathy and wariness.

"Please, all I need is some food and a medic and some sleep. Then I'll leave and go away again. Please?" I can hear the pleading in my voice.

Percy glances to the man beside him. "Dad?"

The man frowns at me, looks at his son, then back to me. There is something odd in his expression. He sighs. "I'm sorry, Goldsmith? That's your name, isn't it? I'm sorry, but we can't help."

Percy looks worried. "B—"

His father cuts him off and speaks more firmly. "No, Percy, we can't. This boy may have been your friend, but now he is no one. Do you understand me? He is no one."

"What do you mean?" The words come out before I can stop them, louder than I had intended.

The man looks around. Fear lines his face, but why? He wraps his arm around Percy's shoulders, pulling him away from me. I lurch after them and grab his coat sleeve.

"Please, why is this happening to me? Why can't you help me? My father—"

The man whirls around, yanking his arm from my grasp. "Your father cannot and will not help you now." I step backward, recoiling from the anger in his voice. His expression softens and he leans in, speaking more gently. "I'm sorry, Goldsmith, I really am. But you do not know what you're asking of me; of us." He shakes his head slightly. "Look, I won't report this to the Metz for another half hour or so. That's as much as I can do. But you can't run forever. Eventually, they'll find you and perhaps, if you were to go willingly ..." His voice trails off.

Then he pulls Percy away and the two of them hurry off down the street, leaving me standing there more confused than ever.

Why are they afraid of helping me? What have I done?

The feeling of raindrops on my face and hands brings me out of my daze. The street begins to turn dark as the water seeps through the porous surface. The sky is gloomy and heavy with cloud.

I shove my hands in my pockets, grateful for the heavy hooded coat, and begin to trudge away from the square. A blur of black makes me jump back, heart hammering. The cat turns and hisses at me before continuing its dash across the street. Something hits me on the top of my head and I back away, arms up in a pathetic defensive stance, before I realize that I've walked into a hanging sign.

Get a grip. Fear and hunger gnaw at my belly, overwhelming rational thought. *What can I do? I can't outrun them forever – not here.* They're probably watching the cameras right now. Tracking me. They're going to find me. It's inevitable, just a matter of time.

Strangely, despair seems to give me energy. *Are there any parts of the city the cameras don't cover?* People's gardens. Gardens with thick shrubs to hide in. There are still some private gardens in the richest part of the city.

Speeding up, I turn down a side street, only to run smack bang into something hard and unyielding. I stagger backward, smarting with the impact, and my hood falls back.

I take a sharp breath as I register in front of me the unyielding black body armour of a Metz officer. We move at the same time. The fabric of my coat sleeve slips through its fingers, a hair's breadth away from capture. Then I'm off down the street, turning left, then right, then left again, trying to gain some precious distance between me and my pursuer, adrenaline overcoming my exhaustion.

At the next intersection, I glance back. There are two of them now, barely a hundred metres behind me, and as I watch, a third joins them from higher up the road. My legs are so weak. I'm not sure how long even terror can drive me on. At least, this maze of passageways makes it harder for them to run flat out and catch me.

The next alleyway kicks me out onto a main road. To my horror, there are Metz officers everywhere. One of them spots me and they begin to run toward me. I have no choice but to run in the other direction.

Ahead of me, bisecting the road, is the Wall. Lost in the maze of tall buildings, I hadn't realized how close to the edge of the city I was. It rises up into the dark clouds, swirls of light protecting us from the Outside. So beautiful and yet so deadly.

A street leads off to the left, another to the right, down toward the swamp. I take the right turn, rounding the corner at a sprint, and skid to a halt. Coming toward me are a line of officers, weapons drawn and ready. I turn back onto the main street, but I haven't taken two steps toward the other side road when I see the figures swarming up it like hornets from a nest. Glancing around, I desperately search for a way out. But there are no other alleyways.

I am trapped.

They converge behind me, the three flows merging into one, forming a barricade of black warriors. Why so many officers for one boy? Surely, they can't expect me to be that hard to take down? There's a shout. An order for me to stop. *Can't they see I'm standing still?* The figures have slowed, they're walking now.

They know there's nowhere for me to go.

I think of the warnings, the fear people had for me. Of me. The fear of what the Metz may do.

It won't be an easy death. Purley's words ring in my head. Percy's dad's face comes to mind, a picture of fear. My chest tightens as my eyes dart from black mask to black mask. So many of them.

Why aren't they shooting? Do they want to take me alive? I wonder if the rumours I've heard are true. Of the Farms. The Labs. What they do to criminals.

There's a sour taste in my mouth. Any hope of a last-minute rescue has gone. They're only ten metres away now. It's strange how fighting for your life is easy when you have hope.

You still have a choice. Not a choice between life and death, but a choice in how you die.

One of the Metz takes a few steps forward. It holds out its hand and says something I don't catch. I glance up at the Wall, wondering how much it will hurt, how quickly it will be over. Then I turn and, without hesitating, run toward the Wall.

7

Aleesha

M urdoch grabs my arm, pulling me to him as if we were a couple out on a walk.

"Oww, get off!" My shoulder's still sore from the abuse I gave it yesterday.

I squirm, trying to pull my arm free, but his grip is too firm. I look around, hoping one of the gang may be within shouting distance, but although I recognize several faces in the crowd, there are none who I can rely on for help.

"Where are we goin'?" I hiss out of the corner of my mouth. Figuring there's no point in being literally dragged along, I try my best to keep pace with him and keep my head down.

"You'll see."

That's all I get out of him. We turn off down a side street and weave our way across Area Four, passing through the Shanksters' territory. My heart begins to hammer in my chest as I realize where we're heading. The Dragons. They're not going to take kindly to me being in their territory. In fact, in my last interaction with them, the guy who's now their leader said he would personally pull my guts out. Slowly.

"Woah!" I dig my heels into the ground, pulling Murdoch to a stop. "Hang on a sec." After jerking my arm free, I twist my hair into a knot on the back of my neck and pull the thin hood of my jacket up over it. *Thank god I wore a hooded jacket.*

"Ready when you are." I hold out my arm theatrically, earning me another silent glare.

Keeping my head down, I focus on the road in front of me. These streets are as familiar to me as the Snakes' territory in Four. I've walked them in the dark, blindfolded and, on one occasion, bundled in a sack on someone's back. I don't have to look around me to know exactly where I am.

We keep away from the main roads, skirting down side alleys and quiet, tumbled-down streets. Purple symbols serve as a reminder that we're in the Dragons' territory. The streets are mostly empty. People in this neighbourhood have jobs and are out during the day. I even spot the back of a Metz patrol as we cut across one of the main streets.

Murdoch stops at the entrance to a small square yard at the back of a row of terraced houses. Pots of tangled brown leaves entwine themselves with vines that cling to the brickwork. There's even a small tree. More plant life than I've seen in one place before yesterday.

"This way." He pushes me toward the back door.

The room I enter is sparse, even by Outsider standards. There's a small sofa covered with a brown striped blanket, and a three-legged stool. A tall man stands by the window, staring out into the yard. In the opposite corner of the room is another door, presumably leading to the front room of the house. I take a step toward it, then stop.

"It's locked. But there's no need to run. We're not going to hurt you." The man's voice is smooth, but kind of rough at the same time. Like he's trying to speak like an Insider, but can't quite lose the trace of his natural accent. There's something about him, the way he holds himself, that oozes power.

Relax.

"I don't think we've met." I force my voice to be casual, lazy, even.

The man cocks his head as if weighing me up. He's dressed casually in jeans and a white t-shirt. A single tattoo winds its way down his arm, barely visible on his dark brown, almost black skin. A chain. The Chain.

"No, we haven't. But I understand that you have some information for us, Aleesha." His tone is calm and deliberate but slightly mocking, as if he somehow knows I have nothing to tell them.

I stand up a bit straighter, not that my five feet and two inches gets me anywhere near his six-and-a-half-foot frame. *Now, how to spin this.*

"You asked me to investigate the Shanksters. Find out whether they were thinking of joining, or already part of the—" I pause for a second but force myself to say it. "The Brotherhood. I managed to get time alone with their new leader."

I weigh up the consequences of lying and getting found out versus not giving them what they want. But I figure if I completely make something up and then get found out, it's going to be the bottom of the river for me, with a handful of bricks tied around my feet.

"He wasn't very forthcoming, but there's no way he would have beaten Drake in a fair fight. The Brotherhood put him there. The Dragons also have a new leader. They held a leadership contest, but it may not have been a fair fight." I force myself not to shudder at the thought of *him* in charge of the gang.

"Are those facts or just street rumours?"

I hesitate for a second. "Rumours," I admit, "but the leadership thing is a big deal. No one cheats at the leadership contests, and to not have one at all ..." *Is strange.*

The leadership contests were originally started by the gangs to prevent them destroying themselves and each other with constant infighting. Whoever wins the contest is accepted as the undisputed leader by everyone inside and outside the gang. Leadership contests are big money-makers for gangs, too; kind of like huge street parties. Not holding a contest means giving up a good number of chits and pissing off the other gangs in the area. All gangs profit from a contest.

The man looks thoughtful for a minute then returns to staring outside. Behind me, Murdoch shuffles his feet impatiently. The silence is starting to get to me.

"Well, if you're not needing me anymore, I'll be off." I turn and take two steps toward the door, but Murdoch blocks my path.

"Not so fast."

"You're smart, Aleesha." The man speaks conversationally, still staring out the window. "Rather *too* smart for an Outsider."

My heart begins to pound.

He surprises me by walking over and placing a finger under my chin, tilting my head so I'm forced to look up at him. His touch is electric, and his eyes bore into me, like he's trying to look into my head. I want to look away, but I can't.

"Too smart to waste your life on tronk." He almost spits the last word and I flinch.

Uh oh, Murdoch told him.

I open my mouth to defend myself, to deny it, but then close it again. He nods in acknowledgement of my defeat and, dropping his arm, turns away again. Strangely, I find myself missing his touch.

"Our deal is off." It takes me a second to process his words, but when they sink in, an icy chill grows in the bottom of my stomach.

"But—"

"We had a deal, Aleesha. You help us, we help you. You've not kept your side of the bargain, so why should we keep ours?"

My face burns with the heat of shame and disappointment. *I'm not giving up that easily. Unless they were lying all along ...*

I turn to Murdoch. "So, you don't know anything about my mother? It was all a ploy to get me to play your game?"

Murdoch looks taken aback, but quickly recovers his usual smirk. "Not at all. I know of someone who saw your mother die. But, as we agreed, you had to deliver your side of the bargain first."

"Die?" I squeak. The chill spreads outwards from my stomach and up to my chest, which tightens, making it hard to breathe.

"You didn't know?"

Dead.

"W-what?"

"You didn't know she was dead?" The tall man's voice is more gentle now.

Get a grip.

"Of course, I knew she was dead," I lie, trying to control the tremor in my voice. "If she wasn't, she would have come back for me."

Cold like ice. Like death.

"Well, we may be able to make another deal."

"Another deal?" My brain feels like it's on go-slow, struggling to piece thoughts together. A voice inside is screaming at me to get a grip, but it's drowned out by the fog.

"How long have you been able to go through the Wall?"

The question comes at me so suddenly that I have no time to think of a response. My mouth's hanging open and I close it sharply, rounding on Murdoch.

"You were following me?"

And I didn't notice? Poor, Aleesha, poor. You're losing your edge.

His lips broaden in a mocking smile. "You wish. Just a coincidence. I happened to be in Area Five when this girl plunges through the Wall and legs it down the street in front of me."

I feel an overwhelming urge to punch the smirk off his face. My hand clenches into a fist by my side.

"How long, Aleesha?" the black man asks again.

"Not long. I fell through accidentally." I pause. "Do … Do you know why? Why I can go through the Wall?"

"No." He frowns. "You're the first person we've found who can do it."

"Can Insiders go through?" I hesitate. "Not that they'd want to, of course. Much easier to use a pod."

"As far as we know, Insiders can't pass through the Wall."

"Has anyone tried?"

"Yes, someone did try!" He rounds on me, his eyes flashing in anger. "And yes, they died. And before you ask, it's nothing to do with the microchips, either. We thought that might be it, that the Wall triggers something in the chip, but we were wrong."

He stares out the window. There's an uncomfortable silence. *There goes my theory.* I look down at my hands, wondering what would compel someone to throw themselves at the Wall just to test whether it killed them or not. Surely, there has to be a better way of finding out?

I fold my arms, trying to keep my feelings under control, but they're bubbling up inside me like a volcano. Anger. Frustration. Curiosity. So many emotions.

"So, what's the job?"

"For now, just scout Inside the Wall. Get to know the area, the hidden spots where there are no cameras. The best places to get in and out without being seen." He turns to look at me. "Don't get caught. Murdoch will be in touch when we have a job for you."

I stare at him in disbelief. "That's it?" *How long do I have to wait?*

"For now." His tone is dismissive. We have clearly come to the end of the interview. Except I'm not done. Murdoch places a hand on my arm and I shake it off.

"What about your side of the bargain? I'm not going to wait indefinitely while you decide whether or not you want to use me."

He takes a step toward me, looking down at me coldly. "You have to prove yourself first." He nods to Murdoch. "Escort our visitor out."

There are so many questions I want to ask, but I bite my tongue. Murdoch unbolts the door leading to the backyard and motions for me to step through it.

"Aleesha?" I turn to look back at him. For a moment I think I see sympathy in his eyes, but I blink and they're cold and hard. I must have imagined it. "Stay off the tronk. You screw up again and there'll be no more deals."

As we leave the small back yard of the house, I realize suddenly that he was playing me all along. They had no intention of letting me go.

Where have these people come from? They don't seem to be Insiders, but they're clever for Outsiders. Better fed, too.

Perhaps I've met my match ... Or, at least, my equals.
Tread carefully, Aleesha. This could be a dangerous path.

8

Trey

The colours of the Wall swim in front of me. They are all I see. It's three paces away.

Now two.

One more step.

But I'm still running. My eyes snap open. *What's happening?* Something looms up in front of me. I hit something hard and am thrown to the ground.

"Oww!" My vision is blurred and I blink frantically. Every part of me hurts. I thought dying would at least stop things hurting.

My vision clears just as the smell hits me. *Jesus, what a stink.* I feel suddenly dizzy and realize I'm holding my breath. *Breathe.* But the foul-smelling air catches at the back of my throat and I roll to the side just in time to heave up what little water was left in my stomach.

Rotting, unidentifiable trash is piled up against a brick wall. The brick wall I've just bounced off. Gingerly, I prod the rising lump on my forehead. Behind me, the Wall sparkles in the rain. Still there, shimmering and glowing. I must have run through it.

But that's impossible. Isn't it?

Excitement surges through me. I went through the Wall. There's no other explanation. And the Wall is now between me and the Metz. This thought causes the fear to return. *Can the Metz go through the Wall?* I don't think so, but I've never had cause to think about it before. *Surely, if they could, they'd be on me by now.*

I take a step back, then another, until my foot sends a metal can skidding down the street. I stagger toward an alley a few metres away that leads away from the Wall. Crumbling concrete walls covered in black and blue graffiti and topped with coils of razor wire line both sides. Down the alleyway, the concrete walls merge into large, windowless brick buildings. The place looks derelict and deserted.

Fear grips me. I'm Outside the Wall. Outside. And everything I know, everything I've been told and read about the Outside fills me with dread.

Trembling, I fasten my coat, pulling the hood over my head as the light drizzle turns to heavy rain. There's a rumble of thunder, then a flash of lightning splits the sky. Inside the coat, I feel kind of protected. Disguised. Perhaps inside it, I can pass for an Outsider.

The alleyway weaves through what look to be warehouses until it eventually opens out to a wider road. The city hum is louder, but in this neighbourhood, at least, there seems to be no one around. Rather than reassuring me, it just makes me feel more uneasy.

A squeal from somewhere nearby breaks through the background noise. It sounds as if it's coming from an alley on my right. Drawing level with it, I peer into the deepening shadows and see a group of people huddled around something on the floor. A man prods it and the thing whimpers. I can't tell if it is animal or human, but the sight makes my blood runs cold and I hurry away before they spot me.

Around the next corner, a group of men huddle under a tin roof. Their clothes are tattered and it looks as if they haven't washed in a year. I think I can smell them from here. *Filthy, lazy tramps.* Smoke stings my eyes from the small fire that's rapidly losing its battle with the water dripping through the holes in the makeshift shelter.

I keep my eyes on them as I sidestep through the shadows on the other side of the road. They're engrossed by the fire. Hands that are dark with ingrained dirt hover above the spluttering flames. *Just keep looking at that fire.* I don't see the rusted piece of metal until my foot connects with it, sending it skidding with a clatter across the street. Five pairs of eyes are suddenly on me.

One of the tramps leaps up and lumbers to block my way. He leans forward to peer into my face and the taste of decay on his breath makes me splutter.

Then they're all around me. Prodding and poking, pulling my hood down, tearing at my coat.

"Who's this?"

"Ee's got a nice coat. A nice warm coat, that is. Bet it keeps off the rain."

"Is he one of *them*? Looks like a' Insider with that pretty hair."

"Not much meat on 'is bones, though. And ee's very pale, isn't he?"

"Get off me!" I lash out wildly with my good arm and connect with someone.

"Stop yer fighting, boy. It won't do you no good."

But they won't let me go. I can barely breathe, the smell of them is so bad. I hit out again and again, trying to make a break in the circle.

More by luck than aim, one of my blows connects with a tramp's nose and he falls back, wailing in pain. Someone grabs my bad arm and I scream before the pain even registers. I yank my arm away, leaving the coat sleeve behind. There's a tug on the other sleeve and suddenly I'm tumbling forward, free.

I can hear the fighting behind me as I run, not daring to look back. I wonder if the coat will survive the fight and who will be the lucky victor. Without it I feel exposed. My shirt sticks to my skin in the rain. A blue shirt in a world of grey and brown. With my white-blond hair, I am a beacon in the dark.

As the last dregs of daylight fade, I slow to a walk. The mud sucks at my shoes, releasing them with a slurping sound that accompanies every step. In places, the water comes up to my ankles and I wonder if I've inadvertently walked into a river. Most of the windows in the tall apartment blocks are dark and only the flicking light of an occasional streetlight stops me from walking straight into a wall. *Surely, they have power out here? There's enough roof space for panels. Unless they choose to live in the dark.*

In these odd patches of light, I catch glimpses of more tramps huddled in doorways or on top of rubbish piles, trying to stay out of the water. Their eyes follow me. An occasional bony hand reaches out to pat my leg, causing me to flinch away into the middle of the road.

A neon pink light from a side alley catches my attention. I strain to make out what it says, its flickered letters dancing in front of my eyes. Hotel. *A hotel?* My footsteps quicken as relief floods through me.

Then I stop. I have no money. No ID chip, nothing.

This is the Outside. I bet you can arrange to pay in the morning, then just sneak out.

It feels wrong, like stealing the coat from the house in the woods. But I have to get out of this rain. Voices spill out from inside. A restaurant or bar, perhaps. I push open the door under the neon sign and walk in.

The bar falls silent as I enter, the swishing of the door closing the only sound. Heat burns my cheeks as I feel their eyes on me, judging me. Then, as if conscious that the silence is too intense, the noise and chatter resume.

The bar is small, filled with a collection of mismatched tables, half made of cheap plastic and the others cobbled together from pieces of junk. A dozen or so people sit around them. Several are playing a game involving metal discs that they slam down onto the tabletop. In one corner a man sits alone, hunched over a small glass of clear liquid, a crutch propped up against his chair. In the opposite corner, two skeletons stare at me with hollow, lifeless eyes, paper-thin skin stretched over their bird-like frames. One coughs and I realize with a start that they're alive. Though by the look of them, not for much longer.

I walk to the bar, leaving a trail of water in my wake. There's only one customer sitting there, a blond-haired man hunched over a glass. Behind the bar, a girl about my age dries glasses with a fraying rag that may once have been white. Her brown hair is streaked with blond and she has a small mole on the right of her forehead. As I get closer, I see her skin is slightly lined. *Perhaps she's older than I thought.* Then I remember that Outsiders may not have access to the skin treatments that can remove any unsightly wrinkles or marks. She stares at me curiously.

"D-d-do you have a spare room?" *Damn that stutter.* Even after years of work it still sometimes comes back.

The girl seems taken aback. "Umm, sure." She looks around as if unsure what to do next.

The atmosphere in the room is tense. As if everyone's waiting for something to happen.

Something's wrong.

"Hey, kid, do you know what this place is?"

The voice is quiet in my ear. I turn to face the blond-haired man. He's about my height but stockier, with tanned, weathered skin and a large, crooked nose. He looks fifty or sixty, but I guess he could be younger. All these Outsiders have so many wrinkles and lines on their faces it's hard to tell their age. He's the first person I've seen out here who's got blond hair and the first who doesn't look like they're half starved. And although he's not exactly friendly, he doesn't look like he's about to try and kill me.

I hesitate for a moment before answering, wondering if it's a trick question. "A hotel?"

The man smiles wryly. "Not the sort you're used to, I bet. In this place, they only rent rooms by the hour."

I'm confused. *What's he trying to tell me?* I glance over at the barmaid who is studiously polishing a glass.

The man sighs and leans forward. His breath is slightly acrid from sour beer. "It's a brothel, son. A whorehouse."

"Oh." I can feel myself blushing. *You idiot. If they didn't already see you as an Insider, they do now.*

"You're new out here, right?" He doesn't wait for an answer. "This isn't a good part of town for you to be in. I don't know how you've ended up here, but you should get back up to the East Gate. Get back Inside."

"I-I can't go back."

He glances down at the blood-soaked pillowcase on my arm.

82

"Why? What have you done?"

"Nothing!" The bar goes quiet again. "I've done nothing wrong," I say more quietly. Desperation loosens my tongue. "Honestly. I don't even know where I am or how I got here. I just need somewhere to stay for the night and a medic." The room seems to suddenly tilt and I close my eyes, reaching for the reassuring solidity of the bar. *No fainting now. Stick with it.*

"You're in Area Four." The man's voice is slightly softer. "Go back to the main street and turn right. At the crossroads turn left and follow that road. It'll eventually get you into Area Five. You'll hit the Wall at some point. Follow it up and you'll get to the East Gate." He looks warily at me. "It's a bit of a walk, though."

I've already forgotten what his first instruction was. "Could you show me?" I ask hesitantly.

His expression clouds and anger flashes across his eyes. "No," he answers shortly. "I have to go." Standing, he pulls on a black jacket and heads for the door.

"Wait!" I stumble after him, knocking over a bar stool in my haste. But as I get to the door, I feel hands grab me from behind and cold, sharp metal against my throat.

"Not so fast, *boy*."

I gulp, feeling the prick of the blade on the lump in my throat.

The man pushes me in front of him, through the swing doors and out into the dark alleyway. Blinking, I can just about make out the blond-haired man, crouching a few metres away, staring into the shadows on the other side of the street. There's a pink glint as the light of the hotel sign reflects off something in his hand. He glances over at us.

"Let him go."

"Make me."

The knife presses into my flesh and I feel a sharp prick followed by a trickle of blood down my neck. My shoe slides on the slippery mud and only my assailant's arm around my chest stops me falling to the ground.

"Stop yer messin' around," he growls in my ear.

A movement in the dark catches my eye. *There are two of them.*

"Stay completely still," the blond-haired man says, still staring at the black-clad figure in the shadows.

Who's he talking to? Him? Me?

The man lunges toward the figure in the shadows, but at the last minute, he twists and something like a sparkling wheel comes flying through the air toward me. The air moves by my right ear and there's a dull *thunk* followed by a gurgling. The knife at my throat drops to the floor.

My assailant staggers back and falls to his knees, clutching at the knife embedded in his throat. Blood sprays the front of his jacket and his eyes bulge as he gasps for air. I stand, muscles frozen, unable to take my eyes off him, only able to watch as blood pumps from his artery, his life draining away. He falls sideways, writhes on the floor, and then is still.

A grunt from the shadows tears my attention away. The blond-haired man is fighting a figure dressed all in black. As I watch, he's thrown back against the wall. He gasps and freezes in place as, with a glint from the shadows, the man in black presses a knife to his throat.

"When will you old dogs learn to give up?" The voice is surprisingly high-pitched with a flat intonation.

"What do you want?"

"Cut out the bull, Mr McNally. We know who you are and what you were doing in that bar. We've been talking to your friend."

"I don't have any friends."

I glance around, wondering what to do. Running would probably be a good option, but I don't know where I'm going and likelihood is I'd end up being attacked again. If I can help the blond man get away, he'll be obliged to help me, or at least show me the way up to Area Five.

The knife my assailant had held to my throat is stuck point-down in the mud. I reach out, then hesitate. I'm not sure I can bring myself to stab anyone. I glance back at the dead man splattered in blood and shudder. *No, I just need to knock him out.*

"Oh, really?" The dark figure sounds amused. "Big black guy, cool tattoos. I particularly liked the one of the lizard on his stomach. The eyes were beautifully done."

There's something lying in the mud just behind the two men. It looks rather like a large club. I take a tentative step toward it, then another. It's a rounded wooden stick, about half a metre long. There's a carved handle at one end and at the other, metal studs. I swallow hard. It looks just as lethal as the knife.

"Take your hand off the knife."

I freeze, my hand outstretched toward the handle of the cudgel. Then I realize that the words were directed at the blond man, not me. *Has he forgotten I'm here?*

"Let go now," the dark figure warns.

Silently, I lift the piece of wood. It's heavier than I had thought and weighted at one end. Normally, I could have lifted it easily, but my arms feel limp and weak and I have to use both hands to hold it steady. The men are three paces away. I hold my breath as I creep forward.

"Good," the dark figure drawls. "Now slowly turn ar—"

Halfway through my swing, I realize the cudgel is going to hit the man's head, not his shoulder as I'd intended. But it's too

85

late to alter the blow, the weight of the cudgel pulling it down. The man crumples to the ground.

I drop the weapon and stand, shaking. In the gloom, I catch the blond-haired man's eyes. *Did I kill him?* I want to ask, but I can't. The thought makes me sick. I don't want to know.

The man stares at me for a second, then pushes past me. He goes over to the dead man and pulls the knife from his throat, wipes it on the man's trousers and sheaths it in a hidden pocket. "Cheers, kid." He nods at me and starts off up the alley toward the main street.

I stumble after him and grab his arm. "Wait! Y-you have to help me."

"Why?"

"I just saved your life!"

He yanks his sleeve out of my grasp. "And I saved yours. I think that makes us even."

"Please, I won't bother you for long. I just need somewhere to rest up. A medic …" I feel lightheaded again and put out a hand to the wall. There's a sigh, then a firm hand grasps my upper arm.

"Fine. But if Abby won't take you, you're on your own."

Who's Abby?

I follow the tug on my arm obediently, stumbling up the alleyway behind the man. He's moving fast and I can barely keep up.

"Are all Insider boys this pathetic?"

"It's been a rough … couple … of days," I pant.

He snorts. "Clearly."

The journey through the dark streets seems to go on forever. It's all I can do to keep putting one foot in front of the other, splashing through the flooded streets, oblivious to my surroundings.

After a time, the streets become drier, although the rain continues unabated, and a few more streetlights appear. We turn off the main road and make our way through a series of smaller streets until finally, the man stops in front of a small terraced house and hammers on the door.

I sway slightly, reaching out to lean against the wall. There are footsteps and the door opens a fraction, shooting a line of light across the street.

"Bryn?" The woman sounds surprised.

The man starts talking to her rapidly in a low voice, but I can't make out what he's saying because everything is spinning and this time I can't stop myself from falling. I'm dimly aware of being picked up and carried inside. A mass of dark hair blocks the bright light and a kind, gentle voice speaks to me. Then I can't keep the blackness away any longer.

9

Trey

When I awake, I'm lying on a narrow bed, blinded by the sunlight filtering in through a tall window. For a moment, I lie disorientated, wondering if this is part of yet another dream. They were some crazy dreams. Or were they dreams at all?

Blinking drowsily, I raise my arm to shield my eyes. It's neatly bandaged with white cloth. Memories surge back. I prod the bandage experimentally. Sore, but not the searing pain I remember. My limbs are stiff and slow to respond as I push myself up on one elbow and look around the small room.

It's bare apart from a battered wardrobe, a couple of shelves with stacked boxes and the bed I'm lying in. Everything about it feels old. It's not just the lack of modern furnishings, but the ancient, worn wooden floorboards and the slight musty smell, though the white-washed walls are clean.

A cup of water sits on the floor beside the bed, next to the bedroom door. I grasp it but my fingers are weak and I nearly drop it. The water has a chemical tang, but it's cool and wets my parched throat. It's only after I've drained the cup that I wonder if it had something added to it. A shiver runs down my back.

I sit up cautiously, my head spinning, and place my feet on the floor. My feet are bare with rosy patches left by healing blisters. *How long have I been asleep?*

A familiar blue shirt catches my eye. My clothes are neatly folded on the floor next to the wardrobe. That's when I realize I'm wearing a thin t-shirt several sizes too big and loose trousers. I wonder if they belong to the blond-haired man. I get to my feet and immediately fall back down on the bed, which creaks in protest. My muscles are stiff and sore. I feel like an old man.

Gritting my teeth, I try again. After limping over to the cracked window, I tap it experimentally. Real glass. *When was Plexiglas invented? A hundred years ago?* The window looks out over a set of back yards. Most of them are bare with puddles of standing water, but the yard of this house has neat beds, some empty, some full of leafy plants, and a covered area in one corner. It's the only splash of colour out there. Behind the yards is a narrow alleyway, another brick wall and more houses: some brick, some concrete.

Gingerly, I take off the oversized clothes and put my own back on. They smell clean, but they're torn and the shirt is covered in dark stains. *Blood.* My stomach gurgles and a wave of dizziness rushes over me. I need food. When was the last time I ate? But more than that, I need to find a toilet.

Opening the bedroom door, I find myself at the top of a narrow set of stairs. Two doors lead off the small landing. One is closed, but the other is half open and reveals what looks to be a bathroom. I relieve myself then head back out to the stairs.

Voices filter up from one of the downstairs rooms.

"What am I supposed to *do* with him? Every moment he's in this house he's a risk. *You're* a risk. It's a good thing my neighbours aren't the nosy types. But if the Metz are after him, it's only a matter of time before someone reports on him."

"Well I didn't ask to pick him up, he just refused to leave me alone," a man replies. The blond man who rescued me, I think. "Oww!"

"Hold still, then. You're going to have a scar from this one."

"Well, if I can get out of here today, I *may* be able to get to a medic facility in time," the man grumbles.

"You'll be lucky. I doubt any of the boats will be going anywhere today after the storm. There you go, all done."

Their voices cover the noise of my footsteps on the stairs. But the woman's next words make me freeze.

"Well, he can't stay here. As soon as he wakes up, you're going to have to work out what to do with him. He's your responsibility."

"How can he be my responsibility? Anyway, I can't stay in London any longer. As you said, he's a risk."

There are footsteps and the sound of water being poured. "You can't just leave. What about the Chain? And Lamar—"

"Don't give me that, woman. Lamar wouldn't have wanted me to take on the leadership. He knew I'd screw it up. One of the others will have to do."

There's a mixture of anger and pain in his voice. Whoever Lamar is, or was, he meant something to this man.

I hesitate for a second, my hand on the door, then push it open and walk into the room. It's a small, brightly coloured kitchen at the back of the house. A large battered table takes up most of the space, with a row of cupboards and a hotplate against the back wall. In one corner is a large antique rocking chair, above which hang bunches of dead plants. The walls look to be painted a yellow ochre colour, but it's hard to tell as any available space is taken up with paintings, driftwood carvings, or unevenly shaped painted plates. In pride of place hangs a strange wooden object with a curved body and a long neck along which runs a series of wires.

"Ah, sleeping beauty awakes at last," the man says sarcastically. "How are you feeling, boy?"

He's leaning against the table in a shirt and underwear, a large bandage wrapped around the top of his right thigh. Dark bruises cover one side of his face and there's a gash on his cheek. From the way he winces as he struggles to pull on a pair of old jeans, that's not the full extent of his injuries.

"B-better, thank you."

My toes scrunch up on the cold tiled floor. Everything about this place is so *old*. It feels like it's from a different century. I think of my London home; the clean, bright, sparsely furnished apartment with floors heated to a comfortable temperature, a proper all-in-one cleaning unit and the food prep unit that can make almost any meal you want. It feels a world away.

"Come and sit down." The woman smiles warmly at me. She's dressed in plain clothes and her long thick dark hair is pulled back into a braid that sits over one shoulder. Her olive skin is lined and worn but almost glows. Like the man, I find it hard to work out how old she is. If she was an Insider I'd guess she was in her seventies, but out here I suspect she's much younger. In her forties, perhaps. Instinctively, I know I can trust her. The man, I'm not so sure about.

"I'm Abby," she says, placing another of the heavy cups in front of me. I peer at the steaming liquid suspiciously. "It's only mint tea." She laughs, breaking the tension that I hadn't been aware of until now.

I lift the cup with both hands and sip cautiously. It's pleasant and hot.

"You've met Bryn." She nods to the man who's slumped back in the rocking chair. He glowers at me. There's a ping from a small food heater. Abby pulls a bowl out and places it in front of me. "Eat. You must be hungry."

I eye the contents of the bowl.

"W-what is it?"

"Porridge. All I've got left, I'm afraid. Here, have some sugar with it." She pushes a small pot across the table. There's barely a decent spoonful of sugar in it. I sprinkle some over the grey mush and take an experimental spoonful. It tastes as bad as it looks.

"Not what you're used to." She sounds embarrassed.

I shake my head, fanning a hand in front of my mouth. "No, it's great. Just hot. How long have I been asleep?"

"Two days and a night," Bryn says curtly. "What's your name, boy?"

"Darwin Trey G—" I snap my mouth shut.

If they work out who my father is, I doubt they'll help me for much longer. Government ministers probably aren't looked on fondly out here.

Bryn snorts. "Darwin? What kind of name is that?"

"Bryn!" Abby gives him a warning look.

He holds up his hands. "Okay, okay, but calling yourself Darwin out here is asking for trouble. Trey is better. My grandfather was called Trey."

I nod silently. Secretly, I've always preferred Trey. Being named after a famous scientist always makes me feel inadequate, a constant reminder that I'm not as clever as I should be.

"So, Trey, what have you done to get the Metz after you, and how did you end up down in the worst part of Area Four?"

How much to tell them?

But I don't have a clue where I am or what to do next. They clearly don't *want* to help me, but perhaps they can fill in some of the gaps in my knowledge.

I tell them everything that happened, from my arm starting to jerk in school, to running through the Wall into Area Four. They listen in silence, though Abby gasps when I describe how I cut the chip out of my arm, and Bryn raises an eyebrow when I talk about going through the Wall. When I finish speaking, the room is silent.

"Sorry, I know you wanted to leave me in the bar." I take another spoonful of the grey mush. It tastes just as bad, but my stomach is demanding food.

"Nothing personal. You just turned up at a bad time. A very bad time." Bryn's face turns dark.

"If there's anything I can do to help …" My voice trails off. *Stupid boy. What could you do to help them?*

Bryn's face turns thoughtful. "Well, perhaps you *can* help. If you dug your chip out completely, then you can't be tracked by the Metz. And you say you came *through* the Wall?"

I nod, dumbly.

"Do you know why you got through? Why it didn't kill you?"

"No. I-I was hoping you might be able to tell me that." It should have killed me, I know that much. *So, why didn't it? What's different about me?*

Bryn looks disappointed. "No. You're only the third person I've come across who's able to do it. And two of you in the space of a week …" He mutters the last part, almost to himself.

My spark of curiosity is quickly dampened by an overwhelming homesickness. "I need to find my family," I say quietly. "Is there anything you can do to help me get home?"

"They're Insiders, right? And you know where they live?"

93

"Yes, but I haven't spent much time in London. We used to take the pods everywhere, but now I can't, obviously …"

Bryn nods. "Okay, well, if you're willing to help us, we may be able to get you back to your family. Though I'm not sure they'll be able to help you if the Metz are after you."

I don't answer. If my father, one of the most senior government ministers, can't help me, then nobody can. But I'm sure this must all be some kind of mistake. He's probably sorting it out now.

Bryn pushes himself to his feet. "Well, I'd better be off. Need to report in with the boss."

I open my mouth to ask him about who he's working for, but he's already gone, banging the front door shut behind him.

Abby grimaces. "Normally, he's friendlier than this, Trey. He's just a bit touchy at the moment. A friend of his … of ours … was killed. Bryn blames himself, even though he nearly got himself killed trying to rescue him. He just needs a bit of time."

She sits down beside me, clasping her own mug of tea. Close up, I notice the dark shadows under her puffy red eyes. She's been crying.

I search for another topic of conversation. "Is it just you and Bryn who live here?"

"Just me. Bryn comes and goes. I hadn't seen him for four years before he turned up with you the other night."

She catches the look of surprise on my face and smiles. "I know, I'm lucky. Seven of us used to live in this house, but they all died or left. It's mine in law, but the only reason I haven't been forced to take others in is because I've helped the local accommodation officer out a few times. I often have sick people staying. Next door, there are three families sharing. Technically, that's over the legal limit, but it's not enforced. Better for people to have a roof over their heads than not, even if it is crowded."

Three families in a house this small? I glance out the window that overlooks the back yard. "I like your garden."

"It's about the only one you'll find out here. It costs almost every chit I have to keep it going, but people help out. It's a resource for everyone, really."

"What do you mean?"

"They're healing plants. Some native species, some that Bryn and others brought me from overseas. It's tricky trying to keep them alive in this climate, but I just about manage." There's a note of pride in her voice.

"Healing plants?" I'm confused.

"Sure. That's how I treated your arm. Although, I did have to give you some pills, too; the infection was too deep-set, even for my skill with herbs." She smiles over at me. "I trained as a nurse years ago, before the medic units and bots took over. Now, I research and use historic plant-based healing methods. They're not as quick as the medics, but they often do the trick."

"But why don't people just go to a medic unit if they're sick?"

"Because not everyone wants the investigation that inevitably goes with a visit to the medic. And not everyone can use the medic facilities. A lot of the time, it's wounds from gang fights rather than sickness that I treat." She shrugs. "Anyway, there just aren't enough medic facilities out here for everyone."

Not everyone can use the medic facilities. People who are unchipped, she means. Illegals. A shiver runs through me as I think of the tales Theo told me about the Outside. Muggers, thieves. Whole areas ruled by vicious gangs who'd kill anyone who didn't follow them.

I have to get out of here. I need to go home.

10

Aleesha

Two days of rain. Endless, incessant rain. After the first day, we're confined to the apartment, the storms having turned the streets into raging rivers. The steps inside our apartment building are lined with hobies seeking refuge. Someone must have let them in. Jay boils them some water – the tank's being topped up by the rain so the neighbours can't complain too much – but no food. We only have his rations between the two of us.

The first night, I snuck the last packet of tronk out of my lockbox while Jay was out collecting water. But he got back sooner than I'd thought he would and I'd barely had a taste before he'd ripped it out of my hand and thrown it out into the corridor, where the hobies fell on it eagerly. Bet they couldn't believe their luck.

He was mad. Raging. Told me that if the storm wasn't so bad, he'd have thrown me out of the apartment, too. I didn't have the energy to fight back. He had a right to be so angry. Tronk is bad stuff. But it's so irresistible.

The weird thing is, you don't get withdrawal symptoms if you don't have any. None of the bellyaches or fits that some of the crap on the street gives you. Which should make it easy to quit. But the thing you really crave when you don't have it is happiness. That's what keeps you coming back for more, again and again. You just want a few hours of happiness. Of peace. To be able to escape from the filth and the mess and the harshness of life out here. Is that so bad a thing?

Tronk has one other advantage: it stops you feeling hungry. And hunger *hurts*. It's a pain that never goes away. But that's also how it kills. It stops you wanting proper food because you want the happiness more. So you trade your rations for more tronk. And more. Until your hair and teeth fall out and you're just skin and bone. And no one can survive for long like that.

Jay is twitchy, constantly pacing the room and staring out the windows, as if he can wish away the rain. He's worried about what's going on at the Snakes' HQ and if Rich is working his way into Dane's favour with his rival trapped by the flood waters.

The apartment is damp, the wall and part of the floor soaked from where the wind has driven the rain through the cracks in the walls and windows. Too wet for mould at the moment, but that will come as it dries out, spreading across the stained ceiling.

Finally, on the second night, the rain stops and by the following morning, the water level in the streets has dropped to something approaching normal. The hobies get ushered out, gloomy and dismal at being forced back onto the streets, but they're as hungry as we are. I leave Jay in the long queue at the ration store, making an excuse that the one further up may have a shorter wait. But instead of heading to a shop, I splash through the mud-covered streets until I'm standing, once again, in front of the Wall.

The pink and blue fabrics I stole are shoved up my jacket. A bit of knife-work has converted the long skirt to a kind of dress.

My hair's piled up on top of my head in an imitation of the style I'd seen a lot of women wearing, and although my features aren't quite perfect enough for an Insider, I'm hoping people will just think my parents chose brains over beauty.

I take a deep breath, trying to stop my hand from shaking as I reach out toward the Wall. Every instinct is screaming alarm bells in my head. At the last minute, I snatch my hand back, heart pounding. *You did it once, why not again?*

The trouble is, I still don't know *why* I can get through. What makes me different, if there's anything at all? Perhaps Jay was right and there was some issue with the Wall that day. I had dismissed his suggestion, but that was because I thought my ability to get through was related to the chips. Or maybe because I had some special Insider blood. But Murdoch's boss had seemed pretty convinced that it was nothing to do with whether someone was an Insider or not, or whether they were legal or illegal.

A shiver runs through me despite the warmth from the sunlight penetrating the dense cloud cover. Is it really worth risking my life for? Just to be Inside? The pull is strong though, stronger even than the cravings for tronk. I want to be among those people, even though they pushed me away; to breathe in the smell of their gardens and taste their clean, pure water.

Once you've seen, you can't unsee. Once you've experienced life Inside, you can't go back to the way things were.

A slight tingling is the only sensation as my arm passes through the Wall. I follow it, stepping once again into the cobbled street behind the long row of houses.

The cobbles are covered in a film of mud. This reassures me. Inside might be clean, but it's not perfect. They must have felt the effects of the storm as much as us. *Though I doubt any Insiders died, unlike those hobies who weren't able to find shelter.* I think of the motionless bodies I'd passed on my way here, sprawled wherever the water had deposited them.

A scuttling noise catches my attention. A small bot appears from the passageway off to my right. I press my back against the wall that runs along the back of the houses and freeze. It looks like a cleaning bot, a smaller version of the kind they use to disinfect areas as part of the Cleanings. *Can it sense I'm here?*

The bot spins, spraying some liquid in an arc around it. It pauses, then spins in the other direction, moving in a crazy dance along the street, in the opposite direction to me. In its wake, the cobbles gleam. I release the breath I've been holding.

On the main roads it barely looks as if there's been a storm. Only the odd broken tree branch and neat pile of leaves are testament to the destructive wind and rain. The windows of the shop fronts are gleaming, a stark contrast to the windows of the shops in Area Four, left opaque by dust and filth.

I stroll through the crowds of people, holding my head high and acting as if I belong. It seems to work; no one gives me a second glance as I explore the streets and squares, creating a mental map. Metz officers patrol, but they're clearly visible and easily avoided.

There are drinking fountains in every square, dispensing clear, clean water. It tastes pure and fresh with none of the aftertaste you get with rainwater. I drink until my belly is full, then sit on a bench beside a playground.

The playground is sectioned into areas. The one nearest me is marked for children aged between five and nine. A group of bored parents stand off to one side, watching the kids run around and fight over the equipment.

It looks more like a well-equipped training gym than a play

area, but as I watch, I realize why. The kids are competing with each other. Goading each other to jump higher, run faster and pull harder. They're strong, too. One of the smaller kids executes a complicated set of manoeuvres hanging from a long bar, a routine that half the Snakes would struggle to complete. I'm not even sure I could do it the first time.

Two men holding hands perch on the next bench along. They're deep in conversation and I try and listen in. They seem to be discussing some kind of model that will more accurately predict the weather. At least, that's what I think they're talking about; I can only understand perhaps one sentence in ten. I look from them to the children in the playground, so much bigger and stronger than the scrawny kids Outside, then up at the large screens that line the square and are currently displaying an advert for a boys' school out in the country.

How could we – I – ever hope to fit in here? It's a different world. No wonder they don't want to let Outsiders in.

My stomach gurgles, complaining of hunger. There's no way I'm going to try paying for food again, but perhaps I can filch some. It's not exactly as if they've got a shortage of it in here. Do these people know what life is like Outside the Wall? That there are children starving to death out there? Or do they know and just don't care?

When I get back to Area Four, I've got two peaches and a small cheese hidden in my clothes. It's been a while since I've needed to filch food, but it's good to know my skills haven't totally wasted away.

The apartment is empty when I get back. I place the food on the table and stash the bright fabrics back in the hidden area under the floorboards. The scent of the fruit sweetens the air in the apartment, making my mouth water.

I've only seen a peach once before. There was a crate of them in the food we liberated during the raid on the depot, though they weren't labelled, so I only found out what they were called today. Dane gave me one. It was far and away the most delicious thing I had ever tasted.

I force myself to clean the two chipped plates on the shelf and sit down at the table. Cutting the cheese in half, I reluctantly place one half and one of the peaches on a plate for Jay. The cheese is hard and white on the outside, but softer inside. It smells odd, almost like it's gone off a bit, but I'm guessing it's fresh as plenty of people were crowded around wanting to buy it. I nibble a bit off the corner. Rich and creamy, but with a salty tang that makes the tip of my tongue tingle.

Next, the peach. Holding it up to my nose, I close my eyes and inhale its perfume, rubbing my finger across its furry skin. The sweetness explodes on my tongue, juice flowing down my throat. It tastes like … like heaven.

I wait for an hour, but Jay still doesn't show. He must be at headquarters. The water has almost drained from the streets as I make my way the short distance to the back entrance. I feel stronger after the food. Even just that little piece of cheese made me feel full again. Jay definitely owes me one for not eating his share.

When I enter the cavernous main hall, I immediately feel the tension in the air. People huddle in groups, talking in hushed voices. At the far end, Jay and Rich have their heads together talking. *More like arguing*, I think as I catch the dark looks on their faces. As I get closer, they break apart, each going to their own group of followers.

"What's going on?"

Jay looks around, surprised to see me. He grimaces. "Rumours of another Cleaning. We're overdue for one and Danny thinks they'll use the damage from the storm as an excuse."

"To create more damage?" I reply sarcastically, getting a scatter of laughs.

Jay looks slightly put out and pulls me to one side. "Look, Dane's still missing," he says in a low voice. "Apparently, he wasn't here during the storm and Rich has been, well, overstepping the mark."

I bite my lip. He doesn't need to say more. Rich must have seen the absence of both Dane and Jay as a chance for him to get a few more people on his side. But Dane missing is worrying. As is the rumour of a Cleaning. "But there's not much either of us can do until we know for sure that—"

The main door flies open with a crash. We both turn to look as a young boy runs in, panting and stumbling. He spots Jay and heads toward us, pushing past anyone in his way. I recognize the kid: one of the youngest gang members who Jay has kind of looked after since his older brother was killed in the raid.

He stops in front of us, gasping out something that's impossible for us to make out.

"Hey, calm down." Jay places a hand on his shoulder. "Get your breath first."

The boy's eyes are wild and his face pale underneath matted brown hair, cheeks tinged red with exertion. He's trembling and not, I think, from the effort of running here.

All eyes in the room are on him as he finally draws in enough air to speak.

"Dane's dead," he announces in a small voice that quavers in the silent room. "They found his body near the river. I-it must have been washed up in the storm."

"What was the cause of death?" I ask.

The kid frowns at me, not understanding.

"Do you know how he died? Was it in the storm or before?"

He shakes his head, looking from Jay to me and back again. Jay gives him an encouraging nod.

"A man said he thought before. The head was all smashed in and he was … was pretty—" He clamps his hand over his mouth as his face turns even paler.

Jay gives me a look and I tug the boy away. He makes it outside the building before puking his guts out against a wall. I rub his back, my mind racing.

Dane's death changes everything. There'll be a leadership contest. If Jay wins, he'll be the new gang leader. If he loses, well, the best he can hope for is disgrace. More likely, death. And without Jay, I lose my lifeline of food. My influence in Area Four. I'd be back on the streets.

I tug the kid back inside, needing to know what's going on. Rich and Jay are talking, the rest of the gang crowded around them. As I approach, Jay raises his voice.

"Rich, Danny and me are goin' to take a look for ourselves. We can't assume anything until we've all seen. Everyone is to meet back here at one-three-zero-zero hours."

He doesn't even glance at me as he strides out of the hall, Rich and Danny hard on his heels.

* * *

As it turns out, I don't make it back to headquarters for the gang briefing. While heading for my rooftop to do some much needed training, Murdoch accosts me. I follow him sullenly, thanking my lucky stars that there aren't likely to be any gang members around to spot us.

We end up at a small house in the northern part of Area Five.

It's nice up here, or, at least, about as nice as it gets Outside. The people who live here are well off, for Outsiders. They have jobs and don't have to rely on government handouts to live.

The streets are noticeably cleaner here than in Area Four. I guess the floods weren't as bad. The drainage systems must work better, or perhaps it's just that all the water flows down to Four. Modern apartment blocks, some with balconies, are interspersed with older brick buildings that are generally well cared for. I used to think this part of the city was luxury, but that was before I went Inside. Now, it just looks like a poor cousin trying to dress itself up.

Murdoch leads us around to the back of the house. The backyard is bare apart from a few brown weeds trying to break through the cracked paving stones. The back door leads into a sparsely furnished kitchen with white-washed walls peppered with damp. In the front room stand a couple of tables and a handful of chairs. The place doesn't look lived in at all.

"How many of these houses have you got?" I want to ask how they got hold of them and why they're lying empty when there are so many people in need of homes, but I don't want to piss Murdoch off just yet.

"A few." Murdoch motions for me to sit in one of the hard-backed chairs.

"Are we meeting your boss again?"

Pain flashes across Murdoch's face so briefly I could almost swear I imagined it. But his face is pale and he stares at the netted window rather than return my gaze.

"No. Another member of the Chain. They should be here soon."

They. More than one person. I'm intrigued. And curious about what happened to the black guy with the striking tattoo. "What's his name? Your boss's name, I mean."

Murdoch exhales sharply. "Lamar. His name was Lamar."

Was. So he's dead. I open my mouth to ask who's in charge now, but I see the expression on his face and close it again.

We wait in silence for about ten minutes, then I hear the back door open and footsteps crossing the kitchen floor. *Two people, one of them limping.* A tall, tanned, blond-haired man enters, glances around and nods to Murdoch. A wary look passes between them, like they don't quite trust one another.

A thin figure wearing a tight winter coat steps out from behind the man and stands awkwardly with his hands clasped in front of him. I presume it's a guy, though the hood of the coat is pulled up, hiding his face.

"How're you doing, Bryn?"

"Been better. This is the girl?"

Murdoch nods. I lower my eyes and peek up at the man called Bryn. He's hot, in an old-man kind of way: scruffy blond hair, muscular body. He looks a bit haggard, but so do most people over forty. Not like Insiders, who have so much skin preservation work that it's impossible to tell how old they are. A dark bruise colours his cheek and he favours his right leg. He catches me looking at him and scowls. I wonder what he's been told.

"So, you can go through the Wall."

It's a statement, not a question. I look straight up at him. *Blue eyes, hiding something. Lots of things. There's pain there, too.*

"Yes."

"A useful ability to have." He seems to be probing for something.

"Perhaps," I answer carefully.

He carries on for a few minutes, asking about where I've been

Inside and how well I know my way around. His accent is slightly foreign, though not distinctive enough for me to place. Finally, he takes a step back. "Trey." He beckons to the hooded figure, who shuffles toward us. Bryn flicks his finger up. The figure hesitates, then pushes the hood back.

I stifle a gasp. He's not so much a man as a boy. An *Insider* boy. The hooded coat makes sense now. Out here, he'd get stared at in the street. Or worse.

He's about my own age, maybe a bit younger. His face is pale and drawn but beautiful. He has high cheekbones and perfect skin that *has* to be genetic enhancement. And his *hair*. So light and fine it's almost white. His eyes are bright blue, but kind of vacant. Like he's seen too much.

"Trey can also go through the Wall. You two will be a team."

I fold my arms and glare at Murdoch. "I told you, I work alone."

He glowers at me. "You proved last time that you can't be trusted on your own. You work with him or the deal's off."

"It's a simple job," Bryn continues as if I hadn't spoken. "We have a contact Inside. We want you to collect some information from them and bring it back."

"What information?"

He looks at me coolly. "You don't need to know that."

Usually, I'm pretty good at reading people, but even his eyes give nothing away. *Perhaps if I push him.*

"What is it you're working toward, anyway? I think you should at least tell me that before you expect me to risk getting caught by the Metz for you. Are you fighting the Brotherhood?"

"What do you know about the Brotherhood?" Anger flashes in his blue eyes as he pushes me back against the wall, the weight of his body squeezing the air from my lungs.

"N-nothing." I manage to get enough room to stomp on his foot and, as he pulls back slightly, push hard on his chest. "Get off me!"

He raises his hands and takes a step back. "Sorry. But I'm serious. Have you had any involvement with them?"

"No. I ... I think they killed Dane. But—"

"Who's Dane?"

"The leader of her little gang," Murdoch butts in.

Bryn doesn't even glance at him. "Well, here's a tip on staying alive. Keep away from the Brotherhood. Have nothing to do with them. Or you'll end up as dead as Dane."

"Thanks, but I'm pretty good at keeping myself alive without your advice. What's it to you, anyway?"

A flicker of pain crosses his face and I catch a warning glance from Murdoch. *Ah, I've hit a nerve.* "Did they get your boss? Lamar?"

It's a guess, but their reactions tell me I've hit the mark. Bryn's face darkens with anger. And pain. *Lamar wasn't just his boss. He was his friend.*

"Yes, he's dead. And if you knew exactly how he had died then you wouldn't be so quick to dismiss my advice. Anyway, to answer your question, no, we are not fighting the Brotherhood specifically. Or, at least, we weren't. Things may have changed now. Tell me, Aleesha, why does the Wall exist?"

The question takes me aback. "To stop us getting Inside. To keep us separate."

"Yes, but *why*? Why does there have to be Outsiders and Insiders?"

I find myself squirming slightly under his gaze. "'Cos they want to keep everything for themselves. All the food, all the water, and with the Wall there they don't even have to look at us. They can pretend like we don't even exist." The words spill out and I sound so harsh, so *bitter*, that I surprise myself.

Bryn nods and stands back, seemingly satisfied. "Well, you're in the right place, then. We want to break down the barriers between those who live on either side of the Wall. Make London society more equal."

Interesting. I wonder what rank this guy has in the Chain. Murdoch defers to him, but from the look on his face, Bryn's told me a lot more than he thinks I should know.

"You'll go through the Wall together tomorrow. Meet at Pollard Square at nine." Murdoch stands up straight and leans slightly towards the door, clearly eager to get away.

I glance over at the boy. Trey. He wanders to the window, in a world of his own.

"Oh, I forgot to mention," Bryn says. "The Metz are after Trey. You'll need to go carefully to avoid them."

I roll my eyes. *Well this is going to be a party. It's hard enough keeping one person away from the Metz, and by the look of him, this kid will only be a liability. They'll spot him a mile away with that hair; it lights him up like a bloody beacon.* "Great."

I push myself off the wall and turn to Bryn. "Nice meeting you."

He nods in reply, but his gaze is still on the boy standing by the window.

"You too, Trey. See you tomorrow!" I raise my voice slightly and the boy starts. As he turns, he disturbs the net curtains and sunlight peeks through into the room. It lights up his hair, making it glow around his face. It reminds me of a picture my mother once showed me in an ancient book. An angel, that was it. A messenger of hope.

I stifle a laugh as I turn to leave, toying with my own dark braid.

I don't believe in angels. Or hope.

11

Aleesha

When I get back to the apartment, Jay's sat at the table, his head in his hands. The plate is empty, but he doesn't mention the food.

"Where have you been?" His voice is gravelly and hard. There are dark rings under his eyes.

"Sorry I missed the briefing. Was it Dane? Is he—"

"Yes, he's dead. Body'd been in the river for days by the look of it." He sighs. "The leadership contest is tomorrow morning."

"So soon," I whisper, my stomach plummeting. *Damn, how can I possibly be in two places at once?*

"Well, there's not much point in waiting. Gang's been in limbo for the past couple of days. It needs a leader." He scowls.

I sit down opposite him and stroke the back of his hand. "Well, you must be the favourite. Who else is challenging?"

"Me, Rich, Miles. Danny was going to but dropped out. Probably wise. He'd be a great second, but he's not up to the leadership."

So, it's really between you and Rich, I think. Miles is stupid to even try, unless his knife skills have improved overnight.

"You'll be there, won't you? Starts at ten, down by the river."

"Of course."

Dammit. The river's at least a half hour walk from where I'm supposed to be meeting Trey at nine tomorrow. How the hell do I wiggle my way out of this one?

He glances up at me, obviously not convinced by my reply.

"You *will* be there." This time it's not a question.

"Wouldn't miss it for the world."

He scowls at my flippancy. "Jonas came to see me. Said he'd seen you hanging around with an Irish guy. Followed you out into Area Five. He's been doing some investigating." He folds his arms and leans back in his chair. "Says this guy is part of the Chain."

Bloody Jonas.

I think quickly. "Look, I didn't want to tell you anything as it may be nothing. I heard a rumour a couple of weeks ago about this new gang crossing boundaries. I thought they may be working with the Brotherhood, that maybe they *were* the Brotherhood by a different name." I pause for effect and look down at the table. "Figured it may be worth trying to find out what they were up to."

I glance up at him, but the expression on his face is unreadable. *Does he believe me?*

"And what did you find out?" There's a trace of sarcasm in his voice.

I sigh. "Nothing definite yet. They're involved in something big, but I think it's wider than just the gangs. They seem to be targeting the government."

Jay snorts. "Well, if that's their game, they're bloody idiots." He leans toward me. "Don't see him again. Ever. And next time, tell me first. Yer *my* girl; you don't work for anyone else, is that clear?" There's a threatening tone in his voice that I haven't heard before. Or, at least, not with me.

"Of course." I walk around the table and rest my hand on his shoulder, but he pushes me away.

"I mean it, Aleesha." He stands and glares down at me. "Don't treat me like a fool and stop yer lying. You'll get yourself – and me – into trouble. Now get out."

It takes me a minute to register what he's said.

"Get out!" The snake on his throat bulges. I've never liked that tattoo. The symbol of loyalty to the gang above all else. I turn and force myself to walk slowly to the door, but every footstep feels like a nail being hammered further into my heart.

* * *

I head for my favourite thinking spot: the flat rooftop of one of the tallest buildings in Area Four. From here, the tops of the glass towers Inside poke up above the Wall. On a clear day, you can just about see all the way across the river to the ruins of towers and buildings on the other side. I always wonder if people live over there. If they're looking back at us.

At the centre of the roof is a rough building, overhung on one side by a metal roof that provides some shelter from the weather. I'm half surprised to see it still there; one of these days a storm will take it. On the side is a wooden beam that I use for knife-throwing practice. I prefer to train up here rather than at the Snakes' headquarters. That way they don't know how skilled I am.

I twirl the knives in my fingers, idly throwing them at the beam, but my heart's not really in it. My mind flits between thoughts of the Inside and the more immediate problem of how I'm supposed to be in two places at once tomorrow morning. If I don't turn up at the meeting point, I can't see the Chain giving me another chance. I've screwed up enough. And if I don't turn up at the leadership contest, well, I don't even want to think about the consequences of that.

It's not a decision I want to make. Shoving the knives back in my hidden pockets, I start pacing around the rooftop.

When I first fell through the Wall, I thought maybe that was it. Confirmation that I had the blood of an Insider. But what was I thinking? That I could just walk up to someone on the street and say, "Hey, I think my father's one of you. Do you know who he is?" Like that was ever going to work. Besides, I'm not an Insider. Compared to the dumbasses in Area Four, it feels like I am. But the strength and speed of those children. There's no way I could compete with that. Even if I was a legal citizen, I'd always be marked an Outsider.

An image of Trey jumps into my head, the sun lighting up his hair. *Now, he's an Insider.* He looked pretty weak and scared of his own shadow, but he's an *Insider*. And if Murdoch's going to force us to do this job together, maybe I can use the opportunity to quiz him. Perhaps he'll have some clue to my father.

I think back to the morning my mother disappeared over twelve years ago. Someone had come to the door. I was hiding in the secret cupboard at the top of the hallway as usual when anyone banged at the door, but I could see through a crack in the door. A boy had delivered a holo message – a private one that I couldn't hear. But I remember her reaction. Shock, then surprise and delight. She'd laughed in a way I'd never heard her laugh before. When she'd lifted me down from the cupboard, her eyes were shining with excitement. What had she said? It was something, something important. It's there at the back of my mind, if only I could remember it.

Frustrated, I storm down to street level, sliding down ladders and jumping through empty windows. I don't even think about where I'm going until I see the lapping water ahead of me.

The river. I come back to myself with a start and look around. A handful of drugged-up hobies look back at me. Others are wrapped up, sleeping. Or dead, perhaps. Sometimes it's hard to tell. This is where they end up, all the people who sink down through society to the bottom of even Area Four's lowly levels. Selling the clothes off their back for a few chits to get their next fix. Wasting away until their bones break and their bodies crumble, their minds having been lost months before.

But right now, I can see the attraction of it. The temptation to escape this miserable existence and find happiness, if only for a few hours. To turn to tronk to take the pain of life away. *Just one taste; what harm can it do?*

"Hey, girl, what you doing down here?"

I turn, looking for the source of the soft, cracked voice.

"Up here." There's a movement from a little further up the street. I walk up, suddenly feeling dozens of eyes on me. A woman sits on the step of a bricked-up doorway, wrapped in a threadbare blanket. A pair of bare, stick-thin legs poke out from underneath the blanket, ending in a bright red pair of heels. They seem out of place, a splash of colour in the grim alleyway, but they make me smile.

"Like my shoes, love? They're beautiful, aren't they?" An impossibly thin arm reaches down to stroke them. "A client gave them to me as payment, and I just couldn't resist. Proper expensive, they are, like the ones those models wear."

And probably stolen off the boats. Or from a guard who was slipped a handful of chits to pretend one of the casements had broken in transit.

"Come sit down here, love. You look lost." The whore pats the step beside her. "I don't bite."

114

"Thanks, but I'm okay. I know where I am. Just wanted to have a look at the river."

She nods vigorously. "Oh, I know. It's nice down here, isn't it? The sound of the water is so soothing."

I go to move on, but something stops me and I look at her again. Scraggly dark hair, what little of it remains, and blue eyes, clouding over but still containing a spark of life. She looks haggard, but if I had to guess, I'd say she's not much older than me.

The woman reaches under the blanket and pulls out a small packet. She tips a tiny amount into her hand and licks it. Her face suddenly relaxes and her lips turn up in a hazy smile, her eyes closing.

My eyes are drawn to the packet in her lap. Before I can stop myself, I reach forward and grab it. The woman doesn't seem to notice. I hesitate for a fraction of a second, then tip a small amount of the tronk into my palm. Just enough to take the edge off the loneliness. An hour of peace. Fumbling, I tuck the packet back under the woman's blanket. She barely stirs. *I'll come back later and give her a chit for it.*

My mouth is dry with want. I can almost taste it on my tongue. I sink down on the step beside her, barely noticing the filth and smell of piss.

I shouldn't. I don't even want it, really. But there it is, travelling toward my lips as if on a predetermined journey.

I can taste the chalk that's mixed in with it. Then the drug hits me, making me slump backward against the wall. It's strong. Stronger than the poor quality crap you'd usually get down here. This is way beyond what I'm used to.

The woman beside me giggles, or perhaps that's me? Why not laugh, after all? A little well of happiness bubbles up in me and

115

I forget what it was I was worrying about, or even why I was bothering to worry at all. Life will take care of itself.

The street starts spinning around me and the scuffles of the hobies, the lapping of the water and the giggling of the whore next to me blend in a loop of music that seems to be getting farther and farther away. And everything is getting dark, even though I could have sworn it was still mid-afternoon. Silly me. It must be evening, which means time for sleep. And happy dreams.

* * *

"Wake up!"

A voice filters through my consciousness. Or perhaps it's still part of my dream. It was such a nice dream. I try and sink myself back into it, retreating back into my five-year-old self; my mother laughing and swinging me around the room.

"Wake *up!*"

The voice keeps digging at me and now I feel a hand shake me. Feelings come rushing back. But still a little bubble of happiness. It's not completely gone.

I crack open an eye and stare into a small round face. *A child?* I open the other eye. A pair of frightened, clear green eyes look back at me.

"Come *on*. You need to get up. They'll be here soon!"

There's an urgency in the young girl's voice that brings me fully awake. I push myself up and look around. It's daylight and feels like morning. *Have I slept the whole night?* I'm sitting on a step and must have fallen asleep in the doorway. The woman has gone, as have the other hobies that crowded the street yesterday. Now it's deserted.

I suddenly feel dizzy, the street blurs and I feel sleep pull at me. It would be so *nice* just to lie back down and sleep. But this child, whoever she is, seems determined to drag me away.

"Oww!"

My vision clears and I frown down at the set of indentations on my arm. "You *bit* me."

"You were sleepin'." She shrugs, unrepentant. "If we don't go now, they'll get you."

I lick my cracked lips. "Who will?"

"The men. They're Cleaning."

"A Cleaning?" My voice comes out in this weird squeak.

The girl looks confused for a moment, then goes back to pulling on my arm. She's small, probably only six or seven.

"Where's your mother?" I say groggily.

Tears pool in the girl's eyes, but she doesn't answer. Just tugs at me again, looking back up the street. I push myself upright, wobble a bit, then lean against the wall for support. I can still feel the tronk coursing through my veins.

"But I like this place ... I think." I'm not really sure of much at the moment. But I would quite like to go back to my happy dream.

The girl looks panicky. "Please, come wiv me?"

Her pleading tone cuts through the happiness, triggering something that clears my head. I take a step and then another, managing to stay pretty much upright. We carry on like this, me lurching up the street, occasionally falling against the wall when I lose my balance, and her, constantly chivying me along. It's kind of cute and annoying at the same time.

She pushes me right down an alleyway, then left, and right again. I don't think I've ever seen these streets so empty. As we walk, I feel the drug begin to drain out of my system and my balance improve. There's a pounding in my head. It doesn't hurt too much, but it's like I have a drum beating between my ears. I poke a finger in my ear, trying to clear it out.

"Don't stop!"

She runs back to me and grabs my arm, pulling so hard that I'm forced into a lurching run. The panic in her voice scares me. And then I realize the pounding isn't in my head, it's all around me. The sound of feet. Many feet, pounding all in time. *Cleaning.*

Now I'm the one almost dragging the girl along with me. I can hear her panting and whimpering. Around one corner, then another. The footsteps are getting louder. We're running right into them. I know now what is happening. What she was trying to tell me. And we can't turn around – they'll run us into the river.

Think. Come on, think. But it's so hard, my brain feels so foggy and thick.

"Here!" I feel a tug at my waist, and when I turn around the girl has disappeared. When I retrace my steps I spot the narrow gap in the wall, just about wide enough to squeeze through.

I follow her, tripping over rubbish that fills the path. After about ten metres, the alley opens up into a courtyard. I scan it quickly and my stomach drops. Glancing over at the girl, I can see her coming to the same realisation. Her eyes widen, and even in the gloom cast by the tall buildings above us, I can see her pupils dilated in fear. There's no way out.

I spin, starting back down the narrow alley, but the pounding is so loud now, so regular that I know by the time we get back to the main street they will be there. I pace around the small courtyard, trying to drown out the noise. The cracking and banging of doors being broken in. A scream, suddenly cut off.

My foot catches on a loose paving slab, sending me flying to the ground. But it's not a loose paving slab. It's some kind of brick border. I yank back what may once have been a fabric sack, the fibres now held together mostly by dirt. It half disintegrates in my hand, but what I see beneath gives me a glimmer of hope. Wood. Frantically I claw at the mud and dirt that's been packed down by heavy feet. More wood appears and then metal – a metal ring.

I pull on it, but it doesn't budge. The girl's choked sobs fill my ears. She's given up hope. I pull again, my back straining with the effort, but still the bloody hatch won't move. Perhaps it's secured from underneath? In which case, we *are* screwed. The footsteps are so close now they must be almost at the entrance to the alley. Marching feet, perfectly in time. A line of destruction. *Cleaning.*

Something is pressed into my hand. A scrap of rope. I feed it through the loop and the extra length allows me to brace my foot against the border of the trapdoor. I put the rope over my shoulder and with every bit of strength I can muster, throw my weight forward.

It sticks for a minute, but then something gives. The hatch lifts slightly, then falls back. Panting, I look around wildly. I grab a scrap of metal and shove it into the girl's hand.

"Stick it under the edge." No breath for more words.

Again, I lift the rope. Again, I pull, wishing for once in my life that I weighed more. The hatch lifts slightly, but it is enough. I hear the scraping of metal on wood and run around to curl my fingers under the edge of the trapdoor. I'm not sure where I get the strength from, but when I push up with my legs, there's a crack like something's breaking and the hatch lifts.

I totter slightly, the door no longer back-breakingly heavy. A rusted metal latch swings gently in the opening. The light from the courtyard doesn't penetrate the dark space below, but at this moment I couldn't care less what's down there.

The girl scampers through the hole without hesitation, but for a moment, I freeze. The pounding footsteps have stopped. A low voice murmurs something and there's a rustling sound. Feet disturbing the rubbish in the passageway.

I drop down and twist myself into the hole, my legs flailing for purchase. They hit something solid and I begin to lower the hatch.

The clean wooden hatch.

Quickly I push it up again and try to pull the fragmented sack back over it. But there's no time. I manage to cover the metal handle, but I know the boards are exposed. Gently, I lower the hatch down, trapping us in complete darkness.

12

Trey

I'm trying to get a grip of the geography of the areas outside the Wall. Abby's house is in Area Five, as is the house where we met Murdoch and Aleesha and the meeting point that we're walking to at the moment. Area Five borders the Wall and extends from the East Gate in the north, down to Central Lane in the south; a road that's unusually wide and straight compared to the jumble of streets and alleyways that make up the rest of the area.

On the north side of the East Gate is Area Six. That's one of the better areas. Some of the boys from school live in Six. According to Abby, people who live there consider themselves to be Insiders and look down at everyone else. To the south of Five is Area Four, and to the east, Three. Areas One and Two disappeared years ago as the waters rose, but there's an area they call the Dogs: an island in the middle of the water, with ancient towers almost as tall as the towers Inside. Bryn calls the people who live there "waterhobies" – homeless people who live on the water.

It seems the further away from the gates you get, the worse the areas are, as if the tendrils of the government and Metz can only stretch so far. Or perhaps it's just that that's where the worst of the Outsiders go. Those who are too lazy to get jobs or choose not to live within the law.

I'd never really thought about what the city was like Outside. From Inside, you can't see over the Wall, except perhaps from the top apartments of the tower blocks. That must be why they cost less than those lower down. It comes up occasionally on the news screens, mainly when there are protests and riots, but it feels like they're reporting from a different country, not part of the same city.

It certainly doesn't *feel* like part of the same city. It's not just the lack of modern buildings and facilities or the absence of pod stations. This place feels lifeless. Dead. There are no birds or insects that I've seen, no animals roaming the streets; not even much plant life to speak of, apart from weeds.

I asked Abby yesterday if she'd thought about getting a cat to keep her company and she just laughed at me. Apparently, out here a cat would be snatched and cooked up for dinner in ten minutes flat. They *eat* cats. Savages.

And now I look like an Outsider, too. My hair's dyed a muddy brown and Abby's rubbed some thick paste into my skin that's changed the shape of my cheeks and made my skin darker. I feel dirty. She couldn't do anything with my eyes, thank god, and just told me not to look anyone in the eye. Still, at least no one will recognize me as the boy on the run.

We arrive at the meeting place right on time. Murdoch's slouched against a dirty grey wall that was once white, glancing repeatedly at the device on his wrist. He nods as we approach and appraises my new disguise.

"Abby's done a good job," he says eventually. "You'll do."

We wait in silence, but ten minutes later, Aleesha still hasn't turned up. Murdoch's becoming agitated. He checks the time again. "Five more minutes. She'll be here," he says, though his voice lacks conviction.

"Heard there was a Cleaning this morning down by the river," Bryn says mildly. "Perhaps she got caught up in that?"

Murdoch snorts. "She's too smart for that."

Another silence. "So, how long are you planning on sticking around for?" Murdoch asks casually.

"As long as I'm needed," Bryn replies.

I look from one to the other. There's a hostile undercurrent in their words. I wonder if it's something to do with the death of Lamar. Aleesha had referred to him as Murdoch's boss.

"You know, Milicent is the logical choice of successor." Murdoch drops his voice so there's no chance of anyone overhearing, his tone still artificially casual.

"It's not up to you – or me – to make that decision. Leader's said he's still deciding."

"But we're wasting time. We have an opportunity now. If we don't take it, the B—"

"Not now, Murdoch," Bryn snaps. "We shouldn't be discussing this here."

Murdoch's face flushes red and his lips tighten into a thin line.

Five more minutes pass, then Murdoch throws up his hands. "Right, well, she's obviously not going to show." He curses under his breath.

"I could go and get it." The words are out of my mouth before I have time to think. "By myself," I add, somewhat needlessly.

Bryn looks surprised, but Murdoch narrows his eyes. "What, and have you disappear Inside? Not a chance. At least *she* has some incentive for bringing it back here."

I feel my face redden. *Was my thinking that transparent?*

Bryn sighs. "Well, you'll have to call it off with Stephens. But unless that girl of yours has a good reason for not showing, we're going to have to think of some other way to get the information. Come on, Trey, let's get back."

As we walk back through the streets, I try and piece together what I know about this organization. The Chain. It seems like their leader – this Lamar – was murdered by another gang. But Bryn mentioned another leader, though it sounded as if he wasn't here. And Abby had hinted that Bryn lived overseas. Is the Chain an international organization?

I'm so lost in my thoughts that I nearly trip over a small child who stumbles in front of us. "S-sorry." I help him up and he stares at me, wide brown eyes in a thin, grubby face.

"Come on." Bryn pulls me past, his grip on my arm almost painful. The kid looked almost half starved and there was no sign of his parents. *Who lets their kids out on their own in a place like this?* As we round the next corner, I realize we've got a tail.

"Why's he following us?" I whisper. "Doesn't he have a home to go to?"

Bryn glances back and gives an exasperated sigh. "He's following us because he thinks you're going to give him something. He probably fell over deliberately to catch your attention."

I stop and turn to face the boy. He looks up at me dolefully and silently holds out a grubby hand. "I'm sorry," I say gently. "I don't have anything." I turn to go, but feel a tug on the hem of my coat.

"Plis?" The kid smiles hopefully.

"Here, kid. I'll give you this, but only if you stop following us." Bryn dangles a small, flat piece of metal out of the child's reach. His eyes light up and he stretches for it. "You going to go home right away?" Bryn prompts.

"Yis." The boy stretches up again. This time Bryn drops the

metal to within his reach. He grabs it eagerly and scuttles off up the street without a backward glance. Bryn gives a satisfied grunt.

"What did you give him?" I ask as we turn into the alleyway leading to Abby's back yard.

"Half a chit." He sees my blank face. "It's the currency they use out here. People don't tend to have much in their bank accounts and a lot of the time people don't want the government to know what they're buying and selling so they trade in chits."

"Oh." I'm getting the feeling there's a lot I don't know about the Outside.

Abby's in the kitchen, kneading something on the table. White powder's scattered everywhere. She looks up as we walk in, surprised. "You're back quickly."

Bryn grunts. "Murdoch's girl didn't show. Waste of time."

Abby brushes her hands together, grimacing at the resulting cloud of dust. "Trey, do you want to make tea?"

I pour some water from a bottle into the kettle and set it on the hotplate to boil. No water heater. Archaic.

After grabbing three of the large uneven mugs, I measure out half a teaspoon of herbs into each. Abby makes the mugs herself. Pottery, she calls it. Apparently, she sells them at the market up in Area Six to people who like old-fashioned, hand-made items.

"Maybe she had a good reason for not turning up," I say. "She can't be all that bad, can she?" An image of the dark-haired girl jumps into my mind. She looked so young, so beautiful. There had been sadness in her large brown eyes and something else that I couldn't quite read. I'd thought perhaps she was an Insider, too – someone else who'd found themselves Outside – until she'd opened her mouth.

Bryn lets out what sounds like a growl and I realize with a

start that I'm blushing. He comes over to me and grabs my shoulders, pulling me around to face him. "I know she's pretty, Trey, but don't go doing anything stupid just because she's a girl. She would probably slit your throat as soon as sleep with you. She's a drug addict. A child of the gutter. And she's from Area Four! The only reason she's survived so long out there is because she knows how to look after herself. And *only* herself. I don't know what Murdoch was thinking taking her on." He gives me a shake to emphasize his point.

"I'm sure Murdoch knows what he's doing," Abby says placidly. "Now, leave him alone, Bryn. Can't you see you're scaring him?"

"Well, he should be scared." But he drops his hands from my shoulders and turns back to lean against the table.

Truth is, I'm terrified. I've been terrified almost every moment since I found myself in this god-awful place. It's like a nightmare I can't wake up from. Home feels so far away right now.

I try and pour the boiling water into the mugs, but my shaking hand splashes it over the surface. I need answers. It just feels like everyone is hiding something. That no one around here tells the truth about anything.

Abby gently takes the kettle from me and pours the tea. I bite my lip, trying to stop the emotion rising in me, breathing into the tightness that's suddenly developed in my chest. I can almost feel the glance they exchange behind my back.

"I just want to go home," I mutter.

"I know," Abby replies, patting me on the arm and leaving a powdery white handprint.

"Is that flour?"

"Yup!" A smile lights up her face. "Bryn bought it for us. I haven't had fresh bread for months!"

She sounds as if she's just won the lottery.

"You *make* bread?" *Why doesn't she just buy it?*

She doesn't catch the disparaging tone in my voice and I feel a flash of guilt. Maybe they don't have bakeries out here. I catch Bryn glaring at me and look away, embarrassed.

I sit down with the tea, rubbing the dressing on my arm absentmindedly. It still hurts occasionally, but it's more itchy than painful now. Abby says that's a good thing. That it means the wound is healing and the drugs she gave me for the infection have worked.

"I'm sorry about your friend, Lamar," I say, trying to be friendly. "Did this other gang, the Brotherhood, kill him?"

"Yes."

"And he was the leader of … the Chain, isn't it? Who's in charge now?"

Bryn snorts. "A very good question." Abby scowls at him and he rolls his eyes. "I was supposed to be meeting Lamar that night you walked into the bar. Except he didn't show; the Brotherhood had got to him first. He had something of value to us, and presumably, them. After I brought you back here, I went after him. They'd captured and tortured him. By the time I found him, he was half dead."

"So, did they get the thing he had?"

Bryn smiles crookedly. "No. Tough bastard kept it hidden. He gave it to me before he died and it's now well away from their clutches. Trouble is, Lamar didn't have a second, so the rest of the Chain are bickering about who gets to lead. They're all pretty useless."

"What about the guy you mentioned?" I hazard a guess. "Is he foreign, too? Abby said you're not from London. Does that mean the Chain is an international gang?"

Bryn shoots a look at Abby that I can't interpret. "We are *not* a gang. And technically, I am from London. I was born here, anyway."

"So, you're chipped then? That's why you can't go through the Wall?"

Bryn shakes his head. "No, kids were chipped when they were older back then – five or six. My parents left before that. Anyway, it's not the chip that kills you. At least, we don't think so. Someone tried it once – a member of the Chain who wasn't chipped – and he died just like anyone else. It was a shame. He was a valuable asset." A muscle in his cheek twitches. "Is there anything for lunch, Abby?"

I'm burning with curiosity. We're taught next to nothing about the world beyond Britannia at school. Some of the kids come from other cities: Birmingham, Manchester, Leeds. But I've never met anyone who lives *outside* the country. I've got so many questions about what it's like in other places, other countries. How does Bryn get in and out of Britannia when all the borders are closed? But it's clear that the conversation is at an end.

Abby places the dough in a bowl by the window, washes her hands and goes over to the food heater. Moments later, it pings and she places three bowls on the table.

"Sorry there isn't much. Rations don't go far when you try and split them three ways." She smiles wryly. "But the bread will be ready in a few hours."

I stare down at the bowl in front of me. More grey mush, this time topped with a lonely sprig of green. It doesn't smell great. But I'm starving, so I dig in, only realizing when I'm halfway through that Abby's portion is a fraction of the size of mine and Bryn's.

"Here, have some of mine." I push my bowl toward her guiltily, but she shakes her head.

"It's okay, I'm not that hungry."

Bryn frowns at her. "I'll pick up some more stuff when I go out this afternoon. I didn't think, sorry."

Abby nods, but says nothing. Another two mouthfuls and I'm finished. My stomach still feels empty. No wonder Outsiders are so skinny.

Abby catches me glancing around the kitchen. Her olive skin darkens slightly and she pulls a chair over to the tall cupboard above the hotplate. Standing on it, she stretches up to the top shelf and eases a tin box off it with her fingertips. She wipes away a thin layer of dust and opens it. Inside is a solitary bar of chocolate. Not proper chocolate, of course, but the fake stuff kids get as a Friday treat. Chocco. She holds it out to me. "Here, have this."

"Thanks." I smile at her, but she just turns away and replaces the box on the shelf. I rip open the packet and offer some to Bryn. He shakes his head, scowling. My heart sinks. *What have I done now?* The plastic texture of the chocco doesn't melt quite right on my tongue, but it helps fill the yawning hole in my belly.

Perhaps I'm supposed to offer Abby some money. Some of these chits they use Outside. But I don't *have* any chits.

"I- I'm sorry, Abby. I don't have any chits to pay you. But if I can find my father, he'll compensate you for this and for letting me stay here." My voice sounds stiff and formal.

Abby looks hurt. "Don't be silly, Trey. It's not about money. It's fine. I'm just sorry I can't feed you properly."

Bryn stands, his fists clenched. "Life is different Outside, Trey. People can't afford the nice food you Insiders get. And there aren't many places you can buy it – only up in Area Six, on this side of the city. Fruit, vegetables, meat are luxury items out here. Some Outsiders can earn enough to buy them as occasional treats, but most have to make do with the factory-made food. Many people just live off the government rations. Have you ever had government rations, Trey?"

Not until I came here, I think, looking down at my empty plate. What's his problem, anyway? It's not my fault I was born an Insider.

"Well, they're fucking shit." Bryn bangs his fist on the table. "Worse than shit."

"Bryn, calm down. It's fine, he's new out here. He doesn't understand."

Doesn't understand what? At least, Abby seems nice enough. Bryn, I'm not so sure about. Why is he so angry at me? It's like I've personally done something to offend him. Pushing my plate away, I stand.

"Thank you for lunch, Abby."

I stumble out of the room and up the stairs. Slumping on the single bed that takes up most of the tiny second bedroom, I hold my head in my hands and try not to cry. I just want to go *home*. To wake up and find this has all been some horrible nightmare. That I'm not being hunted like some criminal. That this world outside the Wall is just a figment of my imagination. To have a decent meal and a hot shower and my old life back.

Downstairs there are angry voices – Bryn's mainly – then a slammed door. A few minutes later, Abby's quiet footsteps pad up the stairs.

"You left your tea." She sits beside me, holding out a steaming mug.

"Why's he so angry at me?"

"It's not you he's angry at. He's just got a lot going on at the moment," Abby replies carefully. "Bryn has a good heart, but he's not really one for responsibility. That's why he's never really settled down. And I think it's partly to do with your …"

She hesitates, her voice trailing off.

"My what?"

"He had a son once. Daniel, his name was. He died, some years back. Bryn was away on a job at the time and blames himself for not being there to look after him, for not spending enough time with him. I think you remind him of Daniel a bit. Just superficially. He'd have been a little younger than you, if he'd lived. So every time he sees you, perhaps he sees what could have been."

She smiles sideways at me. "Don't tell him I told you that, okay? Bryn's a private man. He keeps himself to himself."

I nod, feeling a pang of sympathy for Bryn. "Is he married, then?"

Abby shakes her head. "No, he never married. There was a woman once, here in London, I think, that he was serious about, but she was already married or something. So was Daniel's mother." She gives a short laugh. "Always picks the wrong women, Bryn does."

"Did you and he …" My voice trails off and heat rises in my cheeks as I realize I'm not sure how to finish the sentence.

"We had a bit of a fling, a long time ago." She makes a face. "As I said, he's not one for settling down. Anyway, he's gone out for a bit. Do you fancy learning how to play the guitar?"

"Guitar?"

"Sure. It's a bit of a lost skill now, but I always find it relaxing."

I follow her downstairs, where she lifts the strange stringed object down from the wall and rests the curve of the body on her knee. She runs a finger down the strings, releasing a ripple

131

of sound.

"What is it?"

"A musical object. There aren't many of them left. I think this one is almost a hundred years old. Before electromuse took over, people used to play instruments like this and record the sound onto discs or computers. That's how people listened to music. You could even go and see them perform live."

She turns a couple of small knobs at the end of the neck, strums the strings again and nods, satisfied. "Like this."

Her left hand moves across the neck of the guitar, the fingers of her right moving so fast on the strings that they're a blur. Music fills the room. Simple music – not as complex and multi-layered as electromuse – but it's so rich and pure that it makes the hairs on the back of my neck stand up.

She stops, the notes echoing into silence, and I feel bereft, as if something special's been taken away from me.

Abby laughs. "It gets people like that sometimes, the first time they hear it. Here, you try."

Sinking into a chair, I accept the guitar reluctantly. It feels way too precious to be holding.

Abby hands over a small piece of black plastic. "You may find this easier for strumming. It's called a plectrum."

I lose track of time as Abby shows me where to place my fingers and how to strum different numbers of strings to get different sounds. My efforts are pathetic and half the time I create discords rather than harmonies, but I'm entranced by the sound and the process of creating it. Eventually, my hands are too stiff to continue, and when I look at the fingers of my left hand the skin is blistered.

Abby takes the guitar off me and hangs it on the wall. "I've got some salve for your fingers. They'll toughen up in time. Sorry,

I should have stopped you earlier."

"No, it was amazing. Thank you." I hold out the plectrum.

"No problem. Keep hold of it, I have several. But wait until your fingers are healed before practising again."

I shove the plastic tab into my pocket and begin to rub the pale green cream Abby hands me onto my fingers.

A rhythmic pounding from outside the front of the house makes Abby look up suddenly. It gets louder. "Wait here." She rushes into the sitting room. When she comes back, her eyes are wild with fear. "You have to hide."

My stomach plummets. "The Metz?"

She nods. "Not for you, at least, I don't think so. But they may stop by."

There's a banging on a door. If it's not Abby's then it must be the house next door.

"Come on, quick."

She runs up the stairs and drags a chair from her bedroom, placing it under a small hatch that I hadn't noticed in the ceiling of the landing. "Get up into the loft."

I climb up, wincing as one of the blisters on my fingers pops. The attic is mostly dark, but there's a small, dusty window set into the slanted roof. I make my way over to it cautiously and peer out.

Two Metz officers are standing outside the house opposite. Another two emerge, one holding a screaming red-faced baby, the other dragging out a woman who stumbles and falls to the floor. She's crying and begging, though I can't make out her words, they're too confused by her distress.

What are they doing? A man walks out the house and clutches at the arm of the officer holding his wife. Behind him, a boy of about seven holds onto a younger girl who's also crying.

"Please, take me! Take me instead." The man pulls at the arm, but the Metz just flicks him off with a backhanded swing. He stumbles away, but undeterred, runs back to pull at the woman. "Let her go!"

The desperation in his voice makes my heart pound.

"Take me, please, take me."

The woman goes limp suddenly, then gets to her feet, pushing the man away. "No, John, no. The children. You have to look after the children." She looks toward the two children in the doorway and blows them a kiss.

"Let's go." The harsh, robotic tone of the officer's voice breaks through the screaming of the baby and the sobs of the mother as they drag them both away. The man looks after them, dejected and broken, until the young girl runs over and tugs at his arm. He crouches down, wraps his arms around both children and together they sob.

Ten minutes pass before Abby calls me down from the attic. She's pale and shaking even more than me.

"What was that?"

She looks away. "The baby was an accident. They … they already had two children. Someone must have reported them to the Population Control Officer." Her voice is hard and cold.

"You *knew* they were harbouring an illegal?"

She gives me a defiant look. "I helped her give birth to him. Such a beautiful, healthy boy." A wistful look appears in her eyes.

"But that's breaking the law!" I splutter.

"So is treating injured people without taking them to a medic." She looks at me meaningfully. "Would you have handed them over, Trey? An innocent baby, to be murdered?"

My heart stops. "Murdered?"

"Oh, so they don't tell you about that in your schools, then? Yes, in all probability. If he's lucky, someone may adopt him, but he's only a poor, unplanned-for baby from Area Five; he hasn't got any enhancements going for him."

"What about his mother?" I ask faintly. "Will she be ex-executed?"

"Probably not. She's only an *Outsider*, after all. No need to make an example of her." There's a trace of sarcasm in her voice. "They'll probably take her to the Farms. Of course, that's really just a slower kind of death." Her hand shakes as she fumbles with a mug. "Hopefully, they'll let John keep his job. Otherwise, he won't be able to afford to stay in that place and the rest of the family will be in trouble, too."

I don't reply, unable to think of anything to say. The screams and cries of the woman and baby reverberate in my head. I don't know what's worse: that I never knew this sort of thing happened, or the knowledge that my father – the man I've looked up to my whole life – is the person responsible for overseeing population control in the city.

13

Aleesha

We cower in the darkness, waiting as the footsteps come closer. Three Metz officers. They pause. I can picture their owners scanning the courtyard for doors, escape routes; anywhere someone could be hiding. The girl trembles beside me. Hesitantly, I wrap an arm around her, though whether it's for her reassurance or mine I'm not sure.

Go away, dammit!

If only I could mentally force them to turn around and walk back out of the alley.

The footsteps start again, but rather than going back down the passageway, they're coming closer. Directly toward us. *They've seen the trapdoor.* I try and breathe lighter and then find myself holding my breath as the footsteps stop, right above our heads.

More footsteps in the courtyard, but the officer above us doesn't move. My lungs start to burn and I want to draw breath, but I'm scared in case even this slight noise gives us away. My heartbeat thumps loudly in the silence. The girl is stiff and motionless beside me. *Can they sense we're here?* The Metz are a mystery. People talk of special powers, but I'd always thought the tales were far-fetched. Now, I wonder if they're right.

There's no voice or command spoken, but the wooden trapdoor creaks slightly as the weight is lifted from it. More footsteps, retreating this time. I count them as they go. Three sets. Back down the passageway to the main street.

I sag in relief, releasing the breath I'd been holding. I wait until the next round of pounding footsteps have passed and faded into the distance before I dare to speak.

"What were you doing down there, by the river?"

"I heard someone talking about the men coming, so I came to tell the people by the river. They like me, most of the time. Sometimes if I help them, they give me food. This time, I got a chit." Her whispered voice rings with the pride that only a child can have.

"So why did you stay? Why help me?" *Why would a kid I've never met before risk their life just to help a drugged-out dweeb?*

She doesn't answer immediately. I feel her weight shift slightly as she pulls away from me. When she speaks, it's in a low mumble that I struggle to catch.

"My mum was like you. She took the bad thing."

"The bad thing?" But I know what she's referring to.

"Y'know, the *bad* thing. The thing that makes you muggy and happy. Gives you that nice feelin', like wot you get from the food."

"Where's your mum now?" *And what on earth is she doing letting her kid wander around these areas alone?*

"Gone."

Oh. We sit in silence for a minute.

"My name's Lily," she says eventually. "What's yours?"

"Aleesha," I reply automatically, and then wonder why I've given her – this kid I just met – my real name.

We wait a few minutes longer before emerging from the dark

cellar into the courtyard. They'll be coming back to burn all the rubbish soon, and I don't fancy being trapped in that dark underground space while the courtyard burns above.

There are a few bodies scattered in between the piles of rubbish as we make our way through the deserted streets. Some of them may have been from the flood, but a couple bear the signs of more recent violence. Doors half hanging off their hinges sway gently in the breeze. It's the only time the city is really quiet, after a Cleaning. It feels like a ghost city.

I hope to escape the barricades that mark the edge of the Cleaning zone by going over to the rooftops, but there's no clear way out, or, at least, not one I'd risk with Lily. Instead, we sit on the roof of an apartment block and watch as the bots come through, setting the rubbish alight. The piles burn out quickly. The bodies burn, too.

It's turning into another nice day. The sun shining for two days in a row is almost unheard of in winter. An hour passes, then the cleaning bots finish and the roads are reopened. Back on one of the main streets, I glance up at the clock hanging off the corner of the large apartment block. Nearly midday.

"Where *is* everybody?" Lily's voice breaks through my thoughts, and looking around, I realize she has a point. The street is almost empty and much quieter than usual for this time of day, even after a Cleaning. And then I remember. The leadership contest. Jay. *Damn.* Will they still be fighting? Probably. Jay and Rich are pretty evenly matched.

Other memories return. Of course! I was supposed to be meeting that boy – what was his name again? – and Murdoch at nine. *Double damn.* I slam my hand against the stone wall. *You idiot.* Lily looks at me, surprised.

I crouch down. "I need to go now, Lily. There's a big gang

thing going on today. You need to stay away from it, okay? Have you got somewhere safe to go?"

Her face drops and I feel a sudden stab of what I think is guilt. It's a strange feeling, and not one I like.

"I could come with you? I'd be fine, I'm sure …" Her voice trails off and she looks down at the ground. I look at her now, really look, and realize she can't be more than six. *The same age I was …* But I don't want to follow that train of thought.

I think quickly. "Look, just keep around the main areas. Don't go anywhere near the river or the bar district. They'll be fighting there later. I'll try and come back and meet you here before it gets dark." I point up at the copper sign above us. "Just here. I'm sorry, I have to go. *Don't* follow me."

Then I turn and run in the direction of the bar quarter, knowing she won't be able to keep up with me anyway. I'm already too late to meet Murdoch. With a bit of luck, I won't be too late for Jay.

I don't look back.

* * *

I hear the leadership contest way before I see it. A baying mob of voices; part-cheering, part-booing. I wasn't lying to Lily, the gang leadership contest is probably the most dangerous place in the city to be right now. I reckon a good half of the crowd are only there because they want a fight. I sometimes wonder if that's partly why the Metz never intervene. It's a kind of self-regulating thing. Gets rid of a lot of troublemakers permanently.

The contests for gangs in Areas Three, Four and Five are held in a large square, down near the water. It's the only area of open space large enough to fit the ring and the number of people who turn up to watch. The fights are about the only big events we have Outside and the only source of live entertainment. People bet on who they think will win. Sometimes, the fights go on all day.

Officially, there's a truce between gangs for the day of the event. All participating gangs get a share of the proceeds from the betting and the stalls that sell food and drink, and any gang that starts trouble risks losing their share. At least, that's the theory. But there are plenty of brawls that go on. The gangs may not be allowed to fight, but that doesn't stop everyone else.

I arrive at the back of the crowd a hundred metres back, down one of the main streets leading to the square. They're a shifting, closely packed mob of people. I'd take my life into my hands trying to get through that lot.

It takes me about ten minutes to climb up to the roof of the nearest building and scramble across to the blocks that line the square. I'm not the only one up here. A handful of others are smart enough to realize this is the best and safest view in the house. In the centre of the square below is a roped-off area about twenty metres square. It's lined with guards drawn from the various gangs, then barriers, then the crowd, hungrily pressing forward. Inside the ring, two men circle each other warily. They're both naked from the waist up, and even from here I can see the shine of sweat running off their bodies.

Many years ago, I saw a picture of something called the "Colosseum". It was a great, circular theatre in the centre of which lions and men fought to the death. The leadership contests remind me of that, except there are no animals. Just men.

Jay is easily recognizable, his dark skin and black tattoos standing out even under the dust. The other guy could be either

Miles or Rich, I can't really tell. Jay lunges forward and the guy feints to his left. *Rich. I'd recognize that move anywhere.*

I wonder if Miles is out. Down at the waterside there's a makeshift tent with a few people going in and out. That's where the losers get taken to receive medical treatment. Contestants usually survive, but not always. It depends how hard they fought and how easily they gave in. A lot of the time it's easier for them if they die straight away. Less pain. At Dane's leadership contest, the guy who lost the final bout hung on for two weeks after losing his leg and most of his left shoulder. I heard Dane himself put him out of his misery in the end.

The crowd gasps, drawing my eyes back to the arena. Jay is on the floor! My heart skips a beat. Rich raises his club to deal a final blow, but then he's on the floor too and Jay is rolling back up to his feet. Before he can strike, Rich is up and they continue their circling. I breathe again.

There's a shout from the jury. Time out. The contestants back away from each other to opposite corners of the ring for a ten-minute break. Now's my chance. I have to get down there, to Jay before the end of the break.

I run along the roof, vaulting over the short walls that mark the break between houses until I reach the water's edge. The houses continue into the water, of course, but I really don't fancy swimming in that stuff. Ten paces back from the edge is an access hatch. I drop down the short ladder inside and race down the staircase. In this part of Four, the blocks are usually occupied by squatters or brothels. From what I can see through the odd door that's been left open, this building meets both needs.

As I'd expected, the crowds outside are lighter here. No one wants to get too close to the water. It's easy enough to squeeze my way through the crowd to Jay's corner. A few people push back at me or complain, but I'm smaller than most of them and am gone before they can drag me back.

"Jay!" I push through the guards and lay a hand on his shoulder.

He turns, a mixture of relief and anger on his face. "Aleesha, where the hell have you been?"

He looks so tired and worn that I'm suddenly afraid for him. *What if he doesn't win?*

"Sorry, I couldn't get through earlier because of the crowds. I've been watching everything from up there," I lie, pointing at the rooftop I'd been on for all of ten minutes. "You're doing great, okay?"

He seems to steel himself. "Yeah, though I kind of hope it doesn't go on for much longer." He takes a swig of Chaz, then hands the bottle back to Jonas.

"Hey!"

I turn to see a young boy, perhaps ten or so, being held back by the guards. He's carrying something in his hands and pointing at Jay.

"Let him through!" Jay calls.

The boy runs up to us and silently hands a small parcel over to Jay, who seems to be expecting it. The boy doesn't wait around but rushes back into the crowd.

"What was that all about?" I ask.

Jay smiles and shrugs. "Rations."

He opens up the parcel to reveal a bunch of chocco bars – the good ones that cost an arm and a leg out here. Grabbing them, he pulls the packaging away, but a few fall out of his grasp to the floor. He bends down to pick them up, and in flash of movement slides something down his trouser leg. Before I can work out what it was, or even if I imagined it, he's straightening up and handing me one of the bars.

"Here you go. Not every day you get chocco."

He rips into his own bar, chewing it down in a couple of bites. I stick mine in my pocket for later. The last thing my stomach wants right now is food.

"Hey!" One of the officials is pushing through from the jury's' table toward us. She arrives, panting and scowling. "What was that parcel? You know anything coming into the ring must be searched."

Jay looks chagrined. "Sorry, ma'am, it's just some chocco bars." He holds them out for her to inspect. "Some kid brought them for me; I'm not sure where he's gone." He looks around as if the kid will pop up out of the ground in front of us.

The official frowns and takes the bars, opening each of them in turn and snapping them in half. But even she can't find anything wrong.

"Where's the packaging?"

I pick up the scrap of fabric the bars had been wrapped in and silently hand it to her. She turns it over in her hands, scowling as she can't find anything to argue about.

"I don't want to see anything else coming into this corner," she warns. "You know you're supposed to bring any food in with you at the start."

"Yes, ma'am, I'm sorry."

I'm kind of shocked at Jay's compliant attitude. But it doesn't do to piss off the jury at a time like this. There are twelve of them: seven are members of the Snakes, drawn at random, and the other five are representatives of other gangs. But really, the decision of the crowd is final. The one time the jury tried to cheat the verdict, the crowd went wild and tore them apart. Literally.

The gong sounds again. "Time out over!"

I pull Jay toward me for a kiss, tasting the sweat and blood on his lips. "Good luck," I whisper.

He smiles, takes the weapon Jonas is holding out and strides back into the ring.

Whereas the last round was clubs, this round is knives. The rules state a minimum length of six inches and a maximum length of twelve. I sit down in the chair Jay vacated, keeping my fists balled in my lap to avoid anyone seeing how nervous I am. I just want it all to be over. But if neither of them wins this bout, they'll go on again and again until one of them is too exhausted and slips up. And looking at them both padding around the ring, I think that Jay may reach that stage of exhaustion first. He needs to finish things quickly.

It seems Jay has the same thought as he immediately goes on the offensive, lunging toward Rich, who reflexively blocks the first blow. Jay keeps up the pressure, pushing Rich toward the side of the arena. If he can push him out, the contest is over.

Rich seems to sense the danger he's in and parries, slipping out under Jay's arm. Caught by surprise, Jay's momentum carries him forward. He manages to stop just short of the ropes, sucking his belly in to be sure he doesn't brush them. *He should have seen that coming.*

Rich is quick to press his advantage and for a moment, I think he has him, but Jay somehow uses his own trick against him and is back in the arena. He backs toward me, the two men dancing around each other in a blur of arms, legs and metal. Their feet kick up dust that swirls in a vortex around them, making one almost indistinguishable from the other. It's impossible to tell who has the advantage; one minute it seems Rich is the stronger, but a few seconds later Jay has the upper hand.

They lurch toward me and the thought flashes across my mind that I should move. If they were to crash outside, they'd crush me for sure. But I'm frozen to the chair.

Jay looms up in front of me, his knife raised over his head to block Rich's blow. The light glints off a line of red stones embedded in the handle of Rich's blade. I wonder if Jay's going down, but in an unexpected move, he grabs Rich's free arm with his own, pulling himself around. Rich, off balance, crashes to the floor, but as he falls he tangles Jay's feet, pulling him down on top of him.

Through the cloud of dust, I see them wrestling. They need space to use the knives. Knocking your opponent out first only earns you a stern admonishment and them an easy win. Jay seems to be trying to get his leg up around Rich's neck. *What the hell is he doing?* They're so close I can hear their grunts of effort and their choked, ragged breathing and smell the stench of their mingled sweat and blood.

I'm probably the only person close enough to see Jay's hand through the dust cloud. He brushes his trouser leg, then thumps Rich in the stomach. Winded, Rich falls back, his face twisted in pain, and in that moment, as the dust begins to clear, Jay rises to his knees, brings his knife up and plunges it down into Rich's belly. There's a gasp from the crowd, followed by a silence. Then they erupt in applause for the victor.

Jay raises his arms, blood dripping from the outstretched knife. I frown, still trying to work out what I've just seen. Because as Jay was lifting his knife there was already a dark wound on Rich's stomach. Jay sought the exact same spot with his knife. And as he rises to his feet, he rubs his leg, almost as if it itches. Or as if he's hiding something.

He turns to smile wearily at me, but I find I can't return it.

Jay has won the leadership contest, but did he cheat? And if so, who helped him win?

14

Aleesha

J ay continues his celebrations while the judges confer
before formally announcing him the winner; an announcement that's lost in the baying of the crowd. In front of me,
Rich's lifeblood drains away, the dark stain creeping steadily
closer to the corner of the ring. Astonishment and pain mingles
on his face and he seems to be trying to say something. But
then he gives up and his head rolls back into the dirt.

There's a commotion behind me and the medical volunteers
push past into the ring. They won't be able to do anything for
him. A stab to the stomach out here, away from the rapid access
medic facilities, is a death blow. I suspect Jay meant it that way.
Dead men don't talk, after all.

*Do I call him out on the truth? But if I tell anyone, even others in
the gang, that he cheated, they'll be an outcry. He'll be evicted at the
very least. Probably killed. And if Jay goes down, I go down with
him.*

But the thought stays with me as I watch Jay stagger around
the ring, basking in his glory. In pretty much any other situation,
what he just did would have been fine. Normal, even. But the
contests are sacred. It's the one and only rule of gang life. Once
you're in charge, you can do what you want. But you have to

get there by honest means.

It doesn't feel right that he cheated. And Rich is dead because of it. But if Rich hadn't died, Jay would have. And really, there *is* no one else who's up to leading the Snakes.

The crowd begins to disperse, thirsty for beer and blood of their own. I wonder how the barkeepers in this part of town feel about leadership contest days. How the extra takings weigh up against the cost of damage from the fighting.

Rich is taken away to the medical tent. I look around for his girlfriend, Megan, but don't see her. Did she see him go down? Has she resigned herself yet to her new role on the fringes of the gang, or perhaps outside it altogether? We rise and fall with our men out here. With the odd exception.

I force myself to stand as Jay approaches. He looks about ready to drop with exhaustion. His chest is matted with sweat and dirt, and beads of blood drip from scratches. He almost collapses onto me and I ease him down into the chair, passing him a precious bottle of water, saved for this moment.

He glugs back most of the bottle, pouring the final part carefully into his hand to wash his face. He'll be allowed home to clean up before he officially takes up his new role and the party begins at the gang headquarters.

There's a frisson of excitement in my belly as I wrap the light, black jacket around his shoulders. I am now the girlfriend of the leader of the most powerful gang in Area Four. It feels good.

Jonas and a couple of the guards escort Jay back to the apartment while I run on ahead to fetch some washing water down from the tank. By the time he arrives it's pretty hot. I fill the big bowl and place it on the table with the remainder of our bar of soap.

Jay dismisses his escort and strips, discarding his filthy

trousers in the corner. I wonder if he expects me to wash them. Probably. Stepping into the large tray, he dunks his head straight into the bowl of water and begins to scrub himself, giving a sharp intake of breath as the soap aggravates his cuts and scratches.

Casually, I walk over and pick up his trousers, running my hand down the left leg until my fingers find a slight thickening in the fabric. A hidden pocket. I'm half expecting it, but somehow it still comes as a shock when my finger touches the cold metal blade inside. I draw it out slightly. A fine black dagger, no more than four inches long. But even at that small size it would have been discovered during the full-body search before the challenge began. Which means it *was* slipped to him part-way through the event.

"Can you come do my back?"

I whirl around, dropping the trousers, but Jay doesn't seem to have noticed my inspection. After walking over, I grab the cloth and dunk it in the already filthy bowl of water.

I manage to get two more bowls of water out of the big pan we use only for this job. Normally, we make do with one bowl between us, but this is a special occasion. Plus, no one else in the block is likely to complain about him taking all the hot water in the building and most of the solar energy to heat it now he's the leader of the Snakes. Most of them are probably down at the square. I help towel him down and then apply some of the salve that helps prevent infection to the cuts on his chest, back and arms.

Leaving him to dress, I empty the water outside, flooding the small courtyard with its broken drain. When I return, Jay smiles and pulls me into his arms.

"So, how does it feel, my queen?"

149

His earlier annoyance at my non-appearance seems to be forgotten. I try and smile back at him, but the knowledge of the blade in his trouser pocket is gnawing at my stomach. I have to know.

"Jay, who did that blade come from?"

His face darkens. "What are you talking about?"

No going back now. "The blade in your trousers. I saw you stab Rich with it. Who did it come from?"

His hands grip my arms tight as he pulls away from me. Suddenly, I feel scared.

"The only blade you saw was my knife, Aleesha, do you understand? There was. Nothing. Else." His voice is tight and controlled.

"But the ch—"

"Nothing else, Aleesha." He shakes me hard.

To my surprise there is something other than anger in his eyes. Something I've rarely seen before. Fear.

I mutter an apology, still no clearer about what's going on. Jay sighs and pulls me into him again, hugging me tight. "Come on, it's time to go to our celebration party." It seems I'm forgiven for now.

As we leave the apartment, a thought strikes me, stopping me dead on the stairs. The Brotherhood. Would they have helped Jay win in order to get a hold over the gang? Are the Snakes now in their grasp, too? Fear grips me at the thought of what they may want in return for their help. It could destroy the gang.

Rich's death may only be the start.

* * *

The party is already going strong when we arrive at the old

warehouse. Though it's early-afternoon, half the gang are intoxicated already. Those who drew the short straw guard the perimeter morosely, jealous that they can't partake fully in the festivities.

I hang around with Jay for a while, but I'm not big into parties, and after an hour or so decide to slip away. Jay doesn't mind, he's happy enough being the centre of attention.

On my way out I spot Anelia, Megan's friend, hovering close to the door as if waiting for someone.

"Have you seen Megan?" I ask.

Anelia shakes her head, biting her lip. "She went to the tent where Rich was taken after … you know."

"Did he make it?" I ask, although I already know the answer.

She shakes her head and looks down. "I think it was quick, though. But Megan said she didn't want to be disturbed and wouldn't let me in the tent with her. I told her I'd meet her here, but …"

Her voice trails off and I know what she's thinking. If Megan doesn't turn up at the party it'll be a sign that she doesn't accept Jay as leader. A sign of rebellion. Whatever her feelings for Rich, without the gang, she won't have much of a life left in Area Four.

"I'm sure she'll be here soon." My voice sounds hollow and I search for some reassuring words. "You know what, I bet no one even notices she's not here. And if it gets raised as an issue, I'll speak to Jay and try and persuade him not to make a big deal out of it."

Anelia smiles weakly. "Thanks, Aleesha."

I leave her staring out down the street and wander north through the mostly deserted streets toward Area Five.

* * *

151

I don't really have a clue where to find Murdoch, so I follow the path he'd taken me on yesterday, toward the empty house. I suspect he'll have a way of finding me.

When he arrives about twenty minutes later, he's madder than ever. Not bothering with niceties, he pushes me through the backyard and into the house. Kicking the door shut, he throws me against the wall.

"Firstly, you do not come here without my permission. Ever." He jabs his finger at me. "Secondly, how you have the nerve to turn up I don't know. It's done now, there is no deal. You've screwed up too many times."

He glares down, daring me to speak.

"I'm really sorry I didn't turn up this morning. I meant to, honest, but—"

"But what, you decided you'd prefer a hard night out instead?"

"No!" I glare back at him, then lower my gaze. *Come on, more grovelling, Aleesha.* "It was the Snakes' leadership contest today; there's no way I could have missed it. You know that. I didn't know until last night and couldn't find you to tell you."

"I don't care about some petty gang fight," Murdoch spits. "We had a deal. You didn't meet your end of the bargain, that's that." He leans back against the wall, his arms crossed.

I take a deep breath and walk over to him, trying to bring tears into my eyes. "Please, Murdoch, one more chance? I promise tomorrow I'll turn up at whatever time you need. You have my word."

He snorts. "The word of a drug addict? I'm sure that means a lot."

I'm NOT a drug addict.

I grit my teeth to stop myself saying the words out loud. Instead, I lower my voice to a purr. "Come on, Murdoch, just one more chance." I'm close to him now, and I peek up through my lashes. *Dammit, if only I could cry.* But I've never cried, not since before my mother left.

Murdoch's face begins to soften. Then his lips tighten again and he shakes his head.

"Please? I'll do anything." My voice trembles and I'm close enough to feel his breath on my forehead. I run my hand lightly up his thigh.

"Anything," I repeat.

His eyes widen with lust before he pushes me away with a growl.

"Tomorrow. Nine in the morning, same place. But this really is your last chance. If you don't show then, there will be no other opportunities. And your *boyfriend* will be getting the full story on your illegal status."

I smile at his turned back. It's my last chance. But it's also theirs. If I don't get some information about my mother after this, I'm walking. And they'll be one spy down.

15

Trey

We return to the meeting point the next morning to find Aleesha slouched against the stone wall of the hall. Her eyes widen when she sees us, but she makes no comment on my altered appearance. She's dressed exactly as she was the other day: black trousers and a grey sleeveless top. A small backpack sits at her feet and she twiddles the strap in her fingers as if unwilling to lose contact with it.

Murdoch arrives a few minutes later and raises an eyebrow. "Nice of you to join us today, Aleesha."

She scowls at him and mutters something unintelligible under her breath.

Murdoch briefs us on the square we need to go to and the café where we're to make the pickup. "Make sure you're there for ten. Our contact will be reading a copy of yesterday's newspaper and eating a pastry and orange. When he leaves, he'll leave the newspaper on the table. Underneath there will be a small plastic box."

Murdoch indicates the size with his finger and thumb and looks at me. "Trey, I want you to bring the box back to the second meeting point." He names a street junction, which doesn't mean anything to me, but Aleesha nods. "Do not try and open the box. And Trey? Don't even think about giving it to her." He jabs his thumb at Aleesha, who scowls in response.

"What if your contact is delayed?"

Murdoch shrugs. "Just hang around until he gets there. Look inconspicuous."

Aleesha snorts. "Because hanging around like a couple of hobies is a *great* way of looking inconspicuous," she mutters under her breath.

"Pretend like you're a couple of love-struck teenagers making out," Bryn says. "They'll not look twice at you then."

My cheeks suddenly burn uncontrollably as I catch the smirk on his face. *Stop blushing like a girl, dammit.*

I follow Aleesha through a maze of streets and alleyways toward the Wall. The thought of going back through the Wall twists my stomach into knots. What if it doesn't work again? Maybe it was a fluke I got through last time. I try not to think about it, which, of course, makes it impossible to think of anything else.

We cut through a narrow passageway between two rows of houses and suddenly it's right in front of us. I stop dead. My heart hammers in my chest. *Calm down.* I close my eyes, and when I open them, Aleesha's staring back at me in bemusement.

"Sorry, this is only the second time I've done this." I swallow nervously. The Wall is only a couple of metres away.

Aleesha smiles, and for the first time it seems genuine. "The second time is the worst." Then she grabs my hand and pulls me forward.

Off balance, I stagger forward. The Wall looms up as fear chokes any cry I may have wanted to utter. And then we're through. Aleesha drops my hand and folds her arms, waiting as I reel around trying to get my breath back.

"See, it wasn't that bad," she says. I can only nod my agreement.

This side of the Wall looks remarkably similar to the side we just left. A narrow backstreet behind a long row of houses. Before we move off, Aleesha pulls some clothes out of her bag and begins to put them on over her existing attire. She looks me up and down. "What have you got on under that coat?"

I unzip it, revealing the dark grey top I'd put on this morning. One Abby had "lying around". Aleesha frowns. "We'll have to pick you something up. Come on."

We set off down the alley, and a few doors down, she grabs me some brighter, more appropriate clothing. I open my mouth to admonish her, then close it again. It's not as if I can exactly walk into a shop and buy the stuff now. And to be honest, the dull blacks and greys of Outsider clothing were getting to me.

"So, where's this square, then?"

My heart sinks. "I thought you might know?"

"*You* don't?" Aleesha stares at me. "But you're an Insider. The whole point of you coming along on this job is because you're *supposed* to know your way around Inside."

"Well, I don't, okay?" I mutter sullenly. "I've hardly spent any time in London and we always used the pods to get around. I know some parts of the city, but not this area."

"Great. Well, we'll have to ask for directions, then." She stomps up the road toward the main street.

Aleesha makes me ask for directions; perhaps conscious of her accent. I approach an older woman sitting on a bench in a small park. She reels off a set of directions, but I'm lost after the first few. Glancing sideways, I catch Aleesha nodding slightly, her lips moving silently as she repeats the directions to herself.

We turn to leave, but on a whim I pause. "Is Great Percy Street around here?"

The woman frowns, then nods. "It's a bit further on from the square." She reels off more directions. I make more effort to remember these.

"What's at Great Percy Street?" Aleesha asks as we walk away.

"It's my parents' address in London."

"I thought you said you weren't from London?"

I sigh. "No, I just said I've hardly spent any time here. My school's about fifty miles north, in the country, and as well as the London apartment, my parents have an old house in Wales. They used to pack me off there during school holidays."

"Where's Wales?"

"West coast of Britannia. There's not much out there, hardly any people anymore, just goats."

There's a pause. "Your parents must be pretty rich to have two homes."

"I guess they are, compared to Outsiders. But the Welsh house has been in my mother's family for generations. It's a wreck, to be honest. At some point, it'll fall down completely and they'll have to abandon it."

"I've never been beyond the city." There's a trace of wistfulness in Aleesha's voice. "How did you end up Outside, then?"

I sigh again, more deeply this time. "It's a long story."

We saunter casually along the streets, trying to blend in with the crowd. As much as I hate my dyed hair and the stuff Abby put on my skin, the disguise seems to be working as no one gives me a second glance. I almost relax, until I spot a Metz patrol further up the road and freeze. Aleesha pulls me down a side street. A reminder that there's nowhere I'm really safe.

The smells wafting from the food shops make my mouth water. I almost stop at one before I remember that without my chip, I can't buy anything. But at least water is free. We stop at a drinking fountain and Aleesha sticks her head under it for so long, I have to pull her away before the next person in the queue starts to complain.

She wipes her mouth and smiles. "It tastes so good, doesn't it?"

"Whatever." *It's only water.*

The square the woman directed us to looks vaguely familiar. I remember the large antique clock on the wall of the building opposite, which marks the time as ten to ten. The bright red awning of the café extends out, partially covering the tables strewn out into the square. A handful of people sit at the tables; a couple, three women (two with babies) and a few business types who sit alone, engrossed in work. Another person is invisible behind the newspaper held in front of their face.

We stroll casually up to the blank wall that links the café with the corner of the street. As we draw closer, Aleesha pulls me around so I'm in front of her. She backs up until she's pressed against the wall. There's a mocking gleam in her eye. "So, what was Bryn saying about making out?" she murmurs, pulling me a little closer.

I feel myself blushing again, uncomfortably aware of how close she is and wanting to both draw closer and pull away. "Um …" I flounder for something to say.

Aleesha glances over my shoulder toward the café. "That's him," she whispers.

I twist around, glad of the distraction, and glance over at the man with the newspaper. He wears the regulation blue suit that marks him out as a government official, though probably a fairly junior one. On the table sits a half-eaten fruit pastry and an orange.

The ten o'clock news begins to blare out of the speakers on

the screens dotted around the square. I'm relieved to hear I've dropped out of the headlines.

"Hey." I feel a hand on my cheek, pulling my head around. "We're supposed to be making out, you know."

"Errr, right," I reply, not really sure what to do next. *Bryn didn't really mean it, did he?*

She pulls my face toward her, though I can see her keeping one eye on the café. Her breath is light on my face and smells surprisingly sweet. My stomach feels as tight as it did on the other side of the Wall and my palms are sweating. Her lips are just inches from mine. *What am I supposed to do? I've never kissed a girl before.*

A chair scrapes on the cobbled street. Her lips reach forward and touch mine for the briefest moment before she pulls back. She grabs my hand and casually pulls me around. I can't help but smile as I follow her. We probably do look like a pair of lovesick teenagers.

The man picks up his orange as he prepares to leave, nodding at the robotic waiter. The newspaper sits half folded on the table. As we walk past, Aleesha pauses. "Hey look at this." She picks the paper up and points at a headline, being careful to keep the page horizontal. Her other hand slides underneath. One of the women at the next table glances up in surprise at her accent.

The waiter hovers over to clear the table. "Okay if we take this?" I grab the newspaper and wave it in front of the waiter's camera. It pauses for a moment, processing.

"Of course, sir. Would you like a table?"

"No thanks, we've got to dash."

We move as quickly as possible off down the street, leaving the square and café behind.

"Did you get it?" I say out of the corner of my mouth.

"What do you think."

I pull Aleesha into a narrow passageway off the main street and hold out my hand. "Give it to me."

She stands there, a mocking smile on her face. *Is she testing me?*

"Murdoch said I was to have it." I narrow my eyes, wondering how on earth I'm going to force her to hand it over. But with a slight shrug she acquiesces, dropping a small grey cube into my outstretched hand. I turn, walk back to the main street and turn left, following the directions the woman had given me.

"Wait, where are you going? We need to go back that way." Aleesha grabs my arm, but I pull it away and carry on walking. She runs in front of me. "Where are we going?"

"A little detour to Great Percy Street."

Her eyes narrow. "You bastard. This was your plan all along, right? Get back to Mummy and Daddy and take them the information." Before I quite know what's happening, she pushes me into a dark alleyway and there's cold metal pressing into my throat.

"I knew Murdoch should have let me come alone. Now, give me the cube."

"You're wrong. Get off and let me explain." The knife doesn't move. "Look, if you kill me here someone will see, the Metz will be here in an instant. We're probably on camera right now." I glance up at the corner of the building, though I've no idea if there are cameras or not. "Don't be stupid, *Outsider.*"

She hisses angrily, but pulls the knife away.

"I'm sorry. I just ... I just need to find my father, okay? I'm being hunted, I have no idea why and he's the only one who can help me. Can we please just go and find him? I-I'll make it worth your while, I promise."

She chews her lip, considering. "Fine. But if you decide you're staying with them, I'm taking that cube back. *I'm* the one who's going to get into trouble if it's not delivered on time."

I breathe a sigh of relief.

We walk in silence for a few minutes before Aleesha speaks again. "What do you think it is?"

"The cube? I don't know. But the man we took it from is a government official, so I'm sure it can't be anything good. The Chain said they wanted more equality in the city, didn't they? Perhaps …" I hesitate for a second. "Do you think they're trying to overthrow the government or something?"

"I'm hoping so," she replies darkly. "How did you know he's a government official?"

"They all wear the same kind of suit. At least, all those below a certain level do. You can tell what rank they are by their ties. He was middle rank."

"Oh." She thinks for a minute. "What about women?"

"What about them?"

"Do they have to wear suits, too?"

"Sure. They can choose to wear a skirt instead of trousers. Men can, too. They just have to be the right colour."

She makes a face. "Identikit blue."

"Well, everyone Outside seems to wear identikit black," I reply.

She smirks. "That's because black is practical. Doesn't show the dirt and you don't get seen in the dark. Those jackets look like they're hot in summer, though."

I shake my head. "No, they're coolmax. They cool down your body as well as protecting you from the sun." A slight frown appears on her face. I sigh. "Let me guess, you don't have coolmax Outside?"

She just gives me a look in reply.

We take a right at the end of the wide street, then turn left down a residential street. It opens out in the middle, the houses forming a circle around a fenced-off park. The street continues for a couple of hundred metres after the park, ending at a road lined with more modern, glass houses. We turn right, then almost immediately left. Aleesha pauses.

"Here you are, Great Percy Street! What number is it?"

"Forty-one." I look around, puzzled. This looks nothing like the street we live on. But when I glance up at the side of the house facing us, the sign clearly reads *Great Percy Street*.

Confused, I follow Aleesha down the street, looking around for something, anything, I recognize. Ahead of me, Aleesha pauses in front of a tall, white building that fronts directly onto the street. It has a bright green door with a line of buzzers, indicating that the property is divided into apartments. As I draw closer, I see the polished metal plate with the number of the house. Forty-one. *41 Great Percy Street*. The address I've had memorized since I was five years old as being home. But I am totally, one hundred percent certain that I have never been to this house in my life before.

I stand there for a full five minutes whilst my brain shoots around random theories and ideas, trying to find some kind of logical explanation. There must be two Great Percy Streets. The odd, out-of-place sandstone house with the gargoyles that I *know* to be home must be on another Great Percy Street. Or perhaps I got the number wrong?

But I know I haven't. And there can't be two Great Percy Streets. I can clearly remember having a conversation with my father about street names in the city. He laughed aloud when I asked if there could be two people with the same address. He replied that it wasn't possible; that every single street in the city – be it a main road or a ten-foot alleyway – has its own unique name.

So, why have my parents sent me here, to a random house in an unfamiliar part of town? I find myself walking over to the green door and staring at the labels next to the buzzers on the left of it. Three of the four buzzers have name labels, all unfamiliar. The fourth, for the top floor apartment, is blank. On an impulse I reach out and press it.

It rings for a few seconds then goes silent. I'm about to turn and walk away when a female voice emerges from the speaker.

"Hello? Can I help you?"

I turn back, unsure what to say. "I—" I'm about to give my name, but stop myself. *This person is a stranger.* "Do you know Andrew Goldsmith?"

The voice hesitates a fraction of a second too long. "No, I've never heard of him."

She knows something. I'm sure of it.

"Please, can you tell me where he is?" My words sound more desperate than I had intended. I take a deep breath and force my fists to unclench.

"No, I told you, I know nothing. Now please get off my doorstep." She's angry, too angry for someone who's just had a random stranger turn up at her house. But why would she lie? And who is she?

"I'm sorry," I try and keep my voice calm. "I was given this address to contact. Please, can you tell me who you are? There's no n—"

There's a bleep and an automated voice comes on. "I'm sorry, there is no one at home at the moment. If you would like to leave a message, please press the green button." The robotic words echo around the small porch.

I step back toward Aleesha, who gives me a questioning look. I can't bring myself to speak, so I just shake my head. As we set off down the street, I glance back to the window of the top floor apartment. She pulls back as soon as she sees me watching, but I catch a glimpse of her pale face framed by long, sleek dark hair. There is something vaguely familiar about her, something I can't quite place my finger on, but I am sure I have never seen her before.

16

Trey

We walk in silence, Aleesha leading us back through the streets on a route that avoids the frequent Metz patrols.

Murdoch looks relieved to see us when we get back to the meeting point. "Did you get it?"

I pull the small grey cube out of my pocket and hand it over.

"What *is* it?" Aleesha asks.

Murdoch does some complicated motion with his hands, then opens them to reveal the unlocked cube. A microchip.

"Information." He grins, flashing white teeth.

Aleesha rolls her eyes. "No shit. *What* information?"

"I told you, that's not for you to know."

"Are you plotting against the government?" In my head my voice is firm and demanding, but the words that spill from my mouth are limp and weak.

"I *said*, it's not for you to know." I shrink as Murdoch looms over me.

"Murdoch." Bryn warns. Murdoch takes a step back, flashing Bryn a look of pure hatred.

"We've done the job, now what about *my* information?" Aleesha asks. A look of annoyance flashes across Murdoch's face. "Come on," she presses when he doesn't respond. "We had a deal."

"Fine." Murdoch pulls a small piece of film from his pocket and hands it to her. I catch sight of a name and address before Aleesha shoves it into her pocket after a quick glance. A rare flash of surprise crosses her face.

Bryn raises an eyebrow at me. "You alright, Trey?"

I nod, dejected. I'm anything but alright, but I don't really want to get into the details now. As we walk, I think back to the face at the window. I'm sure the woman knows my father, knows who I am, perhaps. So, why didn't she say? *Because she was frightened.* I stop dead.

Of course. There are cameras everywhere Inside. If the Metz had recognized me, were following me, and I stopped at that house, it would put her in danger. And if I was to find my actual home? Which is probably being watched already, as surely that's where they expect me to go ... Then I'd be walking straight into a trap.

"Trey?" Bryn's looking at me, puzzled. I shake myself and start walking again, my mind whirring. The address was a decoy, but it may have saved me. But I still don't know why my parents gave me a fake address.

Unless they knew that one day, this could happen.

* * *

Back at Abby's with a mug of steaming herbs, my relief at not having been captured is quickly replaced by a terror that still grips my stomach so tight I sometimes struggle to breathe. All I've been clinging to for the past week has been the thought of finding my parents. The knowledge that if I can just find my father he'll fix everything. Now, the one thread I'd been clinging to is broken, and I don't know what to do next.

Abby sits down beside me and places a hand on my arm. "Let me look at your dressing, Trey."

I let her pull up my sleeve and unwind the bandage around my forearm. I glance down as she peels off the dressing and wince. The dark gash is still there, the skin slightly swollen around it. I'll have a scar, Abby told me, though it may fade over time. A never-ending reminder.

Abby prods the wound gently, making me wince again. "It's looking better." She smiles up at me and begins to spread some lotion over the wound. "In a few days you should be able to leave the dressing off. Fresh air will help finish the healing process."

Bryn snorts. "Fresh air? In this city?"

Abby glares at him, then looks back to me. "You know, you were really lucky you missed the muscles and cords in your arm. You could have lost all use of it." She balances a clean piece of cloth on my arm and begins to re-wrap the bandage around it.

"There you go." She ties a knot and pats my arm. "So." She hesitates for a moment. "Where have you been?"

I don't know what to say. I'm not even sure I can speak. A lump rises in my throat, choking me, and tears prick at the back of my eyes. I swallow, trying to focus on the mug in front of me, to gulp down the tears. Only girls cry.

A tear drops onto the table. I sniff and throw my head back, casting my eyes around the room for something else to focus on. But it's useless.

"Oh, Trey." I feel Abby's arm around my shoulder, pulling me into her. Her kindness is the final straw and I begin to sob. The sobs roll up through my body, shaking and rattling every part of me.

* * *

Finally, I can cry no more. I rest, exhausted, against Abby's shoulder for a minute, then push myself upright, ashamed at my outburst.

"What happened, Trey?" she asks gently.

So I tell them. Tell them about trying to find my father, my family, the address I was given. And how the address turned out to be a fake. They sit in silence, digesting.

"Trey, who is your father? Maybe we can help you find him. I have some connections on the Inside, but if you won't tell us who he is ..." Bryn leans forward, balancing on the edge of the chair.

Can I trust him? I'd trust Abby, but she can't help me. She barely goes outside her house and backyard. She seems to trust Bryn, but ... I sigh. Once they know who my father is, there's no going back. But right now, I don't think I have a choice.

"His name is Andrew Goldsmith."

There's a sharp intake of breath from Abby.

"He's the minister in charge of health, education and population control." I don't have to say anymore. There are probably only a handful of ministers Outsiders really know or care about. But Andrew Goldsmith is most definitely one of them.

"And your mother? Brother or sister?" Bryn's voice is rough.

"Miriam Goldsmith. And I have a sister, Ella. She's quite a bit older than me."

Bryn stands up and begins to pace the kitchen. It's so small he can only take three paces before he's forced to turn around.

"And how old *are* you, Trey?"

"Seventeen last month," I reply, puzzled.

Bryn mutters a curse and slumps back down in the large rocking chair. He leans forward, pressing the heel of both hands into his forehead. I glance over at Abby, but she looks as confused as me. And slightly afraid.

"He cares, you know," I say, wanting to break the awkward silence. "He's trying his best to make things better, but his hands are tied." My words sound lame. Like excuses.

Abby pats my arm. "I'm sure he does." But her face is troubled.

I nod silently, the memory of the screaming mother and baby still fresh in my mind. This world Outside is even worse than I'd imagined. *Father couldn't be blind to this, surely?*

But I also remember times when he came home for a rare day or two off and looked so haggard and worn. Conversations with my mother that I wasn't supposed to hear, about disagreements with his cabinet colleagues. With the President himself.

"I may be able to help find them." I glance up surprised and Bryn holds up a hand. "No guarantees," he warns, "but I have a few contacts Inside who are trustworthy."

"Members of the Chain?" I ask, hesitantly.

He nods and frowns. "But I'm afraid they'll ask for something from you in return."

My heart sinks. "What?"

He shrugs. "I'm not sure. But the fact that you're untraceable on the government systems now is useful to us. It may just be errands, like the one you've done already. We'll have to see."

"I'll do anything," I reply, more confidently than I feel. Though I can't help wondering what my father would think. *I don't have a choice.*

Bryn stands and walks toward the back door. His face is pale under his tan, and his usual cocky air has gone. "I'll go and make enquiries now," he mumbles as he pushes past me. The door slams shut. I sink my head down onto the cool plastic of the table.

Abby sighs. "Don't worry, Trey. He's just shocked. But he'll come around. You can't help who your parents are, anyway. But just be careful about what you promise the Chain. Try and stay away from them as much as possible."

I hear her footsteps on the floor and a twang as the guitar is lifted down from the wall. "Now, it seems to me like you need some music." She starts plucking at the strings and I close my eyes and let the soaring melodies wash away some of the pain.

* * *

Bryn returns a couple of hours later, looking more like his usual self. "Come on, Trey, there's someone who wants to meet you," he says without preamble, grabbing the last remaining bread roll from the basket on the table.

"Who?" Abby asks.

"Milicent."

She frowns. "Was there no one else you could go to?"

"Who's Milicent?" I ask, looking from Bryn to Abby.

"She's one of the senior Chain members and she can contact your family. Maybe even arrange for you to meet with them."

Abby barks a laugh.

"I don't get it," I say. "What's wrong with her?"

Bryn rolls his eyes. "Abby just doesn't like her very much. She can be …" He searches for the word. "Pompous, on occasion."

"*Lamar* didn't like her," Abby corrects. "And with good reason. Has she made her bid for leadership yet?"

"She's trying."

"Honestly, Bryn, can you not just take on the role? You know that's what Lamar would have wanted."

"No way!" Bryn takes a bite of the roll and continues whilst chewing. "Dealin' with petty squabbling all day? Honestly, if

Lamar had had a decent team here, we'd have sorted this city out years ago. Besides, I'm ready for retirement."

Abby snorts. "You? Retire?"

Bryn scowls at her. "Yes. Why? Don't you think I've earned it?"

"Well sure, but I can't imagine you sitting in a room all day doing nothing. Besides, no one *retires*."

Bryn points a finger at her. "That's because you have this stupid altruit thing going on here, and everyone wants kids, so no one lives long enough to retire. Honestly, if you Britons weren't so insular, you could sort out your population problem overnight and then everyone could live long and happy lives." He takes another bite of the roll.

"What do you mean?"

Bryn turns to me. "This is what they don't teach you in school. The rest of the world is out there." He gestures expansively. "And everyone here is trapped. And as your government refuses to trade, you're left with what little food you can conjure up from the little land you have left. Sea levels are only going to keep rising and you can't factory-produce everything, it's not healthy."

"But surely there must be some reason they can't open the borders ..."

"I'm sure the government have their *reasons*. But it's not them who are suffering, is it? Anyway, this is why I need to retire. I'm getting old and cynical and cranky. And feeling the aches and pains of old wounds. The sooner I can get out of here and get home, the better."

He pulls out a chair and faces me, suddenly serious. "Look, Trey. Milicent is the best-placed person to help you. That's why I went to her. But she'll want something in return. Are you sure you want to go through with this?"

"What choice do I have?"

His eyes search my face and he seems about to say something, but checks himself. "Right, well, if that's the case, we'd better be going. Just be careful, Trey. I know you think your family can help, but there may not be anything even they can do. If you want to get away, start over somewhere else, well, maybe I can smuggle you out …"

The words hang in the air between us. The thought of exploring a new country and finding out more about the world outside Britannia makes my stomach lurch in excitement. But I can't just leave. I have to find my family first.

"I'm sure," I say more confidently than I feel. There isn't really a choice. *But why is Bryn suddenly so concerned about my welfare?*

We walk north until we reach a wide straight road thronged with people that marks the boundary between Areas Five and Six. The occasional pod flies overhead – the first I've seen Outside – and where the road intersects the Wall, there's a set of tall, black metal gates set into a stone wall. The East Gate.

"Milicent lives Inside," Bryn says in a low voice as we dodge through the flow of people heading to and from the gate. "But we access her house from out here."

The mystery deepens as we stop outside a fabric shop that's part of a row of terraced houses that back onto the Wall. A bell chimes when Bryn opens the door and a middle-aged woman comes to greet us. She's tall, but stoops slightly and limps along with the aid of a cane. She seems to know Bryn and asks us to wait. After a minute, we're shown to a trapdoor at the back of the shop with a steep set of wooden steps leading down into a cellar.

We walk down and the hatch is closed shut behind us. I try to swallow the sense of unease at being trapped underground. I don't think I've ever *been* under a building, though I know some of the ancient houses in the city have cellars. This one is lined with shelves and has a floor of rough stone. The single LED bulb casts the corners of the room into shadows.

"Come on." Bryn beckons impatiently from a small door on the far wall. "We haven't got all day."

I follow him along a narrow passageway interspersed by sets of stairs, all of them leading down. I try not to think about how far we are below ground, and the weight of earth above us. Bare bulbs every ten metres or so cast just enough light to walk by. After a long, straight section we reach another set of steps, this time leading upwards. At the top, we turn right and come across another door.

Bryn presses his thumb to a scanner on the left. There's a bleep and a green light flashes. A moment later, the door opens, held by a man in an old-fashioned butler's uniform. We emerge into another cellar, this one much larger than the last.

"Please, go straight up." The man waves his hand to the staircase that spirals upwards. As we climb, I see a large cupboard swing back in front of the door, hiding its existence.

The butler joins us in a large kitchen and leads us through into a richly furnished hallway. I look around, amazed at the sheer amount of space. There are still a handful of houses in the city that haven't been divided up into apartments. They're owned by the real elites. People who have money and power enough to resist change.

The butler stops in front of a large, white-panelled door. He knocks on it twice, then opens it in response to a call from inside. We step through into a large, bright sitting room decorated in an elegant but slightly old-fashioned style. Light floods in from the tall windows that take up most of one side of the room and look out onto a manicured garden bounded by a tall, dense hedge.

"Welcome, Darwin."

I turn to greet the woman who rises from a large, gold-trimmed chair. Her grey hair is pulled back from her face in a soft twist, and her face is old but almost unlined. She could be ninety or a hundred and thirty; it's impossible to tell. "I am Milicent."

"Trey, please." I take the hand she holds out to me, unsure as to whether I should be shaking it or bowing to her. She exudes a sense of grandeur and power, as if she knows she is the most important person in the room, but her smile is kind.

"Please, sit," she gestures to a low sofa and returns to her chair. "I understand you are trying to get in touch with your parents?"

"Y-yes," I stammer. This woman makes me nervous, despite her kind smile.

"Bryn has told me your father is Andrew Goldsmith?"

I nod, not trusting myself to speak again.

She frowns. "Strange, I wasn't aware Andrew had a son."

"You know my father?"

The smile returns. "Yes, of course. A very nice man. And his wife – so elegant. You have her eyes." She glances across to Bryn and something flickers across her face, too quick for me to catch.

Bryn clears his throat. "As you know, the government are after Trey for some reason. He hopes that his father may be able to help sort his, err, situation out."

Milicent nods. "Of course." She looks at me again. "Your family are safe, Trey, but your home is being watched by the Metz. It's not safe for you to go there; they would grab you before you even got to the front door."

A mixture of relief and disappointment floods through me. *At least they're okay.*

"A contact of mine has been in touch with your father, who is extremely relieved to know you are alive and well. He believes he can visit a mutual friend of ours without arousing suspicion. I can arrange for you to meet your family there, if you like?"

"Yes, th-thank you!" I feel almost giddy with relief. Perhaps this nightmare will soon be over. What will I do first? *Eat a roast dinner. Or a chocolate cake from the bakery. Or perhaps spend a full hour getting massaged, cleaned and exfoliated in the shower unit.*

"Unfortunately, I suspect that your situation will not be resolved overnight."

The bubble bursts.

Milicent looks at me sympathetically. "I know, but the Metz still seem to want to get their hands on you. Hopefully, your father will be able to sort something out soon."

"Why are you helping me?" I have to ask, though I suspect I don't want to know the answer.

"Well, there are two reasons. I know what it's like to lose a child." Her gaze flickers to a portrait on the wall of a smiling man a little older than me. "So, I have some sympathy for what your parents are going through. But there may also be a few small tasks you can assist me with."

Milicent rests her elbows on the arms of her chair, steepling her fingers together. She smiles again, but this time the warmth is gone.

My heart sinks. "What sort of tasks?"

"You will be briefed on them after you've seen your family," she replies, "but in the main, it will be information gathering."

I feel cornered. I'm pretty sure that whatever these "tasks" are, my father wouldn't approve. But as I'd said to Bryn, I don't really have a choice. *Besides, she's an Insider. I'm sure I can trust her.*

"Okay," I say and my voice sounds small in this huge, cold room.

Milicent claps her hands. "Perfect. Well, we'll make the arrangements. You should be able to see your family tomorrow!" She smiles again, but I can't bring myself to return it.

17

Aleesha

T he name on the slip of film reads "Louisa Grady". Mrs Grady. I know the name, but struggle to bring a face to mind. The Gradys lived around the corner from us. There were two boys who were a little older than me; twins, as I recall. I went into their shop sometimes to buy food if Mum had a spare chit or two. To beg for credit if not.

I stand outside the grey steel door, working up the courage to press the button marked "Grady". Excitement and nerves mingle in my belly, but also resignation. At least, I know for certain my mother is dead. That shock has already passed. And now I can find out how she died, and why.

The button beeps twice. I stare up at the tiny camera in the corner of the doorframe. *Yes, Mrs Grady, it's me. Now, open the damn door.*

Finally, there's a click and the door opens. A tall, thin woman stands in front of me. Dark hair streaked with grey is plaited down her back. She hesitates for a moment. "Aleesha?"

I nod. "Mrs Grady." She must have been expecting me.

We stand there, staring at each other awkwardly. She's aged a lot since I last saw her, though I guess that's understandable given it must be twelve or thirteen years ago.

"I'm glad to see you looking well, Aleesha," Mrs Grady says. "I was worried about what had happened to you after …" She pauses.

Not worried enough to look after me, though. I chide myself at the thought. It's not really fair, after all. It's hard enough raising two kids out here, let alone risk taking on a third, illegally.

"Well, you'd better come in."

I follow her in silence through to a small room crammed with a pair of sofas and a bed in one corner. "The boys still live here." Mrs Grady nods to the bed. "Though we're hoping they find jobs soon and get a place of their own."

Most of the large, more modern apartment blocks are owned by the big businesses in the city for their workers. Jobs with them are in high demand and they have their pick of candidates, even for the most menial work. There are still some jobs that are better suited to people than bots.

I'm not really in the mood for chit-chat and pleasantries. "I've been told you know what happened to my mother on the day she went missing. The day she … died."

Mrs Grady nods, not meeting my eye, and glances over her shoulder. "Shall we sit down?"

I perch on the edge of the squishy grey sofa.

"Tea?"

I shake my head. "Why didn't you tell me at the time?"

"Because you were a six-year-old child. No child should have their parent taken away like that."

"You should still have told me she was dead!" My voice is hard and accusatory.

"I-I didn't tell anyone what happened. Couldn't. Not until much later." She looks down at her hands. "I still remember that day, though it must be twelve years ago. Brent had fallen in the playground and cracked his arm so I had to take him to the medic centre. There was a long queue; I think it was the day after a big gang fight, so there were lots of broken bones to mend. I remember noticing there were more Metz than normal on the streets, but I'd assumed they were just there to prevent more fighting. One of my friends was at the centre with her little boy and she offered to mind Brent for an hour. We'd run out of catchan spice at the shop and I wanted to get to the market in Rose Square before it closed for the morning.

"I ended up coming up to the square from one of the narrow alleys. Pearson's Passage, you know it?" I nod in response. "But as I approached the square, I could see it was deserted. Some of the stalls were half packed up, but others looked like the owners had just dropped what they were doing and disappeared. I'd been so wrapped in my own thoughts, worrying about Brent and getting to the market in time, that I hadn't noticed there was no one else about. Something stopped me before I walked out into the square; some kind of sixth sense, perhaps."

She laughs nervously. "Then I spotted a movement on the building opposite. You know, the buildings there have those balconies that run around them? There was someone on the balcony, hiding. Then I spotted someone else – two people actually – on the other side of the square. Metz officers.

"I could see the far end of the square from where I was, where the old town hall used to be. It was that direction your mother came from. She must have come straight from your house, and she seemed in such a hurry, she almost ran into the square. I was about twenty metres from her, close enough to see the excitement on her face that turned to doubt when she realized the square was deserted. I wanted to cry out and warn her that something was wrong, but I was too afraid. I just had this feeling something wasn't right. Th-that something bad was going to happen."

She pauses, smiling at me. "She was always beautiful, your mother, but I don't think I'd ever seen her as beautiful and relaxed as she looked in that moment she ran into the square. It was as if all her cares had been lifted from her shoulders."

I nod stiffly, not able to say anything. I feel like I'm six years old again, waiting for my mother to return. Waiting.

"She took a few more steps toward the statue," Mrs Grady continues, "but then she seemed to change her mind and turned to run back the way she'd come. Perhaps she finally sensed the atmosphere in the place. And that's when the Metz appeared. They swarmed into the square from every direction. So many of them! For one woman? They shouted at your mother to stop and when she didn't, they shot her in the leg to take her down. I-I didn't see what happened next. They were all around her like a swarm of ants—" She breaks off and raises a hand to her mouth, choking back a sob. "I'm s-sorry, Aleesha."

I find my voice. "But *why*? Why were they after her at all?"

Mrs Grady fights to compose herself. "That was the strange thing. I'm almost positive that it wasn't *her* they were after. It was someone else; someone she was due to meet. They kept shouting, 'Where is he?' at her. But I don't think she could have said anything at that point even if she'd wanted to." She looks at me sadly.

"And then?" I have to know this – the end.

I've known in my head my mother is dead ever since that day she didn't come back. I knew she wouldn't have abandoned me. But in my heart, there was always a slight hope that maybe she was still out there. That she was held prisoner somewhere or had forgotten who she was. That I would have a chance to find her again. The last traces of this hope trickle coldly away through my veins.

"They beat her. And I think used the tasers on her. I heard her screams – still hear her screams sometimes, at night."

Tears run down Mrs Grady's face and I see the toll this secret has taken on her over the years.

"But whatever it was they wanted, she couldn't – or wouldn't – give it to them. One of them barked an order and they all fell back. They began spreading out across the square, searching under and around the market stalls. Your mother was still alive, I think, though I could see from the blood on the floor and the way she lay that she was badly hurt. She raised her hand slightly toward the officer in charge. And then he shot her in the head, and finally she was at peace."

Her eyes stare blankly at the wall behind me, her face frozen as she relives the memory. I feel dizzy, then realize I've been holding my breath and release it in a rush. Pain filters into my brain and I look down to see the fingernails of my left hand digging into my arm so hard they've drawn blood.

"That's not the end of it, though."

I glance up at Mrs Grady. This time, when she looks at me, there is fear in her eyes.

"There was a man who walked into the square while this was all going on. I think he may have been a waiter at one of the cafés. Anyway, he obviously didn't notice the commotion until he walked into the square. H-he turned to go, but they grabbed him and shot him there. No questions, nothing. It was enough that he'd seen."

We sit in silence as I try to absorb this. To hear these details … Mrs Grady was right not to tell me all those years ago; the specifics, at least. Though she should have told me my mother wasn't coming back. On a whim, I pull my boot off and untie the amulet from around my ankle.

"Have you ever seen this before?" I hold it out to her.

She shakes her head. "No, but it's pretty. Was it your mother's?"

I nod and retie the trinket back around my ankle. It was a long shot.

"Why didn't you help me? When you knew she was dead. I was only six. Why didn't you come and get me?" I can't keep the bitterness out of my voice.

"I did help you. At least, I did what I could. I couldn't take you in; I already had the boys. I asked around my friends to see if anyone would take you but drew a blank. Especially as they weren't sure if—" She checks herself suddenly, then continues. "Well, then I did the only thing left. I asked the children's home to take you in."

"You did *what*? *You* set them on me?" A fear that I thought I had long since buried rises up in me again. It was in the children's home that I had found out that I was different. Illegal. My first run-in with the Metz. I had been lucky to escape.

She flinches back into the sofa and I suddenly realize I'm looming over her, my short-bladed knife clutched in my fist. I take a step back.

"Do you know what those places do? I was fine on my own."

"You were six years old! No six-year-old is 'fine on their own'. You were clever as a child, I thought you'd do well at school. It would give you an opportunity."

"To what? Get shipped away to the Farms?" I sneer.

"To have a proper life! To go to school, get a job. Not live alone in a dingy basement."

She drops her voice and slumps back in her chair. "Except you weren't a proper citizen, were you? That's why your mother kept you hidden away. You were – are – illegal." She whispers the last words as if even saying them aloud could trigger the Metz to come charging in to arrest us both.

And that's what all this comes down to. The story of my life: Illegal.

Disgusted, I turn to leave, but something makes me pause at the door. "Do you know why? Why she didn't register me?"

Mrs Grady looks up. "No." She hesitates then adds, "But your mother was a good person. There must be some reason she didn't register you. I don't know what it could be, but she must have thought you'd be better off as an illegal child than as a registered citizen."

* * *

"Aleesha!" Lily's squeal of joy and surprise fills me with guilt. It's like she hadn't expected me to return.

"You okay? How did you sleep?" I walk over to sit beside her. She is careful not to cuddle up to me, or even touch me at all, though I can tell she wants to. *She learns her lessons fast, this one.* I think back to yesterday: how she threw her arms around my waist when I returned to meet her under the clock, and how I'd instinctively pushed her away. Hard. The thought makes me wince. *What kind of person am I who throws a child to the ground?*

"I'm okay," she replies, then her expression crumples and she buries her face in her arms.

Tentatively, I reach out and place a hand on her shoulder. "What's wrong?"

Her words are muffled by her arms. "Da … ster rat … cudn't slip."

What? "Lily, I can't hear you. Come on, sit up." I try to keep the frustration out of my voice.

She turns a tear-stained face toward me. "The rattlin' monster kept me awake," she says dolefully.

The rattling monster? I cast my eyes around the bare rooftop, but there's nothing remotely monstrous up here. A gust of wind lifts the corrugated iron roof of the shelter and it drops down with a clatter. *Ah, the rattling monster.*

"The roof, Lily? Is that what you were scared of?"

She nods, her eyes wide.

I sigh and reach out. She hesitates for a fraction of a second before scooting over and tucking herself underneath my arm. I try to remember back to when I first found this place and if the roof had bothered me then. I can't remember being frightened by it. Then again, there were plenty of real monsters to fill my nightmares with; I didn't need to make any up.

"It's only the roof, Lily. It's … it's not a monster at all." I search desperately for something comforting to say. "In fact, it's actually keeping *away* the monsters with all the noise it's making."

"Really?"

"Really."

We stare out across the rooftops. I couldn't think what to do with her yesterday. It was clear she had nowhere to go as she was living on the street. I couldn't take her back to Jay's when I had no idea when he'd return from the party or what state he'd be in. At least, on my roof, she's safe from the Metz and Pop Officers. I say my roof, but of course it's not. I just use it.

I always find it strange how the rooftops stay empty despite the crowded conditions below. They're not all flat, admittedly, and you have to know how to access them, but it's a whole different world up here. I used to come here a lot to train, figuring out circuits of exercises to make me strong enough to defend myself. Practising my knife skills until I could embed the knife in the centre of the wooden plinth of the small three-walled shelter nine times out of ten.

"So, where are you from, Lily? And shouldn't you be at school or something?" *Or have a home.*

"I live wiv me mam, between the old highline and the towers. Or, least, I did." I know where she means. It's on the edge of Area Three. Not the worst part, but there aren't any good parts in Three.

"Mam looked after me, when she wasn't on the *stuff*." She spits the word out. "But then the men came and took her away. The men who gave her the *stuff*. I think they killed her, 'cos she didn't come back." Her voice is emotionless. Either she's tougher than she looks or she hasn't really processed this yet.

"When did this happen, Lily?" I ask gently.

She considers this for a moment, counting on her fingers. "Mebbe ten days? I stayed in the house for a bit by meself, but a neighbour told the Pop Officer 'bout me and they came to take me to the kids' home. I didn't stay long there. At first, they didn't take too much notice of me, and it was nice to be with other kids, but then the 'spectors came to do the testing. And I think I must have done something wrong 'cos they said they'd have to take me away to the Farms, and my mam told me about the Farms and how they do 'orrible things to people and stuff." Her voice rises and her eyes glaze over.

"I thought they were goin' to grab me there and then, but Jack was next in the line and he puked all over the 'spector. So I ran. An' I managed to get out into the street. They came after me, but I'm good at hidin'.

"I just bin on the streets since then. At first, I was just trying to get away from the home an' find somewhere safe. There was a man who said ee'd help me and I cud live wiv him, but he didn't turn out to be a nice man." She stares into the distance, reliving more painful memories.

My chest is tight and there's a lump in my throat. That she's still alive and free is something of a miracle. I want to tell her I've been there, that I know what it's like. That you can't trust anyone, least of all someone who says they want to help you. That she shouldn't be trusting me with this. But I can't find the words.

I stroke her hair gently and am rewarded with a warm smile. I return it and feel a fluttering sensation in my stomach. It's strange but not unpleasant.

I hesitate, wanting to know more about her but not wanting to trigger more bad memories. "What about your father?"

Lily shrugs. "Dunno who me dad is. Mam said he wuz from out of town." She pronounces the words carefully. "He's on the boats. I don't think she was supposed to have me."

"And how old are you?"

She furrows her brow. "I dunno really. Six, mebbe?" My heart pounds. Six and abandoned by her mother. Just like me. "How old are you, Aleesha?"

"Eighteen."

"That's proper old." She snuggles into my chest.

I smile. She really is something.

What do I do with her? There are so many kids on the street and the last thing I need is a tag-along. It's hard enough getting food for one person. And my life isn't exactly without danger, especially now Jay's the head of the Snakes. *But I can't just leave her.* There's something about her – her innocence perhaps – that makes me forget how crap life is.

She reminds me of me. The child I was before my mother left and I was forced onto the streets. Forced to do whatever it took to survive. Six years. That's all the childhood I had. If I don't help her, how long will she survive? And even if she can find a way like I did, it will rip that innocence from her. The sparkle in her eyes that lights up her face will be gone within days.

"I can't promise anything, Lily," I warn her. "I live with someone else, you see, so I'll need to ask him first, but if he agrees, you can try living with us for a bit if you'd like? Only until we can find you a permanent home, obviously," I add, not wanting to make any long-term promises. *Not if I can't keep them.*

Her face lights up. "Really?"

"Really. But I have to check first, okay?"

She nods eagerly.

"You may have to stay up here a bit longer." I reach for my backpack and feel around inside. "Here, I got you some food."

She takes the bread and fake-meat paste eagerly, stuffing it into her small mouth. The daylight is starting to fade, and the first twinkling lights of the glass towers visible over the top of the Wall are coming on. A flash of movement across the roof catches my eye.

"Look, Lily, a bird!" I point at the black creature perched on the edge of the parapet. It's a big, bulky bird, not tiny and delicate like those Inside, but it's rare to see any animals or birds out here. Anything big enough to eat is fair game for killing and it's so barren out here, there probably isn't the food for them.

"Wot's a bird?" Lily asks with her mouth full.

"They're animals that fly. Look!" The black bird takes off and soars over the rooftops in the direction of the Wall. I wonder if they can go through it or fly over it, but it disappears before I can see.

"Wish I was a bird. Then I could fly up an' over the Wall." She flaps her arms in imitation.

"Well, don't go trying," I say, alarmed. "You can't fly, okay, Lily?"

"Oww, you're hurting!" Tears fill her eyes and I realize I'm gripping her arm hard.

"Sorry." Guilt rushes through me. *See, I can't look after a child. I'm useless.* "Just promise me you won't try, Lily?"

She nods, rubbing her arm. "I'm not stupid." She yawns.

"Why don't you have a bit of a nap now?"

She rests her head on my thigh and is asleep in seconds.

I think back to my conversation with Mrs Grady, trying to piece together what must have happened that morning. The holo message had been delivered. My mother had been shocked, but happy. I'd never seen her so excited. What was it she'd said? I rack my brains, then in a flash it comes to me. *Finally, he's come for us.* That had been it. Then she'd tied the amulet around my wrist, kissed me and left.

Finally, he's come for us. Who else could she have meant but my father? And she'd gone to meet him, but walked into a Metz ambush. Had he betrayed her? Or was the holo message a fake by the Metz to draw her out? I shake my head. That doesn't make sense. They didn't want her, they wanted him. The person she was meeting. They didn't even take her in for questioning, they just shot her. But if they didn't send the holo message, then who did?

I'm starting to think there's a lot about my mother that I didn't understand. Did she have enemies I never knew about? Or perhaps she had been wrong about my father and he wasn't the person she thought he was.

I stroke Lily's hair softly as she sleeps. Sometimes, it feels as if we're all just pawns in a bigger game. Expendable Outsiders, whose lives and deaths don't mean a thing to anyone.

18

Trey

We're taken to an apartment on the ground floor of a large house in Milicent's neighbourhood. Getting there requires us to go through the tunnel again, then sneak out through Milicent's garden, over a wall into a back alley, then *back* into the garden of the apartment. It all seems an almighty faff. The grass is still wet with last night's rain. Or perhaps it's dew. The boots Bryn found for me are a size too big, but, at least, they're waterproof, unlike my former school shoes, which have been relegated to Abby's scraps cupboard.

The apartment's spacious and opulently decorated. An overflowing chest in the corner of the hallway hints at children. Two probably. A son and daughter. That's what most people choose.

I think of my parents' apartment, large by most standards, but about half the size of this place. It makes me wonder just how much influence Milicent has. Or perhaps the people who live here weren't told that a wanted criminal needed to use their home.

Bryn knocks on the door to what must be the living room.

"Come in!" a voice calls from inside. My father's voice.

"Go on, I'll wait out here," Bryn says. I turn the handle and, taking a deep breath, push open the door and walk inside.

My father stands with his back to me, staring out the window on the far side of the room. In front of him, both perched on the edge of a long, hard-looking sofa, sit my mother and my sister, Ella.

"Darwin!" Mum explodes from the sofa and runs to wrap her arms around me. I rest my head on her shoulder, breathing in roses and vanilla. God, how I've missed that smell. Tears spring to my eyes and I hold her tight, not wanting to let go, but then Ella is there, too, and my father; his arms enveloping all three of us as he used to do when we were small.

There's a cough from the other side of the room and Dad breaks away, casting a guilty glance over my shoulder. Confused, I turn to see a dark-haired woman lounging on the arm of a high-backed chair. She's dressed in the dark grey uniform of the palace guard, her hair pulled back into a tight knot at the nape of her neck. Something about her is vaguely familiar.

She smiles wryly at me, but no one introduces her or gives any explanation for her presence. Mum pulls me over to the sofa and pushes me down. She keeps hold of my hand and Ella takes the other. Mum looks over me searchingly. "What's happened to your hair, Darwin? And your *face*?"

"It's to make me less recognizable," I say, my voice cracking slightly. I keep forgetting my hair's dark now. Hearing my parents speak my name – my first name – feels slightly odd. I'd got quite used to being Trey.

"I'm sorry it's taken us so long to find you." My father's voice is tired and strained. "I didn't even know the Metz had gone to St George's until they came to the house. The only reason they didn't arrest all of us there and then was because they thought you may find your way home. When the President told me you'd disappeared outside the Wall and there was no news or sightings of you, I thought the worst …" He sits down on the sofa opposite and bows his head, massaging his forehead with his knuckles.

"Your father spent hours Outside looking for you, in disguise, of course. Just wandering the streets, trying to find out if anyone had seen you."

He looked Outside for me? I wonder if that's where he picked up the purple bruise on his cheek and the extra grey hairs. He looks as if he carries the cares of the world on him. I try and reconcile this man that I know and love with the man who, according to Abby, sends children to what most people regard as a fate worse than death. I can't do it. *Abby must be wrong.*

"So, why did they come after me at St George's? Why did my arm start going crazy, like it didn't belong to me anymore? Why did I have to do this? Become *this*?" I raise my arm, yanking down my sleeve to reveal the bandage wrapped around my forearm. My mother gasps and chokes back a sob. My heart pounds. Finally, I'll know the truth.

"I-I'm not sure how to say this." My father sighs and rubs his forehead again. "Darwin, you were – are – an illegal child. We didn't have permission to have you."

"You mean, I was a mistake?" I'm even more confused now. *Dad never makes mistakes.*

"No, sweetheart, that's not what he means." Mum grips my hand fiercely, almost crushing it. "What he means is, we already had two children. And you know the law: only two children per couple."

"That's why we had to keep your existence a secret," my father adds. "And why you spent most of the holidays at the house in Wales rather than here in London. We had to be careful, so careful, to try and make sure no one knew about you who also knew about ..."

"Your other child," I say slowly. *But there's always just been me and Ella. Who ...?* I glance over at the dark-haired woman, only now seeing the resemblance to my father. The same tilt of the cheekbones, the strong jaw and dark eyes. *Of course, that's why she looked familiar.* She smiles back at me, but there's no warmth in her eyes.

"Anabel was eighteen when you were born. She agreed to go abroad to live and work in France. If you knew about her, we thought you'd accidentally say something at school about having two sisters, which would have raised the teachers' suspicions. She's been there for seventeen years, only coming back for occasional visits." He smiles fondly at her.

"She's done amazingly well." My mother's voice is full of warmth. "Come back to take up a position as deputy head of the palace guard. The youngest person and the first woman to ever do so." Her voice rings with pride.

The palace guard is the security force for the palace and government buildings. Metz patrol the perimeter of the buildings but never go inside.

"You left London – left Britannia – for me?" I stare at her.

"Don't worry, little brother, I'll cash in that favour someday."

Her voice is familiar. I've heard it recently. Then it clicks. "You were the person in the apartment, at Great Percy Street," I say slowly.

My father flashes her a puzzled look. "You never said Darwin had turned up there, Anabel?"

The woman looks annoyed. "Well, it could have been anyone at the door," she replies defensively. "I didn't want to put you in danger."

Dad sighs and turns back to me. "As far as our friends in London were aware, we had two daughters and occasional visits from our nephew, Darwin. As far as everyone at St George's was aware, we had a daughter and a son. I managed to change the government records so you were recorded as a legal citizen. It all worked so well until ..."

"Until I came back to screw things up," Anabel cuts in.

"Somehow, the Metz suspected or found out you were illegal. I don't know how. I'd swear on my life that everyone who knows the truth about you is trustworthy." Dad's forehead creases with worry. There are new lines there since I last saw him and more grey in his hair.

"They did some digging and found that Anabel was still alive. In order to fix the Personax system for you to be officially recorded as our son, I had to register on it that Anabel had died." He looks at her guiltily. "I managed to get around the fact that we didn't have a death certificate for her, but that only worked so long as no one looked into the records in detail. Once the Metz started investigating, the discrepancy was exposed. That's when they activated the chip in your arm. They can release a tiny amount of poison from it that causes your arm to jerk about. It's intended to both expose the criminal they're after and partially disable them to stop them escaping."

"So, I'm a criminal now," I say flatly.

My father winces. "That's not what I meant. It's *usually* used for criminals. In your case, they just wanted to catch you."

"But I *am* a criminal, aren't I? That's how they see me." I can hear my voice rising and I take a deep breath, trying to remain calm. Dad's right; getting angry isn't going to help me now. I'm not sure what *can*. Illegal children aren't really talked about, but the law is clear. No expansion on family size is permitted.

"Is there …" I hesitate, not sure how to phrase my question. *Are you going to get me out of this mess you created?* "Can you do anything to help me?"

"Yes!" my mother jumps in. She squeezes my arm. It's like she can't bear to see me go, to lose me again. "You know we'd do anything for you, Darwin," she says softly. There are fine lines on her forehead, too; lines of worry I've never seen before on my mother, who's so keen on keeping up with her skin treatments. She almost looks her age.

I look back to my father. After all, he's the only one in a real position to do anything. Out the corner of my eye, I see Anabel scrutinizing me, as if she's trying to weigh up if I was worth her sacrifice all those years ago.

"What does happen to illegal children? If you'd … handed me over when I was born?" The screaming woman and baby still haunt my thoughts. Perhaps now I can prove Abby wrong.

"Sometimes, they're adopted, but we didn't want to give you away, and besides, there are very few couples Inside who want to adopt now. Most just choose to create a baby from donated genes if they don't want to use their own or if they're a homosexual couple. Otherwise, there's the Metz academy, but we didn't want that for you either—"

"Those inhuman beasts!" My mother grips my arm even tighter. Red marks on white skin.

"What, you mean you didn't want the *honour* of your child being a Metz officer?" Anabel's voice is laced with sarcasm.

"No!" My mother glares at her. "Which is why we kept you from that route, Anabel. At least, the guards are human."

"So are the Metz. All flesh and blood. Well, *mostly* flesh and blood."

My mother snorts. "They may be flesh and blood, but they're

not *human,* not really."

I think of the black and yellow masked figures. The same colour as the wasps father had to periodically smoke out of the roof of the outhouse in Wales. Their robotic actions and single-minded focus. Their ability to kill without seeming to *feel* anything.

I shudder. "Surely, there must be another alternative?"

There's a pause in which my parents look at one another. *Great, what else are they keeping from me?*

"Don't you think we've had enough of secrets?" The words come out sharper than I had intended and I feel my mother flinch.

"Well, if a child doesn't pass the intelligence tests for the Metz, the parents have a choice. Either they can send the child to one of the orphanages at the Farms, or ..."

"Or what?"

"Or they opt for euthanasia. Most go for euthanasia. At least, the child feels nothing."

"Which, of course, we couldn't have done," my mother adds hurriedly. "Besides, with your father's position, if we'd even admitted to having an illegal child, he – we – would have lost everything."

So, that's it. The real reason they kept me a secret. Less about my welfare and more about my family's position. Dad couldn't do without his important job. Mum couldn't cope without her lunches out with friends and her anti-aging treatments.

I pull away from my mother as anger surges inside me. So many secrets and lies. My family, the people I've loved and believed loved me, have been lying to me my whole life. My whole world is not what I thought it was.

Another thought hits me. "So, if you didn't intend to have me, you couldn't have used the gene bank," I say slowly, my mind still working through the implications of this. *She couldn't even have gone to the medic for an abortion. Just becoming pregnant carries its own punishment.*

Usually, couples who want to have a child choose what genetic enhancements they want or can afford, and these are combined with their natural genes to form an embryo that's then inserted into the mother. Presuming she wants to carry the baby, of course. Many women feel it's more "natural" that way, although the artificial wombs are promoted as less risky for both mother and child.

"Which means I don't have any enhancements. All this time, I've been struggling at school thinking it's *my* fault I can't keep up with the other boys, and I've been at a disadvantage all along!" Anger drives me to my feet and I stand there, fists clenched, glaring at my father. *What a hypocrite. Making me feel bad all these years.*

"Genetic enhancements are not the be all and end all," says my father, a trace of anger entering his normally calm voice. "The majority of everyone's genes are natural, and not all of your friends would necessarily have had intelligence enhancements. I seem to remember physique was a popular trend around the time you were born."

"You're a perfectly rounded, natural human being," my mother adds, soothingly. "Just because you didn't have any enhancements doesn't make you any better or worse than anyone else."

Whatever. I glance at Ella and Anabel and wonder for the first time what enhancements they were given. Is there a gene for sarcasm?

I blow out hard, trying to get my anger under control. "Fine, so what happens now?"

"I've been speaking to the President," Dad says. "He's open to a solution that doesn't involve … that suits everyone. But at the same time, he can't let this go unpunished. You're not to blame for any of this, Darwin; he knows that and he's not without compassion, whatever the media makes of him." He frowns. "I just need a bit more time to come up with something that can get us all out of this mess. For now, it's good to know you're safe. We've been so worried."

Safe is not the word I'd use to describe my current situation, but I let it pass.

"How *did* you escape, Darwin?" asks Ella, suddenly lighting up with curiosity. My mother echoes the question. Even Anabel has a look of vague interest on her face.

I tell them the whole story of my escape from St George's, only leaving out Purley's role. I figure that's a secret best kept between me and him. I tell them about finding I could go through the Wall and the conditions Outside. My father hangs his head at this, but says nothing.

When I mention meeting Bryn in the bar of what I thought was a hotel, my mother takes a sharp intake of breath. I glance over at her, but she nods to continue. I explain about meeting Abby and how she's looked after me. I don't mention the Chain. I'm sure they're plotting against the government and Dad should know about it. But … I don't know what to believe any more.

The people I believed were supposed to protect us are hunting me, want to eradicate me, simply for being alive. And it seems like even Dad can't figure out a way to stop them. I swallow down the bitter taste in my mouth.

When I finish speaking, there's a pause. My mother turns my forearm toward her, gazing down at the gauze bandage that covers my self-inflicted wound. I feel a tear splash onto my arm.

Anabel is the first to speak. "Well, you're obviously tougher than you look. I'd always taken you for an underachieving spoilt brat." There's a slight, *very* slight, trace of admiration in her voice that makes me smile.

"Anabel!" My mother sounds shocked.

"Oh, come on, Mummy, we all know the truth. Or is that something else you haven't told him?"

"What do you mean?" Ella sounds as confused as I feel.

What else is there I don't know?

"Anabel." There's a warning tone in my father's voice and he gives her his best "shut up" look. Then he smiles at Ella and me. "I'm sure you have lots more questions, Darwin, and we've got more to tell you both, but I suspect we've already outstayed our welcome here, so it'll have to wait for another time. Darwin, we would love for you to come with us, but I'm afraid it's too dangerous – for everyone. The Metz are keeping a constant watch on us in the hope of catching you. Are you okay to stay with this Abby for now?"

I feel a stab of disappointment. *All this and I still can't go home?* But I know in my heart he's right. I nod.

We say our goodbyes; Mum, Dad and Ella give me big hugs. I just get a nod from Anabel. She doesn't seem like a hugging type.

"Ella, do you want to show Darwin where the bathroom is before he leaves?" my father says, walking me to the door. He opens it and ushers us both outside. Bryn is leaning against the far wall of the corridor, looking bored. My father beckons to him. "Bryn? Could we have a quick word, please?"

As the door shuts behind us, Ella and I exchange a glance. "What was *that* about?" I ask her.

She shrugs. "I'm not sure, but I suspect Anabel's just trying to wind you up. You have to understand, it was a big deal for her. She effectively banished herself to another country for years for a baby she never even thought she'd meet. It's changed her." She glances down at the floor.

"What … what's it like out there? Outside?" She whispers the word.

I shudder. "Horrible. Worse than I'd imagined. I'll kill for a decent meal. And a shower. But it's not …" I hesitate, trying to think how much to tell her. "There's something not right about it all. It's not what we were taught. Outsiders aren't all lazy and stupid, and … well, there's just something not quite right," I finish lamely.

Ella frowns as she leads me through the house to the bathroom. Before she turns to leave, she says, "Look, I love you, Darwin. No matter what, you're my brother. Be safe and come home soon." She gives me a hug, then disappears back towards the living room.

I make the most of having a proper flush toilet, and when I emerge, Bryn is waiting for me. He looks pale and tight-lipped, but when I ask if he's alright he just nods. Perhaps he's angry. I guess he thought he was going to be able to get rid of me, finally.

We walk back in silence, each of us lost in our thoughts. I've never felt so lost. Even when I was wandering around in the worst part of Area Four, at least, I had some direction. I knew I wanted to get back home to my family. But my family aren't who I thought they were. And even if I can go back, home will never feel the same again.

19

Aleesha

I leave Lily up on the roof, huddled at the back of the sheltered area to keep out of the rain blowing in. When I get back to Jay's, I hear voices coming from the apartment, too low for me to make out any words. I shuffle my feet outside to mark my presence, then open the door and walk in.

The room is gloomy, the last grey light of the day coming through the window. Jay is standing by the table. His head whips around as the door opens and his face is tense and lined. Behind him, standing by the window with his back to us, is a tall figure dressed all in black. The hood of his tight, lightweight top is pulled up over his head and his arms are crossed.

"Aleesha. Where have you been?" Jay asks.

I shrug. "Out and about. I didn't want to wake you this morning." *Especially as you'd have been like a bear with a sore head.*

Jay throws a glance in the direction of his guest and begins to massage his temples. He's worried about something. There's a tension in the air, but I can't tell if it was there before I walked in or if I'm the cause.

I look at the stranger, intrigued, then Jay catches my eye. "Go!" he mouths silently.

I step back uncertainly. "Well, I won't disturb you. I'll see you in … in a bit." I take another step back, my hand still on the door handle.

"Wait." The voice is deep and smooth. It's not shouted or barked, but it's a command all the same. A flash of fear crosses Jay's face. *Fear for me or for himself?*

"Shut the door and sit down, Aleesha."

I shut the door and walk over to the table, but remain standing. The figure turns to face me. Under the hood, white eyeballs stare out. His skin seems to absorb light. As I meet his eyes, a shiver runs down my spine.

He gives off a strange smell. Not unpleasant, just unusual. Fresh damp earth, sweet wood and a slight freshness, like the needled trees in the Insiders' gardens.

"I don't think we've met." I'm impressed at how calm and relaxed I sound, despite my stomach tying itself in knots.

"No, we haven't."

Fine, not one for conversation, then. Or names.

Jay looks from one of us to the other, obviously not sure if he should intercede. There's an uncomfortable silence. Finally, the man breaks it. "I have a proposition for you, Aleesha."

From the blank look on Jay's face I can see this is news to him.

"I know who you're working for, and why. They are not friends of ours, the Chain. And if you knew the truth about them, I suspect you would not agree with their ambitions, either."

Who is this man? I can't remember ever seeing him before. Damn it. I've been so careful about being followed when I go to meet Murdoch since Jay let slip Jonas had spotted me. I could swear I hadn't been followed. I glance at Jay out of the corner of my eye. His face is tight-lipped. *I'm going to pay for this.* Anger surges through me, but I'm not sure how to play this. *Denial? If I don't deny it, then that implies it's true.*

"I'm not sure what you're talking about. Perhaps you have me confused with someone else?"

There's a flicker of anger in the black man's eyes. "Don't be stupid, girl," he says shortly. "If you want me to provide evidence to your *boyfriend*," he says with a sneer that makes me bristle, "I can. But I don't have time to argue, so let's just take it as fact. Like the fact you are able to go through the Wall undetected."

I glance over at Jay.

"No, he didn't tell me," the man continues. "But we've been keeping an eye on you for some time. We keep a look out for people who may be useful."

I don't like his phrasing. It sounds remarkably like what Murdoch said when he first recruited me. It's not a bad thing, to be useful, but I'd rather get to pick and choose who I work for.

"So, who are you, and who do you work for? And what d'ya want from me?" Even as I say the words, the final piece of the puzzle clicks into place in my head and I know what he's going to say before the words leave his lips.

"I am part of the Brotherhood. I expect you've heard of us." One corner of his lips twists up in an ironic smile. "Your boyfriend," he inclines his head toward Jay, "has agreed to an alliance between the Snakes and the Brotherhood. I have to say, he's been much more amenable than his predecessor."

Dane. So that's why he ended up slashed to pieces in the river. Like the other gang leaders who've disappeared in mysterious circumstances. Those who refused to bow to the Brotherhood's demands. *The secret blade that allowed Jay to win the contest. It was all set up.*

Jay is studiously avoiding my eye. *You fool, Jay.*

"As for what you can help us with," the man continues, "we're interested in finding out what the Chain's plans are. I want you to report back anything you find out. Particularly, anything that relates to the government. Anything you're told to get, bring to us first."

"Why should I?" The words are out of my mouth before I can bite them back. *Damn. Open admission of guilt.*

"Because if you don't, I will deliver you in person to the Metz headquarters. I suspect they'd be interested to know you're able to breach the Wall." He places his hands on the table and leans forward. "Believe me, Aleesha, I can make things very difficult for you, not to mention your new little friend, if I choose to." His voice is calm, but the undertone of menace makes my blood run cold. *How does he know about Lily?* "Plus, I wouldn't want anything to damage our promising relationship with the Snakes."

"Of course, she'll help you," Jay breaks in, looking up at me. "Won't you, Aleesha?"

I feel trapped into a corner. "If I betray the Chain, they'll hand me over to the Metz, and if I don't help you, you'll hand me over to the Metz," I say, folding my arms. "Doesn't seem like much of a choice to me."

"I'm sure you're ... smart enough to figure something out. Just bring us whatever you find. And don't go thinking you can wiggle your way out. We'll be watching you."

Somehow, I don't doubt his words. I remember Bryn's warning. *Keep away from them. Or you'll end up as dead as Dane.* Easier said than done. And now it's not just my life that's at risk.

"Now, I must be going," the man says. "Remember what I said,

Jay?" Jay nods. The man strides over to the door and opens it. "I look forward to a long, happy relationship with both of you." He flashes a set of bright white teeth and departs, closing the door behind him.

I move to the window and watch as he leaves the building and walks down the street. He blends into the shadows, avoiding the few streetlights that cast a pale glow over the mud. Then I sit down opposite Jay, who has sunk into a chair and is resting his elbows on the table, his head in his hands.

"Who the hell was he?"

"Never mind who he was. I told you to stay the hell away from the Chain." Jay's voice is angry and when he looks up at me, his eyes are hard. "After I've given you all this," he waves one hand around the dirty, unkempt room, "you go and betray me? Betray us all?"

"No, Jay, that's not it," I plead, grabbing his hand in both of mine. "I've not been betraying the gang at all, honest." He pulls his hand away, hard, and I know I don't have long to convince him.

"The Chain know something about what happened to my mother. About what happened when she disappeared. They're giving me the information in exchange for doing some work for them. And it's nothing to do with the gang, just a few jobs going through the Wall. I made them swear it was nothing that could harm the Snakes."

"Yeah? And what's their *word* worth?" Jay stands, pushing back his chair so hard it crashes to the floor. He doesn't bother to pick it up. "I'm sick of your excuses, Aleesha. You should have told me about this first." Before I can apologize he storms over to the door and yanks it open. "I'm going for a walk."

I rest my head on my arms, the table cool beneath my forehead.

How did I end up in this mess? More importantly, how do I get out of it? Tiredness washes over me, flooding the emptiness inside. My limbs are so heavy, and it takes a huge effort to lift my head.

Just need to escape.

Dropping to the floor, I crawl over to the loose floorboard and prize it up. *But Jay threw out the last of the tronk, didn't he?* I tip the contents of the metal box out on the floor, desperately pawing through it. There are a couple of stale protein bars and some vitamin tablets, but I don't want them now.

My fingers grasp what at first I think is an empty packet, but when I bring it closer and squint, I make out the slight residue of powder. I stick my tongue inside and lick up what I can.

Replacing the box, I go and curl up on the bed and stare at the rain running down the window, willing the tronk to take effect. But it doesn't fill the gaping emptiness inside, or take my mind off the shadowy, threatening figure. I don't know what deal Jay's done with the Brotherhood, and the worst thing is, I don't think he realizes what the consequences will be.

For all of us.

* * *

When Jay returns an hour later, he's a little calmer, though still pissed. I set down a mug of hot water with the last scrapings of the sweetener he likes and apologize profusely.

"You just have to accept your mother is gone," he says, somewhat mollified. "Your life is here now, Aleesha. Live in the present, not the past." He bangs his fist on the table for emphasis. I nod, pretending to agree.

"So, you swear you won't have nothin' more to do with 'em? Not properly, I mean. You may have to pretend for a bit, but when you don't bring back anything useful, he'll forget about you."

I shake my head. Jay glares at me. "Okay, I promise."

It's not like there's much the Chain can offer me now. I'm no further to finding out who my father is, and I doubt they have any other witnesses they can drag out. Jay's naive to think the Brotherhood will get off my back that easily, though. A dangerous underestimation.

"So, who was that guy?"

Jay sighs and looks out the window. "He came to see me a few weeks ago before Dane disappeared. He said the Brotherhood was wanting to unite the gangs to create peace so we can work together. Apparently, he'd already spoken to Dane, but he wasn't keen to cooperate."

That doesn't surprise me. Dane was the stereotype of an Area Four gang leader. Stubborn and wedded to violence. Cooperation was not a word in his vocabulary.

"He hinted that Dane may not be around for much longer and that if I supported their cause, they would support me in becoming the leader of the Snakes. To be honest, it wasn't really as if he gave me a choice," Jay admits. "I reckon if I'd refused, they'd have gone to one of the others and I'd have ended up in the river like Dane."

"So, they sent the boy to you with the blade." I say. Jay's eyes snap up, a mixture of anger and guilt on his face. "I saw what you did," I say carefully. "But really, I'm just glad you made it through alive."

I reach out and squeeze his hand, hoping the words don't sound too false. Obviously, I *am* glad he's alive, but the fact he cheated still feels wrong.

I could have stopped this. If I'd said something ... But what then?

Someone else would be gang leader, someone even easier for the Brotherhood to manipulate.

"And now? What do they want now you're in charge?"

Jay pulls back, shaking me off. "Give part of the Chapel district to the Shanksters. He said we're killin' each other needlessly, but it's gonna to be tough trying to convince some of the boys 'bout that."

The Shanksters' patch covers the eastern part of Area Four, extending across into Three. They've been trying to take over parts of our territory for months now.

"I managed to get a …" He frowns, then gives up. "Got him to agree to draw a line down Castlemain Street. Oh, and we're to take some people off Cleaning watch."

This immediately sends alarms ringing in my head. "Why? How many?"

Jay shrugs. "Just a couple each shift. He said we'd need 'em for something else." He screws up his face in concentration, then shrugs sheepishly. "Can't remember what, though."

I bite back a retort and try and keep my tone neutral. "A couple is half a watch, Jay. We can't cover the whole area with two people *and* get a warning out in time."

The Cleaning watch is the main reason the gangs are accepted by the community. We listen for rumours, keep a constant watch for any sign of a Cleaning. Then warn people so they have time to get out before the Metz arrive.

"It'll be fine. We'll make do." But there's a tremor in his voice. *You didn't think of that, did you, Jay?*

"What's his name, the black man?" I ask, changing the subject.

Jay shrugs. "He calls himself Samson."

It's an unusual name. Not one I've heard before, but I won't be forgetting it.

208

"Anyway, enough talk of him." Jay pulls me to him and tugs the fastening around my ponytail loose. My hair falls down my back. He always prefers it down. "If yer wanting to apologize, I can think of a way you can make it up to me."

Our mouths meet. I lick the residue of sweetness off his tongue and slide my hand up the back of his tight top. He lets out a gentle moan.

I pull back slightly. "Jay? There's something I need to ask you."

"Can't it wait?" he replies, leering down at me.

"No." I push myself away, but he pulls me back into him, his arms tight around my waist. I try and wiggle away and he raises an eyebrow.

"If you're trying to cool things down, you're having the opposite effect." His eyes close as he pushes into me.

I roll my eyes. "Wait a sec." I take a deep breath. "I nearly got caught up in a Cleaning the other day, actually, when I was on my way to your leadership challenge. A young girl helped me. She … she saved my life. She's on the streets at the moment. Can she come and stay here for a few days?"

Jay opens both eyes, wide. "You want to bring a kid here?"

"Please, Jay, she's only six and she has no one; no parents or anything."

He steps back, pushing me away from him, causing me to stumble back against the table. "What are you thinking, Aleesha? We're not some … some *home*. There are plenty of lost kids on the street and you've never looked twice at them."

The anger's back in his voice and I could kick myself. *I should have gone about this some other way.*

"What are you trying to play, some kind of happy family? Because that is *not* how things work around here."

"Hey, calm down." I take his arm, stroking the inside of it

gently, the way he likes. "That's not what I mean at all. You know I don't give a damn about kids. I just need somewhere safe where she can sleep for a few nights until I can find someone to take her in. I promise it won't be for long and she won't get in the way."

Reaching up, I cup his cheek, turn his face to me and kiss him hard on the lips. He responds, momentarily distracted from his anger. I wrap my arms around his back, feeling the wave of muscles move under my hands.

"Please, Jay? I've never asked for anything before and I *promise* she won't get in your way. 'Sides, she's pretty smart for a six-year-old. You may even like her."

Jay grunts and begins to slide my top up. My skin tingles under his cold hands. He steps backward, drawing me with him into the bedroom.

"Well, if it's only for a few nights, but she has to be out of this place during the day. I'm not sure who'll be coming around and I'm not conducting my business with a kid playing games in the corner."

I smile, relief washing through me. "Don't worry, I won't let her cramp your style."

Jay begins to kiss my neck. He pauses and smirks at me. "And she most definitely sleeps *out there*."

I laugh and kiss him back as we fall together onto the bed.

20

Trey

I'm practising bar chords on Abby's ancient guitar when there's a bang on the back door and a distorted face presses up against the window. The plectrum falls from my hand, the strings vibrating the last of their doleful chord into the silence. *Bryn, back already?* It can't be. When he left last night he said he'd be away for at least two days.

The Plexiglas mists up, giving the face a ghostly look. My muscles are weak; I'm paralyzed by indecision. *Do I answer it? Should I hide?* But whoever it is must surely have seen me. "Don't be an idiot," I say to the empty room. It's probably just someone looking for Abby. A customer.

I carefully rest the guitar up against the wall and go to open the door. Then I pause and go back to fetch the sharp knife Abby uses for chopping herbs. Just in case.

The face has gone from the window. Perhaps whoever it was got fed up of waiting. But my relief is short-lived. I open the door a crack, enough to see Murdoch's angry glare and his foot tapping impatiently on the worn flagstone. He reacts quickly, pushing the door so hard I stagger backward into the room, the knife dropping uselessly to the floor with a clatter.

Murdoch snorts. "Going to stab me, were you? Thought you

were going to keep me out there all day."

"I-I didn't know it was you." I stammer. *Should have thought to put something heavy behind the door. Idiot.*

"Where's Abby?" Murdoch crosses the room and peers into the hallway.

"At the market."

"Good. We need you to do a job for us tonight," he says without preamble. "Do you know your way around the government headquarters?"

I stay silent, not sure where this is going.

"Talk to me, boy!" He scowls angrily.

I nod, for once wishing Bryn was here. Murdoch scares me even more than him. "A little. I-I've been there two or three times, but only to certain parts. It's a maze in there."

"Have you ever been into the basements?"

"No."

"Did your father ever speak about them? About what was down there?"

I shake my head, confused. "I didn't even know there were basements. How do you—"

"Never mind. Let's go."

He grabs my arm, pulling me toward the back door.

"But Bryn said nothing would be happening for the next few days," I blurt, stumbling after him. *What job is this? What's in the government's basements?*

"Bryn was wrong," Murdoch says shortly. "Now, come with me, we don't have much time."

It's mid-afternoon, but the air is damp and cold; a gloomy mist envelops the tops of the taller apartment blocks. Almost everything out here is housing, I've come to realize. Apart from the government stores and a handful of shops scattered along the larger streets. Even the ancient churches and mosques that still survive have been taken over, officially or unofficially. But despite that, there still seems to be a shortage of places for people to live.

I knew population control was still an issue, despite the stringent laws that have been in place for decades, but I never realized it was this bad. I ask Murdoch about it as we skirt through the narrow streets and back alleys.

"It's not as bad as it was thirty years ago," he replies. "Then, you could hardly move for hobies on the street. People kept coming in, thinking it would be better in the city than the surrounding areas. Those who'd lived on the upper floors of flooded buildings in the south of the city ran out of the food they'd hoarded, so they came, too."

I think back to my history classes and the map of what they called Greater London before the Flood. So big it would take days to walk from one side to the other. Now, what had once been the south part of the city was separated by a vast body of water, crossable only by pod. The currents are too strong for small boats, and the water too shallow and dangerous for the large ships that bring supplies in from other parts of Britannia. People still lived on the other side, but all the business, all the jobs, had moved to the main part of the city in the north.

"And the water still rises," I say aloud.

Murdoch nods. "Slowly, but every year it gets a little higher and more people are pushed into a smaller area.

"Why haven't they built more to the north? Extended the city that way?"

"A good question. Perhaps you should ask your father that. They say they don't have the money. But they'll have to at some point. The water's going to rise a lot more. Reckon they'll have to pack up and move the headquarters in the next ten years or it'll be underwater."

I get the feeling Murdoch's a bit of a pessimist at heart, though he doesn't sound gloomy about his prediction. In fact, quite the reverse.

"Have you always lived in London?"

"I was born here. Area Four. But my family are Irish. They fled Dublin because they thought they'd have a better life in London, but it turned out to be just as bad here."

"Do they still live here?"

"Nah, we moved back when I was ten. Government were glad to see people go at that point. Fewer mouths to feed."

"How did you become involved with the Chain?"

Murdoch's eyes flicker with irritation. "D'ya always ask so many questions, boy?"

I shrug. "I just like knowing things. This is all new to me. I-I hadn't even been Outside before ..."

"Finally getting to know your own city, eh? The Chain helped free Dublin. It was one of their first big successes. It was a bit like here before the Wall went up. There were good parts and bad parts and a lot of inequality and a government who didn't give a damn. The Chain took down the government, made things fairer. And there were a good few years with the crops, which helped with the food supply. It's not perfect, but it's a lot better than what it was."

"And that's what you're trying to do in London?"

"In a manner of speaking. London's a much bigger beast than Dublin, though, and we didn't have the Metz to contend with."

"The government aren't all bad, though. It's not that they don't care, it's just the problem's so big—"

"Look, kid. I know you've been brought up an Insider and

fed all this crap by your dad about how they're doing their best, but compare this," he waves his arm, taking in the line of hobies huddled in their ragged jackets, the shuttered windows and the mud-streaked buildings, "to what you've got Inside. Does this really look like an equal distribution of wealth to you?"

I see his point. But if Outsiders aren't contributing to society, surely they shouldn't be entitled to *all* the same benefits? Otherwise, what motivation has anyone to go to work? But I suspect Murdoch's not going to see this side of the argument.

I decide to change the subject. "So, why didn't you stay in Dublin then, after things got sorted out?"

"My sister decided to come to London. I didn't hear from her for a while. We didn't know the comm lines had been blocked. So, I followed her over."

His voice is tight and he picks up the pace as if wanting to get away from my questions.

"And?"

He stares straight ahead, his eyes hard and cold. "She'd got caught up in one of the gangs out here. The leader wanted her, she refused, so they gang raped her. That leader had … disturbing tastes. She didn't survive the experience."

"I'm sorry." I swallow hard, trying to push away the unpleasant picture forming in my mind. "Which gang was it?"

Murdoch shrugs. "It doesn't exist anymore. This was years ago; gangs come and go. I found the man and killed him. Hunted down each of those involved. The Chain helped me find them and gave me a place to stay. I've been here ever since."

A shudder runs down my spine. I wonder if that's where he got the scar that runs along the right side of his jaw. *How lucky I've been, growing up away from all this.* I wonder how my life would have differed if I'd been born an Outsider, however high up.

"So, the Chain's been around years, then?"

"Stop with all the bloody questions, won't you?" He scowls at me, then relents. "Yes, in one form or another. But it's only since the Leader came in that action across countries has become more coordinated. We have access to more resources now. London's time has come."

We turn into the alleyway leading to the back yard of the white house. *London's time has come.* The words make me shiver. Suddenly, I don't want to ask any more questions.

* * *

Aleesha's waiting in the front room, staring out the front window, when we walk in. She's wearing a grey long-sleeved top to go with the ubiquitous black trousers and boots. Perhaps her wardrobe is so limited she doesn't have anything else. The tight-fitting clothes emphasize the angles of her body. She seems all bone, with a thin layer of muscle. I'm used to people being slim – there's no excuse for being fat when there are so many medicines you can take – but like most Outsiders, Aleesha looks like she's half starved. I think again of the blank-eyed tramps and children wandering the streets. Perhaps she is.

She gives me a half smile as we walk in, which I return. She had helped me find what I thought was my home, after all. And she didn't make any sarcastic comments at my failure. Bryn's words come back to me. *She would probably slit your throat as soon as sleep with you.* Surely, she can't be that bad, can she? Besides, I don't intend to sleep with her.

I catch Murdoch's raised eyebrow out the corner of my eye and realize I'm blushing. *Dammit.*

"So, what do you want us to do?" My attempt to sound calm

and in control fails miserably.

"Go exploring."

"Inside?"

"Kind of." He pulls a piece of paper – real paper – from inside his jacket and, unfolding it, places it carefully on the table.

"There's an old system of tunnels that were used hundreds of years ago for transport. The Tube, they called it. Everything was underground in those days: sewage disposal, electricity, comms, the lot. The city must be riddled with tunnels. Many were destroyed, of course, in the Great Flood or were deliberately collapsed, but we think you may be able to use them to get across the city."

He traces a path on the paper with his finger. "All the way through to the government headquarters."

"You're bloody mad," Aleesha says finally, breaking the silence. "You think you can break into the main government building by *going underground*?"

"Well, we don't know yet," Murdoch replies. "That's your job to find out."

I think about the government headquarters. It's not just one building; the whole block is surrounded by a barrier similar to the Wall that reaches up to the second-floor windows. There's a main gate at the front, and a back gate for staff and deliveries. Both are heavily guarded by the Metz and their dogs in addition to the palace guards.

I stare at him in disbelief. "I can't believe the government would miss that out of their security plans."

He shrugs. "Perhaps not, but I bet they don't have the same level of security as above ground. After all, no one really knows about the tunnels. I bet the most they have is some sensor nets. And most sensors detect people's chips. Which means you two should be able to pass through them unnoticed."

"But how do you know these tunnels even exist?" Aleesha peers at the paper with its brightly coloured squiggles.

"They do exist." The words fall from my mouth. Murdoch and Aleesha both stare at me. "The London Underground. I-I saw it in a book once."

One of the ancient paper volumes stacked on the dusty shelves of St George's library. I'd asked the librarian if I could take it out to read, but she'd taken it off me and said it was for library use only. When I'd gone back to look for it, it was no longer on the shelves. *Is this another thing we're not supposed to know about?*

"They were built in the Victorian era, some of them, when the underground trains first started. Though the deeper tunnels were constructed a hundred years or so later. The deepest parts were two hundred feet below ground."

"Really?" Aleesha's voice wobbles for a second and her face pales. I don't blame her. The thought of being that far underground frightens the life out of me. But I'm also curious to see what these old tunnels are like.

"We've been trying to align the map of the tunnels with the city as it is today." Murdoch pulls out a thin roll of film and places it next to the paper. "We've made a copy for you to take. We've done our best to decipher the station names from the old map, but some were just too worn. You'll have to just make the best of it."

I stare down at the map. Coloured lines run across the page, each neatly labelled. A yellow one seems to go around in a circle in the centre. According to the list to the right of the page, this yellow line is called the "Circle". How descriptive. Where the lines intersect there are small circles, each with their own unfamiliar name.

"What the hell am I supposed to do with this?" Aleesha stands up and folds her arms. "This isn't a proper map and I've never heard of any of these places. They could be out of a fairy story for all the good they are."

"Calm down," Murdoch snaps. "It may not be geographically accurate, but once you're in the system of tunnels, it should be easy enough to find your way." He points to one of the circles on the map, which has grey, yellow and green lines running through it. "We know the old government area used to be called Westminster. A lot of it is underwater now, but if you can get to one of the stations further from the river – Charing Cross or Green Park, perhaps – there may be a service tunnel you can pick up that takes you underneath the current headquarters."

He traces his finger back to the right of the page. "I think we're around this area." He circles his finger around some stations on an orange line. Hoxton. Bethnal Green. Shoreditch. "Only problem is, these are marked as being an overground line. To be honest, I think you may have more luck down here in Area Four. We think Aldgate East may be just outside the Wall, in the southern part of Four."

"Aldgate," Aleesha murmurs thoughtfully.

Murdoch gives her a sharp glance. "You've heard of it?"

Her brow wrinkles in concentration. "I've seen the name somewhere … It'll come to me."

"So, you want us to break into the government building and do … what?" I ask.

"Nothing, yet. Just see how far you can get before something blocks your way. Don't go up to the main levels. I don't want you getting caught and them figuring out what we're up to. We know from the building plans that there are basements under the building, so presumably, there's access up from there. If we can get into the basements, the rest should be doable."

Aleesha's head snaps up. "Building plans?"

Murdoch curses under his breath.

"Was that the information we got from the government official? It was, wasn't it!"

Murdoch glares at her. "It's none of your business. Your job is to figure out a way through to the basements, not to ask questions. You can check if there's any additional security to get up to the main levels," he adds, almost as an afterthought.

"And what's in it for me?"

Murdoch looks taken aback at Aleesha's question.

"I don't work for free, you know. Now I've spoken to Mrs Grady, I'm not sure there's anything else you can offer me."

Murdoch sighs. "Fine." He pulls a small pouch from his pocket. It clinks. Aleesha eyes it hungrily.

"Ten chits and another twenty when you report back. Plus, there are a couple of bottles of water and some food in that bag." He points to a small backpack under the table. "And a couple of flashlights, but I want those back when you're done, okay?"

Aleesha nods, pocketing the money.

"And don't think you're getting anything," Murdoch says, rounding on me. "We've done enough for you."

I shrink back under his gaze, but my mind is racing. *What are they up to? If there's a weakness in the government security systems, father needs to know about it. At least, if I go along, I can find out what it is.*

Murdoch hands Aleesha the film map and begins to carefully fold up the original. "Report back tomorrow morning at ten. Not here, at the statue in Rose Square. The government are moving fast. Which means we need to move faster."

For what?

"Figured out where you're going yet?" Murdoch asks as we leave the house.

Aleesha nods. "I'm sure I've seen the name somewhere down in the concrete jungle, in the south part of Four."

"Good. Find it and see if you can access the tunnels there. If you can't, we'll have to think of something else. Though you won't get your chits, of course."

Aleesha gives him a dirty look, but Murdoch shrugs and turns to leave. "Tomorrow, at ten."

The mist is even thicker as Aleesha leads the way south. I recognize the first few streets, but as they get filthier and more crowded and the buildings even more rundown, I realize we must be getting into the heart of Area Four.

"Pull your hood up," Aleesha hisses. Not that anyone can really see us in the gloom. Eventually, we reach a break in the buildings and I can vaguely make out a large open area in front of us, though it's hard to see much. Off to our right, the Wall still glows through the fog.

"Be quiet now, and follow me *exactly*," Aleesha whispers.

"Where are we going?"

"To see a friend. But bad people live in this place – *really* bad. Just … don't do anything stupid, okay?"

I nod and follow her across the open space toward an enormous pile of rubble. I clamber up it, watching carefully where Aleesha places her hands and feet. The large concrete blocks are surprisingly stable, however haphazardly they seem to be stacked.

"Hide here."

Straightening, I look around, but the fog has hidden the surrounding buildings and all signs of life. When I look back, Aleesha is gone.

21

Aleesha

"Giles!" I hiss into the dark, crouching inside the rough entrance to the makeshift tunnel. Pieces of rusted metal and Plexiglas sheets hold back the rubble. Mostly.

This jungle is just a huge mound of broken debris. Rumour has it, it's haunted. I don't believe in ghosts, but it's not a safe place to explore; the rubble's been known to shift unexpectedly, trapping people inside, and the few people who do make their home here are some of the most unsavoury characters in Area Four. And that's saying something.

Fortunately, one of these unsavoury characters owes me a favour.

There's a soft scraping noise behind me; the sound of someone catching their arm on a piece of metal. I turn my head and there's a pale ghost of a face not four inches from my own, its yawning black mouth open in a horrific parody of a grin.

I throw myself backward to the ground, my legs pedalling furiously. The scream that rises in my throat turns to a pathetic squeak as I try and fight the instinct to call for help.

"Miss Aleesha?" The ghost face appears in the tunnel entrance and resolves itself into a normal human face. Though I'm not sure if you'd call this hairless chalk-white creature normal. "Giles." I sit up and begin to dust myself off. "What do you think you're doing sneaking up on me like that?" I glare at him while trying to calm my pounding heart.

He smiles that strange open-mouthed smile of his and shrugs. "My home, Miss Aleesha."

I guess he's right. "Can I come in?"

He moves back into the darkness and I crawl inside the entrance again. No further. I'm not keen to find out what he has back there in this place he calls home. His eyes, as pale as the rest of him, are bright in the dark.

"Giles, do you remember when I was last here? We were looking under the rubble and there was a sign that said 'Aldgate' or something like that. Can you remember where it was?"

He nods vigorously.

"Aldgate East? Yes, I know that. And Aldgate, too, but that's on the other side." He giggles nervously.

Were there two Aldgate stations on the map? I can't remember and I don't want to get it out now.

"Can ... can you get underground there? Like, properly underground, to a tunnel?"

He is silent for a moment. "Yeees, there is a way underground," he says finally, his voice hesitant. "The tunnels are deep though, and dark."

"It's okay, I have this." I pull the flashlight from my belt to show him. He cowers away, whimpering. "Hey, it's okay, it's just a light. Can you show me how to get into the tunnel?"

"Yeeees." Again, that slow, drawn out response. Like I'm pulling the word from his throat, one letter at a time. "But why do you want to go down there, Aleesha? The tunnels aren't a place for you."

"I've been asked to explore them. Try and find a way through."

"To the Inside?"

"Perhaps."

He considers this for a minute. "And if I show you the entrance, then we're even?"

"Yup, we're even."

This time I see him nod in the darkness. "Let's go."

Trey is waiting outside. He jumps to his feet, eyes widening when he catches sight of Giles. I place a finger to my lips and shake my head slightly.

"Who is this, Miss Aleesha?" Giles hisses, cowering behind me.

"It's okay, Giles," I whisper. "He's a friend."

Giles doesn't look impressed, but he leads off through the concrete jungle. Somehow, he knows which blocks of concrete are okay to stand on and which to avoid. In some places, he stops and literally points out each step to us. I wonder if he's learnt this from experience or if he's rigged up some traps to dissuade people from exploring his territory. I wouldn't put it past him. He's quite well known in this part of Area Four – they call him the albino because his skin is so white and his eyes so pale. There are lots of rumours about where he came from. Some say he was an Insider, abandoned by his parents because of his mutation. Or that he was a third child, naturally conceived but not wanted. Others say he was born underground and that's why he's so pale. That he murdered his parents when he was just a child.

After half an hour of picking our way through precariously balanced pieces of rubble, we emerge at the northerly edge of the jungle. The last traces of daylight are fading into the evening gloom. *Why bring us this way? It would have been much quicker to walk around the edge.*

As if reading my mind, Giles gestures with his thumb. "The Boots Brothers live that way. You wanna stay away from them. They don't like going into the jungle proper, but if you're on the outskirts they'll have you in a flash. A pretty girl like you they'd have a field day with," he warns. "When you come back out, head straight for the Wall and follow it up. They don't like the Wall. And don't use that flashlight to draw attention to yourself." He eyes it warily.

"Sure," I reply, looking around for the sign I remembered seeing.

"It's down here," Giles says, climbing down from the large block we're standing on. It feels the most solid thing in this place. I follow him. *This is the spot.* There's a faint pattern on the block that makes me wonder if there was once a carving on it, now weathered by time. To the right, covered in dust and half buried in rubble, is the sign. I run a finger over each letter, brushing the dust off. A-L-D-G-A. I give it an experimental tug to see if the sign will come loose, but it doesn't budge.

"Here!"

I look around for Giles, but he's disappeared.

"Down here!" A white arm appears from underneath the block. There's an entrance about two feet high. I have to get down on my belly to crawl in, but once inside it opens up below me. I twist to land on my feet and look up at the small portal of daylight.

"Come on, Trey, follow me."

The dust from his scrabbling catches at the back of my throat.

"This way." Giles is already heading off into the darkness. Coughing, I switch on my flashlight and follow him down a rough tunnel that runs underneath huge slabs of concrete. It drops down into a larger space. I shine the beam of light around until a picture on the far wall catches my eye. A red circle, cut through with a blue line. The symbol on the map Murdoch gave me.

"This way!" Giles's head appears around the corner and I hurry down a short flight of steps, Trey right behind me. I follow the sound of scuffles in the dark, hoping its Giles and not a rat. The tunnel opens into a larger void, collapsed in at one end.

"See," Giles says happily, pointing to a sign on the wall. "Aldgate East."

I shine my light around. To the left is what looks like some kind of controlled access barrier. Two sets of stairs leading down into a blackness my light can't penetrate.

Giles taps my shoulder, making me jump. "Aldgate East, Miss Aleesha. I can go now?"

"Have you been down there, Giles?"

"Once," he replies reluctantly. "You can get down to the old train tracks. Can I go now?"

"Yes, fine," I reply, exasperated.

He nods, then pulls something from his pocket and holds it out to me. "This'll help you find your way back."

A flo pen. I smile at him. "Thanks. I'll return it later."

"Don't worry, I have another." He stands there awkwardly for a moment. "Well, I'll be seeing you." Then he turns tail and disappears back up the tunnel.

I take a deep breath, suddenly very conscious of the weight of the concrete and rubble above me. *This must have been here for hundreds of years; it's not likely to collapse now. Get a grip.*

"Who was *that*?" Trey asks, coming over to peer at the barrier.

"Giles. He's a little odd, but you can trust him." *I think.*

"So, this is an old Underground Station."

"Yeah." I run my finger through the thick layer of dust on the barrier, revealing a flash of yellow. "Pity they couldn't afford cleaners."

"Huh. Where do we go from here?"

"Down."

I vault over the barrier and start toward the right-hand set of stairs. Eight steps, then a short platform, and then another thirteen. At the bottom, a long platform leads into the dark, dropping off to the left. There's an identical platform on the other side of the trench.

I run my hand along the wall. The smooth tiles are cold. A pattern of red and blue. The same symbol, this time with the words "Aldgate East" emblazoned on the blue line. Balancing my flashlight on a bench, I pull out the roll of film. The coloured lines are bright in the dark.

"Any idea if we're on the pink or green line?" I ask.

"Nope, but these seem to be the only platforms. Maybe the trains ran on the same track?"

I sigh. "Well, let's go one way and see what we find."

Turning, I play the flashlight beam over the entrance to the tunnel behind me. At least, it's bigger than I feared; as wide as many of the larger streets Outside and more than double my height. But my heart's pounding in my chest and I have to wipe the sweat off my hands before lowering myself into the trench. *Don't think, just do.*

"Here goes nothing," I say. The words echo down the tunnel ahead. *Nothing, nothing, nothing.*

We wander through the tunnels, using the ancient map as a guide. I soon realize that the distances on the map bear no relation to the actual distances between stations. And there are platforms and sidings that aren't marked on the map, some covered in rubble, others untouched as if waiting for the day the trains run again.

The tunnel for the green line – the District Line – is blocked, so we have to take the more convoluted route via Liverpool Street Station. The tracks are full of rubble, but I manage to find a route around it by breaking through a door that leads into a large underground room full of pillars. From there, a sign points us down, deeper into the earth to the red "Central" line. At every junction I mark a circle and an arrow with the flo pen. The glow of the symbol in the dark is reassuring, like a lifeline guiding us back.

"So, what do you reckon the Chain are really after in the government headquarters?" I ask as we walk along the empty train tracks.

"I don't know," Trey admits. "Maybe they want to assassinate the President or something? From what Murdoch said, they've been in the city a while."

He recounts the conversation he'd had with Murdoch earlier. "That's strange, I'd never heard of them until Murdoch turned up in Four." *And blackmailed me into working for him.* I frown. "I guess they could have been in one of the other parts of the city, but if so, why move? I wonder who their new leader is, too."

"I don't know. But I get the impression he's not from here – from London, I mean. Bryn's friend, Lamar, was in charge until recently, and now Milicent seems to be taking over."

"Who's she?"

"An Insider woman. Old. Very rich. She lives in this enormous house in the best part of the city, by herself, I think."

How does he know all of this? I feel suddenly annoyed. It's my job to find out this stuff, but somehow he's managed to get more out of Murdoch in one trip than I've got out of him in a month.

"How come you're still here, anyway? Haven't you found your parents yet?"

"Yes, Milicent helped me meet them." He sounds hurt. Perhaps my tone was a *little* harsh. "I-I can't go back yet, though."

"Did you find out why the Metz are after you?"

"Yes." There's a pause. "Apparently, I shouldn't be alive. I was ... born illegally."

I stop dead. *Trey? Illegal?* "What?"

His feet shuffle in the dark. "Yeah, crazy, right? Mum and Dad already had two children. I've got a sister I never knew about."

Somehow this makes me feel a bit lighter. *So much for his perfect Insider life.* "Well, it's not so bad, being illegal," I say breezily.

"Don't be stupid, of course it is. They want to kill me, or send me to the Farms. What's good about that?" he asks bitterly.

"Well, okay. But it's not *your* fault. It's nothing you've done, it's your parents fault for not having got sterilized like you're supposed to." I pat his arm. "Come on, better keep walking."

After a few minutes, there's a cool breeze on my skin. An air vent? I step forward and it disappears, but further up, there's another one.

"But Dad *is* sterilized." Trey sounds puzzled.

"What?"

"Dad's sterilized. I remember him saying he got done after they had Ella. It didn't click at the time, but that doesn't make sense at all ..."

"Well, maybe it didn't work. Or perhaps your mother had an affair or something. It doesn't really matter, does it?"

From the uncomfortable silence, I get the impression that it does matter. *At least, he has parents.*

229

Eventually, Trey breaks the silence. "My father says Outsiders are always fighting. Was he right?"

"We're not *always* fighting. Most people are just trying to survive. But when there aren't enough resources, what do you expect? People fight over food. Water. Firewood – what little of it there is." I catch the bitterness in my voice. "You don't know what it's like."

"No, I don't," he says quietly. "I don't know how you're so brave the whole time. It's like nothing ever scares you." He sighs. "Whereas I'm scared of *everything*."

I shrug. "It's not that I'm not afraid. You just learn to hide it. Fear is a sign of weakness. It gives your enemy something to exploit."

"I suppose that makes sense." He laughs nervously. "Easier said than done, though."

There's another silence.

"Did you find out about your mother?"

"I found out she was murdered."

"I-I'm sorry."

"Don't be," I reply, more sharply than I had intended. "I mean, don't say you're sorry just to be polite. That's an Insider thing. Trying to be polite all the time. Like the government people. Outside we just say it how it is. Much simpler."

"I really am sorry." His voice is sincere. "I don't know how you survived on your own as an—"

"An illegal?"

"Yeah."

I sometimes wonder that, too.

I have no idea of time or distance this far underground, but it feels like we've been walking for miles when we finally arrive at a station called Tottenham Court Road.

"It says 'Tottenham Road' on here, but they've probably copied it down wrong," I say squinting at the map. "We need to find the black line."

Trey wipes his sleeve across a black smudge on the wall. A black arrow emerges, and a word. *Northern.* "This one?"

We follow the arrows through a series of tunnels to another platform. Holo screens line the wall – dead and grey now, of course – the products they were advertising part of another time. Back down onto the tracks and into yet another large tunnel. I stifle a yawn. We must have been down here for hours.

The next station is too damaged for us to tell what or where it is. Rubble fills the platform, spilling down onto the tracks. We have to climb up and over it. The blocks of concrete and stone move unnervingly beneath our feet.

At the next station, I stop and check the map again. "This should be Charing Cross."

There seems to be a vague pattern under the dust-covered wall; a picture of some kind. Trey brushes at it, raising a cloud of dust. When it clears the words "ING CROSS" are visible. We made it.

"Now what?" Trey asks.

"Now, we try and find a way in."

We spend what must be an hour searching the tunnels, corridors and staircases in the station. All end in either water or rubble. The place is a maze. Without the flo pen we'd have ended up walking endlessly in circles. Weariness fills me, my limbs feeling heavy and unresponsive, and I sink down with my back against the wall of one of the tunnels.

"Here." I offer Trey some of the water from the backpack Murdoch had given us and he gulps it down.

A scuffling noise further up the tunnel makes me freeze. *Rats.*

I *hate* rats. There aren't many of them Outside anymore. They taste terrible, but meat is meat.

"Hey, come and look at this. The rat went through this grate." Trey tugs at the metal, but it doesn't move.

The grate is perhaps a metre square and set out from the wall slightly. *Air ventilation?* I curl my fingers under one of the flutes and give it a yank. It gives slightly but not enough. "Give me a hand!"

This time, something snaps and the grate falls back toward us, revealing a dark opening. *Great, an even more confined space.* Taking a deep breath, I crawl inside, shining my flashlight in front and fervently hoping the rat has moved on. *Just keep moving.*

A glint ahead. Another grate. This one crashes back with one hard shove. A cloud of choking dust rises as it hits the ground. On the other side is another tunnel, tall enough to stand up in and walk two abreast. It's rougher than the ones in the station. Old cables of some sort run along one side. *A service tunnel, perhaps?* A flash of white catches my eye.

"Well found, *Insider*," I say as Trey emerges, coughing, from the opening. He's grey with dust, and I suspect I'm the same.

"Are we in?" His voice is tinged with disbelief.

"Looks like it." I focus my flashlight on the small white sign. It's a different symbol to the one they use now, but the words are clear enough.

UK Government.

22

Trey

The rough tunnel leads to another, then another. Finally, we reach a set of small rooms, most of them filled with metal cabinets. I try to open one, but it's locked. There's a label stuck to the front, too faded to read.

"Maybe they're archives."

"Archives?"

"Stores of old information. Otherwise, why keep them locked? They don't look like they've been touched for a while."

The next room is much larger and filled with tables and chairs, all of them covered in a thick layer of dust. An empty mug with the words "Dad's mug" in a child's scrawl looks like it's growing something inside. I wonder how long ago someone left it there and why they didn't come back.

"It's pretty dingy down here," Aleesha says. Dust particles dance in the beam of light.

"I can't see any security precautions, unless ... unless they're invisible?"

"Guess they thought people were unlikely to go crawling around with the rats. Especially, if no one knows about the tunnels."

There are more metal cabinets in here, some of them with a

small, rusted sign. The only word I can make out is the last one: Access.

"Hey, this looks as if it may be a way up?"

Aleesha's standing in front of a door. At the top, there's a white sign with a green man running up a stepped line.

She tries it. "Locked."

"Wait, what's this?" There's a small black box on the side of the door with a tiny amber light in the top right corner. "It's a fingerprint scanner."

"There's your security."

I examine it briefly. "It's an old-style one. I don't suppose you've got a KBox, have you?"

"A what?" She looks at me blankly.

"It's a basic device you can use to interrogate information systems."

"You've lost me." Annoyance flickers on her face.

"You can use the KBox to pull off the fingerprint algorithms stored in the scanner's memory, then recreate it and feed it back to the scanner electronically. Basically, you trick it into thinking an authorized person has placed their finger on the scanner. We did a tech project on it a couple of years ago."

Aleesha frowns. "Doesn't seem very secure if kids get taught how to hack into it."

"Exactly. I mean it would stop some people, I guess—"

"Outsiders, you mean."

Fortunately, it's too dark for her to see my cheeks redden. "I—"

She waves her hand. "I was kiddin' you."

"Oh. Anyway, the scanners currently used set off an alarm whenever you tamper with them. There's no way I know to hack into them."

"So, why haven't they replaced these?"

"I don't know. Mind you, we don't know what's on the other side of that door," I say darkly. "If they've got all sorts of killing devices, updating a simple fingerprint scanner isn't really necessary, is it?"

"Okay, well while we're here, let's see if we can find any other access doors. And have a look for cameras."

"Cameras?"

"They'll be hidden, obviously. Look for tiny lights …" Her voice disappears as she goes into the next room.

I roll my eyes. *Right, look for cameras. They're basically invisible, but …* I wander back over to the cabinets and idly pull at the doors, my eyes running along the ceiling looking for any tiny dots of light.

Locked.

Locked.

Locked.

Open.

A jolt of excitement runs through me as my fingers curl around the rusted edge of the door. I pull it again. A screech of metal against metal. It was locked, once, but the rust has damaged it so much that my slight tug was enough to break it.

Inside are rows upon rows of hanging dividers, each jammed full of films. There's even the odd piece of paper, but these have mainly disintegrated. Most are neatly stacked, but others look like they've been hurriedly crammed inside, without thought as to order.

I pull out one of the folders and set it down on a table. They've used hard film, which makes sense, but some of the films are folded or crushed. Whoever filed these didn't do a very good job.

Balancing my flashlight, I start to flick through them. They're mostly records of meetings and old policy documents. They're decades old, some from before the Great Flood even, and not even date ordered.

A handwritten document catches my eye. Most of the other films have a classification imprinted at the top of the page. But not this one. Just the word "Confidential" scrawled across the top.

"Found anything?"

I look up guiltily. "Err, I didn't see any …"

Aleesha rolls her eyes, the effect made scarier by the ghostly pallor of her skin in the light. "I'll check again."

Her beam of light flashes around the room.

"What are you looking at, anyway? Are they papers?"

"They're films. Though some look as if they're copies of paper documents. I-I think there's some important stuff in here." The dates of the papers are from the years after the Great Flood. The dark time. The time we don't really get taught about. And some instinct inside me says that this stuff is important.

"Isn't everything on the information bank?"

"Yeah, but back then they used to keep physical backups as well. To be honest, I reckon someone put them down here during an office clear out and no one's bothered to remove or destroy them since. They've been locked in these cabinets for decades."

The flashlight pauses in its dance. "I think it's clear. Can't see any cameras. Come on, let's go." Her voice has an edge to it.

I hesitate, torn between wanting to stay and read through the papers and wanting to get back home. I've lost track of time, but it must be the early hours of the morning. The thought of traipsing back through the tunnels is not appealing.

"There's so much here …"

"Just take them with you."

"What, *steal* them?" *Government papers? That's got to be a crime.* But curiosity makes my fingers straighten out the edges of the pile, discarding the papers that look irrelevant.

"Why not? It doesn't look as if they care about them that much."

"Fine." The atmosphere in here is starting to get to me, too. Just because Aleesha didn't find any cameras doesn't mean they don't know we're here. They could have motion sensors or something. "Let's go."

I tuck the pile of films inside my jacket, zip it up tight, and replace the rest in the cabinet, pushing the door shut. We follow the glowing marks on the wall back to the grate, Aleesha erasing them as we go. Then we're back on the platform at Charing Cross station.

"Argh!"

I whirl around. Aleesha's huddled in the trench, her face laced with pain.

"What is it? What happened?"

She shakes her head. "It's okay. Just landed wrong. Give me a minute."

I hover, anxious. *Am I going to have to carry her back? Or get help?* But after a few minutes, she gingerly gets to her feet and tries walking.

"Hmm. It'll be alright, I think. Just a bit of a sprain. Good thing I have bendy ankles."

"You sure?"

She nods. "Yup. Come on, let's get out of here. I hate this bloody darkness."

* * *

237

It's still dark when we emerge from the tunnels and follow the Wall up into Area Four.

"Do you want to come to the river to wash?" Aleesha laughs at my expression. "It's not *that* bad. Or, at least, parts of it aren't. It won't get you clean exactly, but it'll get the worst of the dirt off."

She gives me a pointed look. Even in the dim light I can see we're covered head to toe in dust. It sticks to my face like clay and stings my eyes.

I shrug. "Guess I need it, then. Does your hair itch as much as mine?" It feels as if insects are crawling over my scalp.

We walk through the quiet streets to the river, Aleesha trying to hide the fact that she's limping. *Is this part of the "no sign of weakness" thing?* Probably.

The water is cold, but it tears the worst of the dust and dirt from my arms. Aleesha pulls her boot off and sticks her foot in.

"Is it bad?"

"Na. Just a bit sore. It'll be fine in a day or so. At the moment, I can't feel it at all." She laughs.

It feels good to scrub my hair, though some of the dye momentarily stains the water.

"You'll be blond again soon," Aleesha comments.

The sky begins to lighten. The grey mist of the previous evening must have dissipated overnight. Silhouettes of towers stand proud, far across the water.

"What's on the other side?" Aleesha asks, staring out.

"Houses. Apartment blocks. The water flooded a lot of the south part of the city, but there's still the southern outskirts. I guess there are people living there, though a lot of them migrated up here after the Flood."

"You know what I've always wondered?" The question seems

rhetorical. "What happened to Areas One and Two. I guess they must have existed once. It doesn't make sense to start at three."

I nod. *Does she not know this? But of course, she probably hasn't been to school.* "They were further east of here. When they created the areas, after the Great Flood, they still existed, but as the water levels rose further they slowly drowned. They built the docks out there – the only dry land for miles around."

"Maybe this will all be under water eventually," Aleesha says sadly.

I don't tell her that she's right, and that day will come sooner than she thinks.

Something glints on her ankle as she lifts it from the water. "What's that?"

She rests her ankle on the opposite knee, massaging it gently.

"This?" She fingers the trinket. "It's something my mother gave me. Apparently, my father gave it to her."

"A triquetra." I lean forward, intrigued.

"A what? Do you know what it is?" Her hands fumble with the cord and she pulls it apart, holding the amulet up to me.

"N-no," I stammer, taken aback by the urgency in her voice. "I mean, I've seen the symbol, but not this piece."

"Where? What does it mean?"

"You find it carved into gravestones sometimes, or in churches."

"So, it's a religious thing." She sounds disappointed.

"Kind of. In the Christian religion it usually represents the Trinity."

Aleesha looks blank.

"God, Jesus and the Holy Spirit. But it was used more widely before that, as a sign of special things or of three people bound together." I trace my finger over the amulet. "The circle represents unity of the three."

"Hmm." Aleesha looks thoughtful as she ties the cord around her ankle again and puts her boot back on.

I yawn, suddenly overwhelmingly tired. It hits me that we've been up all night. "Can you show me the way back?"

"Sure."

By the time I get back to Abby's the sky is light. Knocking gently doesn't work, so I bang on the back door until I see her through the window.

"Trey!" The worry lines on her face ease when she sees me. "Where on Earth have you been? I was so worried. The knife …"

"Murdoch dragged me away," I mumble. "Sorry, I've been up all night. Just need to sleep."

"Of course …"

I stumble past her and through the house up to my room. *Need somewhere safe for the papers.* I look around, but eventually just shove them under the mattress. It'll have to do for now. Stripping off my filthy clothes, I leave them in a heap on the floor and collapse onto the bed, sleep dragging me down.

* * *

The sound of angry voices in the kitchen below wakes me up. I feel groggy and heavy with sleep. Sunlight filters through the window, but from the angle, I don't think it's yet afternoon. Closing my eyes, I begin to float back into the depths of sleep when there are loud footsteps on the stairs and the door flies open.

Instinctively, I pull the sheet up to cover my naked body. Murdoch stands over me, his expression fierce. "Get up. Now." There's a lighter footfall and Abby appears beside him in the doorway clutching my wet, but clean, clothes. She gives me an apologetic glance and drops them on the floor by the bed. I look pointedly at the clothes, and with a grunt Murdoch leaves the room, half closing the door behind him. *What does he think I'm going to do? Jump out the window?*

I sit up, wincing at the aches and bruises that have materialized whilst I've been asleep. But I dress quickly, not trusting Murdoch to give me privacy for more than a few minutes.

I've barely finished lacing my boots when he barges in again and grabs my arm, practically hauling me down the stairs.

"What's wrong?"

"You were supposed to report straight back to me."

I stop, yanking my arm out of his grip and stare at him in what I hope is an expression of defiance. "We were out all night. I haven't slept. And believe me, anything I said to you when I got back here wouldn't have made much sense at all."

Abby presses a bar into my hand as I'm marched out the front door and down the street. I eat it quickly, but it does little to fill the empty space in my stomach.

To my surprise, we don't go to the usual white house, but instead walk further north, almost into Area Six. We stop at the back of a large building that looks like a school. Two men guard a small door. They nod at Murdoch and wave us through.

Murdoch guides me up a short flight of stairs and into a small sitting room furnished with a couple of sofas and a low table. Aleesha is already there, perched on the edge of a high-backed chair.

"Come in, Darwin. Please, sit down." I'm surprised to see Milicent standing by the table. She waves me to sit down next to Aleesha and takes a seat opposite me. Murdoch closes the door behind us and stands with his back against it.

I lick my lips to try and moisten my mouth, but they're so cracked and dry even my own saliva stings. I'm not sure if it's hunger or nerves, but my belly feels like it's tied itself in knots. I glance over at Aleesha; she doesn't meet my eye.

Milicent clears her throat delicately. "Darwin—"

"Trey. My name is Trey."

She smiles slightly as if amused. "Sorry, *Trey*. Now you're both here, can you tell us if you found a way through last night?"

I start describing the route we took through the tunnels. Aleesha butts in occasionally to correct me when I get the name of a station or line wrong. When I tell them about finding the cut-through into the basements, Murdoch crows.

"Yes, I knew there'd be a way!"

Milicent glares at him, but he continues, unabashed.

"What security was there? Did you get up into the main part of the building?"

"I couldn't find any cameras," Aleesha takes over, "but they could have been well hidden. There was a fingerprint lock on a door that may lead up to the main building. We couldn't open it, but Trey thought he might be able to hack it."

All eyes are on me. I shrug. "It should be pretty straightforward with a KBox Model Three. Even a Model Two should do it."

"Well, we can get one of those, no problem." Murdoch licks his lips.

"There's something else. The basements seem to be used as archives. There are some films in there, copies of papers from the time of the Great Flood and just after. I-I took some of them. I haven't had time to look at them yet, but I think they're important. They talk about the Population Regulation Ac—"

"Old documents, not relevant today. The Great Flood was

decades ago. I'm sure they might be of interest to a historian, but we are dealing with the present, young man," Milicent interrupts.

"But I've never heard of this Act. And from what it looks like, there's information in there that people should know. I think … perhaps the government haven't told us the truth."

"About what? Something that happened sixty years ago? We need to focus on the lies they're telling now. We can't change what happened in the past, but we can change what happens in the future." Murdoch's voice escalates as he speaks.

"But you still haven't told us what it is you *are* planning to do," Aleesha butts in. "Why do you want to get into the government headquarters?"

Murdoch hesitates, looking over to Milicent, who shakes her head.

"We can't tell you," she says gently. "It's for your own protection. Your youth is in your favour. If you get caught and genuinely know nothing, they may go easier on you."

"But why would they catch us?" Aleesha asks. "Unless …" Her eyes narrow. "You're going to send us in again, aren't you?"

My breath catches in my throat.

"Perhaps," Milicent says finally.

"Well, I'm not doing anything unless you tell us what you're trying to do." Aleesha sits back and folds her arms.

I'm beginning to recognize that attitude.

"And even then, don't bank on my support. On that note, I think you owe me some chits."

Murdoch rolls his eyes and tosses her a bag. She weighs it in her hand, then pockets it.

There's a pause before Milicent speaks. "We are looking to gain access to the government's central information system. As you may know, there's no way of hacking into it remotely. We have an expert who has the skills to get what we need, but he may need some support getting into, and out of, the building. That—"

There's a bang from outside and the sound of raised voices. The door flies open and Bryn enters. Grime is set in the lines on his face and his matted hair hangs in dreads. There are bags under his eyes and his clothes are filthy.

"What are you playing at?" He glares from Milicent to Murdoch and back again. "You said nothing would be happening for the next two days. Then I get back to Abby's and the first I hear is that Trey got dragged away by you," he jabs a finger at Murdoch, "and has been out all night."

"Bryn. You look … tired," Milicent says delicately. "Unfortunately, whilst you were away, things moved on somewhat. We received word that Mikheil and his father are already on their way. They'll be here tomorrow. We needed to find out if it was possible to get into the building via the tunnels."

"Well, why didn't *you* go then," he says to Murdoch, "or one of your other minions?"

Murdoch shrugs.

"We knew these two could pass through the Wall. They were the most likely to be able to get the furthest."

"Trey, Aleesha, thank you for your assistance." Milicent stands. "Murdoch will escort you home."

We walk back outside, blinking at the relative brightness of the daylight after the dark room.

"I can take Trey back home if you like?" Aleesha volunteers.

Murdoch looks torn. He obviously wants to go back and join the shouting match Milicent and Bryn are having, but also doesn't trust Aleesha.

"It's fine, we can find our own way back." I smile weakly.

"Well, okay, if you're sure," Murdoch acquiesces. "But I want you both staying close to home for the next few days. You especially. No disappearing." He jabs his finger at Aleesha. "And stay off the drugs."

"Don't worry, I've quit." She smiles sweetly back at him.

Murdoch raises an eyebrow. "I doubt that very much."

Instead of going back the way I'd come, Aleesha pulls me up the street, away from the guards and into a small courtyard. "Quick, up here. We should be able to listen in." She pulls herself lightly up onto the roof of an outbuilding and pads across to a small window that's cracked open. I follow, rather less gracefully.

"This wasn't Lamar's plan." Bryn's words float up from the other side of the window.

"Lamar isn't alive anymore." Milicent. "And we can't wait for the Leader to make up his mind forever. We need to act now, before the government gets wind of us. We have an opportunity t—"

"Look, we can get some reinforcements in a few days. Trained operatives from the continent."

"We don't have a few days. The Brotherhood are on our tail and the government seem to have ears everywhere. If we strike now, we have a chance. If they find out what we're planning, then anyone going in will walk straight into a trap."

"Which is why you should be sending in trained operatives, *not* kids."

A snort of derision. Murdoch. "They're practically adults, Bryn. Besides, they know this city; at least, Aleesha does. She knows how things work. Think about it: a six-year-old unchipped kid. Odds are ninety-nine percent that she'd have been picked up by the Metz within days. She's probably better at surviving than most of your *operatives*. She's had to be. As for the boy, well, he's a bit wet, but he's an Insider and the son of a senior minister. If they do get caught, he may be able to talk his way out of it."

"That's a long shot. Besides, his father is in enough trouble as it is. I doubt he'll be a minister for much longer."

My blood runs cold at Bryn's words. *Is Dad going to lose his job? Or worse ...*

"Sure, it's a long shot, but we don't have many other options."

"You're playing with their lives. Using them as pawns in your game."

"That's part of our job, Bryn." Milicent. "Sacrifices have to be made. Who else do you suggest we send in? We still don't know what's behind that door. Logic dictates the security would be a barrier similar to the Wall."

"We *have* to find out how the Wall works," Bryn mutters. "It's the crux of the whole problem."

Their voices drop and I struggle to make out any more words until Milicent raises her voice again.

"Well, you can ask the Leader if you want, Bryn, but I'm sure he said you weren't to get involved in any direct action. Something about him already having lost one of his best men ... Murdoch and a couple of the others will go with them. We may not even have to use them."

More murmurings.

"Right, I need to get back." Milicent again.

There's a tap on my arm. Aleesha nods in the direction of the courtyard. *Time to go.*

"What's a pawn?" Aleesha asks when we're safely back on the road to Abby's.

"It's a piece in a chess set. An old game my father taught me to play. The pawn is your sacrificial piece. They're expendable."

"Like us." There's a trace of sarcasm in her voice. "Expendable."

I shudder. "Well, you don't have to go along with their game."

"No, but if they are breaking into the main information bank, I may be able to persuade this expert of theirs to do some more digging." She looks thoughtful.

"About your father?"

She nods. "My mother was killed by the Metz. It was a big operation, they were waiting for someone. There'd be a record kept of something like that, wouldn't there?"

"I'd have thought so."

We walk in silence until we're around the corner from Abby's. I'm starting to recognize the streets.

"Trey … the films you took. Will you tell me what's in them?"

I nod. "Sure. Though I'm pretty knackered and it'll take me a bit of time to read them. Shall I meet you tomorrow?"

"Great. Do you know how to get to Rose Square?"

"I think so. Or I'll ask Abby to show me."

"I'll see you there, by the statue at three."

"See y—" But she has already gone.

A yawn wracks my body. *Time for sleep.* And whatever it is the Chain have planned, it can wait until at least tomorrow.

23

Aleesha

I slump against the wall at the bottom of the stairs leading up to Jay's apartment, tiredness washing over me. I'm hoping Jay will be out and I can curl up with Lily on the bed for a sleep. But when I walk in, Lily's not there.

"Ah, you're back."

"Where is she?" I glance around, but there's barely any furniture in the room. No place for a child to hide. There's an odd scent that triggers something in my mind, but I'm so tired and distracted I push the thought away.

"I asked Jonas to take her out for an hour," Jay says coming over to me. "Don't look at me like that. You can't just leave her here and expect me to babysit."

I force my face to relax into a smile and stand on my toes to kiss his cheek. "Sorry. I'll go find them now. Which way did they go?"

The atmosphere tightens and I become suddenly aware of someone else's presence in the room. Jay's hand clenches my arm.

"Wh—"

"Hello again, Aleesha."

That deep, melodic voice. My legs twitch, fighting the urge

to run. My limbs are frozen in place. I open my mouth, but it's so dry I can't get any words out. *Samson.*

He steps out from the bedroom. No hood this time, but still dressed all in black; the tight clothes emphasizing his muscular arms and chest. Thick dreadlocks hang down his back, exaggerating the size of his head.

"You have something for me?"

"N-no." I take a deep breath and force myself to look away. I glance at Jay. He's uneasy, but not, I think, from anything specific. Just being in the presence of this man is enough to make anyone uneasy. *What has he told him?*

Tap, tap, tap. Samson's foot on the floor. "You found the underground tunnels, then?"

I swallow, trying to moisten my mouth. "Why are you asking me if you already know?"

His laughter bounces off the wall. "It was an educated guess. What were you doing?"

However good I am at lying, this guy's not going to be fooled. But how much of the truth to tell him? "The Chain told u—" I stop myself, then continue, "told me about some tunnels that run under the city. From before the Great Flood. They wanted to know if the tunnels were intact and if it was possible to get through to the government headquarters."

"And is it?"

"I'm not sure. I got through to some underground rooms. Basements. But no one had been down there for years, and I've no idea where I was in relation to the buildings above." I shrug. "That's it."

"So, they're planning to break in? Why?"

"I don't know. They wouldn't tell me. They said it was best for me not to know." That much is true, at least.

249

Samson narrows his eyes and I force myself to meet his unblinking gaze.

"Did they say when?"

"No, not exactly." I swallow, rubbing my sweating palms on my legs. "Not right away, I don't think. I got the impression they're waiting for something, but I'm not sure what."

He falls silent, considering this.

"What about the boy who was with you."

"What? What boy?"

My response is too quick. High-pitched. Even Jay casts me an enquiring glance. *Dammit. He's getting under my skin.*

"Defensive, aren't you?" He smirks. "You know the boy. Dark-haired kid. Doesn't look like he comes from around here."

My shoulders are tense, hunched up to my ears. I force them to relax. "He's just a boy. He's not from Four. Too posh for these parts."

Samson takes a step in my direction, then another. It takes every inch of willpower I have not to step backward. "I don't feel like you're being very helpful, Aleesha," he says slowly, deliberately.

"I-I'm sorry. I can only tell you what I know."

"That's exactly what I mean." His voice is low. Dangerous.

Laughter from outside shatters the silence. Lily's voice on the stairs. I make a move to the door, but a look from Samson stops me.

"Tell … tell them to go out again, Jay." I give him a pleading look.

"No, Jay. Tell them to come in. I'd like to meet this young lady." Samson's teeth glint white.

Jay hesitates for a moment, then walks to the door and opens it slightly, so just he can look through. He says something to

Jonas, too low for me to catch, then there are footsteps on the stairs again. Closing my eyes, I breathe a sigh of relief.

"Aleesha!" There's a pitter-patter of feet and small arms are thrown around my waist.

My eyes snap open and my body begins to tremble. I run a hand gently across her mass of curls. "You okay?"

She nods, then presses her head into my belly. "Missed you." She glances around and pulls back, curious. "Who's he?"

"It doesn't matter. Now, why don't you go and play for a bit out on the landing? One of the other kids may be around." I push her gently in the direction of the door.

He moves in a flash, so quickly I barely register the movement, am only just reaching out for her, when she's snatched out of my reach.

She doesn't make a sound, too frightened to scream. Her eyes are wide, one arm twitching nervously. The blade pointing up under her chin looks too big for such a small girl. There's a faint squeak of fright, but it doesn't come from Lily. It comes from me.

"The boy, Aleesha. Who is the boy?"

"I-I told you."

A single red drop of blood falls to the floor. Tears brim in Lily's eyes, but to her credit she manages to hold them back.

"He's an Insider. The son of a government minister," I say in a rush, my eyes not leaving Lily's. "His name is Trey. He-he's being chased by the Metz for being an illegal."

"Ah, the illegal boy. That's interesting. I didn't recognize him." He sounds faintly amused, but I'm not sure why.

He releases Lily, pushing her forward, and she stumbles across to me. I kneel and wrap my arms around her as sobs wrack her small body. I clutch her to me, my heart pounding.

Samson brushes his hand over a black device on his wrist and an image of Trey, as I'd first seen him days ago, with blond hair, appears in the air. He's smiling and dressed in a blue shirt with some kind of logo on it.

"This boy."

I nod.

"Darwin Trey Goldsmith. Son of Andrew Goldsmith, Minister of Education and Health. Bet he didn't tell you *that*, did he?"

I shake my head, unable to speak. *Andrew Goldsmith is Trey's father? The Andrew Goldsmith? The man responsible for the lack of medical facilities. The children's homes. The Population Control Officers.*

I feel an odd sense of disappointment. And betrayal. I'd almost been starting to like him. Though, perhaps that was just the novelty of being able to talk to someone properly. Someone intelligent. Who wasn't trying to use you for something.

Samson chuckles to himself. "When they contact you again – if they ask you to go into the government headquarters – I want to know. *Before* you go. Do you understand?"

"Yes."

He moves toward the door, surprisingly graceful for such a large man.

"Wait! How do I get in touch with you?" I straighten, still not letting go of Lily.

He pauses in the doorway. "Tell Jay. He knows how to reach me."

We stare after him, waiting for the sound of the door at the bottom of the stairs to open and close. Jay moves to the window. "He's gone."

Lily stops crying. I settle her on a chair and give her one of the chocco bars still left from last night. Then I join Jay at the window.

"What the hell have you got involved in, Jay? That guy … he's dangerous. Really dangerous. You're going to get us all killed!"

"*I'm* going to get us killed?" he hisses. "You're the one lying to him, screwing around with this other gang and that boy; whoever *he* is."

"He's just a spoiled Insider. Smart enough, but useless out here."

I immediately feel bad, then chide myself. I'm not the son of the evil minister, after all.

"Samson's scary, but I'm not sure the Brotherhood are all that bad. They're trying to stop the fighting between gangs for one thing, and that can't be bad, right?" Jay says.

"Depends how you go about it. If you murder everyone, there's no one left to fight."

He huffs. "How do you know the Chain are the good guys in this anyway? Seems to me they're the ones being all mys—" he struggles with the word "—*mysterious* about what they're up to."

I bite my lip. He's right. The Chain and the Brotherhood seem to be on opposite sides of some war, but I don't know which of them is on the right side. If there is a right side. "Look, I'm sorry, okay. I just … I just don't like him, that's all."

"Yeah, well, you don't exactly *like* many people, do you?"

His sarcasm hurts, but I try not to show it. "I'll take Lily out for a bit," I say quietly. "Give you some peace."

He nods. "Better make it a couple of hours. I've got someone coming around. Business." He stares out the window, refusing to meet my eye even when I turn his face to mine for a kiss. I brush his lips, but he doesn't respond. I wonder if he knows something about Samson that I don't. Or about the Chain, perhaps. I'll find out tonight.

Lily's keen to go out again and races down the steps in front of me. I turn at the door and look back, but Jay is still staring out the window, as if watching for someone.

* * *

After an hour of wandering the streets, Lily is tired and grumpy. Eventually, I give in to her pleas to go home. *I'm sure we can wait in the bedroom while Jay sorts his business out.* The thought of lying down is overwhelmingly tempting.

"Stay down here," I whisper to Lily, who nods, her eyes wide.

I tiptoe up the remaining stairs to the apartment door. It's closed, but not locked. There's a murmur of voices from inside, but they're too indistinct to make out.

Sod it. I turn the handle and push the door open, surprised to find the room inside empty. Well, not quite empty. There's an unfamiliar coat slung over the back of one of the chairs. Too small to be Jay's.

As I step inside, there's a laugh from the direction of the bedroom. No, not a laugh, a *giggle*. A high-pitched, I'm-so-feminine, *female* giggle. Then a murmur – I recognize Jay's voice – followed by a squeal.

It feels like my heart skips a beat, then it's beating so loud I can barely hear anything else. Coldness seeps through me despite the warmth in the room, and I have a sudden urge to sit down, but my legs carry me onwards, toward the open bedroom door.

I see them before they see me. Jay is on top, her underneath, hidden by his bulk. They're entangled in the grubby sheet, her pale hand wandering around the dark skin of his back. Jay lets out a moan and arches his neck.

She notices me first. I'm not sure how long I've been standing there – it feels like minutes, but must only have been a few seconds – when Jay pulls her up the bed slightly and she spies me over his shoulder. Her blue eyes meet mine and widen.

She's pretty. Perfectly straight nose, unlike my own stub nose. Cascades of brown hair, though it's the grubby kind of brown. Wide eyes, like an innocent doll. Pretty, yes, but not beautiful.

Jay picks up on the tension in her body and turns. A flicker of apprehension crosses his face when he sees me standing in the doorway. He pulls away from the girl and she grabs at the sheet to cover herself, but not before I catch a glimpse of her perfectly-formed large round breasts. Much more of a handful than my own pair. *Is that why he went for her?*

I turn my back and walk to the table. My limbs move mechanically, like I don't own them anymore. Like I'm just an automated bot.

"Aleesha, wait!" Jay calls after me. But he doesn't understand. I'm not going anywhere, not yet. The ice in my veins is replaced with fire, a burning anger that bubbles in the pit of my stomach, overcoming even the pain that radiates from my chest. I reach for the nearest item – an empty Chaz bottle – and launch it with all my strength into the bedroom.

It smashes on the wall above the bed, sending fragments of glass raining down on the girl. Jay is already halfway to the door when my next missile – an empty tin can – catches him in the chest. My hand reaches for something else to throw, but finds the table bare. I pull a knife from the hidden pocket on the side of my trouser leg, but Jay's quicker than me and grabs my arms, pushing me back against the table.

"Stop it!" He shakes me. "What the hell do you think you're doin'?"

"What am *I* doing?" I suddenly find my voice. "What are *you*

255

doing? And who the hell is that whore in *our* bedroom?"

He releases one hand to slap me across the face. I'm not expecting it and the iron-tang of blood in my mouth comes as a surprise. He leans in close and speaks slowly, between gritted teeth. "She is *not* a whore."

His naked body presses into me and a sudden surge of desire mingles with my anger. But only for a second. I bring my knee up, hard, between his legs and he crumples, cursing me. I push him away and pull the knife out, holding it in front of me, but in self-defence, not attack. When he's angry, Jay scares even me, and he's pretty mad right now.

He looks up and all I see in his eyes is anger. I stand my ground and stare right back at him, but inside my fear grows.

"You're going to regret that," he says quietly.

He stands up and takes a step toward me. I take a step back – I can't help myself – but at that moment the girl appears in the doorway, the sheet wrapped hastily around her.

"Jay, stop."

Her voice is soft but compelling, and to my surprise he does stop. But he doesn't take his eyes off me. "Stay out of this, Beth."

She walks over and stands behind him, one hand on his shoulder. She doesn't trust me, then. Smart. "Just let her go." She kisses his shoulder.

This riles me. "This is my home," I hiss. "*You* should be the one leaving. Jay?" I glare at him, hoping, really hoping, he backs me up on this. That it isn't over.

But he turns slightly, reaching one hand back to caress her leg. "No, Aleesha, this isn't your home." His voice sounds tired now, the anger draining out of it. "It never has been."

And then it hits me that he's right. This place has never been what you'd call home. Just a place to stay. Like every other place

I've stayed. Temporary. Transitory. And me: just a temporary girlfriend. A fling.

My arm drops to my side, the knife falling from my hand. It clatters to the floor and I bend to pick it up, my body working on autopilot.

"You can come back tomorrow morning to pick up your stuff," Jay says. "Now go."

He steps toward me to usher me out of the room, but my eyes are fixed on *her*. Beth. She smiles at me, but it's a smile of pity, not malice. Which makes it even worse. The anger rises in me again, all-consuming. The knife flies from my hand. It whistles past her ear, exactly as I'd intended. Not to hurt her, just to wipe that smile off her face.

"Aleesha." Jay's voice is a growl. His eyes are on fire. "*Go!*"

A moment later, I'm staring at the green, peeling paint on the door. There's a click as the door lock is activated from inside, and I'll bet my last chit my code doesn't work anymore.

"Aleesha?" Lily's voice tremors up from the bottom of the stairs. I wonder how much she's heard and how much of that she understood. "Is Jay mad? A-are we goin' somewhere else?"

I nod, starting down the stairs. The pain in my chest is deeper now, though whether it's from Jay's betrayal or my humiliation, I'm not sure.

"Yes, Lily," I say, reaching out to her. "We're going somewhere else."

24

Aleesha

We spend the night up on my roof. I don't know where else to go and, at least, up here, there are a couple of blankets. Lily wraps herself in one and lies down, resting her head on my outstretched leg. Her breathing slows as she falls asleep.

My body is tired and aching, crying out for rest. But my mind won't settle. It just replays the same scene over and over again. Jay's apartment. Jay in bed with *her*. His anger. Her calmness. She calmed him in a way I thought impossible.

It gnaws at my insides, that mixture of pain and jealousy. The pain is real enough, though not enough to make me cry. Nothing is enough to make me cry. Sometimes, I wish I could just release all the pent-up anger and hurt inside me in one great fit of sobbing.

I always knew, deep inside, that Jay's apartment was never truly home; that one day he'd tire of me and I'd be back out on the street again. But I should have seen it coming. Why didn't I spot the warning signs? Do I care for him that much?

Who is this girl? Beth. I haven't seen her before and her accent is different. Softer. *Surely she can't be an Insider?* I shake my head. Even Jay wouldn't get that lucky. But maybe she's from

258

Area Five, or Six, even. Brought up properly, with a mother and father. With a home.

I roll Lily's curls around my fingers. She looks just like an angel when she sleeps. A baby angel. I need to find somewhere safe for her. But where? I can't stay around Snakes' territory, not with Jay in charge and *her* hanging off his arm.

It's all too much to think about. Too overwhelming. I close my eyes, leaning my head back against the wall. If I can sleep, perhaps something will come to me in the morning. It takes a while, but eventually the thoughts swirling around my mind transcend into dreams. Dreams of tunnels, piles of film covered in words I can't read, and the writhing figures of Jay and Beth.

* * *

When I awake, it's morning. Lily sits beside me, her arms wrapped around her knees. Her arms have little bumps all over them and I realize that in my rush to leave the apartment yesterday I'd forgotten her coat. I unfasten my jacket and wrap it around her, pulling her close to me to warm her up.

"I'm hungry," she says, cuddling up against me.

"Me too, Lily. We'll go find some food in a minute." My stomach rumbles in agreement; I can't remember the last time I ate. Too long ago. Everything – the rucksack, my chits – is back at Jay's.

"Wuz it me, Aleesha?"

"Huh?" I look down at her, confused.

"Wuz Jay mad at me? Is that why we left?" Her eyes are full of tears.

I hug her tightly. "No, it was nothing to do with you. Don't think that. It was me. My fault."

I feel even more sombre this morning. Depression hangs over

259

me like the grey clouds blanketing the sky. It seems the brief sunny period we had is over and we're back to the rain. I try to think of all the people who owe me favours, but it's a pretty short list, and none of them are people I'd consider leaving Lily with.

Yawning, I lean back against the shelter. Sleep hasn't left me feeling any better rested. Perhaps I can just doze for a bit.

But Lily has other ideas. She starts walking around the rooftop, my black jacket wrapped around her shoulders like a cape. She's mumbling something to herself and staring out at the towers. Every now and then she looks back at me, checking whether I'm still pretending to be asleep. Eventually, she comes over and grabs my hands.

"Come on, Aleesha. Time to go."

I slump back, resisting her efforts to pull me up. "Just another minute."

She lets go of my hands and kneels beside me, wrapping her small arms as far as she can around my chest. "I know you're sad, Aleesha, an' Jay's angry at us. But mebbe today he'll be happy again?"

Her optimism tugs at my heart and I can't help but smile. *I have to be strong. For her.* "I don't think so, Lily, but come on, let's go find some food."

The streets below are full of people. There's a buzz about the place, as if some big event is about to happen. We head to McGinty's place. He's usually pretty good about giving me food on credit when I don't have any chits to hand. At least he knows I will pay him back. Sure enough, he writes down our purchases on a scratched piece of film and, with a toothy smile and a wink, slips Lily a lemon fizzle.

I lean over the counter and drop my voice. "So, what's going on, McGinty? What's happening?"

He glances nervously around and takes a step closer. I try not to recoil at the stench of his breath. "Rumours of a Metz raid. At least, most tell me it's a raid, but others are saying the government are planning a Cleaning."

My blood goes cold. "Another one?"

He grimaces. "I know. But it's just rumours, so who's to know? *They,*" he jerks his thumb in the direction of the Wall, "could have started them just to spread fear. T'keep people from attacking the compounds."

As we leave the shop, I wonder if he's right. I'd heard there had been more attacks on the supply vehicles that take the government rations from the depots in each area to the government stores. There had even been attempted raids on the depots themselves. Hunger forces people to do desperate things.

We walk to Rose Square and sit on the steps of an old statue. Breaking a grey bread roll, I hold one half out to Lily. She wrinkles her nose as she takes it and pops the lemon fizzle in her mouth instead.

I stare out in front of me. *This is where it happened. Where she died. But who were they really after?*

"What are we going to do today?" Lily asks, sucking on her sweet.

I shrug. I just feel so *tired*, as if I could sleep for days. We should probably go to Jay's and pick up my things. I should get some chits from him, too. He must be rolling in chits now he's head of the gang, enough to see us through the next few weeks. Maybe even enough to rent space in a room.

But all of this just feels like too much hard work. So, I close my eyes and lean back, letting the warmth of the day seep into my bones.

"Why is everyone going toward the river?"

"I don't know, Lily." *Do all children ask this many questions?*

"Some people are running, Aleesha." Fear touches the edges of her words.

I crack open an eyelid and frown. She's right; the flow of people moving across the square has a panic in it.

"Okay, let's go, then." I sigh and stand up, reaching down to pull her to her feet. I kneel down in front of her. "Look, I'm sorry I'm so grumpy today. I'm just upset about Jay and stuff. I promise I'll sort us out somewhere else to live, okay?"

She smiles at me trustingly. "Course you will."

Hand in hand we make our way across the square to join the people heading toward the river. Normally, I'd be more alert, listening in to people's conversations to try and find out what was going on. After all, following the crowds isn't always the safest thing to do. But today, I just feel tired and numb, so I don't pay attention to what people are saying as we get carried on the tide.

After a while, the flow of people seems to slow and disperse. Coming out of my daze, I look around and realize we're on Dellom Street. Home of whores and dens. And *it*. Suddenly, I can taste the tronk in my mouth. The sweet tang followed by a slight sour taste. And then happiness.

That's what I need. Not food or money or clothes. The craving is strong now. So much has happened in the past few days to take my mind off it, I almost hadn't missed it. But the black cloud is so heavy on me. I begin to walk faster, dragging a protesting Lily behind me.

You promised her – promised them – you'd quit. Urgh, that little voice of conscience in my head. But I'll only have a little bit, just enough to take the edge of the depression away. It'll help me think straight again. Figure out where we can go.

"Aleesha, stop!" Lily's voice is frightened and she trails behind me, pulling on my arm. "This place is bad!"

No, this place is good. "S'okay," I mumble. "We'll just be a few minutes."

She starts to cry. I stop and kneel beside her, wracked with guilt. *What am I doing to her? She'd be better off without me.* I wrap my arms around her and try to calm her sobbing. But the need is still there inside me. I just need to get some of it. Just a quick hit.

Gradually, she calms down. I glance around, wondering if there's somewhere I can leave her, just for a minute, but the sides of the street are littered with beggars and drug addicts, most of them off their heads. No wonder she's terrified.

"Hey, what are you doing down here?"

I look up, blinking as the dark silhouette above me comes into focus. Jonas. I breathe a sigh of relief and stand up. "We got caught in the crowd coming down from the square and ended up here." I wonder if he knows about Beth and decide on balance he probably doesn't.

"I need to go and speak to one of the dealers; to take a message from Jay," I lie. "Could you keep an eye on Lily for me, just for a couple of minutes? I don't want to have to take her in there."

He frowns suspiciously. "I didn't know Jay had anything to do with this part of town."

"He doesn't, but this guy owes him money. He doesn't want to start a fight by sending in you or the other guys, so he thought I might be able to persuade him to hand it over."

Jonas seems to accept the story, and actually smiles slightly when Lily gazes up at him. Her smile is enough to melt the hardest heart. "Okay then, but five minutes. No more. I have stuff to be getting on with."

I bend down to Lily. "I'm just going to be a few minutes. Jonas will look after you until I get back."

She sniffles. "Please, don't go. Let's just go back to the square."

"Two minutes. I promise I'll come back for you." On an impulse, I lean forward and kiss her on the forehead before standing and striding toward an open door covered in orange graffiti.

* * *

The room inside is dark and damp. It's more a concrete shell than a building. Window-shaped holes, empty of glass, let in some meagre light. Inside, it stinks of sweat, piss and worse. People lie around the edges of the room, some propped against the wall; others appear to be sleeping. They stare vacantly at nothing.

You see, this is what it does to you. This is what you'll become.

I walk through into the next room, which is much the same. Two men slouch against the wall on either side of an empty doorway. Underneath their relaxed postures, I can see they're alert. As I get closer, one of them moves to block my path.

"I'm here to see Mitch," I tell them.

He doesn't move. "I don't think Mitch is expecting you."

I smile sweetly at them. "Probably not, but he'll not want me to be left standing here while you pair debate the matter."

They glance at each other. You can almost see their little brain cells trying to work this out. Finally, the one standing in the doorway nods. "Follow me."

I follow him down a narrow corridor that ends in a small room. This one has some furnishings, if you call a wonky table and a couple of disintegrating armchairs furniture. Behind the table sits a man with slicked-back hair and scarred hands. He's jotting notes on a piece of paper, but looks up when he hears us enter. A flicker of annoyance crosses his face, but it's quickly replaced by his usual blank reptilian stare.

"Aleesha. It's been a while." He stands, motioning me to one of the chairs and nods at the henchman, who leaves.

I move to stand by the side of his desk. "Business going well, Mitch?"

I glance down at the paper on his desk. There are some big numbers on there. Business must be going well indeed.

Mitch quickly pulls the paper out of my sight, folding it away in a drawer. "So, what can I do for you?"

"You owe me a favour," I say, getting straight to the point. I do some quick calculations in my head. "About ten ounces worth of a favour."

His eyes narrow. "No favour is worth that much. Besides, I thought you were off the stuff."

"Oh, it's not for me." I wave my hand breezily. "And don't worry, I'm not going to be treading on your turf. I just need to do a few trades, is all."

Mitch frowns. "You can have three ounces, and that is more than you're owed."

I give him a pained look. "Really? Is that all your life is worth to you? All your *business* is worth?" I glance significantly in the direction of the drawer containing the piece of paper.

He leans forward, but I stand my ground. "I would think twice before threatening me."

I move so fast, he doesn't have time to react. His eyes widen as the point of my knife presses into his stomach. "And I don't like to be threatened," I say in a low voice. "But, as I know you'll keep your word, I'm happy to take two ounces as a down payment today. I'll come back for the rest another time."

He thinks for a minute, then nods. It's a no-brainer, really. He'll give me the stuff and warn his heavies not to let me in again. But that's fine for now. Two ounces is plenty. Some to sell, and a little whiff to improve my mood.

I pull the knife away slightly and nod to the cabinet in the corner where he keeps his stash. I follow him as he walks over, looking for any signs he's going to pull a fast one. But he doesn't try any funny tricks and a few minutes later, I have a carefully weighed pouch of white powder sitting in my pocket.

I walk backward toward the door. "Pleasure doing business with you, Mitch."

He inclines his head toward me. "As always, Aleesha."

I turn and walk a few metres down the corridor. My hands shake with anticipation and my mouth is dry. Pocketing the knife, I fumble to draw the pouch out. Carefully, I open it and tip a bit of the powder into my palm. More comes out than I really need, but it's too much hassle to try and get it back in the packet and too precious to waste.

I tip my head back, letting the powder fall into my mouth, licking my palm to get every last bit. Then I re-seal the pouch, replace it in my pocket and lean back against the cool wall, waiting for it to take effect.

It takes barely a minute. The surge of bliss begins to melt the tension in my body; happiness slowly pushing aside the black cloud of depression. *At least he's given me the good stuff.*

I smile, thinking of the fun Lily and I will have today. Maybe we'll go up to Area Six. Try and find a playground. She'd like that.

I push myself away from the wall and concentrate on walking

down the corridor back toward the guards. *Must focus on walking straight.* It's harder than you think. The drug affects your balance and it's hard not to giggle when you fall to one side.

As I stagger back through the doorway into the second room, I become aware of a commotion outside. One of the heavies is looking out through the hole in the wall, back up the street.

A man rushes in, tripping over an outstretched figure in his haste. He stops, panting, in front of the heavies, his hands on his knees.

"Let ... me ... through ..." he gasps, though one of them is already pulling me aside from the doorway.

"What is it?" the other one asks.

"Raid. Metz are coming," the man answers, then runs down the corridor toward Mitch's office.

A raid? The thought cuts through my island of happiness. *Raids are bad. I should get out of here.* I force my legs into motion and stumble toward the door, but others in the room are stirring and they block my way. Outside, there are screams and cries of fear and a familiar, rhythmic pounding of feet.

I make it through to the first room, but here people are more alert and aware that something's going on. They block the doorway, all fighting to get out, not having the sense to realize they'd get out quicker if they just held back a bit. Outside, people are running down toward the river.

Think. THINK. But the drug is working its magic, numbing my thoughts and sending jolts of happiness through my body. *I have to get out of here. There's some reason ... Think!*

I get pushed up against the concrete wall at the front of the building and reflexively kick back into the mass of people. Light streams in from a hole in the wall above me. Stretching up, my fingers just reach over the edge. With a grunt, I pull myself up and swing a leg over.

From up here I can see the surging crowd of people. And behind them, just coming into view, rows and rows of black and yellow helmets. *Metz.*

"Aleesha!"

I look around for the source of the voice. *Lily. Of course, that's why I need to get out of here. To get Lily. I promised her.*

My eyes find her, perched on Jonas's shoulders. Jonas looks annoyed and afraid, trying to keep the crowd from pulling them down the street. He doesn't see how close the Metz are behind them; how near the danger is.

"This way!" I holler at them, waving for them to move. I drop down from my perch, but then I too am caught up in the river of people. I try and fight my way against the flow, but my strength and reactions are slower than normal. Fear cuts through the happiness as I lash out with my elbows, inching my way up the street.

"Lily!" I scream, but my voice is lost in the tumult and I'm too small to see them over the crowd.

I give up trying to force my way across the street and instead work my way along the side of the buildings where it's a bit easier to move. I reach a set of steps that lead to a doorway and, standing on my toes on the top step, can just about see them above the heads of all the people.

I watch as Lily spots the black figures of the Metz and says something to Jonas, who turns. But as he does so, someone pushes against him and he falls to the ground, Lily tumbling from his back.

I plunge down, back into the crowd, my only thought to get to Lily before she's trampled underfoot. But the Metz are so close now, barely twenty metres away. Their feet pound, all in time, as if they are one body. They herd the crowd in front of them, batting with their black rods anyone who doesn't get out of their way fast enough. I'm carried down the street again, away from them. Away from her.

And then, suddenly, the press eases. People slow down. The rhythmic pounding has stopped. I'm about ten metres from the edge of the crowd, but by jumping up, I can catch a glimpse of what's happening. The Metz have formed a circle and are dragging people out from the surrounding buildings. I recognize a handful of the drug dealers and their allies. Mitch isn't among them, but the two heavies who were guarding his den are. And in the centre of the circle, lying motionless on the floor, is Lily.

My heart stops. At least, it feels like it does. I elbow my way through the crowd towards the Metz. People move to let me pass. I'm about three metres away when I hear her scream. Fear mingles with relief. *She's alive.*

Over the shoulders of the people in front of me I spy her, surrounded by a ring of Metz. She stands alone, her eyes wild with terror, searching for someone who may be able to help her.

The Metz move forward, pushing the men and women into a line. *No, oh, god no.* I've seen this before, just once. It was enough. The purpose of a raid is to spread fear and remind people of the punishment for disobeying the rules. *Surely, they wouldn't shoot a child?*

"Lily!" I yell, frantically trying to push aside the people in my way, my eyes fixated on her. I don't know if she can hear me above the noise: the shouts and struggles of the people being forced to kneel on the ground around her. They've probably guessed their fate.

Just as I break through the crowd, I feel a hand on me, pulling me back. I turn to see Jonas, his face battered and bloody.

"Let me go!" I try and pull my arm away, but he holds firm.

"Don't be an idiot. There's nothing you can do for her," he hisses. "Don't draw attention to yourself."

I kick out, catching him on the kneecap. He doubles over, swearing, but his grip on my arm eases enough that I'm able to pull free. I'm nearly through the crowd again when the first shot rings out.

There's a collective gasp, then a second shot. *Surely, they're not going to shoot them all?* I search for Lily and see her standing in front of a Metz officer. He's holding a black collar above her head.

"Lily!" I scream, and this time she hears me.

Time slows. Her face turns to me, eyes wide in terror. "Aleesha!"

As I push aside the man blocking my way, she begins to run to me. But each small leg moves so slowly, takes so long to strike the ground, that she has only gone a few paces when another officer grabs her and throws her back into the circle.

"No!" The word hangs in the air. Everyone is suddenly silent. Watching. Waiting.

I move, but my legs are heavy and slow, like I'm running through a swamp of mud. One step. She's pulled to her feet. The officer brings the collar down around her neck. Two steps. *There's still time, there must be.*

The knife is in my hand, though I don't remember it leaving my pocket. There's no glint from the weapon in the officer's hand. Like the rest of the uniform, it seems to absorb light. My aim is true. The knife strikes the back of the officer's hand. It bounces harmlessly to the floor.

Lily's hands claw at the collar. Her shrill scream of pure terror cuts through me. The officer takes a step back and reaches for something on its belt.

Three steps. A shot rings out. My breath freezes in my mouth, all the blood in my body suddenly turned to ice. Her small body crumples to the floor. A dark stream of blood runs from her forehead down onto the filthy street. Her eyes still stare at me, but the sparkle in them – the life – is gone.

A murmuring rises up around me. People are angry. But the noise comes from far away. They surge past, toward the Metz. Toward Lily.

As my legs buckle under me, I feel wetness on my cheeks. Tears.

25

Trey

I awake with a start from a strange dream in which I was climbing a staircase. I had to reach something, but I'm not sure what, and I was being chased, all the time, being chased.

It's still dark and there's a patter of rain on the window. I try the light switch but nothing happens. Electricity must be down again.

There's no use trying to get back to sleep. I feel wide awake and must have slept a good ten hours. I barely stayed awake long enough to eat and wash before collapsing into bed after getting back from Milicent's interrogation.

Murdoch's flashlight is on the floor by the bed. It lets out a faint beam. Enough to read by at any rate.

I retrieve the wad of films from underneath the mattress and climb back into bed, using the pillow to prop myself up against the wall.

Where to start? Most of the films are date stamped. I shuffle them until they're in chronological order, then pick up the top paper and start reading.

It's an extract from notes of a cabinet meeting a few months before the Great Flood. There's a list of attendees, but most of the names mean nothing to me. Only one stands out: Purcell, the Prime Minster. That was what they called the President back then. I start to read.

Some time later, I put down the film and stretch. There's a crick in my neck that I hadn't noticed developing. Outside, the sky is lightening. Not enough to see by, but not far off. Walking to the window, I try to take in what I've just read. If they weren't official government documents and I hadn't personally found them, I'd have thought it a fictional story, made up by some enemy of the government. It's all so very different from what we were taught at school.

They had all the warning signs. The hot summers, the rapid rise in sea levels, a report on the possibility of the imminent collapse of the Greenland ice cap. Forecasts for a storm surge coming down the North Sea that could over-top the flood defences. The storms that had saturated the ground and left rivers brimming.

It's all there in the papers. They'd had time to prepare. And they'd argued about the balance of probability. Scaremongering. The risk of panic. Until it was too late for anything to be done.

There's only one mention of notifying the states on the other side of the North Sea of the risk. But the papers are incomplete, and I can fill in the gaps from what we *were* taught in history. We – Britannia, or Britain as it still was then – were responsible for forecasting, assessing and disseminating weather reports. And for some reason, the government chose not to share the forecasts.

I stare out the window, wondering how different the city would look if someone had made a different decision back then.

Half the cabinet stated people needed to be evacuated from areas at risk in case the surge was as bad as forecast. The other half thought they shouldn't: that there'd been so much chaos and loss of life as a result of the last false alarm, they couldn't risk it again unless they were certain. But who could ever be certain with the weather?

I go back to the bed and pick up the handwritten film with "Confidential" scrawled across the top. It's a transcript of a conversation between the Prime Minister and the Secretary of State, written on paper headed with the Prime Minister's Office. The Secretary of State tells him that, due to the inland flooding, there aren't the police resources to effect a safe evacuation. That to evacuate would certainly lead to loss of life and thousands of people stranded between the flooded interior roads and the coast.

Is that what made your mind up, Prime Minister Purcell? What made you decide to bet the lives of a million people on the weather forecast being wrong?

Stretching, I sit back down and continue reading. There are a couple of papers covering the immediate aftermath of the flood. Mainly lists of statistics: estimated deaths, number of homes destroyed, how many days' worth of food and fuel remained.

The next film is dated five years later. The style and heading is different. There's a new government. Still a cabinet, but no Prime Minister anymore. Instead, there's a President.

The film records a debate around the passing of emergency legislation in Parliament titled the "Population Regulation Act". I've never heard of it. The debate seems surprisingly short and non-controversial, but then I notice in the footnote, the abbreviation "ed." after the report number. *Is this an edited version of the discussion?*

There's a copy of the legislation attached to it. It's pretty hard to wade through and I have to read it twice to check I'm interpreting it right. Even then, I'm not sure. *Surely, this can't be legal?* I shiver, the room feeling suddenly cold, and get up to

274

pull on a jumper from the small pile of clothes that Abby found for me. Then I sit down and read the Population Regulation Act for a third time.

When it's fully light outside, I get dressed and head downstairs. There's a familiar smell in the kitchen.

"Are you making pancakes?" I ask incredulously, peering over Abby's shoulder. They actually look like proper food.

"Good day at the market yesterday. I still had a bit of flour left a—"

"Don't tell me," I interrupt. "I don't want to know what's in them. Let me pretend they're real." At least, it's not the usual grey mush. After what I've been reading this morning, I don't think I could face it.

Bryn looks better this morning. Or cleaner, at least. I'm curious to know where he's been, but he circumvents my questions, eventually flatly refusing to answer them, though he does say he's been helping my father out, which seems strange. *Unless whatever he's been doing is something to do with me?*

The pancakes are tasty; the best food I've had for, well, as long as I've been out here. As Abby stacks the plates, Bryn clears his throat.

"Trey, I ... I need to tell you something."

This sounds ominous. My skin crawls. Bryn sounds serious and I get the feeling this isn't good news. "Are they alright?" I ask.

He looks puzzled.

"Who?"

"My family ..."

His face clears. "Oh, no, they're fine, I think. As far as I know, anyway. I need to see your father today."

There's a pause. Abby wipes the dishes and replaces them in

275

the cupboard, then starts to clean the sink.

"What is it you need to tell me then?"

"Oh, right, yes."

Bryn reaches up to brush a hand through his hair, then drops it again and clears his throat. Beads of sweat form on his brow.

"When you saw your family the other day, there was something they didn't tell you. I – we – thought it might be too much to throw at you all in one go. We were worried about you. But now, well, I think you should know."

Another pause. *What's he on about?*

"You see, Trey, I actually knew your mother, a long time ago. Before you were born. I was working Inside then, before the government found out about me. Anyway, I met your mother at a party and we hit it off."

Abby stops scrubbing and stands stock still.

"Miriam, your mother, was – is still – so beautiful. I loved her from the moment I saw her. And she ... I do believe she loved me. Your father was barely at home at the time and she was lonely. We started seeing more of each other and, well, one thing led to another."

His tanned face flushes and he looks down at the table.

"Bryn, w-what are you saying?" There's a wobble in my voice. My mind is telling me the logical conclusion I should have reached, but I don't want to believe it. My mouth feels dry.

"I'm saying that, well, I'm your father, Trey. I-I didn't know at first. I had no idea at all until you said who your father was. And then, well, I knew from what Miriam had said years ago about how sensible and responsible he was, that the chances of him accidentally fathering a child were practically nil. And you were about the right age, and you don't look at all like your father, and indeed, rather like Daniel ... Like me."

I stare at him, Aleesha's comment comes back to me. *Perhaps your mother had an affair or something. It doesn't really matter, does it?* But it does matter.

"You knew this and you didn't tell me?" I stand up, not caring that the chair crashes to the floor.

"I didn't know, it was just a guess. It was only when I confronted your mother, the day before you saw them, that she admitted it. Back then, I just got this note from her saying she didn't want to see me anymore. That she'd decided to stay with your father and I should leave." He looks at me sadly. "She wanted the best for you, Trey. And with your father, you could have the best. I'd have been the worst person in the world to bring up a kid. Daniel was proof of that," he adds bitterly.

"I … you … you should have told me! *They* should have told me!" I shout and storm out of the room, slamming the door behind me. I slump on the stairs, pulling at my stupid, dyed-brown hair. *Has my whole life been a lie? What else am I going to find out about myself that isn't true?*

Abby's voice comes through the door. Sharp, angry. And Bryn's. Trying to calm her down. Curiosity draws me to the door and I press my ear against it to listen.

"He's not my responsibility, though. I didn't even know I *had* a son until four days ago."

"You're still his father, Bryn."

"Only biologically."

"That counts!" Abby sounds furious. "Look, Daniel's death wasn't your fault—"

"Don't bring Daniel into this." Bryn's voice is angry.

"Why not? You can't hang on to that guilt forever. You need to grow up and take responsibility for your actions. This isn't just about Trey. The Chain is falling apart. Without Lamar to bring them all together, they'll do more harm than good, you know that. I'm worried about what Milicent has planned. She's clever, but too … too driven. It blinds her. And I don't know what they're going to get Trey doing next."

"It's not my job. I'm just a messenger. I don't know the ins and outs of London. I haven't been here for years, and a lot has changed in that time."

"But Lamar trusted you. He believed in you to do what was *right*."

"And what is right, Abby? I just don't know anymore."

The back door slams.

I lean against the wall, closing my eyes. *My father isn't my father, and the man who is doesn't want me. Where do I go from here?*

The door opens. "Oh, you're here! You heard that, then."

I nod.

Abby sighs. "Come and sit down. I think we both need some tea."

We sit in silence for a while, clutching our mugs of steaming herbs.

"You okay?" Abby asks eventually. "It must be a lot to take in."

I nod. *Even more than you realize.*

"It's just … everything is different from what I believed. I always thought Father and the government were helping people, but from out here, it looks like they're doing nothing. And now I find out he's not my father at all. It feels like everything I've ever been told is a lie."

"Hmm. But have you ever felt like your father, or mother, treated you differently? That they didn't love you as a son?"

I shake my head reluctantly. "No, I-I think they love me."

"Then they do." She reaches over the table and covers my hand.

"And love can't be faked or lied about. Your father may not be your biological father, but he loves you as a son. He was just trying to protect you."

"And he risked losing everything ..."

"Exactly." She smiles. "I know it feels like everything's falling down around you, but just remember that. Your parents love you. And that's more than a lot of people have."

I try to smile. "I guess."

Abby lifts her mug to drink. "So, what's life like Inside?"

"To be honest, I didn't spend much time in London. I lived mainly at our house in Wales. In the middle of nowhere. Now, I know why."

"Tell me about Wales. I've never been outside London."

So I do. She wants to know everything about the plants and trees and sheep. In some ways, it would probably be her ideal home. Lots of things to grow. Not many people. Or any, actually.

"Didn't you get lonely?"

"Not really. I had Ella, my sister, though she's eight years older than me. And a lot of the time I was working. Trying to catch up and retake exams so school would take me back."

She frowns. "But you're clever!"

"Not clever enough." I sigh. "I've always been a disappointment to my parents in that regard."

"Well, you're your own person, Trey. And you're nearly an adult, right? Old enough to make your own decisions. Your parents can only guide you. They don't control your life. And if I were your mother, I'd be very proud of you." She smiles warmly.

"Did you ever have a child, Abby?" I ask cautiously. It seems rude to pry, but I want to know more about this kind woman who's looked after me.

Her eyes sadden. "No. That wasn't to be for me." She smiles, too brightly. "I never found the right man."

Did you love Bryn, Abby? The wanderer who would never settle down.

"Anyway, I need to go to the market later, but first, I feel in need of music." She sniffs and wipes the back of her hand over her eyes, then smiles at me again. "Shall I play, or you?"

I make a face. "You, definitely. I'm still struggling."

"Nonsense, you're a quick learner," she says, lifting the guitar down from the wall. She settles it on her knee and starts gently strumming. The melody runs through my head, pushing down the thoughts and worries so I forget all about my father and Bryn and the Population Regulation Act and just focus on the soothing music.

26

Aleesha

I cradle Lily's limp body in my arms, rocking back and forth, barely able to see through the tears that run down my face and soak her thin t-shirt. Strange things, tears; I wouldn't have thought I had this much water in me, but still they keep on coming.

Grief and guilt wrack my body. *Is this what it feels like to care? Why do people love when it hurts this much?*

This was my fault, my stupid fault. If I hadn't been so weak, so foolish, she would still be alive. If I'd listened to her when she begged me to leave, she would still be alive. If I hadn't been so selfish, she would still be alive.

I clutch her tighter as if by doing so I can somehow force life back into her body. There's a pain in my chest that feels like a knife between my ribs. If I believed in a god I would offer anything – my own life, even – to bring her back. I should have held her more when she was alive. Given her the affection she so desperately craved.

Should have. Could have.

Jonas stands by the window, looking out. The sound of fighting filters up from the street below. People fighting each other, now that the Metz have gone. Any excuse for violence.

"Why did they kill her?" Emotion chokes my words.

He shrugs. "Dunno. Maybe they just thought it wasn't worth taking her with them. If they think at all."

He had got us both out. Pulled me from under the feet of people streaming in both directions. Rescued Lily's body from being trampled on as the crowd fought with the Metz officers. Brought us up here. The crowd fighting the Metz. *Has that ever happened before?*

"I need to go," his voice cracks slightly.

I wonder if he feels guilty for the part he played in her death. Though at least he had tried to hold her up, tried to keep her above the crowd. "Will you be okay?"

I nod. *Will anything ever be okay?*

Jonas pauses at the top of the rough concrete staircase that leads back down through the shell of the building.

"What are you going to do with her?" he asks.

There is nowhere to bury bodies out here. If you die in Area Four you either get taken to the crematorium in Three or get put in the river. The crematorium is out of the question, and I can't bear to give her to the river. To have her body swell up and decompose slowly. *No. Let her burn brightly, and let the winds take her remains.*

"She will burn on a pyre, down by the river, and I will scatter her ashes to the wind."

He doesn't reply. Doesn't make any comment on the impossibility of my suggestion, but just nods and leaves.

I'm sorry, Lily. I thought I was doing the best for you, but I wasn't. I was doing what was best for me.

I stroke the light brown curls that fall to her shoulders. The collar is still around her neck. I can't bear for her to wear it – a prisoner in death – but I can't figure out how to get it off. An

282

image of the Metz officer comes to mind, standing over her. The collar. The gun.

You will be avenged, Lily.

* * *

I collect the wood myself, scouring the banks of the river and climbing up and over huge concrete blocks to get to the places people don't normally go. Driftwood is a precious resource. Most people fight over the scraps washed onto the streets by the lapping water, but I manage to find about as much dry wood as I can carry.

It's not enough, though, and even after raiding some of the more rundown buildings, my pyre is pathetically small. But as morning stretches into afternoon and the day begins to fade, Jonas arrives with a couple of other guys from the gang, all of them carrying armfuls of wood, plus a can of fuel. I don't ask where they got it all from. I don't want to know.

Silently, they pile it up. At least, the sky has cleared. There will be no rain to temper the flames. I lay Lily out on the stone block and smooth down her clothes. I've washed the blood from her face, but there's nothing I can do to hide the hole in her forehead.

The pain in my chest has faded to a dull ache. I wonder if it'll ever go away completely. I hope not. Not if it means forgetting her.

Someone approaches and there's a clunk as another piece of wood is added to the pile, then another. Looking around in surprise, I see people – some I recognize, some I don't – walking down to the shore. They each have a contribution to make. For some, it is only a torn-off bit of board, but others donate huge armfuls of driftwood. They don't say anything, but when they've added their contribution, they stand back, forming a semi-circle around the pyre. This carries on for maybe an hour, until a huge crowd has gathered.

All to say goodbye to one small girl.

The last rays of the sun hover behind the towers that rise from the water like lonely sentinels. It is time.

Jonas comes up behind me, holding the fuel can and a piece of iron wrapped in cloth. He plunges the cloth into the fuel and holds it away, dripping.

"It's time."

I nod and step forward, slipping the small packet of white powder from my pocket and tucking it underneath her. It feels wrong, as if I'm tainting her purity with my guilt, but it's also a promise. I whisper to her, "Never again, Lily."

With you I was happy. Not the superficial happiness from tronk. The happiness that is easily given and just as easily taken away. Really happy.

I gently press my lips to hers. "Sweet dreams."

Stepping back, I take the carton from Jonas and soak the wood at the base of the pyre with the fuel. There's more wood here than I've ever seen in one place before. Someone lights the torch and hands it to me. It burns fiercely.

I plunge the iron bar into the pile of wood. It catches instantly, the flames spreading, and soon she is encased in a raging ball of fire. For a moment, I feel an irresistible urge to join her. To burn with her. But a hand on my arm pulls me back, and the feeling passes.

"Let her go," Jonas says softly.

A woman near me begins to sing, and others pick up the tune. It's a children's song; one of the few I remember my mother singing to me. I don't join in. I've never been one for singing.

But as the flames roar, sparks fly up into the darkening sky to mingle with the rising voices. It seems a fitting tribute to a small girl who, when she lived, had never meant anything to anyone.

Except me.

* * *

The fire burns for hours until eventually it's just white embers, glowing in the dark. The crowd gradually disperses until I'm left alone, a solitary figure down by the water's edge.

A slight breeze is already carrying the white flecks of cremated wood inland. The air is warm around me and I'm glad of the thick soles on my boots as I approach the concrete slab where I'd placed Lily's body. Small, charred bones sit on a bed of ash. The collar has toppled onto its side now the support of her neck has gone. It's unscathed by the flames.

"Do you need this?"

I whirl around, wondering how I could have missed the footsteps creeping up behind me, and see Jay holding a painted box. It's one of Bisham's works; the beautiful, and expensive, wooden boxes that Insiders buy as a trinket and those of us Outside aspire to own.

A surge of annoyance rushes through me. Anger that he won't even leave me in peace to grieve. Anger at the role he played in Lily's death. He looks shamefaced, not meeting my eye as he extends his hand to offer me the box.

"For her ashes," he says. Then, "I'm sorry." Though he does not say what for. For betraying me? For chucking us out? Or for Lily's death?

I don't want to take anything from him or feel like I owe him in any way, but I have nothing else to put her in and I will not have her remains blown back across the drug dens and whorehouses she hated. And she would have loved the box. I can almost see her tracing the pattern of flowers and leaves with her small finger.

I take the box from him and return to the pyre, wondering if Jonas would have been so helpful and understanding if he'd known that I was no longer the favourite of his gang leader. Using the edge of my knife blade, I carefully scrape the ashes and broken bones into the box. I suspect there's a fair bit of wood ash in there too, but I don't think she'd mind. I close the lid and stand there, awkwardly, holding the box in front of me.

"I've taken your stuff to Jonas's place," Jay says, glancing up at me. "Figured you wouldn't want to come back to the apartment."

A spark of anger takes light inside me, burning as suddenly and fiercely as the torch. "So, that's how it works, is it?" I spit, "Pass me on to your mate now you're done with me?"

I regret saying it instantly. It may be true for all I know, but now is not the time.

He looks hurt. "No, don't be stupid. He just offered you a place to stay for a few days."

I bite my lip, unsure as to Jonas's motives. The fire still burns inside me. I hug the box to my chest, wondering what to say.

Jay clears his throat. "What are you going to do?"

About what? I think. But then I realize that what he's really asking is if I'm going to make trouble for him. Or defect to one of the other gangs. Tell them where he lives, reveal the Snakes' secrets.

I shrug. "I'm not sure. Maybe I'll head up into Five. See if I can get a job or something." We both know how hollow that comment is. Who would employ me?

"Maybe you could get a job Inside?" He sounds serious, and I remember he doesn't know that the moment I presented myself to anyone on the Inside I'd be found out as an illegal. The corner of my mouth turns up.

"I don't think so," I say, "but thanks for the thought."

To my relief, he doesn't hang around. Making some excuse about "gang business", he quickly walks back up the street. I sit down a little way from the pyre to avoid being covered in the ash that blows back off it, and rest my chin on my hands. *What next?*

I've been sitting there for perhaps half an hour when a moving beam of light tells me someone's approaching. They're also making enough noise to raise the dead (so to speak), but I don't turn to see who it is until I know for sure they're heading to me.

The flashlight is focused on the uneven surface, but I recognize him by his boots.

"Trey?"

"Hey," he says, collapsing on the concrete block next to me, breathing hard.

"Turn that thing off, will you?"

The light disappears. "So, this is the rough part of Area Four?" he jokes. It's lame, but makes me smile all the same.

"One of them. How did you find me?"

"I was worried when you didn't show at the meeting point. People were talking about the Metz raid. I asked around, someone mentioned a child had been killed. It took a while, but finally someone recognized your description and sent me down here."

There's a pause before he speaks again. "I'm sorry about the girl. Was she a friend?"

"Yes." *She was a friend.*

Another pause. "People are talking about rebellion. They're saying it's not right that a child should be killed for no reason.

Why ..." He hesitates. "Why did they kill her?"

"Because she was there," I reply bitterly. "Because that's what *happens* out here, Trey. People – innocent people – get murdered by those brutes. Right under your nose, if you bothered to look beyond the Wall."

"I-I'm sorry, I—"

"You should be," I spit, fury raging inside me. "All this time, you were pretending to be my *friend*, pretending to be shocked at life Outside, and all the time you *knew*."

"What do you mean?" There's hurt in his voice. *Good.*

I take a deep breath, clenching my hands to stop them shaking. "Why didn't you tell me your father was Andrew Goldsmith?"

I feel him tense beside me. "I-I don't know. I didn't know what you'd do."

"You *lied* to me. Or, at least, you didn't tell me the truth."

"And do you always tell the whole truth?"

The comment takes me aback, and for a moment the fire inside me dims.

"Look, my father isn't the person you think he is. He's not a monster, I swear. But he also hasn't been honest with me. I knew nothing of all this." He waves his arm into the darkness behind us. "I didn't know things were so bad out here." There's a pause. "I never thought to look."

We sit in silence, both lost in our thoughts. Two ghosts sitting by the water.

"Don't you need to get back to your boyfriend?" Trey says finally.

"Not my boyfriend," I reply. "At least, not anymore."

Then I tell him everything, the words tumbling from my lips faster than I can think of them. And at some point, I start crying again, and the tears somehow soothe the anger inside me, as if

I can't be sad and mad at the same time. I'm crying for Lily. I'm crying for me. And for all the injustice in this city; for everyone who's ever suffered and loved and lost.

Trey just sits and listens, not saying anything. Tentatively, as if he's not sure whether the gesture is welcome, he hooks his arm around my shoulders and I lean into him, soaking his shirt with my tears.

Eventually, I'm all cried out. Drained and exhausted. I let my head rest against his shoulder for a moment longer. He smells like air and fresh water and the slightly sweet smell of the green trees inside. Closing my eyes, I inhale once more, then sit up.

"I'm sorry."

He shrugs. "Don't be."

An awkwardness descends, neither of us knowing what to say.

Finally, Trey breaks the silence. "The drug, what did you call it?"

"Tronk." The word is bitter on my tongue.

"Do you know its full name? The proper name for it?"

I stare at him. "How would I know? Out here it's called tronk. Or sometimes trock"

Trey screws up his face in concentration. "Co-trodprethine … No, that's not it … Co-tronpurthine, co-trockpurthine, co-tronkpretine. That's it!"

He turns to me, his face lit up in excitement.

"What are you talking about?"

"When I was reading through the files. The term 'tronk' was used once, kind of as a brand name, but mostly they used the scientific term to describe it."

"To describe *what*? You're saying there's something about tronk in those ancient films? Why?"

289

"Because they were the ones who developed it," he says quietly. "The government made it."

Shock snatches the breath from my mouth. *The government made tronk?*

"They developed it for the food. Look, it's probably best if I start at the beginning. The films I took, they only had bits and pieces of information. It took me most of the day to piece it together, along with what I already know. Or, at least, what we were taught. It started with the Great Flood – no, before that, really. When the population was out of control."

He begins to explain. The Great Flood has always just been an event to me. No one ever talks about what caused it – or talk much about it at all. Thinking about the past doesn't put food in your belly.

"So, they told people it was safe to stay in their homes when they knew they were going to die?" I say, scarcely believing what I'm hearing.

"They didn't *know* they were going to die," Trey says. "There was a fifty-fifty chance the storm surge wouldn't breach the defences, and they didn't have the resources or time to evacuate safely. If they'd told people to evacuate, there would have been panic and people would have been killed or injured."

I snort. "So they just crossed their fingers and hoped for the best?"

"Something like that. But the most interesting bit comes after that." His voice is earnest, as if he's giving me a lecture.

The most interesting bit? A million people die and that's not the interesting bit?

"The Flood decimated the population, but it still wasn't enough. It wasn't just Britannia; the population was out of control everywhere. There just wasn't enough food in the world to feed everyone. The Union kicked up a fuss about Britannia not warning them about the Flood. After that, the world turned their back on us. Our imports of food and fuel – we still relied on oil for a lot of things back then – stopped overnight. Shops ran out of food in a few days and there wasn't enough being produced to replace it, especially as a lot of our prime agricultural land was under water. That's when the dark years happened."

"The dark years?"

Trey nods. "We learned about it in school. A little, anyway. There were riots. The government were overthrown; literally torn apart by a mob. The security forces at the time could do nothing. There was no one in charge. And then a couple of the countries we'd angered decided to bomb us. The flooding had been even worse on mainland Europe. We didn't warn them and it nearly wiped out whole countries. Millions died … I guess they wanted to make completely sure we couldn't screw them over again. They focused on the food-producing factories, of course. Left us to starve.

"Anyway, at some point, some order started to develop. I'm not sure how, but a new government formed. The Metz were created, and gradually a new kind of order emerged, in London, at least. But food supply was still a major issue. So, the government passed this emergency legislation called the Population Regulation Act."

He takes a deep breath. "The Act had a couple of different provisions. The first was to stop the population expanding – that's when they introduced the law about reproduction. That a family can only be a certain size across three generations."

"You mean the altruits?" I butt in. "That's common sense, hardly controversial."

"It was then. They didn't even have euthanasia back then," he replies.

Eutha-what?

He catches the expression on my face. "Like you couldn't choose to die if you were terminally ill or in pain. The doctors had to keep you alive as long as possible. And before the Great Flood, the whole country was crippled trying to look after all the elderly people. Of course, after the Flood they all, well ..." His voice trails off.

"Anyway, that was considered a long-term solution. But they needed a short-term fix. They had to feed all these people with something, otherwise there would be more riots. The Act legalized the use of some 'alternative foods' that had been developed in labs. Engineered food. Basically a load of vitamins, minerals and other chemicals injected into a carrier that looked a bit like bread, or meat, but wasn't."

"Sounds like the government rations," I joke.

He looks at me.

"Oh. That's what the government rations are?"

"Yeah. But you kind of know that, right? That it's not proper food?"

I nod.

"One of the chemicals they put in there was an appetite suppressant. It tells you that you're full, even if you aren't. And it made you happy, so you wouldn't care that you hadn't had a proper meal. That's what they called co-tronkpretine. They dished this food out to everyone. Well, apart from those who could afford what limited *real* food was available. But most people had to depend on the rations."

"Wait a minute." My mind's whirring, trying to process what he's saying. Something's nagging at me. "Lily said tronk gives you that nice feeling, like you get from food," I say. "So you mean, they put tronk in food and got people addicted to it?"

"I think so. At least, I don't think they meant to get people addicted. It was only ever supposed to be a short-term fix, until they could figure out how to produce enough proper food to feed everyone.

"But there was a paper alongside the document that doesn't appear to have been raised in the discussion. A note from the medical advisor. It said the chemical hadn't been fully tested, that it wasn't safe to issue to the general population yet, that they needed more trials. That there could be a risk of long-term side effects on brain function."

"What do you mean?" It feels like Trey is speaking in riddles. There are so many words I haven't heard before.

"I think ... I think the drug in the food – tronk – may be part of the reason Outsiders are more ..." He searches for the word.

"Stupid?"

"Yeah. I don't know if it's still put in food today, but if people take it in a purer form ... Plus, I don't know if there's a hereditary element: if the damage is passed down to children.

"There's one more thing. The third part of the legislation. Genetic enhancements were quite rare in those days. They could rule out inherited diseases and things, but were just starting to discover how genes affect other things, such as intelligence and skill. The legislation introduced greater regulation for genetic enhancement, so you had to be on an approved list to get it. Priority was given to couples who could demonstrate they added value to society. Or that they'd commit to their genetically enhanced children being of use to society. Basically, if you were rich, healthy, and smart, your children could be genetically altered to make them even more intelligent."

"And if you weren't?"

Trey shrugs. "Do you see? That's how all this started." He waves his hand around, nearly hitting me on the head. "They may have just been looking for a way to avoid starvation, but the Act led to this separation of society. Between the people who could afford real food and to have their children genetically enhanced, and those who were forced to live off the government rations."

He stops, panting slightly from the tirade.

"If this is true ..." I say, still trying to take in everything he's said.

"Then everything us Insiders have been told about Outsiders is a lie." He frowns. "Except it can't exactly work like that. I mean, *you're* clever and you eat the government rations, right?"

I nod. *And the pure stuff.*

He waves his hand. "Maybe you're resistant to it or something."

"From what you're saying, this has been going on for decades; possibly made worse by the effects passing down generations. So people new to eating the rations wouldn't become quite as dumb, right?"

"That seems logical," he says. His eyes widen. "Do you mean, you're *not* an Outsider?"

I shrug. "I was born Outside. My mother was an Outsider. No idea about my father." I laugh. "Maybe he had such good genes it forced the stupid ones out."

"I'm not sure it works quite like that ..." Trey wrinkles his nose.

"Whatever. Anyway, I've been Inside, remember? There's no way I'm half as smart or as strong as you lot." *And that's a fact.*

"Aleesha, people have to be told about this. We've been living in the dark."

I shiver, but not with the cold.

It's all a lie. They feed us this drug, control us, terrorize us.

"It has to stop."

27

Trey

It's late and the streets are almost deserted, but it feels safer having Aleesha beside me. When I was trying to find her earlier, there had been times I'd wondered if I'd escape Area Four alive. If I hadn't been so lost, I'd have hightailed it back to Abby's. She makes me wait on a street corner while she hides the painted box somewhere safe. I huddle in the shadows, desperately trying to look inconspicuous and count the minutes before she returns.

The screens in the square just around the corner from Abby's are displaying the eleven o'clock news. A scrolling headline catches my attention. *Did I read that right?*

My heart begins to pound as I wait for the headline to come back around. *It can't be ...*

"What's up?" Aleesha asks, looking back at me.

"The news. I think ..." I swallow. "I think it said something about a government minister being murdered." My voice cracks.

Dad? Is this because of me? I should have just given myself in.

The edges of my vision begin to blur. I blink, trying to focus on the screen.

"The Secretary of State has been murdered whilst checking security arrangements in Area Three." Aleesha reads the words slightly awkwardly. She lays a hand on my arm. "S'okay, Trey, it's not your father."

The world clears, though my heart still feels like it's beating at a hundred miles an hour. I read the words that run across the bottom of the news screen for myself. Straining my ears, I can just about make out what the newsreader is saying.

"… the Secretary of State was thought to be on her way back from inspecting a detention centre in Area Three when her pod was brought down and attacked. It's not known who the assailants were, but the Metz say investigations are ongoing. The President has paid tribute to his colleague …"

I can breathe again. *It's okay. He's okay.*

"Come on." Aleesha pulls at my arm, looking around nervously. "I'll take you home."

She's still subdued, but there's a tightness to her expression that makes me think she's bottling something inside. I get the feeling she wants to get rid of me so she can go and beat someone to a pulp.

There are more Metz on the streets than normal for this time of night. We're about two streets from Abby's house when a swarthy man materializes from the shadow of a side alley to block our path. Before I've even registered there's someone there, Aleesha has her knife out and is standing, poised for attack.

The man holds up his hands. "Murdoch sent me to find you," he says quickly. "You're to follow me."

"Like hell," Aleesha replies.

A flicker of annoyance crosses his face. "Really. He said to give you this." He holds out a scrap of film. Aleesha takes it and passes it to me, her eyes never leaving the man's face.

I brush my fingers over the film and read the words that

appear. "Aleesha, if you're not here within ten minutes, I'm going to personally dump your sorry ass in front of the nearest Metz patrol. And don't even think about sticking a knife in my messenger – he's more valuable than you." I look up. "Sounds like Murdoch."

"Anyone could have written that."

The man shrugs. "Suit yourself." He seems to throw something and Aleesha yelps, her left leg buckling. She throws her knife as she's falling, but the man has already ducked forward.

"Sorry," he says, not sounding in the least apologetic. "He said you might be difficult to persuade."

Aleesha curses. "What have …?" Her eyes roll back in her head and she flops limply to the ground.

I stare at her in shock. "What …?"

"It's just a stun dart." The man hooks his arms under Aleesha's shoulders, lifting her torso. "Grab her legs, will you? It'll be easier with two of us."

"What? No!" I grab Aleesha's knife from where it's fallen to the floor and move toward him. The effect would probably be more threatening if my hand didn't shake so much. "G-get away from her."

The man rolls his eyes. "Look, Trey, we don't have time for this. There'll be a Metz patrol here in minutes – they're swarming the place looking for the people who killed that minister. I'm not going to hurt you, or her, I just need to take you to Murdoch. He can't come out right now."

I look from him to Aleesha, who's still out cold on the floor. Her chest gently rises and falls.

"She's fine, really. She'll be awake in ten minutes and I'd rather get her somewhere safe than end up fighting her here."

He does have a point. And if he wanted to hurt her, he could quite easily have knocked her over the head or something. There's a shout from up the street. *Metz*. I slide the knife into my belt and pick up her legs.

We carry her into the side alley just as the first black figure appears at the end of the road. I try and keep track of where we're going, but get lost as soon as we cross the street back into Area Four.

After about ten minutes, the man knocks on the door of a ground-floor apartment. The building is grimy and rundown – like most in Area Four – and a strong smell of mould emanates from inside. From the apartment above comes the sound of a baby crying.

Murdoch opens the door and ushers us in. He looks like he's been in a fight. One side of his face is swollen and bruised and there's a split on his chin. He's favouring his right leg, as if it pains him to stand on it. The door closes behind us.

"She didn't come willingly, then?" he says as we place Aleesha on the floor, the only chair in the room being occupied.

There's a food heater in one corner along with a couple of small cupboards; the doors hanging at jaunty angles. An open door leads to what looks to be a bedroom. The apartment is tiny. *What must it be like for a family crowded together in here?*

A slim woman with short brown hair leans against the far wall, toying with a gun holstered on her belt. She stares at us curiously. On the chair slouches a man of about twenty-five with an angular face and dark hair that hangs over his large forehead. He's very pale and his eyes flit nervously around the room.

I clear my throat. "What's going on?"

"We've had to bring forward our plans," Murdoch replies, leaning over Aleesha. "We need you tonight."

"I thought you said it would be a few days?" My heart sinks. "Where's Bryn?"

"Busy," Murdoch says shortly.

He's lying. I bet Bryn doesn't even know we're here.

Aleesha moans slightly, her eyes flickering.

"Good, she's coming round."

Suddenly, her eyes snap open and she sits up, almost headbutting Murdoch. Anger flashes in her eyes and he catches her fist just inches from his face.

"You *bastard!*"

"Calm down. If you'd have just followed Sanders, he wouldn't have had to put you under. Here." He shoves a brightly wrapped bar into her hand. "Eat this. It'll make you feel better."

Aleesha glances at the bar, then tears it open and chews it hungrily. "You have no right to bring me here like that!" She glares at him. "I'm not your ... your *pawn.*"

Murdoch ignores her and limps to the small table in the centre of the room. "We were hoping we'd have a bit more time. But we've heard rumours that the government are worried about an uprising following the riot earlier today and the assassination of one of their ministers. They're planning to pre-empt it with a Cleaning. Of the whole of Area Four."

Aleesha's eyes widen and she stops chewing.

"What's a Cleaning?" I ask, feeling stupid.

Murdoch looks at me. "Is that another thing they don't tell you about at Insider school?" he sneers.

I grit my teeth. I could say that yes, we were told about Cleanings. That they were events held to clear up the rubbish that accumulates in the slums and scrub graffiti off the walls. I could say this, but I don't, because Aleesha's reaction tells me the truth is quite different and I'm fed up of being the stupid

Insider.

"It's a slum clearance," the woman on the far side of the room says. "The Metz go through an area clearing out the population as they go. Pulling families from their homes, breaking down doors if they're not opened for them. Anyone they don't like, they collar and take away. Anyone who resists is shot dead. Then they send bots in to disinfectant the streets and burn the rubbish."

My blood runs cold. "So, how often are these clearances carried out?"

"Every now and then," Murdoch replies, "It's supposed to prevent disease spreading. But there's never been a Cleaning of an entire area."

"When?" Aleesha's voice is tight and her fists are clenched in her lap.

"Tomorrow."

"And you can stop it?"

"Yes. At least, we think so." Murdoch waves at the man in the chair. "This is Mikheil, a colleague of ours from out of town. He doesn't speak much English, but he's a whiz when it comes to the language of computers. Our job is to get him into the headquarters, let him do his thing in the information bank and get him out again.

"As long as there aren't any security barriers, Sanders, Matthews and me will accompany him. You just need to show us the way in and get us through that door." He tosses me a small black box. "KBox Model Three, as requested."

I pocket the device, relieved that I'm not going to have to actually break in to the highest security building in the city.

"If you're hacking into the information bank, I'm going in," Aleesha says, getting to her feet.

Murdoch's eyes narrow. "This isn't an opportunity for your personal vendetta. I'm not having you along if you're going to screw things up again."

She raises an eyebrow. "Well, without me, you'll have trouble getting in. I bet Trey can't remember the way back through the tunnels."

Heat rises to my cheeks as they turn to look at me. *She's right.*

"Fine, you can come. But Mikheil gets the information we need first before doing any snooping on your behalf."

"Deal."

She's back to the focused Aleesha I recognise, like she just needed some task to channel her anger and emotion into. To help her forget her boyfriend's betrayal and what happened to Lily.

"Right, let's go," Murdoch says. "Mikheil?"

The man on the chair looks up.

"Rea-dy to go?" Murdoch enunciates each syllable. The man nods.

"Wait." Everyone turns to look at me and I feel my cheeks flush. "Y-you're not going to hurt people, are you? I mean, you're not planning to murder the President or anything ..." *Or my father.*

Murdoch sighs. "No, Trey, we're not targeting your father or the President. We just want to stop the Cleaning and show them that their plans aren't working. Make them really listen for a change. Now, let's go, before there are Metz everywhere."

But the Metz are already everywhere. We make slow progress, working our way down through Area Four, sticking close to the Wall until the faint glow illuminates the towering heap of rubble. Aleesha takes us to the gap that leads down to Aldgate East station.

Once inside the tunnels, we move more quickly; even Murdoch, with his injured leg, doesn't hold us back. When I ask him if he's badly hurt, he just shakes his head, inviting no further comment. Not long after, we're crawling through the air duct into the rough tunnels that lead to the archive rooms. It's all the same, the only difference from when we were last here being the disturbance of dust on the table where I'd sat.

Murdoch shines his flashlight around the door with the exit sign. "Okay, Trey, do your thing."

It takes me about twenty minutes to trick the fingerprint sensor into opening the door. I would have been quicker, but fatigue and the watchful gaze of five pairs of eyes mean I fumble the code.

"Nice work," Sanders says when the door clicks. He pulls it open, shining his torch inside. "Staircase leading up." He steps through.

"Wai—" Aleesha cries, but her words are lost in Sanders' scream of agony that cuts off as abruptly as it starts.

For a moment, we're all frozen in shock. Murdoch is the first to move, cautiously shining his light around inside the doorway, his face lined in anguish. Then Aleesha moves to join him, pointing at something a few feet inside.

"See, if you angle the light just so ... It's a barrier. But almost invisible. I only spotted it as ..." She stares at the ground.

My legs feel weak, but morbid curiosity pushes me to my feet to look through the door. Sanders is sprawled on the floor. Or, at least, the bottom part of him is. From his chest upwards there is nothing. As if something has sliced clean through skin, muscle and bone. As Murdoch puts his light on the floor and reaches for the man's ankles, I catch a glimpse of what Aleesha meant. Just a flicker of white in the air, like a wisp of smoke. Gone so quickly that I wonder if I've imagined it.

As Murdoch pulls Sanders' body back into the room, I gasp. His body is intact. Including his head and shoulders.

"W-w-what?" I stammer.

"There's a barrier there – like the Wall – but not designed to be visible," says Aleesha, thoughtfully. "It must be showing an image of what's on the other side, to make you think there's nothing there."

Murdoch is hunched over Sanders, checking for a pulse. Beside him, Matthews is fighting back tears, her hand shaking as she grips the dead man's hand possessively.

"Was there another way in?" Murdoch asks harshly, looking up at us.

Aleesha shakes her head. "None that we found."

"He eeezzz de-ad?"

They're the first words I've heard Mikheil speak. His accent is foreign and he struggles to form the English words.

"Yes, he's dead."

Murdoch stands and looks around, as if wondering what to do next.

"Well, I guess there's only one way to test this," says Aleesha, walking forward through the doorway.

Murdoch moves to stop her, but she slips through his fingers and disappears into the dark.

"Aleesha?" I grab Murdoch's light from the floor and shine it along the corridor. It looks empty. There's no one there.

Then a disembodied hand appears, apparently coming out of thin air.

A faint gurgle escapes my lips and I step back, nearly falling over Sanders' body. An arm follows then the rest of Aleesha steps back through the barrier. She's smiling.

I hear Murdoch's sigh of relief. "You idiot," he growls.

I feel their eyes on me and swallow hard. "My turn?" My voice comes out as a squeak.

Murdoch lays a hand on my shoulder. "Only if you want to try, Trey. No one's going to blame you if not." There's a quiver in his voice that I haven't heard before.

Curiosity and fear war against each other. Hesitantly, I take a step forward. Then another. Then I close my eyes and walk forward.

One step.

Two steps.

I open my eyes. The torch is still in my hand, illuminating a narrow staircase leading up. Just what we'd seen from the doorway. I turn around to look back, but all I see is a closed door. There's no sign of Murdoch or Aleesha.

I walk back again, this time, keeping my eyes open. My vision blurs slightly then clears, and I'm back on the other side, in the archive room. Cold droplets of sweat bead on my forehead.

Murdoch turns to Mikheil, beckoning him forward.

"How do you know he can go through?" Aleesha asks.

"We don't," Murdoch says grimly. "But someone else from outside London, who'd never set foot in the city before did manage to get through the Wall unharmed."

"One person? You've tested it on one person?"

Murdoch's jaw is set. "Yes, it's a risk. But it's been explained to Mikheil. He's willing to try it."

Mikheil looks even paler in the glow of the flashlight. His face is almost expressionless, like he's wearing a mask. His long limbs move slowly toward the door. I hold my breath, waiting for the scream of pain. But he just disappears. The same way Aleesha had.

Murdoch sags against the door frame. "Thank god."

Mikheil comes back and stands next to us in the room.

"Okay, it's down to you two." Murdoch looks from me to Aleesha and back to me again. "I'm sorry, Trey, but there needs to be at least two of you in case anything comes up."

He picks up Sanders' weapon from the floor and hands it to Aleesha. "You know how to use this?"

Her eyes widen as she cautiously looks it over.

"There are three settings. Stun darts, taser and bullets. The safety catch is on. Don't use it unless you have to."

"Trey, you'll need these. This is to help get through the security doors in the main building." He hands me a small box and a combined mapping and comms wristband. "Mikheil has the access code to accompany it. The location of the room you need to get to is programmed into the unit, but there's a physical copy of the blueprints in case anything goes wrong."

He hands Aleesha a roll of films, which she shoves inside her jacket.

"The comm unit won't work here, so you'll be on your own. Just get him," he nods at Mikheil, "in and out again safely. You understand?"

"What happens if we can't get through to the room?" Aleesha asks.

"You try a different route. Figure out how to get through the security system. Kill whoever you need to kill. You *do not* come back without him. And put these on, they'll have cameras in there." He pulls a handful of black fabric hoods from his backpack and hands one to each of us.

Matthews stands and holds something out to me. *A gun?* I stare at it blankly.

"Take it, you may need it." She smiles weakly.

"But I've never used one ..."

"It's easy. Just point and shoot." She shows me the different settings and the safety catch.

It's heavier than I'm expecting; bulky and cold in my hand.

"Here." She unbuckles the holster from her waist and hands it over. "Murdoch, what are we …? We can't leave him here."

Murdoch looks torn. "Okay. We'll take him back out to the entrance to the tunnels, then come back." He looks at us. "We'll meet you back here. If for any reason we're not here, get out and make your way to the white house in Five."

He pats me on the arm and smiles. "Good luck. We're counting on you."

My stomach churns and a wave of nausea washes over me. Closing my eyes, I swallow it down. *Breathe.* When I open them again, Aleesha's staring at me.

"Ready?" she whispers.

I nod, wondering just what we're letting ourselves in for.

28

Aleesha

Once we're through the barrier, I pull out the gun and turn the setting to stun. Shining my light around the inside of the passageway, I pad gently up the first flight of stairs. Mikheil follows me, his large feet noisy on the steps.

I squint into the darkness, looking for any sign of a trap, my ears straining for any unusual noise. A scratching ahead makes me freeze. Mikheil bumps into the back of me, and for a second his sour breath heats my neck before he pulls back.

The three of us stand in silence. I aim the weapon and flick the safety catch off. Another scratching. Then a sudden movement in my torch beam. I fire. In the round beam of light, a rat keels over, a red dart protruding from its side.

A rat. I laugh inwardly. *Get a grip, Aleesha.* But my hand's shaking as I flip the safety catch back on. "Just a rat," I whisper to Mikheil, and he passes the message back to Trey. I take a couple of deep breaths and close my eyes, trying to slow my racing heart. *Stop being so jumpy.*

I push the rat to one side, rolling it over so the dart's no longer visible. Perhaps I should pull it out, but however many times I've eaten rat stew, I still can't bring myself to go near the things.

Strangely, I feel calmer now. The false alarm has settled my nerves rather than making them worse. My hand is steady, holding the weapon out in front of me as we set off again up the passageway. I focus on my breathing and the task in hand. If there's information about my mother's death anywhere, it'll be in the information bank. The emotions that raged through me earlier are gone, locked away deep inside. Avenging Lily will have to wait.

Another set of stairs, a turn and another long corridor. There are a couple of passageways on either side of the tunnel, but I keep walking until there's a tap on my shoulder. I glance back to see Trey pointing to the left. I turn obediently and the beam of light reflects off something in the tunnel ahead. I turn it off, then on again. The same flicker as before.

"Another barrier," I murmur.

I walk closer, until I'm a foot or so away, and extend my fingertips carefully toward the barrier, ready to pull back. There's a tingling sensation as they brush the surface of the barrier then plunge through.

The passageway on the other side is identical, but when I look back at the barrier in the dark I see neither it nor Mikheil and Trey. It's invisible, but at the same time opaque. Like the last one. I poke my head back through and motion for the guys to follow me.

We take a right turn and end up at what appears to be a blank wall. The plan of the building glows in the air above the band on Trey's wrist. The blue line runs through the solid wall in front of us, into the passageway on the other side and then left.

There's a tap on my arm and Mikheil points to something on the wall in front of him. It looks like a spot of grease, but as I bring the light closer, a faint shadow appears. I run my fingers over it. There's a slight indentation. A catch. I can just about grasp the tiny disc between two fingertips. When I twist it, it turns a half turn before stopping. I give it a tug, but nothing happens.

"Up." Mikheil whispers in my ear, and I follow the direction of his pointing finger. There's another grease spot higher up the wall, and Trey crouches down to discover another near the base. Each one turns out to be a tiny catch, and when all three are unlocked, with a slight pull, a whole section of the wall swings toward us.

We turn off the flashlights. A faint glow emanates from the cracks around the edge of the door. I open it a little, peering through, but the corridor's empty. To the left, a closed door blocks the way, and to the right the corridor continues for about ten metres before turning a corner.

I pull the section of wall back fully and step out, padding silently over to the closed door. There's no handle, and when I prod it experimentally, it stays firmly shut. Then I notice the small pad at eye height on the left-hand side. There's a tiny orange light, like the one on the fingerprint sensor Trey disabled. I catch his eye and point to it.

He nods and indicates the top of the door. When I look up, I see there are words inscribed above it. I mouth them out to myself, breaking them down as I'd learned to when my mother taught me to read. AUTH-OR-IZED PER-SON-NEL ONLY. And two letters at the start: IT.

Well, we knew we weren't supposed to be here. I shrug and point again to the black pad. Trey pulls out the small box Murdoch had given him and carefully opens it.

He immediately recoils, snapping the box shut. For a moment, I think he's going to spew everywhere.

"What's the matter?" I whisper, glancing around. My hand grips the gun a little tighter. They must have cameras down here. We need to get a move on.

Trey doesn't answer but turns the box toward me and opens it. An eyeball stares out at me, bobbing as Trey's shaking hand jolts the liquid underneath it. My stomach flip-flops. I take a deep breath and look back up at him. His eyes are wide through the slits in the black hood.

"W-who's is it?" he stammers.

I shrug, though I can hazard a guess. It can't be coincidence that the Secretary of State was murdered a few hours ago. And Murdoch was looking rather the worse for wear.

Trey shoves the box into my hands. "You do it." He closes his eyes and starts breathing deeply.

I hand my flashlight to Mikheil, who's staring up at the sign above the door, and reach into the box. The eyeball is slippery. I adjust my grip, trying not to think about what I'm holding.

I lift it up to the black door pad. The orange light flashes for what seems like an age. Then, finally, it turns green and there's a faint click. I drop the eyeball back in the box and push the door open with my shoulder. It makes a strange sucking sound. The air on the other side tastes different. Fresher.

We're in a short section of corridor that ends in another closed door. This one also has a sign above it. I mouth the words: SER-VER ROOM. The sign is lit up green. On the right wall, a few metres before, is another door, this one unlabelled. There's another retina scanner, a fingerprint scanner and an access keypad covered with numbers and letters. The door itself is plain and nondescript. It looks like a storage cupboard.

Trey checks the building plan and points to the door. "That one," he mouths.

I step closer. Slashes of light shine from a small angled grate in the top of the door. A faint humming noise comes from inside. It stops, then starts up again. I glance at Trey, puzzled. He shrugs and goes back to checking out the pads on the side of the door.

A slight twinkle, like a tiny piece of glass reflecting the light, catches my eye. I blink and it's gone. I scan the base of the green words, looking for it again. And there it is. A tiny camera – so small it's almost impossible to see – scanning the corridor.

Dammit. What are the chances we haven't been seen yet? I feel Trey's hand on my arm, but I shake him off and pull out the roll of wound tape I carry in my pocket. Tearing a strip off, I stand on my toes and reach up toward the camera. *Too short. Damn.*

I turn back to see Mikheil looking at me curiously, ignoring Trey's tugs on his sleeve. I beckon him over and point to the camera, then grab his hand and place the piece of tape on one finger. He looks puzzled.

I stand on my toes again, pulling him down so I can whisper in his ear. "Camera. Up there. Cover it."

His eyes brighten, but he screws up the tape and sticks it in his pocket. Then he pulls out a small tube, about a centimetre across and, pointing it in the direction of the hidden camera, presses the top of it.

He smiles at me. "Camera gone," he whispers.

Huh? Has he managed to disable the camera? Or perhaps block the signal so it doesn't see us ...

"Hey," Trey hisses at us. He's beckoning frantically and pointing at the door. Mikheil frowns and presses a finger to his lips.

"What?" I mouth, walking over to look at the security access pads he's pointing to. But I see the problem at the same moment he whispers in my ear. "There are three access pads but we only have data for two. We can't get in!"

"Can't you disable the fingerprint one?" I whisper.

He shakes his head. "This one is a newer model. And looks like it's only recently been installed."

There's a faint trail of dust on the wall under the third pad. Above the retina scanner is a notice. "Multiple authorization required for access. DO NOT try and access alone."

My mind races. We have an eye for the retina scanner and I guess the keypad should accept Mikheil's code, but we need a fingerprint from a different person to access the room.

A faint scraping sound comes from inside the room, like someone pushing back a chair. Then a cough. I freeze, straining my ears for any further sound.

There's a crackle, then a man's voice. It sounds distant. "Greg, there's something funny going on with the camera down your end. Can you check nothing's in the corridor?"

There are a couple of noises I can't make out, then footsteps. I grab Mikheil's arm and pull him back against the wall beside me. He keeps pressing the black tube in his hand, seemingly unaware of the danger we're in.

The footsteps pause for what feels like an eternity. I hold my breath until it feels as if my lungs are about to explode.

"Nothing there, mate. Of course, I can't see much of anything out of this grate."

"No worries. It's probably just a blip in the system. I'll report it to the techies tomorrow."

The man on the other side of the door yawns. "How long 'til you're coming to take over?"

"Another half hour."

"Can't come soon enough."

There's another crackle of static followed by footsteps, a large burp, then silence.

My breath comes out in a rush. *Half an hour.* Sounds like a shift changeover. I catch Trey's eye and he nods. We creep back along the corridor and into the hidden passageway, closing the panel shut behind us and turning on a flashlight.

"Urgh." I roll my head, massaging the back of my neck. "I hate waiting. What is that thing?"

Mikheil looks at me quizzically.

"Oh, never mind. It seems to work, anyway."

"What do we do now?" Trey whispers.

"Wait until this other guy comes along and they open the door, then stun them both? I can't think of another option."

He's silent for a moment. "I guess not."

"Why do they have security guards anyway? I'd have thought the Metz would be more reliable."

"Perhaps, but the government buildings are offices, even if they're high security ones. Would you really want to go to work and be surrounded by Metz all day? It would feel like being in prison." He shudders. "Besides, they're too big. These are old buildings with narrow corridors. The Metz would struggle to get down half of them."

I think of the oversized figures that tower above even Insiders. *Is it their armour that makes them that big or are they that size underneath?* "Who ... what *are* they?"

Trey glances at me in surprise. "The Metz? They're people, or, at least, mostly people." He frowns. "They must give them some growth hormones or something to make them that size, but I've never spoken to one. At least, until they started chasing me ..."

"Some people say they're bots."

314

Trey shakes his head. "That's just rumour. I think. It's actually quite an honour if your son or daughter is selected for the Metz."

"An honour?" I stare at him in disbelief.

"Sure. Who w—"

Mikheil waves frantically in front of us, pointing to the wall. *Were we making too much noise?* I strain my ears and then I hear it. Footsteps. They get louder until it sounds as if they're right outside. There's a pause, a faint bleep and the sucking sound of the door being opened.

I spring to my feet, gently pulling back the panel. The corridor is empty. The door closing slowly behind whoever's just walked through. Switching the safety catch off my weapon, I creep out and slide my foot against the door to stop it shutting.

Adrenaline surges through me, sharpening my senses. There's a voice from the other side of the door.

"Okay, Greg, you coming out?"

A snort in reply. "Too right, John. About time."

I sense Trey and Mikheil behind me. The door is open a few millimetres. Not enough to see through, but hopefully John won't notice that the door didn't close behind him. I listen impatiently.

A bleep. Two bleeps. Then the click of a lock.

"Hey—"

I push the door open, taking aim in a split second and firing at the back of a stocky man. In front of him, the opening door halts.

"What th—"

In two paces, I'm in front of the opening. I fire blindly, but the dart hits the mark as the man inside stumbles forward, then crashes to the ground, his body holding the door ajar.

I breathe out and lower the gun to my side.

Stepping over the man in the door, I grab him by his feet and start pulling him into the small room. He's short, but well-built and heavy.

"Give me a hand?" I pant.

Mikheil appears around the door, his long arms lifting the man's chest and head. Together, we manage to get him inside, then we go back for his friend.

Trey is just standing, his mouth gaping, looking at the bodies. I drag him into the room and shut the door behind us with a click.

"You shot them," he says eventually.

"With darts. They'll come around in a few hours."

"Oh." He gives a weak laugh. "I thought … Never mind."

The room we're in is small enough that it may have been a storage cupboard once. It's also really warm, even with the cooling unit buzzing in the corner.

We're surrounded by black and grey boxes that hum gently. Flashing lights flicker across them. In the far corner, there's a shiny black table with a single chair, which Mikheil's sitting in. He runs his fingers over the surface and holos flash up in the air above it, coloured words and numbers. It makes no sense to me, but he seems to know what he's doing.

He pinches his fingers and one of the displays disappears. He seems to work between the holo display and the table itself, moving data around, sometimes typing on a strange pad that's appeared on one end of the table, oblivious to anything around him.

"What's he doing?" I whisper to Trey.

"Accessing different systems in the information bank, I think. It looks as if he's changing the code, but I can't keep up – he's too quick."

A new display jumps up. This one has a name in large letters at the top. PERSONAX. Trey tenses beside me.

"What's that?"

"It's the population database," he murmurs. "Everyone's personal records. Everyone who's chipped, that is."

I look closer. It looks like a series of records. Names, dates of birth, locations, ID numbers.

Mikheil stands and stretches, pulling a chip storage device out of his pocket. He inserts it into the side of the table and types a few more commands. A progress bar appears above the table.

"What are you doing?" I ask him.

Mikheil frowns. "Moving data. From here to here." He points to the table and then to the chip.

"Why?"

"Eh?" He shrugs.

Does that mean he doesn't understand or he doesn't know?

I lean forward, pointing toward the list of names. Mikheil's hand closes on my arm.

"Back," he says sharply.

"Can you search?" I ask. I point at the records, then at me and back at the records. "Find?"

"Ah." He taps on the display and a narrow box pops up. "Type." He gestures to the keypad on the table.

It's a jumble of letters and numbers all mixed up. I hesitate, then tap my finger on the letter "M". It appears in the box. I find the letter "A". It's frustratingly slow but eventually she's up there. Maria Ramos.

Mikheil taps the box again and a list of five names appears. Only one has a date of death.

I reach out, my finger trembling, and tap on the name.

An image of my mother appears in the air. My breath catches in my throat. She looks just as I remember her. Smiling. Alive.

There's a bleep and Mikheil's attention shifts suddenly. My mother is gone, replaced by a cube of numbers and letters.

"Hey!" I reach forward, but he pushes me back, holding up a finger.

"One min."

I drum my fingers on the side of the table, until he scowls at me. *Come on.*

Another progress bar appears. I'm guessing it shows how much data's moving to the chip.

Mikheil taps the table and suddenly she's there again, smiling out at me. Beside the image are lines and lines of text. My heart sinks. I start at the top, slowly mouthing the words, cursing my slow reading.

There's a heading labelled "Family". Her parents are listed; both deceased. There's no mention of a husband. Or a daughter.

Some information on her schooling comes next, then employment history, but it's the next section that catches my eye. *Criminal record.* It's pretty bare. In fact, the only thing mentioned is a suspected connection to "LC100". *Is that a person? An organization?*

The text flashes slightly. I point to it and look at Mikheil. "Link?"

He frowns, not understanding. I jab my finger again and his expression clears. "Ah!"

He taps the link. The display disappears. Everything disappears. A red box with large bold letters flashes up. "ALERT TRIGGERED: UNAUTHORIZED ACCESS ATTEMPT."

At the same time, the room is filled with a high-pitched, wailing alarm.

29

Aleesha

Mikheil curses. I look from him to Trey's stricken eyes to the red light flashing above the door. *Dammit, I was so close ...*

"We need to get out. Now."

Trey is already halfway to the door, but Mikheil is still frantically tapping at the table. I pull on his arm. "Come *on*, Mikheil. Guards. Coming. Soon."

"Not finish." He points at the screen, his face tight with fear.

"No time." I reach past him and pull the small chip out of the table.

"No!" He launches himself at me and I stagger toward the door, his arm grasping for the chip in my hand.

"Hey, it's okay, I don't want the damn thing." I give him the chip and grab his arm, pulling him toward the now open door, but he digs his heels in. *We're wasting time!*

Trey obviously has the same thought. He steps behind Mikheil and pushes him. Off balance, Mikheil staggers forward and I manage to pull him out into the corridor. Trey slams the door behind us. Mikheil bangs his fists against it, howling like a man possessed.

I grab his head and bang it against the door. "Listen, you idiot.

If we don't get out of here this minute, all three of us will be dead and whatever data you have managed to get on that thing will be useless. We have to go *now*."

Stupid idiot is going to get us all killed.

He looks disorientated for a moment, then slowly – achingly slowly – he begins to lumber down the corridor.

The sign above the IT room has changed from green to a flashing red. *Dammit, why were you so impatient? Mikheil may have been able to find a way around the alert to access the file.*

Running ahead to the door, I bang the quick release button and throw it wide open for Trey and Mikheil to follow. The panel in the wall swings inwards on the first push.

Come on, guys. I lick my lips, my muscles tense and ready for action as I stand guard in the corridor. Trey climbs into the passageway and as Mikheil follows, I catch the sound of running footsteps.

"The door," I gasp, diving through after them.

Trey is already on it. Just in time, the panel swings shut. Footsteps thunder past us in the direction of the server room.

Trey's flashlight flickers on, illuminating the rough corridor.

"Wait!" I whisper, pulling his arm. *Did I hear something or was I just imagining it?*

He looks at me, surprised, but I press my finger to my lips. *If we hear nothing, we move on.* I count silently to ten, and this time I can see from their faces that they both hear it too: a soft padding sound on the steps below us.

Quietly, I get to my feet, but I fear we've already made too much noise. Either they know we came this way, or they're just covering all possible escape routes. *Did we miss any cameras in the passageways?*

I hesitate for a second, torn by indecision. Do we stay and

fight here, or go back out into the corridor? The last thing I want to do is run blind through the building where there are cameras tracking our every move. But if guards are coming up from below, we could end up trapped.

The padding sound stops. Trey turns off his torch, plunging us into darkness. I want to tell him that that's no good, that we're now as blind as mice, whereas the people coming for us will surely have night-vision equipment. And in a fight where one side can see and the other can't, there's only one likely outcome.

I find Mikheil in the dark and press my mouth up against his ear. "The black thing. For cameras?" I feel him nod. "Press it. Don't stop." He nods again.

Running my fingers across the wall, I find the edge of the hidden door and pull it toward me. The corridor outside is empty. I step out silently and Mikheil and Trey follow; Trey carefully pulling the panel back into place behind him. Mikheil has his hand in his pocket and I hope he's pressing that damn button for all it's worth.

We pad silently along the corridor, me in the lead, Mikheil in the middle and Trey bringing up the rear. He's got the building plan up and I'm hoping he's finding us a way out of this maze.

Each time we get to a corridor I look back at Trey, but he shakes his head. We've been going about five minutes when I hear a shout from behind us and something whistles past my head.

Mikheil barrels into me, pushing me around the corner. I push past him. "Go!"

I switch the weapon to bullets and send a volley of shots back down the corridor. If they know we're armed, they may be more cautious about approaching us.

We run, our positions reversed. Trey in the lead. Me bringing up the rear. I don't know if Trey has a plan for where we're going or just blindly taking turnings by instinct. I stop twice at corners, waiting for our pursuers. I send one down, a stun dart in her arm, but there are at least three others, maybe more. And they're gaining.

"Do you know how to get out?" I pant, catching the guys up after another failed shot. I'm out of the stun darts now, just the taser pulses left. *And the bullets.*

Trey shakes his head. "There's a staircase up ahead. If we go up two levels we'll be in the area I know – where my father works." He stops to catch his breath, then makes a sharp turn right onto a wider corridor. "I can't figure out where the passageways are when we're running. The holo keeps twisting and turning."

We barrel through another door and I spot a narrow table against the wall. I grab it and wedge it in against the door, hoping it'll buy us a few seconds. When I turn, Mikheil and Trey have disappeared, but I can hear their footsteps ahead of me.

I catch them on the staircase and we pause a floor up. Mikheil's face is bright red and he's breathing hard. From the way he's shaking, I'm not sure how much longer he can keep going.

They need more time. "You guys go up," I say, gasping for breath. "I'll lead 'em off this way." I point to the door leading to another featureless corridor.

Trey shakes his head. "We can't split up."

"We have to ... No. Choice."

I can see the fear in his eyes. And something else. Worry. Worry for me? A warm feeling spreads through my chest. It cuts through the fear. It makes me feel brave.

"I'll be fine. You have the information they need." I glance at

Mikheil. "You have to get him out of here."

"But—"

"Go!"

There's a smash as the table breaks. "Go," I say again, more softly.

He hesitates as if he's about to say something, but then turns and starts to pull Mikheil up the staircase. I switch the weapon to bullets and fire a couple of shots back down the staircase to disguise their footsteps. Then I wait for the guards to appear.

They're quicker than I thought and I barely manage to leap out the way of their shots. The bullets thud into the wall. *Bullets. They're shooting real bullets.*

Pushing the door open, I run down the corridor. Doors lead off to each side, but I don't have time to stop and test them. Besides, I don't want to get trapped in a room. *Must keep moving.* I can see the first turning ahead. It's further away than I'd thought and I try to make my legs move faster. My lungs burn and the acid in my legs begins to weigh them down.

The door bursts open behind me. I hear the shot a fraction of a second before the bullet whistles past my ear. I start to weave, deliberately making my movements jerky and unpredictable. Another bullet flies past my head. *Just a few more metres. Please, god.*

Despite my assurances to Murdoch, I'm not that used to guns. Most people Outside can't afford them for one thing. It's more of a knives-and-clubs type of place. Hand-to-hand combat rather than shoot-outs. Occasionally, a government crate will be intercepted and a rack of guns will get loosed on the street. And those times, well, they're *bad* times.

I don't slow as I reach the corner, bouncing off the wall. My heart sinks. *Another long corridor.* But more options. I dive down a turning to the right, nearly tripping over my own feet. Immediately, I know I've made a mistake. There are no lights in this corridor. The only illumination comes from behind me. For a second I think I'm at a dead end and my heart skips a beat. But in the gloom I make out that the passageway continues to the left.

Behind me, footsteps thunder past. *Perhaps they've missed me.* But there's a shout and they're back on my heels. I keep running, dim emergency lighting flickering into life. *Dammit.* If they didn't know I was down here before, they do now.

A wave of dizziness washes over me. I can't draw in air fast enough to feed my muscles. There are no side turnings off this corridor. I will my legs to put on an extra burst of speed and sprint around the corner. Right into a wall.

I spin around. There's a door on either side of me. I check them. Both locked. Both with fingerprint readers. *Damn.*

The footsteps have slowed. I think they're at the end of the corridor. It's only a matter of time before they find me. Surely, they must be able to hear my breathing? My eyes search every inch of tight space, desperately seeking a way out. There is nothing. Even the ceiling is solid – no loose panels or air ducts.

Fear seeps through the adrenaline that's been coursing through my body. I slump against the wall, my hands shaking uncontrollably. How many of them are out there? *They have to come down that corridor to get you. One at a time. There's still a chance you can take them out. If you kill them.*

The thought makes me queasy. Truth be told, I've never actually killed anyone. Stabbed people, yes. Maimed people, quite a few (mostly men). But not actually *killed* anyone. Apart from maybe that thug who'd tried to rape me; I'm not sure if he survived or not.

But these men, these women, they're just doing their job. *I'm the one who's broken in here. I'm the one in the wrong.*

I suddenly become aware of a stinging in my ear. When I reach up, my fingertips come away wet. *Guess that bullet didn't miss after all.*

Heat flushes through me and I clench my jaw. They're trying to kill, not capture. The anger I've been holding in, anger at Lily's death and the betrayal of Outsiders by the government, seeps out. I push off from the wall, stand up straight and roll my shoulders back. My hand on the gun is firm and unwavering.

If they're going to play with bullets, let's see how they like getting hurt.

There's a shout from the end of the corridor. Footsteps coming toward me. Slowly, though. They must know this is a dead end. I check the setting on my weapon. Taser. I count three more steps, then point the weapon around the corner and fire.

A scream of pain tells me that I hit my target. *One down.* How long will a taser knock him out for? Ten minutes? No longer. The weapon vibrates in my hand. I'm out of charge.

More footsteps. Before I can think about it, I flip the switch to bullets, swing the gun around and fire. My first two shots go wide, but the third hits a guard in the shoulder. I flinch at the high-pitched scream. A woman.

I pull back, a volley of bullets thudding into the wall in front of me. My heart's racing and my breathing's fast and shallow. I taste blood in my mouth and realize I've chewed through my own lip. Risking a glance around the corner, I see four dark shapes and my heart sinks. So many? How many bullets are left? I have to keep at least one back. *You can't let them take you alive.* The thought makes me sick. Am I brave enough to do it?

Or perhaps I should just step out now and take their fire.

Not while there's still hope. I turn the corner and fire. A man jerks and falls to the ground. But there are too many. I fire again and again until, suddenly, there are no more bullets.

Not even one for me.

I reach for my knife, but they're on me so fast. Two of them. They pin me to the ground, one kneeling on my chest so hard I struggle to breathe. My vision blurs. Then I feel the cold metal on my skin as the collar closes around my neck.

30

Trey

I hear the shots below us as we pound up the stairs, through some double doors and down yet another corridor. I pray to whatever god may be listening that she's quick enough and smart enough to figure out an escape route.

A side corridor comes up on our left and I pull Mikheil into it. "Need to check route," I pant, bringing up the holo of the building plan. He nods and I suspect he's as glad of the rest as me. Even in this faint light, he doesn't look well. Sweat soaks the hood covering his forehead and cheeks and his eyelids twitch. Leaning over, he puts his hands on his knees and gasps for breath.

I try and manipulate the holo to work out where we are, but my hands are shaking so much it takes three attempts. A flashing dot displays our location. We're on the second floor, in the area of offices outside the secure inner sanctum where the President's office lies. And my father's.

Biting my lip, I try and decide what to do. We can't get into the inner ring of offices – I remember from my visits here that there are scanners on the door – but from the map it looks as if we can weave a way around them to a large hallway. There may be another way down to the basement from there. Or are we better off hiding? I wish Aleesha were here. She'd know what to do.

"Come on," I whisper to Mikheil, pulling him up. His hand is cold and clammy and his eyes plead for just a few minutes more rest. But there's no time.

As I step out into the main corridor I hear a door slam. Instinctively, I pull back and something whistles through the air where I had just been standing. There's a shout from the end of the corridor. I meet Mikheil's eyes and see my fear mirrored in them.

"Run," I say. And we run. Down the corridor and around a corner. Footsteps pound behind us. I slow my pace, waiting for Mikheil to catch up. For a tall man, he moves slowly. *Come on, Mikheil.*

Looking down at the plan, my mouth goes dry. It looks like we're being driven into a dead end.

Or is it? I zoom in on a faint dotted line that seems to join one of the outer offices with one of the inner offices. There's no passageway or corridor there. *What is it?*

More shots as we dive around another corner. Mikheil's gasping and clutching at his chest. "Can't ... can't ..."

I glance back, alarmed. He's reeling like a drunk, staggering from side to side. I grab his arm and pull him along. "Come on, not far."

That dotted line had better mean something. Otherwise, we're running straight into a trap.

"One more turn. That's it," I pant. My heart's racing. Adrenaline surges through me, powering me forward. Mikheil lags behind.

They must be nearly on us now. I turn the corner. It's a dead end. But there's the door to the office as expected.

A single shot rings out, followed by a shill cry of pain. Mikheil limps around the corner, holding his leg.

He collapses onto me and I nearly fall to the floor under his weight.

"Come on." I manage to put his arm around my shoulders and pull him forward. "Quick."

We hobble along for a few steps. The door to the office is ten metres away.

I prod Mikheil in the ribs. "That door. We just need to beat them to that door, okay?"

I don't know if he understands me, but he seems to summon up some energy from somewhere and hops along, dragging his injured leg behind him. The footsteps behind us have slowed. Do they know they've got us cornered?

Mikheil's hand starts to slip from mine, our mingled sweat making it difficult to keep hold. I focus on the door, hoping it's not locked. There's no door pad – a good sign.

Three metres, then two.

I drop Mikheil's hand, still keeping an arm around his waist, and twist my body to grasp the door handle. There's a loud pitter-patter and I duck instinctively as bullets thud into the door and walls around me. Mikheil gasps and sags against me.

Pushing the door open, we half fall through into the room beyond. Mikheil falls to the floor groaning as I slam the door behind us. *Need something to block it.* A filing cabinet.

It lands with a crash in front of the door. Footsteps pound down the corridor as I pull over one of the heavy desks that are crammed into the small room. My back muscles scream in protest. Wires snap as I topple it over in front of the door. Just in time. The door reverberates as someone slams into it from the other side.

"Mikheil?"

He's lying face down on the floor, not moving. I reach down to shake him. The back of his shirt is stained, and when I raise my hand it's covered in blood. My legs crumple.

"M-Mikheil?" I roll him onto his back. Fumbling at his neck, I try to find a pulse, but all I can sense is my own heartbeat, thudding in my ears. I place my cheek to his mouth, praying for a breath of air. Nothing.

A smash at the door forces me to my feet. I stumble away, retching, but there's nothing in my stomach to come up. *Get a grip. You have to get out of here.*

A flashing dot catches my eye. *The holo.* Moving across the room, I find the section of wall indicated by the dotted line on the map and tap it experimentally. It sounds hollow, compared to the solid *thunk* of the surrounding wall. But there's no crack or hidden door that I can see.

Of course, it's probably designed to be opened from the other side. An escape route out, not a way in. If there's anything there at all.

The top of the door starts to splinter. Picking up one of the strong but lightweight desk chairs, I run at the wall. It dents the plaster. I run again, ignoring the pain where the chair edges press into my shoulders and stomach. This time, I break through.

Behind me, the guards begin to methodically smash through the top of the heavy wooden door. Again and again, I run at the wall. Finally, there's a space big enough for me to squeeze through. There's a void just large enough for a person to stand in, then another wall. I'm about to bash through it when I freeze.

The chip. I glance to the door, then down at Mikheil's body. I could just leave it – the Chain couldn't blame me for running – but then Mikheil's death would have been for nothing.

I struggle back through the hole. The plasterboard catches on something around my waist and there's a clatter. I look down at the gun. *How could I have forgotten about it?*

I pick it up, fumbling to find the safety catch and flick it off.

"Keep your hands up and turn around."

I whip my head around. My arm lifts automatically. A guard's face, framed by the triangular slash in the door. There's a shot and for a split second a look of surprise crosses his face. Then he falls back. My gaze comes to rest on the gun in my outstretched hand.

Oh god, no.

I stumble forward, then back again, unable to think. *I shot him.*

More shots, not from me this time. I fall to the floor, crawling over to where Mikheil lies. *The chip.*

I claw at his pockets, my hands slick with sweat and blood. I'm about to give up when my fingers close over a small object. Shaking, I raise the gun and fire at the door, pressing the trigger again and again. I run, knowing I don't have time to smash the other side of wall down and just hoping that my intuition is right.

I throw my full weight against the blank, dark wall in front of me. It gives way, sending me tumbling into the room beyond. My head collides with something that makes it spin. A desk.

A bullet whistles overhead. I fire back, blindly. Shoving the chip deep into my pocket, I head for the door. Glancing back, I freeze.

Footprints follow me across the floor. My footprints. I see the glint of blood on my boots. With shaking hands, I quickly unlace them, creep out of the room in my socks and start running up the corridor.

Light spills from an open doorway ahead. I hesitate for a second, but there's no time to turn back. As I draw level, I realize it's my father's office. He's sitting inside, typing on his computer, a deep frown creasing his forehead. Relief floods through me.

"Dad!"

He looks up as I run in, shock and fear registering on his face. "What the ..." He reaches under his desk and I wave my hands frantically to stop him.

"Please, help me." My words come out in sobs and I'm shaking uncontrollably. I pull the hood from my head.

"Darwin?!" His voice is incredulous. "What the hell are you doing here?"

"They're chasing me."

"Are you hurt?" He gets to his feet, moving around the desk toward me.

Both our heads jerk up at the sound of shouts from the corridor.

"Quick, get under the desk."

I duck under, trying not to touch anything. My father opens the door.

"What the hell's going on?" I hear him ask someone angrily.

"Has anyone come past here?" A female guard.

"No," my father replies. "I heard a bang from down the corridor and was about to call down to security."

There's a pause. "Okay, sir, sorry to have disturbed you. I'd advise closing and locking your door. We've had a break in and are still trying to locate the final criminal."

"Of course. Make sure you get security to call up to me when it's safe. The President?" He leaves the sentence hanging.

"He's fine, sir. Three people broke into IT, but we've captured one and another is dead. We're closing in on the third one. It shouldn't be long."

My father thanks her. The door closes and the lock clicks shut.

One captured and one dead. My heart sinks. *She didn't make it out.*

"Darwin?" My father peers under the desk.

I crawl out and stand in front of him. Relief mingles with shame as I stare at the floor, waiting for questions. For punishment.

"Here, drink this." Dad pushes a glass of water into my hand. I gulp it greedily, suddenly feeling more alert.

"It's a stimulant I use sometimes when working late. Now, what on earth are you doing here? Are you sure you aren't hurt?" His eyes flick over me, looking for the source of the blood.

I shake my head. "I-it's not my blood, it's his. The guy they shot."

Cold hits me, right in the core of my body, and the room seems to shift around me.

"Darwin?" My father's voice comes from far away.

Mikheil's dead. And I shot someone. Killed a man.

"Darwin!"

I look down at my hands. *Will the blood ever come off?*

"Darwin!"

My head whips to the side. There's a slap and my cheek tingles.

"Huh?" I start out of my daze and stare at my father who's standing with his hand raised, a look of fear and concern on his face.

His hand begins to shake, and he lowers it. "I-I'm sorry. I thought you were going to pass out for a minute." He looks guilty. "We need to get you out of here. Has anyone seen your face? Have you had the hood on the whole time?"

My cheek is hot to touch. "No, I mean, yes, I've had the hood on."

"Thank goodness, that's something, at least. Now, tell me, what are you doing here?"

I spill out my story, once started, unable to halt the flow of words. The Chain, our mission. The alarm going off. Running from the guards.

My father just listens in silence, a focused expression on his face.

"When I get my hands on Bryn …" he growls. "What were they thinking, putting you in this situation!"

"But were they right?"

He grips my shoulders, looking me directly in the eye.

"What the Chain have told you … it's not what you think." He sighs. "We're not monsters, Darwin. We're trying to do our best. There's just … there's just a lot you don't understand."

"But the Metz. They shot dead a little girl. And I've seen *Outside* now, Dad. I've seen how bad it is. You never told me—"

He holds up a hand and glances nervously toward the door before lowering his voice. "Look, we don't have time for this now. If they find you here, not even I will be able to save you." His voice shakes and his hands tremble. "W-we've got a lot to talk about, but I need to make sure you're safe first.

"The cameras are out in this section of the building; they haven't got around to fixing them yet. I can get you to the kitchens and find you a cleaner's uniform. You can clean up there and hide until morning when you've got a better chance of escaping. Or perhaps there might be a way out from that part of the building to the basement."

A way out. I take a deep breath. One thing at a time. *Just focus on getting out.*

"But what about A—" I stop myself. "My friend?" I ask.

"He'll have to fend for himself," my father replies grimly. "I can see how the Chain used you, and I know it's my fault you ended up in this situation, but I'm not risking your life and mine to help any member of that gang."

"She's not part of the gang. They're using her just like me." There's a flicker of surprise on his face. I take a deep breath and straighten my spine. "I'm not going anywhere without her."

He reaches out to grip my arm, then removes his hand when he sees the blood on it. "Don't be stupid, Darwin, there's no way I can get her released. I know you always look to me for the answer, but there's nothing I can do this time." His face is twisted with worry.

"You could find out where she's being held, at least? Please, Dad?" I stare at him and finally, he nods.

"But you have to understand, there's no way we can get her out."

He strides to his desk and presses the comm.

"Goldsmith here. Is it safe to come out yet? What, you still haven't caught him …? What about the others …? Captured? I hope you've got the Metz coming to take her away … He said what? But we're not a prison! … Fine, okay. Let me know when you get the other one. I'd like to get out at some point tonight … Ah, fine. Thanks."

He looks up. "They're taking her to one of the store cupboards down by the kitchen as we speak. Apparently, the President told them to keep her here tonight. He wants to question her again tomorrow before handing her over to the Metz."

"Are there cameras down there?"

"I'd imagine so. There are cameras everywhere in this place."

"Okay." *We're just going to have to make a run for it.*

"Darwin, is that a *gun* you're carrying?" My father appears to see it for the first time.

"Uh, yeah." I'd kind of forgotten I was carrying it. I put the safety on and stick it back in the holster.

My father gives me a strange look that I can't quite read. "Come on, let's get you out of here." He moves toward the office door.

"Wait!" I look down at my feet. "Do you have any shoes?"

He opens a cupboard that he seems to be using as a wardrobe and throws me a pair of black shoes. I put them on hurriedly, thankful that we're the same shoe size.

We walk out of the office and around the corner. Father pushes open the door to a small kitchenette. There's a dumb waiter at one end.

"This goes all the way down to the kitchens. They use it to bring food up. You should be able to just about squeeze in. If you're lucky, there won't be anyone close enough to hear it. There's a door to the outside from the kitchens, but it'll be alarmed and you won't make it out past the barriers. Your best bet is to either try and get down to the basements or steal a uniform and find somewhere to hide until morning."

"And the store cupboard?"

He sighs. "I think it's on the corridor leading away from the kitchen. But Darwin, don't do anything stupid, okay?" His face looks anguished. "I-I can't lose you again."

A pang of guilt hits me in the stomach. He's risked everything for me. A child who's not even his own.

"Dad. I … I know. Bryn told me."

A frown creases his forehead, then comprehension dawns. He shakes his head. "That doesn't mean anything, Darwin. You're my son, whatever your genes."

"I know. That's just what I wanted to say. In case, well, in case something happens."

He grasps my face between his hands and kisses me on the forehead, something he hasn't done since I was a small child.

"I love you, Son," he says gruffly. "And I've managed to persuade the President to grant you a pardon, with some conditions. I've been trying to get hold of Bryn. I thought … Well, never mind. But if you're found here, I won't be able to save you. So, make sure you get yourself out of this building, alright?"

I nod, tears welling in my eyes.

"If you make it out, meet your mother and me at Bunhill Fields at eleven in the morning. We'll sort everything out then. Now go."

He helps me climb inside the metal box and pulls down the grate. "Be safe," he says.

"Dad?"

"Yes?"

"I love you, too."

He smiles. "I know."

He presses a button and the dumb waiter begins to rattle down into the dark.

I pull the black hood back over my head and try to figure out some way of getting Aleesha out of the cupboard. I may have let Mikheil down, but I'm not leaving Aleesha behind.

31

Aleesha

"Where are the others?"

I wince as the guard pulls my head up by the hair before slamming it into the floor. Black spots dance in front of my eyes. I can't breathe.

"Where are the others?"

"No others," I wheeze. "Just. Me."

My arms are pulled together roughly and I feel metal cuffs clip securely around them.

"Get off her. She can't breathe with you sitting on her." The voice is gruff. Another man.

The pressure on my chest eases, but it's not much of a reprieve. The hood is ripped off my head. A dark figure looms over me.

"What did you say?" He shakes me roughly.

The other man – the one with the gruff voice – is on his radio. "No, just the one. A girl ..."

"Where are they?" A slap around the face sends me reeling. My nose is dripping and my mouth tastes of iron. A painful lump forms in my throat. The collar is cold on my neck and forces my chin up. *The collar. This is it then.*

"There's no one else, just me."

"Do you think we're stupid? There were three of you on the

cameras."

"You must have been wrong." I spit blood into his face, earning myself another slap.

My captor frowns. "I think this collar's defunct."

The guy on the radio looks over and shrugs. "Well, try a different one. We're to take her to the President's office."

My captor is surprised. "What's he still doing here?"

"Stop asking questions we don't need the answer to. Now get her up."

They march me back down the corridor. The woman I shot in the shoulder is bent over a blood-covered figure, trying to open a dressing with her uninjured arm. I can see from the dark stains across the man's chest that it's no use. *I killed him.* I stumble as my legs forget how to move and fall to my knees.

Strangely, the pain doesn't register. I'm pulled roughly to my feet again and dragged down the corridor. *I killed him. He's dead because of me.*

We go down corridors, up a set of stairs, then more corridors. I stare at my feet, focusing on moving one in front of the other. Not because I want to get to where we're going any faster, but because I know that if I don't focus on this one little thing, I will fall apart.

I'm dimly aware of us entering a brightly lit section of corridor. The light makes me blink. Then there's a door and space opens up around us.

"Is this her?" a new voice asks. This one doesn't sound like a guard. His voice is smooth and polished, an Insider for sure.

"Yes, sir."

"Has she been searched?"

"N-no, sir, we were told to bring her straight here." Gruff-voice loses his composure for a second.

"Well, do it."

Hands start to pat me down. They roughly unzip my jacket. The roll of film blueprints fall to the floor and the man with the posh voice orders the guards to hand them to him. I sway on my feet, nausea rising in my throat. There's a voice in my head trying to be heard, but it's like the rest of my mind is made of soup. It's so thick the voice can't get through. There's only one thought going around my head. *I killed a man.*

They killed Lily. The voice finally makes itself heard. I feel the hands on my back, then running over my chest. Nothing hidden there, boys.

Not him. He didn't kill her.

But they did. The government. They're all the same people.

The hands run down my legs. I count off the knives as they find them. They miss the stiletto – the finest of blades hidden in the seam of my trouser leg. My last resort.

Get a grip. You need to think. The voice is getting stronger as the fog in my head clears. The room comes into focus. It looks like an office or reception room. There's a large desk at one end and a set of comfy looking chairs on the opposite side.

Gruff-voice makes me sit on one of the chairs while they take off my boots. My socks are stained and slick with sweat. For some reason, this makes me slightly embarrassed. The guy with the posh voice stands to one side, averting his eyes. He's dressed in a blue suit and tie. The suit is government regulation. The tie is not.

"What's this?"

There's a tug on my ankle. The amulet.

"J-just a trinket," I stammer. "It's worthless."

The guard glances over at the man in the government suit. He frowns then nods slightly.

The guards push my boots back on and lace them up. The sock's rucked up inside my left boot. *That'll lead to blisters.* Not that I'm likely to be running anywhere soon.

I flex my wrists, but there's no give in the cuffs. They're tight; my hands are already puffing up slightly. I can see no joint or hinge. Like the collars, there is no weak point.

I get pulled up onto my feet again.

"She's ready," the guard says to the suited man. He nods and opens a door. He speaks to someone inside, then pushes the door fully open and motions for us to go in.

The room we walk into is huge, with a richly patterned carpet so thick my feet spring off it. The walls are wood-panelled in the lower part, painted cream above. At one end of the room is a large, polished oval table surrounded by high-backed red chairs. At the other end are sofas set around a low table, and in the middle of the room is a large, imposing desk. Four families could easily live in this space, and would, if this was Outside.

A movement in the corner of the room catches my eye. A large, dark figure disappears through a doorway, too quick for me to catch any details. The door closes, but not completely.

A short man, dressed in a plain shirt and trousers turns and beckons us over. I'm expecting it, but the sight of him still turns my breath sour and sends my heart racing. *The President.*

I stumble as I'm pushed forward, my legs momentarily forgetting how to work. I keep my gaze on the floor, too afraid to look up into the eyes of this evil man.

As we get closer, a familiar smell hits me. It's faint, and almost lost to the other smells in the room: upholstery, fresh flowers, wooden furniture. I close my eyes and try and capture it again, but it's gone. I'm sure it was there, though. And I've only ever smelled it once before.

Samson.

But that doesn't make sense. *What would he be doing here?* I must be mistaken.

A hand on my shoulder halts me.

I look up. The President is not a tall man, perhaps a foot or so taller than me, and slightly built for an Insider. He's staring at me, his expression blank, but his eyes … His eyes are curious; sad and angry at the same time. And there's something else there, something I can't quite place.

"So, you're the girl who's been causing all this trouble," he says finally. "What's your name?"

"Yasmin," I lie.

The corner of his mouth twitches. I try to meet his gaze, but can't. There's a long silence.

"You're, umm, working late," I say finally.

"Well, when one of your top ministers gets murdered, some overtime is often required. I seem to be sleeping here more than in my own bed at the moment." He sighs. "Perils of the job. So, *Yasmin*, are you going to tell me where your friends are and what you were doing breaking into my building?"

"It was just me. There's no one else."

"Sir, we think the collar she has on is defunct," the gruff-voiced guard interrupts. "We were going to fetch another one but were told to come straight here."

The President laughs softly. "I suspect it's not the collar that's the problem, gentleman."

I search his face, looking for the cruelty in his eyes. This man who is the ultimate cause of everything that's wrong in our society, or, at least, the one with the power to change it. But all I see is a man who's old before his time. Tired skin losing the battling with the anti-aging treatments I'm sure he's had.

The corners of his mouth droop; the false bright smile I'm familiar with from seeing him on the big screens is absent. His dark hair, usually slicked back, is thin in places, as if he's given up on the regeneration treatments and is letting nature take its course in a rather unsympathetic way.

"You don't have a chip, do you." It's a statement, not a question.

I look him straight in the eye. "I don't know what you mean."

He chuckles softly. "You're so good at lying. *Aleesha.*"

My heart stops.

"That's it, isn't it? Aleesha. Your little friend shouted for you, just before, well ..."

Time slows. Fire inside. Every muscle tenses. An inhuman scream. *Is that me?*

I tear away from the man holding me, suddenly stronger, more powerful than I've ever felt.

"You murderer!"

My hands – still cuffed – reach for his throat.

He doesn't even flinch. Just as my nails tear at his skin, I'm pulled back and thrown to the floor. Rage clouds my vision. I kick out, thrash around wildly.

My head is slammed to the floor. One slap. Then another. A trickle of blood stains the light carpet. I lie, panting.

"She wasn't chipped, you know." His tone is conversational, as if he were discussing the weather, not the death of an innocent girl. "Which makes her an illegal citizen, even if the punishment was a little ... harsh. The officer concerned has been spoken to. They caught you, you know, on their cameras. You came up as a match for the bread thief. But they were too busy trying to control the crowd at that point to take you in.

"I saw what records you were trying to access. You're more interesting than I thought."

Interesting? What's that supposed to mean?

"Who was she, the young girl? Not a sister, surely. She looked nothing like you."

I don't reply. Just stare at his shoes. Brown. Patterned. Expensive.

He sighs. "Get her up."

I'm dragged to my feet again. He places a finger under my chin, forcing me to meet his gaze. His eyes are hard.

"Every entrance to this place has a security screen, even the old forgotten passageways down to the basements. I got the security team to check. They're all working fine. The fact that you managed to get through them means it's impossible that you're chipped. And that—"

He checks himself suddenly and leans toward me, our faces just inches apart. "It's interesting, isn't it? I always knew there may be a chance someone would be able to get through our barriers, but to have three of you find each other and break in together? Well, that sounds like a plot against the government to me. And you know what the penalty for treason is?"

I nod, not trusting myself to speak. *Death. A long, slow, drawn-out death. And he knows about the others.* I just have to hope I've bought them enough time to find a way out.

He steps back, folding his arms. "I lost one of my best ministers today, Aleesha. Do you know who killed her?"

I'm surprised at the sudden change in subject, but I keep my face blank as I shake my head.

"We do," he replies, "or, at least, we know why. When our system notified us that she – a dead woman – was trying to access our most secure area, well, the reason for her death became clear."

I stay silent. *The eyeball. They should have thought they'd be*

344

tracking access to the information bank. I wonder what else the President knows about the organization. About me. *If the figure who'd slipped from the room had been Samson, then ...* I shake my head. It's impossible.

The President sighs and turns, walking toward the soft chairs in the corner of the room. He motions for me to follow and, after a prod from behind, I obey. I try and perch on the edge of the chair, but it's so squishy it envelops me and I lose my balance, falling back into it. It really is comfortable; more comfortable than any bed I've slept in. Too comfortable. I think I preferred it when we were standing up.

He takes a seat opposite me. "Whenever there's a government in power, there are others who try and take over. Who feel that they can rule better. History shows us that this is rarely the case and all that happens is that a lot of people get killed and the situation stays broadly the same.

"I'm not saying our society is perfect – far from it. There is far more poverty than I'd like. But we – the government, that is – are doing our best to sort out these problems. And quite frankly, having to deal with attempted coups distracts us from tackling the *real* problems in this city."

He sounds sincere, but he's a politician; they're programmed to *sound* sincere. The anger in me bubbles over and I can't stop myself rising to his bait.

"Doing your best? Have you actually been Outside? Seen how people live?"

"I have, actually," he replies calmly, "and I have people dedicated to working out a long-term solution—"

"And what's your solution? You think if you just kill all the poor people, or take them away to your Farms, that you'll suddenly end up with a perfect society? Your *answer* to the problem is the death and destruction of people whose only crime is to have been born in the wrong place."

I bite my lip, angry at myself for the outburst. For losing control.

He looks at me for a few seconds then sighs. "Ah, the naivety of youth. You're just like your mother. So passionate."

It takes my brain a few seconds to register his words. My breath catches in my throat.

"What did you say?" I whisper.

The corner of his lips twists in an odd smile. "I said, you're just like your mother." He searches my face and nods in satisfaction. "I didn't know she had a daughter. Until now. But why else would someone be accessing her personal files? And you look so much like her." His voice drops and his face suddenly twists in a spasm of pain. "Her eyes."

Just as swiftly, he recovers his composure.

My mind's a jumble of thought and emotions. Closing my eyes, I take a deep breath, trying to make sense of this revelation.

"You knew her?"

He nods. "Many years ago. We were at school together."

"You were at school … Wait, my mother was an *Insider*?"

"She *was*. Until she was exiled. Her life could have been completely different if she'd made better choices." A trace of anger enters his voice.

"Why was she exiled?"

"She broke the law."

Breath hisses between my teeth. "You ordered her death."

"No!" He takes a deep breath. "I was only a junior minister then, and it wasn't even my department. Besides, I never wanted to see her killed. It-it was her own fault with the company she kept."

"My father …"

President jumps in, his voice suddenly urgent. "Have you heard from him?"

"What? Who? My father?" I shake my head, confused. "No, I don't even know—" I slam my mouth shut. *Shut up, Aleesha.*

The President laughs. A sudden, harsh laugh. "You don't know who he is, do you? Is that why you were looking at her records?"

What do I say? He knows! But how to get him to tell me.

Curiosity overcomes my caution. "I-I don't know for sure. I mean, he was never around … Do you know who he is?"

He scrutinizes me for a moment. Then he leans forward, steepling his fingers in front of his chin.

"Not for certain. But I have a strong suspicion. And I would be *very* interested to know where he is and what he calls himself now."

Disappointment floods through me.

"As you are not a registered citizen we have no records of your parentage or your DNA. You may not even be your mother's daughter, although the resemblance is uncanny. Your father, or at least the man who may be your father … He … he tricked your mother into loving him. He promised her the world! But he ran from this city a wanted criminal. Make no mistake, she died because of *him.*"

He spits the final words, a string of saliva forming at the edge of his mouth. The knuckles of his fingers, still clasped together, whiten.

"So, who is he?" I ask in the silence that follows.

My words seem to jolt the President from his memories. His face regains its usual blank composure. He even smiles slightly as his voice takes on a lighter tone.

"Believe me, Aleesha, you're better off not knowing. But if you're determined to know, I'll tell you. On one condition."

"What is it?"

"I'm willing to make you an offer. The organization you're working for are proving to be ... troublesome. They do not have the best interests of this city's citizens at heart."

"Insiders, you mean." I can't help but butt in.

"*All* citizens," he emphasizes. "Think what would happen if the Wall were to disappear this minute." He clicks his fingers. "Poof! How long would it be before the whole city was overrun by people out for what they could get. Carnage. Chaos."

"But the Metz would stop ..." My breath catches as the realization hits. *This is what the Chain were planning all along. What all their talk of a more equal society was about. They're planning to take down the Wall.*

He gives me a meaningful look and sighs. "Exactly. Carnage. Anyway, back to my point. I would like you to help us take down the Chain, help us find your companions who are currently running riot in my headquarters and assist us in finding and bringing your father to justice."

I swallow. "And in return?"

"I will make you a legal citizen. And tell you everything I know about your father."

I stare at him. *A legal citizen? He'll make me a legal citizen? I could get a job, be able to buy real food, not steal it. Perhaps even get out of Area Four. Maybe – if I can bargain hard enough – get a room Inside. And to find out about my father ...*

"What's the catch?"

He smiles and opens his hands, palms upwards. "There isn't one. Your companions will be caught eventually. The Chain, well, they got you into this mess, didn't they? As for your father, well, you don't owe him anything. But if we can find him and bring him here, you can ask him all the questions you want."

I bring my knees up to my chest, hugging them and resting my feet on the edge of the chair. There's a cough and movement from behind, but it stops at a look from the President. *Everything. He's offering me everything.*

But if you agree, you'll be one of them. And they killed Lily.

Then something dawns on me. "I'll be chipped?"

He looks surprised. "Of course. That's the only way you can access food, health care – all the benefits of being a legal citizen."

I bite my lip. *They'll be able to follow me, wherever I go. My every movement. But that's what everyone puts up with, right?*

Indecision rages inside me. If I agree, I'll be betraying Trey and Mikheil. *And Lily. And everyone else in Area Four if the Chain can't get the data they need to stop the Cleaning.*

"And if I don't agree? What then?"

"You know the punishment for traitors," he says quietly.

An impossible choice. Life. Or death. Knowing. Or not knowing. Betrayal. Or sacrifice.

I clench my fists. *He's not even offering me freedom. He's just using me. I'm just a pawn in his big game. And I'm done with being used.*

I stand and glare down at him. "No."

Shock flickers across his face. "No?"

"I don't accept your offer."

"You understand what this means?"

I nod. "Yes." *I die.*

We sit in silence for a moment.

Finally, he sighs.

"Take her away. Don't report it to the Metz yet. I want you to keep her here overnight."

"But, sir. We don't have any containment facilities ..." the guard says nervously.

"I'm sure you can find a locked cupboard somewhere." He waves his hand and yawns. "I'll decide in the morning what to do with her, once I've had some sleep. Make sure you keep a close watch on her, even when she goes to the bathroom. You can take off that collar, it's no use on her. Oh, and give her something to eat. She looks half starved."

I'm pulled to my feet and pushed toward the door. I stumble forward, too exhausted and emotional to fight anymore.

"Aleesha?"

I glance over my shoulder.

"I would advise you to learn from your mother's mistakes. Think on what I said. It's a good deal."

The guards drag me from the room and back into the endless maze of corridors. *My mother's mistakes.* It seems I didn't really know my mother at all. But was he telling the truth? Or was it all a lie? Just another trick to get me to switch sides.

32

Trey

I climb carefully into the kitchen. Artificial light streams through the high windows that line the top of one wall, but apart from that, it's dark.

The kitchen is actually a series of rooms: one with food heaters across one wall, another looks to be a preparation area, and a third contains numerous fridge units.

I try and make sense of the floor plan. To my right, a large door leads into a corridor. It seems to be the only way in and out on this level, apart from a set of double doors that lead outside. There are two other doors in this room, but they just lead to store cupboards. A door in the next room catches my attention. Steps lead down from it. *To the basement?*

I pad across the polished floor. It's a plain, unassuming door. No lock or security pad on it. I open it, step through and shut it behind me.

It's pitch black inside and I fumble for my flashlight. Steps lead down into a rough room that's piled high with food crates. The line on the building plan goes down through it and into the tunnels underneath the building. I've found our way out.

Back in the kitchen, I creep over to the main door. I'm about to open it when I hear muffled voices and footsteps. I freeze.

Are they coming here? The door is opaque with no window or viewing panel to look through. No handle either – it must be one of those that swings open from either side. My heart pounds and sweat beads on my forehead. *Stay or run?*

The footsteps stop. I press my ear to the door, trying to pick up something from the conversation. Two voices, both male.

"This one? It's just a store cupboard."

The other voice says something I don't catch.

"What does he think we are, prison officers?" A snort of derision.

"Oww!"

Aleesha!

"Ah, she's still awake, at least."

I push the edge of the door. It opens silently. I freeze as the voices start up again, but they're just moaning about something. Another inch and I'll be able to see around it.

"In you go."

There's the sound of footsteps and a thump as something – someone – hits the floor. A door slams shut.

In my slit of vision, two guards stand in a dimly lit corridor, in front of a door.

"Here's the new code in case you need it."

"Cook's going to be mad that we've changed it," the other one warns.

"Tough. We'll brief the next shift to tell him. Anyway, you'd better go and heat her a burger. He wanted her fed."

"Why me?" the other guard grumbles.

"Because I've gotta look through all the bloody camera feeds from the last two hours. And with John still recovering from that stun dart, we're short-handed. Boss is on her way in and she sounds mad." He shoves a small box into the other man's hands. "Go on, kitchen's just down there. They'll be a food heater in there somewhere."

He kicks at a metal grate at the bottom of the door. It falls off into the corridor. "You can put the food through that so you don't need to open the door."

Slowly, I let the door fall back into its neutral position. Then I turn and, not knowing where else to hide, run for the dumb waiter. I climb in and manage to slide the grate shut just in time. As the door swings open, I shrink back into the shadows.

Through the grate I see the guard walk in and throw the box down onto the nearest work surface. It's a Steakhaus burger. Fake, factory-produced meat, but tasty all the same.

"Just go along to the kitchen. Give the girl a burger," he mimics. "Don't know why *he's* the one who has to review the feeds. If he'd been watching properly, we wouldn't be in this mess."

He finds a heater and yanks open the door, shoves the burger box inside and punches a button. The heater lights up and starts to hum. The guard stretches and begins to stroll around the room.

I hold my breath, wondering if he can hear my heart pounding. If I could only knock him out. But he's bigger than me and I've always been terrible at wrestling.

The gun. Of course. How could I forget. *Stupid.*

I feel for the holster. Silently, I pull the gun out. It's too dark to see what setting it's on. I can't remember what I was firing back at the guards when I was being chased, it was all too quick.

Finding the safety catch, I flip it off, the guard's footsteps disguising the slight noise. He comes closer. *What if I miss?*

My hands tremble as I lift the weapon, waiting until he crosses my path. The food heater pings. The guard stops right in front of me. At least, he's too big to miss. I fling up the grate and fire.

There's no sound from the gun, just a thump as the guard hits the floor.

Paralysis seizes me for an instant, but then it's gone. The guard lies face down, a tiny red dart impaled in his back. Searching his pockets, I find a thin piece of film with a code written on it in an unpractised hand.

Stripping him is hard work. He's a big man and I'm sweating from the effort by the time I've removed his trousers, shirt and jacket. They're far too big on me, but I tie the belt as tight as I can and it stops the trousers falling around my ankles. I wonder about the lack of armour, but then I remember that these are the camera guys, not the armed guards who were chasing us. He does have a lightweight protective cap on, though, and I pull this over my head, hoping it'll hide the black hood from the cameras.

I hesitate, wondering whether to try and drag his body into the lift. But I'm not sure I can actually move him and there isn't much time. Grabbing the burger box from the heater, I head to the door, take a deep breath, and push it open.

I stride down the corridor, hoping I look more confident than I feel. At the door to the cupboard I pause, listening for a second. There's a small shuffle from inside. A keypad covered in numbers and letters seems to be the only lock.

Bending, I push aside the broken grate and slide the burger box into the room. *The moment of truth.*

"Aleesha?" I whisper. My mouth feels dry.

"Trey? Is that you?" She sounds surprised – and jubilant.

"Are you okay? Can you run?"

"Y-yes, but what—"

"Shhh! I don't know if they're listening."

Standing, I quickly type in the code from the film, praying

I've got the right one. I wonder if I've already been spotted on the cameras. That they've realized I'm not the real guard. If they're already on their way down.

The door clicks open.

Aleesha stands in the doorway. Her hair is messed up and her face cut and swollen with bruises.

I grab her hand. "Come on, let's go."

We run down the corridor and through the double doors into the kitchen, all pretence at stealth gone. My hand slips on the handle to the basement door, but it opens on the second try and we race through.

"Stop!" I gasp, fumbling for my flashlight.

I switch it on and we run down the stairs in the cellar room. The light flies over the rough stone walls. Just stone. No door.

"Trey, there's no way out!"

Shaking, I bring up the building plan. *It was on here, I could swear, there was something.* My fingers twitch causing the holo to jump around. "Dammit." I take a deep breath and manage to bring the holo back to the room we're in.

There is a line on the plan. I zoom in closer. But it goes through the floor of the room, not the walls.

"It must be a trapdoor." I look around at the piles of stacked crates and move a couple of paces to my right. "Under these."

Aleesha curses and reaches for the first one. We pull them down. There's a noise in the kitchen above. *The guard waking? Or have we been found out?*

We lift the last crate. Under it is an old wooden trapdoor. It lifts on the first try. I could cry with relief.

Inside is another, rougher staircase. Aleesha goes first and I close the trapdoor behind us. At the bottom is another basement room, but this one leads out into a corridor. In another few turns, we're back in a place I recognize.

"The archive room is just up there."

Aleesha nods and starts running in the opposite direction. A few minutes later, we're at the ventilation tunnel through to Charing Cross station. As I replace the grating on the other side, relief floods through me. Finally, we're safe. I never thought these horrible, dark tunnels would feel so welcoming.

"Want some?" Aleesha lifts the brightly coloured box with a grin.

"You took the burger?"

"Sure, I'm starving." She opens it and takes a bite. "This is good," she says, her words muffled by the food

I can't help but smile. A race from certain death, and all she thinks about is food.

My stomach growls. Maybe she has a point. "Sure."

We walk back through the tunnels, updating each other on what happened after we separated on the stairs. When it gets to Mikheil's death, my voice breaks.

"I-it's my fault." Emotion chokes my words. "I should have used the gun – shot them."

Aleesha reaches out and squeezes my hand. "It's not your fault. They shouldn't have sent you in anyway. I mean, you've never even used a gun before, right?"

I shake my head and wipe my eyes with the back of my hand.

"You did your best." Her voice sounds uncertain, but she gives my hand another squeeze and this time, doesn't release it. "Thanks for coming to get me. You … you didn't have to."

I smile at her. "No problem. That's what friends do, right?"

She smiles back at me, hesitantly, almost shyly. "Right."

We walk in silence for a time. Back through Tottenham Court Road and onto the red Central Line. I wonder what it must have been like to rush through these tunnels on trains. Noisy, I bet. And hot.

"D'ya think we should give them the chip?"

I turn to her, surprised. "Why not? Wasn't that the whole point of this?" *Why else did I risk my life going back for it?*

"But they still haven't told us what they're going to *do* with it."

"They said they were going to stop the Cleaning."

"Yes, but *how*?" She sounds worried. "I'm sure I remember Murdoch – or was it Bryn – saying something about bringing down barriers. You don't think they're planning to take down the Wall, do you?"

I try and think back, but I don't remember the conversation. "I don't know. But would that be so bad?"

"The President said it'd cause carnage if they took down the Wall. I think that's what he thinks they're going to do. And ... he's right, Trey. If the Wall just disappeared, it *would* be carnage. Everyone would just go wild."

"Hmm. But if we don't give it to them, then we can't stop the Cleaning."

"I know." She stares down the dark tunnel. "That's the problem."

"Well, let's not tell them we've got the chip right away. If they can offer us a good explanation as to why they want it, we'll hand it over."

Aleesha considers this for a moment. "Okay, that sounds good." She smiles at me. "But you'd better let me do the talking. You always blush when you lie."

* * *

I spot a light in the tunnel ahead. Quickly, I turn off my flashlight and we creep to the side of the tunnel.

"Should we run?" I whisper in Aleesha's ear.

Her hair brushes my lips as she shakes her head. "Let's wait and see who it is. If it's not Murdoch, then we run. Give me that gun."

It is Murdoch, accompanied by Matthews. Murdoch's look of relief changes to anger as he sees there are only two of us.

"Where's Mikheil?"

I take a deep breath. "He didn't make it."

Murdoch curses, walks to the side of the tunnel and slams his fist into the wall. Matthews glances at us awkwardly and shrugs. Her eyes are red. I wonder what they've done with Sanders' body.

"Right, let's get you two back," Murdoch says, coming back over to us. "You've got some explaining to do."

We walk in silence through the tunnels, emerging into daylight. My eyes water in the brightness.

"What time is it?"

"Just before nine in the morning," Murdoch replies.

We're marched north, passing straight through Areas Four and Five. By the time we get into Six, I'm stumbling all over the place, scarcely able to walk in a straight line. My mouth is parched and the small chip is burning a hole in my pocket.

"How much further?" I gasp.

"Not far," Matthews replies, giving me a sympathetic look.

Not far. What do I do with the chip? I'd suggested keeping it secret, but surely the first thing they'll do is search us. *But what to do with it?*

I'm running out of time.

We're taken to a large old house that's tucked away behind a residential street in Area Six. If you didn't know it was there, you'd probably walk straight past the tiny alleyway that leads to it. Steps lead up to the door; a man and woman loiter at the bottom.

They stiffen at our approach, but relax when they see Murdoch and Matthews. The man gives me a curious glance as I stagger up the steps. *I hope they're at least going to give us a drink before interrogating us.*

We're shown into a small room on the ground floor and told to wait. Matthews stays with us. I collapse into a chair and Aleesha follows suit. My head's throbbing and I just want to lie down and sleep. Even the floor looks tempting.

"Here, looks like you need a drink." Matthews pushes an open bottle of water into my hand. I gulp it gratefully as she hands another bottle to Aleesha and dishes out some wrapped protein bars. She makes a face. "Sorry, I haven't got anything better. Once they're done with you, hopefully you can get a proper meal. You must be worn out."

I smile gratefully as she sits down opposite us. Her brown hair is grey with dust and she clenches and unclenches her hands in front of her, staring at the wall as if going over something again and again in her head.

"I-I'm sorry about your friend," I say, hesitantly. "Sanders. He seemed nice."

I realize how hollow the words are as soon as they're out of my mouth. How would I know if he was nice? I'd barely met him. But her gaze flicks to me and she smiles slightly.

"Yeah, we'd been together a long time. Since school. He was …" Her voice trails off and she stares at the floor, her eyes brimming with tears.

We sit in silence after that. Until the door opens and Murdoch walks in.

"Come on. It's time."

359

33

Aleesha

We're led up the stairs and into a large room that looks out over the street. It's dominated by a battered wooden table. Eight people sit around it. Milicent sits at the head of the table. Bryn is nowhere to be seen.

Murdoch motions for us to sit. Everything in the room feels old. Once richly decorated, the colours have faded over time and now it all just looks a bit sad.

I perch on the edge of the seat cushion, conscious of how filthy I am. My clothes are ripped and covered in dust and blood. There are scratches on the backs of my hands and one nail is torn clean off. From the look of shock on Trey's face when he'd opened the prison door, I suspect my face doesn't look so great, either. Despite the protein bar, I feel sick and empty inside as the adrenaline that's kept me going begins to seep away.

I swallow nervously, feeling Milicent's eyes boring into me. I've always been good at lying, but it feels as if somehow she'll know when I'm telling the truth and when I'm not.

The rest of the group wait for her to speak, but she takes her time before breaking the silence. "I presume the fact that Mikheil is not with you means that he is no longer alive?"

"He was shot by the guards while we were trying to escape," Trey blurts out.

So much for me doing all the talking.

A dark-haired man sags and buries his head in his hands, sobbing quietly. The woman next to him pats his shoulder awkwardly.

"And did you manage to get the information we were after?"

"Yes," I say, before Trey can speak. "At least we got some of it." I can feel him tense beside me, but I carry on. "They were waiting for us. Or, at least, waiting for someone. There was extra security on the room with the computers. They know you murdered the Secretary of State." Murdoch curses at this point and slams his fist on the table. "I think when we used the eye-scanner it alerted them. Mikheil had nearly finished downloading what he needed when the alarms went off. Then we had to run."

"And the information? Surely you didn't leave it behind?" interrupts a man I don't recognize.

I shake my head. "No, Mikheil grabbed it before we left. But the guards were chasing us. They were shooting bullets, not stun darts." There's a flash of pain and I realize I've been fingering the wound on my ear. I snap my hand back down beneath the table, wondering how to phrase the next part. *I need to find out what their game is.*

"Mikheil was shot – right in the chest. We managed to get into a room and barricade the door, but we couldn't save him."

"I tried." Trey stands, leaning over the table. The anguish on his face tugs at something deep in my chest. "I'm sorry. There was just so much blood and ..." His voice trails off at the stony-faced stares and he slumps back in his chair.

"We took the chip and ran. We got separated and the guards

followed me. I managed to take down three of them, but then the gun ran out and they captured me." I hesitate, not sure how much to tell them.

"What else." Milicent's eyes narrow. "You're not telling us something."

Damn that woman. "They ... they took me to the President's office."

There's a murmur of voices from around the table. A door bangs beneath us and there's the sound of people arguing. I catch Murdoch glancing worriedly at the door to the room.

"And what did you tell him?" Milicent asks calmly, seemingly unaware of the rising tension around the table.

"I swear, I didn't tell them anything about you, or what we were after." I surprise myself with my own vehemence. "After all, I didn't really have anything I could tell them. You still haven't told us what the data was, or what you were going to do with it!"

"And given that you managed to get yourself captured, you can understand why," Murdoch puts in.

"I didn't see *you* breaking into the most secure, well-defended building in this city, breaking all kinds of laws, and risking *your* life to get some stupid data!" Trey shouts, jumping to his feet. It's like a fuse inside him has just blown. I've never seen him angry like this. Blood rushes to his face as he glares at Murdoch.

"We nearly died in there today. Mikheil did die. Do you know just what the odds were of us even getting to that room, let alone getting the data and escaping from there? Slim to bloody well none, that's what. And you were happy enough to send us in there to be killed, so I think, at least, we deserve some answers!"

The room falls silent as he glares at the people around the

table. I stifle a smile. I've never heard him curse before. But his anger ignites my own and I have to fight to keep it from exploding out. Anger at the Chain for treating us as expendable pawns. Anger at the government for their lies and cruelty. And anger at myself for failing to protect Lily.

I hide my hands under the table so they can't see my clenched fists, and focus on taking deep breaths.

Milicent looks about to speak when footsteps pound up the stairs and the door flies open. Bryn storms in, his face clouded with rage.

"What the hell has been going on!"

He glares around the table, his gaze finally coming to rest on Milicent, who flushes slightly.

"Nice of you to join us, Bryn."

"Nice of you to *invite* me," he spits.

Uh oh, Milicent's in trouble. I feel a faint gleam of satisfaction.

Bryn glances across at us. "You pair okay?"

We both nod.

"You have gone one step too far this time." He begins to pace around the table. "You may have a level of autonomy in London, but this is *not* just your fight. The Leader has a personal interest in bringing down the government and you've kept your plans from me – from him." He pauses behind Milicent's chair. She sits ramrod straight, her eyes still on us; not flinching at his words.

"If the government catches you, not only do you fail, but years of planning will have been wasted." His voice is dangerously low.

Milicent seems to recover herself. "Well, we're not certain we have failed yet, Bryn," she says tightly. "We were just hearing what Aleesha and Trey had to tell us when you came in. Why don't we let them finish before jumping to any conclusions?"

Bryn looks about to argue, then changes his mind. "Fine." He takes a seat by Trey.

"I think *you* were just about to tell us exactly what your plans were," I say as Milicent's gaze rests once again on me.

"Ah, yes." She looks at Trey. "You have to understand that we couldn't tell you everything, particularly with your father being who he is. We weren't sure of your loyalties. Still aren't, if I'm being honest."

Trey puts his head in his hands. "I don't know what to believe anymore," he says, sounding tired. "But I know that what I've seen here, Outside, is not what I believed it to be." He looks up and meets her eye. "Things need to change."

Milicent considers him for a moment, then nods. "And you, Aleesha? Where do your loyalties lie?"

"Well, if you think I have any sympathy for the government, you're frickin' mad!" I take a deep breath. *Control, Aleesha, control.* "They kill, just because they can. It has to stop. People need to know the truth. The *real* truth, not government lies. If that's what you're about, then I'm in."

"Good. As you know, our aim as an *organization*," she stresses this word, as if to make it clear to us that they don't consider themselves a gang, "is to create a more equal society. London has been divided for too long and the gulf between Insiders and Outsiders has been growing for decades. The Wall is symbolic of this. Whilst it exists, there is no way for the two societies to coexist and no reason for Insiders to face up to the truth."

A wave of dizziness washes over me. *Was the President right?*

"We still do not know how the Wall kills or what makes up its composition. We believe the holo image you see is just that – a physical screen – but our tests to date have been fruitless."

I remember Murdoch's comments about those who had died in the belief that they might be able to pass through the Wall. He had sounded remorseful about it. Milicent sounds as if it was just an inconvenience.

"We think it can be brought down by cutting the electricity supply. I believe you managed to do this on a small scale when you attacked one of the depots, Aleesha."

I nod cautiously. It was just after Murdoch had approached me and blackmailed me into helping the Chain. Even the memories of that night make me shiver. We'd managed to take down the barrier by taking out the electricity supply to it, but the effect was only temporary and the cost of our success had been high.

"Unfortunately, it is nigh on impossible to cut the supplies to the Wall. There are multiple supplies and re-routing possibilities to overcome any attempt, even if we could locate and access the cables. Most of them are buried under tons of earth. But there is an alternative.

"Mikheil's grandfather was one of the brains behind the Wall. The government had moved him and his family over from Poland based on his technical expertise, but once the Wall was up and running, they banished them all back to Poland. They didn't want anyone around who could possibly compromise the system. Poland was not a good place to be at that time – it still isn't – and Mikheil's grandfather resented being sent back. He was also unsure ethically about whether what he had created was right. So, before he died, he told Mikheil's father and Mikheil what he knew."

She glances at the small, dark-haired man who'd been sobbing earlier. The resemblance to Mikheil is uncanny. Though his hair is thinner and his face more lined.

"He didn't know how the Wall worked – the government had

different experts working in isolation on different parts of the setup – but he knew that a set of override codes for each section of the Wall are stored in the main information bank. They're only accessible from inside the system. There's no way we can hack into the information bank, which is why you had to go into the headquarters. But Mikheil had figured out a way of altering part of the recognition system so that once we had the codes, an external device he'd created could be used to target the individual towers controlling the sections of the Wall."

"So, you were going to take down the Wall?" Trey whispers, his face pale.

Milicent shakes her head. "Not all of it. Just the section along the border of Area Four. Mikheil was going to recode the towers so they couldn't get it back up again."

"And then what?" I ask, finding my voice at last. "Your army goes in and takes over?"

Milicent smiles. "Well, in a sense. Our army is the people. Those who live Outside the Wall, who've suffered under the current government." Her voice rises, becoming more strident. "Unrest has been growing. The people are ready to rise up and overthrow their government." There's a fanatical glint in her eyes and some of the people around the table shift nervously in their chairs.

"Then, once it is over, they will look for direction, and that's when we will step in. A new government with people from both Inside and Outside the Wall. Together, we will bring down the rest of the Wall."

"With you as the leader?" I try, but I'm not quite able to keep the sarcasm from my voice.

Milicent doesn't seem offended. "No, of course not." The power in her voice has gone and suddenly she looks what she is again: a frail old lady. "I know I wouldn't be an acceptable candidate to those people who live Outside. Besides, I'm too old and tired to be leading a country. No, it needs to be one of them."

She smiles down the table at us and spreads her hands in a gesture of openness. "So, there you have it. I'm sorry we couldn't have been more open with you from the start, but I'm sure you can appreciate the need for secrecy."

"That's a stupid plan."

The voice rings loud in the room and it takes me a second to realize it's my voice. Milicent glares at me. I gulp and look away, catching the smirk on Bryn's face. *He's bloody well enjoying this.*

"I'm sorry?" Milicent's voice is like ice.

"It would be a massacre." Somehow my voice is bold, even though I'm quaking inside. "You're assuming people are going to do what you say."

Frown lines appear on her brow. "I would have thought they would appreciate an opportunity to improve their situation in life. This gives them a chance to go Inside, to see what they've been missing all these years. To *show* the government that they matter."

"If it was in Area Six, maybe. They're practically Insiders, but things don't work like that in Four. You can't just explain things to people in your complicated language and expect them to understand and follow orders. These are people who only know how to survive. How to fight." Somehow, I'm on my feet, gripping the edge of the table. *I have to make them understand.*

"These people, my people, are violent and desperate. They've been starved, had their children taken away from them, and half of them don't even have a place to call home. They won't hesitate to kill, 'cos in Area Four, you *don't survive* unless you're prepared to fight. The Inside will be heaven to them. And yes, they deserve everything that's in there, but *this is not the right way to go about it.*"

I take a deep breath and look around the table. There are still some cold stares, but a few people are frowning, one even nodding. "If you take down the Wall and just shove them in there, they will loot and destroy and kill anyone who gets in their way. And Insiders, well, they may choose to be blind to what goes on beyond their perfect lives, but they're still people. And they will *die.* Unless ..."

My voice slows as my brain catches up with my mouth. And then the horrifying realization hits me.

"Unless the Metz descend and kill them all," I say flatly, sinking back in my chair. The air feels suddenly thick and hard to breathe.

"Not if we're able to disable the Metz." She smiles.

So, that's her winning card.

"I wasn't aware that the device had been tested yet." Bryn leans forward, frowning.

A man with hooded eyes and short black hair coughs nervously. "It hasn't been tested yet, no, but we have a prototype ready to test."

"Did you not think you should start with something a bit smaller? What if it doesn't work?"

"That's why you're choosing Area Four, isn't it? Instead of Five or Six? In case it doesn't work. You think it doesn't matter if the people of Four die. They're not as important as other Outsiders." I stare along the table at Milicent who, for once, refuses to meet my gaze.

Bryn bangs his fist on the table. "That's enough. I refuse to authorize this plan."

"With the greatest respect, Bryn, we do not need your authorization. You may be the Leader's messenger boy, but you are not in charge. No." She waves her hand to cut off Bryn's next words. "You have no right to intervene. Now, Aleesha, please hand over Mikheil's chip."

"We don't have it."

"I thought you said you took it from Mikheil?" Her voice is cold and hard now.

"I did. But it was taken off me when I was captured and searched." I lock eyes with her and fold my arms defiantly.

The tension grows in the room. Bryn looks about to say something, but stops himself.

"Search them."

Murdoch and a woman rise and move over to us. The woman pulls me roughly to my feet and starts patting me down. Her fingers dig into the depths of my pockets, emptying the contents onto the table. She pokes between my breasts and up my butt crack. She finds even the stiletto blade the government guards missed.

"She's clean," she announces and stomps back to her chair. I can sense her disappointment.

Murdoch is slower. He's still working through Trey's jacket. I see the fear in Trey's eyes and my heart sinks. Murdoch pushes his hand down into the pocket of Trey's trousers. His fingers pause, and when he pulls them out, there's a small black object in his grasp.

34

Trey

For a moment the room is silent, then Bryn erupts in laughter. Murdoch glowers at him and tosses the plastic plectrum onto the table. He continues searching through my pockets. There isn't much in there.

"I don't see what is so amusing, Bryn," Milicent says sourly.

"Your faces … you thought … it was the chip," Bryn pants, wiping his eyes.

"It's a guitar plectrum," I volunteer.

Murdoch completes his search and shakes his head. "Nothing."

"I told you we didn't have it," Aleesha says. I can tell she's holding back a smile.

I sink back into my chair, oddly sad that my plan worked. I wanted the Chain to be able to *do* something, but it turns out they didn't have a plan, or, at least, not one that would have worked. Or perhaps it would have worked, but at too high a cost. *It's not our place to play with people's lives.*

"Can we go now?" I ask. It must be getting on for eleven. I don't want to keep Dad waiting. Strangely, the thought of going home doesn't fill me with the same sense of joy and excitement as it did a week ago. Too much has happened.

"Not just yet," Milicent says and my heart sinks.

"You were told to get Mikheil in and out safely," she continues. "You failed. And you not only lost the chip, but you got captured. You're known to the government now – at least, you are, Aleesha. You'll be on every Metz officer's screen before long. Useless Inside and next to useless Outside. And I don't believe you've told us half of what went on with the President. As for you, Trey—"

"Don't blame them," Bryn interrupts. "The plan was flawed. We'd agreed that Trey would not have to go into the headquarters." He glowers at Murdoch, who shrugs.

"Plans change. And we didn't force him, he had a choice."

"It's time for Trey to go back to his family. You've got no further use for him."

Mikheil's father clears his throat and slowly gets to his feet, his neck and shoulders hunched. "They should not be punished." His English is clearer than Mikheil's, though he still speaks with a strong accent. "I believe they did their best to save my son. H-he was sick anyway and would not have lived out the year. Perhaps it was better this way. They are only children. They have been through enough." He nods to Milicent and sits.

So, that was why Mikheil struggled to keep up. Tears prick at my eyes and I dig my fingernails into my palm to stop them spilling out.

"Thank you," Milicent replies. "But in our eyes, they are adults. We have treated them as such and they should be punished as adults."

Several of the people around the table frown at this, including Murdoch, and there's a murmur of low voices, but only Bryn speaks out.

"As you wouldn't let me speak earlier, Milicent, perhaps you will now. You have no authority to make these decisions." He places a small black box in the centre of the table. "I have a message from the Leader that he wanted to deliver in person."

Murdoch launches himself from his chair and grabs Bryn's arm. "Wait! The risk!"

Bryn shakes him off. "Don't worry, it's a pre-recorded message. There's no signal to track." He presses a button on the box and the head and shoulders of an elderly man appear in the air above it.

The face is familiar and I frown, trying to remember where I've seen it before. When it comes to me, I gasp and lean forward. *But that's impossible!*

There's a hand on my arm. Bryn shakes his head silently. Then the figure begins to speak.

"Members of the Chain in London. I was deeply saddened to hear of the death of Lamar. He was a great man and a personal friend. I have appointed a new person to lead the organization in London and am confident they will be able to work with you to free the city once and for all. Until they arrive, Bryn McNally is temporarily in charge and has full authorization to execute orders on my behalf. Anyone who does not comply with his leadership will be considered a traitor to the organization. Thank you all for your continued work. London's time is near."

The holo blinks, then disappears.

Bryn stands and smiles wryly. "It was not my intention on coming to London to be taking on this responsibility. But I was also not intending to lose a man who was a good friend to all of us. He, more than many of us, believed in the aim of our work here. To plan and carry out an operation that would help create equality, not lead to a bloodbath. To work for the greater good, not one person's personal aims."

He's not looking at Milicent when he says this, but he doesn't have to. She looks like a broken woman, slumped in her chair, her face full of sorrow and loss.

"Now, if you give me a few minutes to escort Aleesha and Trey out, I suggest we have a reasoned conversation about our next steps. Get yourselves a drink and be back here in ten minutes." He jerks his head to us and walks toward the door.

At the top of the stairs, he points down the corridor. "Clean yourselves up in the bathroom, both of you. You can't walk around the streets in that state. Then meet me downstairs."

* * *

Five minutes later, I join Bryn at the bottom of the stairs.

"Bryn, that man. On the holo. Wasn't that Nelson Mandela?" *As in, the South African revolutionary who died over a century ago.*

"It was an image of him. The Leader uses it as an avatar to protect his identity. Uses his voice, too. Apparently, Mandela embodied the spirit of freedom and equality that we're fighting for." He shrugs. "Or, at least, that's what he's told me."

"Who is he really?"

"I can't tell you." He holds up his hands at the look on my face. "Really, Trey. I can't tell you."

"Can't tell him what?" Aleesha walks up to us.

"Oh, nothing," I say. "So, you're not leaving just yet?"

Bryn sighs. "No. Looks like I'm going to have to wait a bit longer for retirement. You know your father is waiting for you?"

I nod.

He hesitates, then puts a hand on my shoulder. It feels heavy and reassuring. "Abby would like to see you before you go, if you get a chance."

"I'll try. I'm hoping I can come by and visit sometime."

"Maybe." He smiles. "Though I think there were some conditions to your pardon. Something about staying out of London."

"Oh." My heart sinks. "Bryn, I've been meaning to ask. Has Abby always lived out here? She seems …"

"Too intelligent? No, she was brought up an Insider. That's where she got her medical training."

"Why did she have to leave?"

"It's not really my place to tell you, but I think she chose to leave. Thought she could do more good helping Outsiders."

"Has she ever regretted it?"

Bryn smiles. "You'll have to ask her that. She hasn't had an easy life, Abby. She deserves better." A fleeting expression crosses his face, but it's gone before I can read it. "Anyway, I need to get back. Can you make your way okay from here? One of the guards will be able to give you directions." He nods at the figures slouching at the bottom of the entrance steps.

"Bryn?" Aleesha's voice is urgent. "What about the Cleaning?"

Bryn frowns. "What Cleaning?"

"There's a Cleaning planned for today. Murdoch said—"

"Wait here a minute." Bryn runs up the staircase.

Two minutes later he's back. "There isn't a Cleaning. Or, at least, not one that we know about. Murdoch made that up to get you to cooperate."

Aleesha's face darkens and she turns toward the stairs. "That ba—"

"Leave it, Aleesha." Bryn grabs her arm. "I'll have a word with him. And honestly, he's feeling pretty bad about it all at the moment. Sanders was a good friend of his and he feels responsible for his death, and Mikheil's. He's an ass, but not a bad man."

"I can check with my father as well," I intervene. "If there was, or is, a Cleaning planned, he'll know." *It's his department after all. My father, the murderer?*

There's a moment of awkward silence. Aleesha glances at Bryn then me.

"I'll see you outside, Trey."

We watch as she walks down the steps and out onto the street.

"So, this is it then?" I ask.

Bryn shrugs. "Not necessarily. If you agree with your father's plan, then we'll be seeing each other again soon." He smiles at me.

"You know what's going to happen to me?"

He nods. "But it's not my place to explain. He's your father at the end of the day. The one who's been there for you." He hesitates for a moment then places a hand on my shoulder. "Any father would be proud to have you as his son," he says gruffly.

Then, with a sad smile, he turns and walks back up the stairs.

I join Aleesha outside and we weave our way in silence through Area Six. At one point, I lag behind to retrieve the chip I'd hidden in a flowerbed whilst pretending to fix my boot. I'm still not sure what to do with it. We continue through Area Five and to the border with Four.

"So, is this it? Are you going to be able to go home now?" Aleesha says finally.

"I guess so," I say. "Dad said he'd persuaded the President to grant me a pardon." I look down at my feet. "From what Bryn said, I don't think they'll let me stay in the city, though."

"So, I won't be seeing you again?"

I can't tell if she's disturbed by this thought or not. She refuses to meet my eye at any rate. On an impulse, I take her hand. "Look, will you meet me here in, say, an hour? Whatever happens, I'll come back. To say goodbye."

Aleesha smiles slightly. "Sure. See you in an hour."

"An hour," I echo and, dropping her hand, turn and walk down the narrow alley that leads through the Wall into the heart of the city. When I look back a moment later, she has gone.

* * *

I'm half an hour late, but Dad is waiting anxiously at the gate to Bunhill Fields. He sags against the stone pillar when he sees me, then composes himself.

"You're alright." He gives me a tight smile and a hug, then pulls me through into the graveyard.

It's a secluded spot, shut off from the world. Even most Insiders aren't allowed in here. Only those who have relatives buried here centuries ago. Tall trees surround the garden of ancient stone gravestones battered and worn down by the years. On a bench set along one of the paths that weaves between them, my mother sits, bent over.

As she spots us, she springs up and runs toward me. There are fresh tears on her cheeks. She wraps her arms around me and presses her wet face to my own, rocking me back and forth.

"I've been so worried about you. Thank god you're alive."

My father places a hand on my shoulder. "It's over now, Darwin, you're safe. You don't have to run anymore."

I gently disentangle myself from my mother and turn to look at him. "Father, is there a Cleaning planned today? Of the whole of Area Four?" I finger the chip in my pocket; the chip I will use as a bargaining device, if I need to, to get this stopped.

His brow furrows. "A Cleaning? No. There are no Cleanings planned today, and we certainly wouldn't look at Cleaning a whole area in one go – it would cause chaos!"

I let out the breath I'd been holding. Giddiness bubbles up in me. *It's okay. It's all okay.* "Never mind. It was just a rumour."

We sit down on the bench, the three of us side by side. My mother is the first to speak.

"You … you know about Bryn?"

I nod.

"You must be so ashamed of me." She wipes a tear from her eye. "I'm ashamed of myself. But I was so lonely at that time. And Bryn, well, he just swept me off my feet. I knew he felt more for me that I did for him, but I didn't realize that he'd fallen in love with me. It was always just going to be a fling. And then he suggested that I leave – abandon London and my family – and go abroad with him."

She sighs. "Of course, that was out of the question. And then I realized I was pregnant and I didn't know what to do. I told your father and he was so understanding." She flashes a sad smile at him. "And Bryn left. I never saw him again, until the other day.

"But I want you to know that I have never, for a single second, regretted having you. We are so proud of you." She cups my cheek and turns my face toward her, and I see such love in her eyes that I know she speaks the truth. But I still can't hold her gaze.

Instead I look at my father. "And you forgave her?" I regret the words as soon as they're out of my mouth. The bitterness in them. My mother flinches away as if I've slapped her.

"It was a long time ago," my father replies, but his face is tight and he refuses to meet my eye.

There's a sudden tension in the air that wasn't there before. *Perhaps some hurts never completely heal.* I look down at my arm; the bandaged wound hidden under my jacket.

My father coughs. "Anyway, about you, Darwin. Bryn has been very helpful. He used his contacts in Birmingham to find you somewhere to finish school. That was one condition of the pardon: that you couldn't come back to London. But you could have gone to university there. Studied history, like you wanted to."

I'm confused. *Why is he talking about my future like it won't happen?*

"But unfortunately, since the events of last night, the President has changed his mind."

A cold dread seeps through me. "What do you mean? I try and swallow but there's a lump in my throat. *I killed a man.* The thought bounces around inside my head, haunting me. *Was it all for nothing?*

My father sighs. "Somehow he knows you were involved in the raid on headquarters. I don't know how – I certainly didn't tell him and you're not identifiable from the cameras. He has no proof. But he seems convinced. Perhaps your friend told him."

"Aleesha wouldn't have said anything," I reply hotly.
Would she?

"Well, somehow he knows. And he knows you helped her escape. I'm not sure what he's angrier about, to be honest. Anyway, it took a lot of bargaining to persuade him not to publicly execute you as a traitor. Just to give *them* a warning."

"What was the agreement?" I swallow hard. "Does he know you helped me?"

"I think he suspects. We'd already agreed I'd be demoted to a more junior position in the government." He looks at his hands. "That's what I was doing last night, preparing the files to hand over to my successor. Now, he's pushed me down another few notches, but at least I still have a job. That's more than I deserve. And Anabel gets to keep her job."

Anabel. The palace guard. "Does she know?"

"No. Ironically she's in charge of the investigation into the security arrangements. I suspect there'll be a few people calling for the Metz to take over security at headquarters, but most of us don't want them patrolling the corridors." He shudders.

My father is a tall man but seeing him now, his shoulders hunched and his face unshaven and lined, he looks shrunken, a shadow of his normal self.

My mother reaches over and clasps his hand. He smiles at her. *How can he still love her, after what she did?*

"I still don't know why he had to treat you so harshly. You've done so much for this country."

"Harsh? I got off lightly."

"But you've lost everything! Your job, our apartment ..."

He pats her hand. "I still have my life, though," he says quietly. "He'd be well within his rights to execute me for what I did. And we have Darwin."

He turns to me, his face serious. "I'm afraid you have to leave the country, Darwin. It was the only alternative he would agree to. You leave and don't return. Ever. In effect, you will disappear."

My jaw drops. *Leave? Forever?* I stare at him unable to speak. I feel like the breath has been knocked from my body.

"I'm sorry, it's the only option. And I'm sure Bryn will have some contacts overseas. Hopefully, he can help us out; again." There's a slight bitterness in his voice.

"I'm going to miss you so much," my mother interrupts, placing her hand on my clenched fists, "but, at least, you can have a life. And hopefully, we'll be able to visit ..."

"So, I'm to be exiled," I spit, finding my voice at last. I lash out, knocking my mother's hand away. *How is this a solution? It's just a way for me to conveniently disappear from their lives.*

"Your life is to be spared," my father says quietly.

"But I've done nothing wrong!"

"I know, but that's not how the law works."

Why does he make it all sound so ... so reasonable?

"Well, have you ever thought to question the law, Dad? You're in the government, you have the power to change these things." I push myself up off the bench and glare down at them.

He laughs harshly. "You think any one of us really has that power? There's no alternative, Darwin. If you don't accept – if you stay here – they'll keep chasing you, and when they find you, your life will be forfeit. The President made it quite clear. This is your only chance."

Leave and live, or stay and die. I kind of know how Mikheil's grandfather felt now. It's a choice that isn't a choice.

"Is that what you tell yourself about your work as well, Dad? Your excuse for what's going on out there?" Anger takes over, the words spilling from my mouth. "Because you know what I've realized in the past few weeks? Everything we are told is a lie. Our society hasn't always been like this. You – the government – created this division. You made Outsiders stupid. Then you put up the Wall so you didn't have to see the dirt and the misery and the death that goes on out there."

"Darwin, how *dare* you!" My mother leaps to her feet, anger in her face.

"Calm, Miriam." Father touches her arm. He massages his jaw. "I'm not sure what you've heard or where you've heard it from, and I don't *want* to know. Personally, I agree with you, to some extent. Governments in the past have made some bad decisions. But we have the benefit of hindsight. This country has been through some desperate times; worse than we can imagine. They didn't know then what the consequences of their decisions would be."

"But why not tell people the truth? Do you not think that even the Insiders would want to change things, would want to know how bad things are out there?"

"I suspect most people are quite happy not knowing, Darwin." My father shakes his head.

"But you were in charge of things Outside. You could change things."

"I can't change the work of decades with a click of my fingers! Besides, all decisions have to go through full cabinet. And get past the President." He rubs his forehead with his fingers. "And now I can't even do as much as raise an issue for discussion."

I stand, my mind made up. I can't seem to get through to him that what they're doing is *wrong*.

"Thanks for the offer of *exile*, but I think I'll stay."

My mother gasps. "No, Darwin, you can't!"

My father grabs my arm, his face flushed. "Don't be stupid, Darwin. Think seriously about this. You can't stay. Do I have to physically hand you over to Bryn myself?" He glares at me, daring me to defy him.

I gently prise his fingers from my arm. I know he wants the best for me. He just doesn't understand.

"Trey."

"What?" He looks confused.

"I'm Trey now. Not Darwin. Just Trey. And I'm old enough to make my own decisions."

Father's right, the government doesn't really have the power. The people do. And if the people are told the truth, if they demand change, the government will *have* to listen. He just doesn't understand that.

I walk away from them, then. Walk through the streets Inside, away from my life before, and cross through the Wall to my new life. There's an emptiness inside me, like I've left part of me behind in the graveyard. But I know that this is the right choice. People – those who live Inside and Outside – need to know what has been done to them and for them.

They need to know the truth.

35

Aleesha

I pace the alleyway by the Wall. Four steps forward. Four steps back. Perching on a low wall, I try and steady my breathing, but my body doesn't want to be still. In my hands, I clutch the small painted box that contains Lily's ashes. I'm hoping Trey has time to come with me to scatter them. I'm hoping he turns up.

He's five minutes late, but I hear him coming, running up the alleyway. "Sorry I'm late," he pants.

The tension in my body suddenly evaporates. "It's okay. How did it go?"

There's a pause while he catches his breath.

"They'll let me live, but only if I leave London and never return."

I feel a strange sense of disappointment. "Well, that's what you thought. Are you going back to school, then?"

He shakes his head. "No, I mean, not just leave London – leave the country. I'd be exiled. Banished to go and live somewhere on the continent. Anyway, I refused."

"You did what?" I stare at him.

He smiles – that quirky little half smile. "I refused."

I can feel my mouth lying open in shock and shut it. "But

why?"

The smile falls from his face. "Because this, this is all wrong." He waves his hand in the direction of the Wall. "I know the Chain's plan wouldn't have worked as Milicent thought, but something has to change, and, at least, they're trying to do something about it." He runs his hand through his hair and sighs. "I'm not sure what I can do to help, but, at least, here I can try and do some good. Better that than ending up at another school where I'm the dumbest kid in the class."

"That's only because they've got enhanced genes. They have an unfair advantage."

He rolls his eyes. "Tell me about it. Now I know how you Outsiders feel."

I thump him hard. But secretly I'm glad he's staying.

"I thought the President had agreed to pardon you, though?"

"He had." A troubled look crosses Trey's face. "But he changed his mind. Apparently, he's convinced I was involved in the raid last night, though he has no proof; my face wasn't caught on any of the cameras. And he's really mad that you escaped."

He grins at me, but I can't return it. The thoughts click together in my mind like pieces of a gun. *Samson. Holding a knife to Lily's throat. I told him about Trey. And that smell in the President's room. Just a faint whiff, but unmistakably him. But why was he there?*

"Aleesha, are you alright? You look like you're about to faint."

I blink. Trey's waving a hand across my face. *He's never going to forgive me. But if I don't tell him, what kind of person does that make me?* I swallow hard. Something in my chest swells. It feels like I'm bruised, but on the inside.

"Trey, I ..." I start again. "There's something I need to tell you."

His face falls. "Oh, *you* told him?" There's a momentary silence before he speaks again. "It's okay, I mean you were in front of the *President*. And they beat you up." He lifts his hand as if to touch my battered face and I recoil automatically before realizing that he's not going to hit me. Trey looks hurt. I curse inwardly. *You idiot.*

He looks away. "I'd have broken, too. I just wish you'd told me."

"That's not it, I mean, not exactly. I didn't tell the President anythin'." My fingernails dig into my palms.

"What then?"

"It all happened before that. The Brotherhood …they have some connection with the President." I explain about how Samson had threatened me and Lily unless I told them everything, including that Trey was the son of a government minister. The holo he'd shown me of Trey. About the black figure I'd glimpsed in the President's office and the lingering smell. Samson's scent. He must have been listening in on the whole thing.

"So, you see, it's all my fault." I slam my fist into the rough concrete wall, tears rising to my eyes. *Not again. Bloody waterworks.* "If I hadn't told Samson about you, the President would never have known and you'd have been able to stay in this country. Gone back to your family."

I hang my head, staring at the grey stains on the cracked paving slabs in front of me. My body feels like it's a battleground of emotions. Anger. Frustration. Guilt. Now there are no more missions, nothing to focus on, I can't seem to shut them away.

"Hey." Trey sounds uncomfortable. "It doesn't matter, really it doesn't. Besides, I don't think I *could* go back now. It would feel wrong. It already feels like a different life."

He smiles at me. A rare ray of sunlight makes the blond roots of his hair glow. It reminds me of the day I met him, when I thought he looked like an angel. Now he's a fallen angel, but just as beautiful.

"I bet you wish none of this had ever happened."

He cocks his head to one side, reminding me of the delicate little bird I'd seen the first time I'd gone through the Wall.

"No, I don't think so. I think the old me would have wanted to believe in happily-ever-afters. That my parents were my real parents. That what I'd been taught at school was the truth. But now, well, I'm glad I know. Or, at least, know that what you think is the truth isn't always." He makes a face. "Does that make sense?"

"Kind of. Though, you know, a life of happiness and pleasure inside the Wall is not to be sniffed at!" I force a smile onto my face.

"Well, I never really fitted in there." He frowns. "But the President offered you all that. To make you a legal citizen and help you find your father? And you turned it down?"

"Yeah. I mean, I did *think* about it. But I couldn't do it. It would feel like betraying Lily again. And I figured I'd screwed you over enough. I ... I didn't realize I'd already done the damage."

"Would it have made a difference if you'd known?"

"No." I hesitate. "You don't betray friends, right?"

"Right."

His smile turns to a frown. "But what are the Brotherhood doing talking to the government? I thought you said they were an Outsider gang?"

"They are. Though, perhaps they're something more. I think the Chain know more about them than they're letting on."

"*That* wouldn't surprise me."

He nods at the box. "Lily's ashes?"

"Yeah, I was hoping you might come and scatter them with

me?" I grin. "It may be a bit of a climb."

"I'm intrigued ..."

We set off through the back streets. Trey raises an eyebrow when we go through the Wall, but doesn't say anything. I have a place in mind.

"Did you ask your father about the Cleaning?"

"Yes. He said there weren't any planned. I believe him, too. It's his department, or, at least, it was."

"Bloody Murdoch."

It leaves a sour taste in my mouth. I'm used to being lied to – in fact, being told the truth is something of a rarity – but usually, I can see through them. It's a knack I have. And the fact that I didn't see through this one makes me uneasy. *Am I losing my touch?*

"You know when the alarm went off?" Trey says.

"You mean when I screwed up the job?"

He laughs. "Yeah. Well, did you manage to finish reading your mother's file?"

I shake my head. I was so impatient to find out about the mysterious "LC100" mentioned that I didn't even read the part about my mother's death.

"Well, I did. There was a Metz operation – Operation Nightshade – focused on capturing a person code named LC100. Anyway, your mother was caught up in it. They never meant to kill her. But they did somehow know that she was going to meet this person and where." He pauses.

I stop, my feet rooted to the ground. "So, they used her as bait?"

"I'm not sure. The record said the operation failed. The Metz attacked too soon, or maybe they knew the other person hadn't turned up. I can't quite remember. But there was a link to the

Metz operation file. It will be classified, but if there's some way you could get access to it, it may tell you who LC100 is and what link your mother had to them. Unfortunately, I think it'll be on the Metz system, not the main information bank."

"Hmm," I reply noncommittally. A week ago I'd have scoffed at him for even suggesting I'd be able to access a file on the Metz system. But then, I'd have scoffed at anyone suggesting it was possible to break into the government headquarters and make it out alive. *Perhaps there is a way.*

We continue walking until we reach the base of a narrow spiral staircase attached to the back of an office building. I point up. "To the roof."

The building's five storeys high, and by the time we get to the top of the stairs, my calves are aching. I stand on Trey's shoulders to get from the staircase to the roof, then lean over to take the box and pull him up.

"It's a good job I don't mind heights," he says as he rolls onto the flat roof, panting.

I walk over to the far side of the roof and look out over the playground. There's a stone parapet, about two feet high, that runs around the roof. I sit on it and dangle my legs over the edge. Trey comes to join me, relieved to see a balcony three metres below. "I thought you were about to jump off the edge, then."

The sound of children laughing and screaming in exhilaration drifts up from the playground below. Parents push them higher and higher on the swings. There's a girl about the same age as Lily who catches my eye. She leans forward in her swing, as if willing herself to go higher and higher. A hard lump forms in my throat.

I wonder if these children even know about the world Outside.

That there are children there who don't have swings. Children who rarely laugh and play.

There's a light breeze, and it's blowing in the right direction. My fingers fumble the catch on the box, but finally I get it open and tip it, the ashes immediately taken by the wind. We watch as they disperse, the wind carrying Lily's final remains high above the children playing below.

"She said she always wanted to fly …" My voice cracks and I stand and walk across the roof. I close my eyes as a single tear rolls down my cheek. *I will avenge you, Lily. I promise.*

The resolution gives me strength. Brushing the water from my eyes I push my shoulders back and crack my knuckles. A flash of black on the street below catches my eye. A Metz patrol. Their bulky figures move perfectly in time. Trey said they were human. I'm still not convinced. But it doesn't matter. I will find a way of making them pay.

Trey joins me. "There's something else we need to do." He holds up a small black piece of plastic that glints in the light.

"You had it all along?" I ask.

He shakes his head. "I hid it on our walk back from the tunnels, then picked it up on my way to meet my father. I figured I could use it to bargain with him to stop the Cleaning." He tilts his head to one side. "Do we keep it or destroy it? Mikheil died for this …"

"But while we have it there's a risk that the Chain could get hold of it." I grimace. "I don't know. The Wall has to come down. But not now. Not in *this* way."

There's a tinkle as the chip hits the floor. Trey stands on it, twisting the toe of his boot until the chip is crushed into tiny pieces. "There. It's done now." There's a tremor in his voice. "I'm not sure I could carry it around any longer; it feels like a ticking bomb." He scoops up the remains and throws them off the roof, where they're caught in a sudden strong gust of wind.

We sit back down on the edge of the roof and stare out at the landscape of glass towers and white apartment blocks.

A thought strikes me, and I give a short laugh. "And after all that's happened, we still don't know why we can go through the Wall and other people can't."

Trey frowns. "No. I don't think even my father knows, though I wish I'd asked him."

"Maybe we've just got some immunity to it or something."

"Maybe."

"What are you going to do now?" Trey asks after a pause.

"Find somewhere else to live, I guess. Get some food." My stomach growls in agreement. "Survival first."

Then revenge.

"What about you?"

"I don't know." He sounds forlorn and part of me wants to reach out and comfort him, but I don't know if it would be welcomed. Then his face brightens. "We still have the films."

It takes me a second to work out what he's talking about. "The ones you took from the basement?"

He nods. "If there's some way we could make people aware of the information in them …. I'm sure most people who live Inside know nothing of how we ended up like this. And they're good people mostly. They'd see that what was done in the past was wrong and challenge the government to *do* something to fix it."

I look dubiously at him. "But will they want to know? I mean, it's not likely to make their lives better, at least, in the short term, is it?"

"They *need* to know. They have a right to know."

I suddenly feel like I have the weight of the world on my shoulders. He's right. But what we know – if we tell people – it'll change everything. And while Trey seems confident, I'm not so sure. The Outside is unpredictable. People could swing one way or the other. *It could start a war.* But if we keep it to ourselves, we are as guilty as the government.

"So, how do we tell them? I can't see people taking a couple of kids seriously."

Trey smiles. "The screens. If we could get something broadcast on all screens at once, everyone would see it. Or, at least, enough people to spread the word."

"Right. We just go to the press. Who will instantly recognize us and turn us straight over to the Metz. My face is on every screen now as well as yours."

"Not if we go to Theo. He's a friend of mine from school. His father runs the main broadcasting agency. He's got access to all the screens Inside and Outside the Wall. And I bet he'd sell his own son for a scoop like this. We just need to find him." He shrugs. "Can't be too hard, right?"

I can't help smiling at his optimism.

The girl on the swings has been pulled away. She's complaining to her mother about having to leave. The woman picks her up, swings her around and plants a kiss on her nose. Trey *is* right. People need to know the truth. There can't be more Lilys. More children killed simply for the crime of being alive.

I find myself leaning into Trey and, after a moment's hesitation, he wraps an arm around me. I rest my head on his shoulder momentarily, closing my eyes to inhale his fresh, sweet scent, trying to capture this moment, this feeling, so I'll remember it. Then I pull back. I'm not sure what he feels for me. If he feels anything at all. But I can't get involved.

You will only hurt him.

He glances at me questioningly but makes no move to touch me again.

An image of Lily jumps into my head, smiling up at me as she sucks a sherbet lemon. And my mother, her face lit up with joy on that morning when my whole world had been upended and my life turned into a daily fight to survive. Both of them murdered for being in the wrong place at the wrong time. And my father … Is he really a criminal, as the President said? Or was that another lie?

At least, they think he's alive. There is hope. A fluttery feeling develops in my chest like a tiny bird trying to get out. I breathe in deeply and straighten my back.

Operation Nightshade. LC100. My father.

I will find you. Somehow, I will find a way.

If you enjoyed Expendables...

Please leave a review!

As an independent author, reviews are really important to me. They help make my books visible to people who are browsing Amazon or other sites and they help readers decide whether they'll enjoy reading my books.

I also take into account the reviews my books get when deciding which series to continue with and what stories to write next.

If you enjoyed reading *Expendables*, I'd really appreciate it if you could take five minutes to leave a review. You can jump straight to the pages using the links below.

Amazon: myBook.to/ExpendablesReview
Goodreads: http://bit.ly/goodreadsexpendables

Thank you!

Alison

Join my Readers' Club

Would you like to receive fortnightly updates from me with free short stories, updates on new releases, giveaways and book recommendations?

Sign up for my Readers' Club today and get a FREE copy of *Outsider* (the prequel to *The Wall Series*) as a welcome gift.

Interested? Sign up here: bit.ly/alisoningleby-outsider.

If you're a fan of dystopian fiction, come and join my private Facebook group, The Last Book Café on Earth (bit.ly/Last-BookCafe). We share book recommendations, fun quizzes and futuristic news.

I look forward to having you on board!

Alison

Author's Note

The idea for the world that *Expendables* is set in first occurred to me when I was listening to a radio programme about the ethics of genetic engineering. This led me to wonder what society would emerge if genetic enhancements to embryos were legal and dependent on the wealth or status of individuals. The separation of Insiders and Outsiders in *Expendables* was my interpretation of an extreme situation, but, I hope, one that is imaginable and realistic.

The Great Flood

As an emergency planner, disasters and how we respond to them have always fascinated me. All the events and people in this story are works of fiction and are not intended to reflect any individuals or the response to any real emergencies. In the UK, the government and other agencies work together on a daily basis to plan and prepare for a range of risks, including flooding. Find out more by searching for your Local Resilience Forum.

The London that is depicted in this series has experienced a sea-level rise of around thirteen metres based on present-day levels. This is significantly higher than current climate change projections for the remainder of this century and would require significant melting of the Greenland and Antarctic ice caps to occur. If you're interested in the scientific predictions of sea level rise in the UK, I'd recommend you look at the UKCP09 report on Climate Projections (ukclimateprojections.metoffice.gov.uk).

Flooding from tidal and fluvial sources, as well as heavy rain, poses a significant risk to London. As a dystopian author, I like to imagine the worst-case scenarios, but you can get a current assessment of risks in London from the London RiskRegister (www.londonprepared.gov.uk).

'Tronk' (co-tronkpretine)

Tronk is a fictional substance. However, the idea for it arose when I was browsing an exhibition in the Science Museum in London about food technology. The exhibition talked about how food production may change in the future, the increase in synthetic foodstuffs and the use of drugs to control people's eating habits.

The London Underground

I lived in London for four years and, like many Londoners, had a love-hate relationship with the Tube. The London Underground map is famous for its symbolic representation of distances and directions and there are many disused stations and unmarked tracks that do not appear on the map. Although I travelled along Aleesha and Trey's route from Aldgate East to Charing Cross station many times, when travelling on a high-speed train in the dark, it is impossible to take everything in. If there are inaccuracies and omissions with some details, please accept my apologies for these.

Acknowledgements

Bringing a book from an initial idea to a finished project is a huge job and I wouldn't have got here without the help of the following people.

Thanks to my amazing team of beta readers: William McCullough, Isabel Hosier, Meg Cowley and Anni Willis. Your comments were invaluable in helping me improve my manuscript.

I was lucky enough to work with Sophie Playle of Liminal Pages who did a fantastic job of editing my manuscript, both at a developmental and copy editing level. Thanks also to Ed, my proofreader, for your work on polishing the final draft and picking up on the typos I'd missed.

My gorgeous cover was designed by Meg at Jolly Creative Cover Design (bookcovers.megcowley.com).

Writing and publishing a novel is a process fraught with hidden dangers. I've battled with crises of confidence, my inner critic and perfectionism and there have been several times I thought this book would never make it out into the world. There are many authors who have helped me along the way, but special thanks go to Meg Cowley, for providing the inspiration that I could do this and the metaphorical kick up the butt I needed to get it done. And thanks to Joanna Penn for making me believe it was possible.

Publishing a book also incurs costs. I was lucky enough to get some financial contributions from friends as a wedding present which helped cover some of the costs associated with producing *Expendables*. You know who you are — thank you.

Finally, thank you to all my family and friends, who have patiently put up with me working evenings and weekends to get this done. And especially to Sam, for his unfailing support and faith in me. I couldn't have done it without you!

About the Author

Alison Ingleby is an author of sci-fi and fantasy fiction for young adults and adults who are still young at heart.

Alison holds a Master's degree in Geography from the University of Cambridge and a Master's degree in Emergency Planning and Management from Coventry University. She's worked as an emergency planner and sustainability professional in cities across the UK and now happily spends her days as a freelance writer, specialising in helping businesses who love the outdoors as much as she does.

When not writing or curled up in her reading chair with a cup of Yorkshire Tea, Alison loves climbing up cliff faces, running across the Yorkshire moors and hiking up Scottish mountains. Her dream is to live in a Scottish castle by a loch. (Preferably one with central heating and hot water.)

You can find out more about Alison, sign up for her Readers' Club and get a free story by visiting her website: https://alisoningleby.com/

Alison's Books

The Wall Series:
Outsider (prequel)
Expendables (Book One)
Infiltrators (Book Two)
Defenders (Book Three) - coming autumn 2018

Short stories & novellas:
Red Sun Rising: A Story from the Alteruvium Expanse
The Climb (featured in the *Future Visions Anthology Vol. 1*)
The Faerie Flag - coming summer 2018

Printed in Great Britain
by Amazon